MEDICAL

Pulse-racing passion

Bound By Their Pregnancy Surprise

Louisa Heaton

Sparks Fly With The Single Dad

Kate Hardy

MILLS & BOON

BOUND BY THEIR PREGNANCY SURPRISE
© 2024 by Louisa Heaton
Philippine Copyright 2024
Australian Copyright 2024
New Zealand Copyright 2024
First Published 2024
First Australian Paperback Edition 2024
ISBN 978 1 867 29957 8

SPARKS FLY WITH THE SINGLE DAD
© 2024 by Pamela Brooks
Philippine Copyright 2024
Australian Copyright 2024
New Zealand Copyright 2024
First Published 2024
First Australian Paperback Edition 2024
ISBN 978 1 867 29957 8

Published by
Harlequin Mills & Boon
An imprint of Harlequin Enterprises (Australia) Pty Limited
(ABN 47 001 180 918), a subsidiary of HarperCollins
Publishers Australia Pty Limited
(ABN 36 009 913 517)
Level 19, 201 Elizabeth Street
SYDNEY NSW 2000 AUSTRALIA

Printed and bound in Australia by McPherson's Printing Group

Bound By Their Pregnancy Surprise

Louisa Heaton

MILLS & BOON

Louisa Heaton lives on Hayling Island, Hampshire, with her husband, four children and a small zoo. She has worked in various roles in the health industry—most recently four years as a community first responder, answering emergency calls. When not writing, Louisa enjoys other creative pursuits, including reading, quilting and patchwork—usually instead of the things she *ought* to be doing!

Visit the Author Profile page
at millsandboon.com.au for more titles.

Dear Reader,

When Kate Hardy and myself were asked to come up with a cozy vet duet, we had great fun brainstorming our ideas. We chose to set our story in the Yorkshire Dales and I already knew that my heroine would be called Halley, after Halley's Comet. With this, it meant I knew something about her parentage and so I made her father an amateur astronomer, who used to take his daughter up onto a hill to show her the stars—a treasured memory for Halley.

So, when it came time for Halley to return to the village of Burndale, I knew this memory of happier times would draw her there and an idea formed in my mind of Halley meeting another great love in her life—our hero, Archer. Being on that hill would change *both* their lives in many ways. And I loved exploring the idea of how *one small decision* can greatly affect someone and I happily explored that in this book.

I hope you enjoy their story.

Louisa x

DEDICATION

For our vet, Kevin. Thank you for saving Mango's life x

CHAPTER ONE

He thought he'd be alone.

He wanted to be alone. It was what he was used to, after all, and he was comfortable in his own company, so to come up here, to Rookery Point, and to find someone else was parked up here to watch the meteor shower? He kind of felt annoyed *and* intrigued. Annoyed that he'd probably have to get through an hour of inane, awkward conversation with a stranger, but also intrigued as to who it would be. It could be someone from the village. From Burndale. But he really didn't know of anyone else who was interested in the stars.

Archer didn't recognise the car. An old four-by-four with a large dent in the rear bumper. Switching off his own headlights, he killed the engine and looked up to the point and saw the silhouette of a woman, sitting on a blanket of some sort, whilst she fiddled with a small telescope. A stranger, then. But how did she know of this place? Not many people did, unless they were locals. He saw her turn to look at him, but he couldn't see her face because of how dark it was, though he thought he could tell she had long blonde hair.

It was the perfect night for staring at the sky. It was clear and cloudless. No breeze. The heat of the day still hanging on, so he only wore a tee shirt and jeans, though he did have his jacket in the car if it got cooler.

He got his own telescope out of the boot. His camera. Wondering if he ought to set up far away from this woman on her own, so as not to be intimidating, or whether he should just say hi, introduce himself and set up right beside her. He didn't want to be rude, so he decided he'd say hello, gauge how talkative she wanted him to be and then decide, so he began to hike up the hill towards the top. There was a small trail between the trees and he ducked to avoid branches and brambles and then he was passing Malcolm's memorial bench. Malcolm Campbell. Halley's father. This had been his spot. Where he'd stare at the stars, too.

Archer paused to stare at the words etched into the wood.

Dedicated to the memory of Malcolm Campbell Husband. Father. Dreamer.

He swallowed hard. He'd wanted so much

to be able to go and speak to Halley after it happened. To tell her he knew what it felt like to not have a dad. That she'd be okay. But he never could. She hadn't really known Archer even existed! They'd not moved in the same social circles at school. He'd been this weird, gawky kid with glasses and an air of neglect, whereas she had been…well…a goddess. Beautiful. Popular. Adored by all! He remembered sitting in the back of the one class they'd shared and staring at her beautiful hair, wondering what it might feel like to touch it. But he'd simply never had the nerve to *tell* her anything. Not even a *hello*, never mind a *Hey, you'll be okay, you know.* He'd not had a dad either.

He cleared his throat as he approached, just to let her know he was getting closer.

She stood up. Turned. 'Hey.'

And the moonlight lit her face.

Archer stopped in his tracks, heart pounding, not sure his voice box would work, but… 'Halley?'

She stared back at him, confused. 'You know me?'

'Er…yeah, I do… I mean…we went to…' He laughed, unable to believe that this was happening. Meeting the girl he'd loved from afar, for all those years, never believing he would ever have the chance to talk to her, ever, and yet…here she was. In this place. Of all places. On this night. Because she'd left the village. Gone to Scotland apparently, vowing never to return. 'Archer. Archer Forde. We shared a class once. Science. We dissected a frog. Well, you dissected it and I watched and barely spoke because you were you and I was just a…' He laughed nervously again and held out his hand in greeting. 'I work in the veterinary surgery in Burndale.'

She frowned as she took in all the information he'd just launched at her, but she reached out to shake his hand. 'I remember that frog, but I don't remember…' Now it was *her turn* to laugh nervously. 'You don't look anything like the kid I dissected it with.'

'Well, the years have been kind. Glasses got switched for contacts. Grew a bit. Fixed the teeth. Found a decent barber to tame the hair.'

'I can see that.' She smiled warmly, almost shyly, and it was as if his heart exploded in his chest and all the feelings he'd ever had for this girl came rushing back.

Archer had been the perfect angsty teen watching Halley from afar and dreaming what it might be like for her to notice him and be his girl. But which boy at that school hadn't?

Halley had been the most popular and most

beautiful girl there and her life had seemed as golden as her hair. She lived on a children's farm, so was surrounded by cute bunnies all day when she was at home. She had an older sister, Hillary, who was cool and clever and admired by all and they had a good relationship, so Halley knew all the older kids, too.

She knew how to wear the school uniform with her own touch of style and made it look good. She could sing like a lark, she got all the lead roles in the school plays, but she wasn't just beautiful, she was smart, too. Her hand was always up first to answer the questions. She did well on her tests and her exams. She loved to read and Archer could remember her sitting on the low wall at school some lunchtimes, with her face stuck in a book, her lips moving slightly as she read.

Halley's life had been amazing until her dad died when she was fifteen. In those weeks she was away from school, he'd wondered how she was. If it would be wrong of him to write her a letter, maybe? Only he'd never been brave enough and so he hadn't. And when she'd come back to school? She'd been different. Less sparkly. A little subdued. But he'd still loved her from afar.

'I didn't know you were back in Burndale,' he said.

'I'm not. Well, not permanently, anyway. My mum had hip surgery and needed someone to help look after her and run the farm whilst she's getting back on her feet. We don't need her slipping in the mud. My sister was doing it, but she's got kids and a full-time job, so…'

'So you came back to help? That's great. I mean, I'm sorry your mum hurt her hip, I knew she'd been in hospital, but… I'm glad you're back. I've not seen you since—' And he stopped talking because he felt she probably wouldn't want him to bring up the last time he'd seen her. Standing there, in the village church in her wedding dress, staring in shock at the woman who had brought an abrupt halt to her wedding.

Was she blushing? Halley looked down at the ground. 'Since I embarrassed myself in front of the whole village? I didn't know you were there.'

'I was at the back.'

'Well, believe you me, I'm not intending to stick around and have people gossiping about me again.' Her voice sounded odd. As if this wasn't what she wanted at all, but she was trying to be brave about it. 'I'm going to work the farm, help Mum and then, when she's better, I'm out of here. Back to Edinburgh.' Again, she tried to make Edinburgh sound as if it was her safe place, her home, but her voice was strained.

'Edinburgh? That's where you're living?'

'Living. Working.'

'What do you do?'

'I'm a trained veterinary nurse, actually, so, same industry as you.'

A veterinary nurse? He wished he had a vacancy at the practice so he could hire her, but they didn't. The only vacancy he'd filled lately was one of partner. Max had retired and now an old college friend, Jenny, was going to join him.

'That's great!'

She nodded and an awkward silence descended.

'So, I guess your sister is watching your mum right now?'

'Yes. They both knew how much I wanted to come and see this.'

These were the most words he had ever said to her, and he knew he had so many more trapped inside him that he could never say to her. Could never say to any woman, but especially not her. Sticking to the obvious seemed better. 'So, you're here to watch the meteor shower?'

She nodded. 'I am. You?'

'Yeah. Would you mind me setting up next to you?'

She smiled. 'Not at all. It'll be nice to have the company.'

Watching the meteors skim the surface of the Earth's atmosphere was the most beautiful thing she had ever seen in this world. There was just something magical about sitting there and staring up at the sky and feeling that sense of wonder. Of watching something leave a glittering silver trail of sparks in the darkness. A brief moment of beauty in the dark. It made Halley realise how all her concerns were just so petty. How little they actually mattered.

When she'd first left, she'd not wanted to return to Burndale ever. This village simply reminded her of all the terrible things that had happened in her life. All the heartbreak and the humiliation and the longer she could stay away from it, the better! But then Mum had had her fall, slipping in mud on the farm, and Hillary had called to say she couldn't cope on her own and it wasn't fair and that Halley had to come back and take on her share of the caring responsibilities. The farm was getting neglected and it needed work and Hillary couldn't do it.

'I've got the twins to look after and Ste-

phen's on the oil rig for at least another three months! Please, Halley! Come home. Mum would love to see you, and you know how to look after those animals better than me, anyway. You're trained and qualified. You've got the knack. You always have.'

There had never been a knack. Hillary had just always preferred different things. The finer things that didn't include muck and manure and birthing baby animals in the middle of the night.

Halley had loved all of that, but, more than watching baby goats being born, she'd enjoyed the hours in the middle of the night that she'd shared with her dad, watching it happen. That was their special time. Just her and her dad, whilst Mum and Hillary slept. She'd get up and don her coat and wellies and they'd sit and talk in the barn, whilst waiting for a labouring mother to do her thing.

But if only I'd noticed the pain he carried. Why didn't I? Why do I never see the truth in people's hearts?

Suddenly, three or four meteors skimmed across the sky. 'Wow! Beautiful.'

Halley turned and smiled at Archer. *He* certainly was. Nothing like the boy she remembered from the frog dissection, who'd been quiet and gangly, with a wild mass of frizzy, blond-brown curls. The boy who'd hardly ever been at school, if she remembered him correctly. Now why was that? She couldn't quite remember.

Now his light brown hair was tamed. Short. His eyes sparkling. Jawline square. A short, trimmed beard. He was cute! More than cute. The type of guy who she would let buy her a drink in a bar. A guy who was so easy to talk to. As though she knew him. Which, she guessed, she kind of did.

Why don't I remember much about him?

'You know I used to come up here with my dad?'

He nodded. 'Is that why you had the bench put up here?'

'Yeah. He used to love showing me the stars. Pointing out Orion, the constellations, telling me how they got their names.'

'I used to clamber out onto the flat roof of our house and stare at the stars.'

'Your parents didn't do it with you?'

'No. I never knew my dad and Mum was always too sick. Whenever I needed a break from her, or my little brother, I'd go out there, if the sky was clear, and look up. I didn't get a telescope until I was fourteen. I saved for it, bought it second- or third-hand with my own money after I took on a paper round.'

She nodded, trying to recall if she remembered him. But she couldn't see him at all. 'Did you whizz around the village on a bike?'

'I never had a bike.'

'Never? Whereabouts in the village did you live?'

'Opposite side to you. On Crab Apple Lane?'

She didn't say anything about how he knew where she lived. Most people knew she grew up on Campbell's Children's Farm. Crab Apple Lane was located on the other side of the village.

'I guess we moved in different circles?'

'We most certainly did.'

'We don't now,' she said with a smile. 'You work with animals. So do I. You like gazing up at the universe. So do I. You're here on Rookery Point. Alone. With me.'

'Yeah.' He looked at her so wistfully then, she felt something hit her squarely in the gut and she realised, with shock, that it was utter lust overtaking her. Whether that was because of the way he looked, or the romantic nature of having stared at the stars together, or because they were alone, up here, on blankets on Rookery Point...or because she'd not been with a guy for so long and felt a primeval urge to do something stupid and reckless, she didn't know. But she did know she was having the feelings with him looking at her the way that he was.

He liked her, too. She could tell. But this could be all kinds of dangerous unless she took control of it.

'Are you single, Archer?'

He stared back. 'I am.'

'So am I.'

He continued to meet her gaze, trying to read her intentions.

'You know, it strikes me that we could take advantage of this unique situation.'

Archer looked a little flustered. 'What did you have in mind?'

She smiled, unable to believe she was going to propose such a thing, but she believed in making her own luck. Grabbing at life when it was offered, because you never knew when you might get a chance ever again. 'Like I said, we're here alone. On blankets. It's a beautiful night. We're both single. Some might say this is romantic…'

'What would *you* say?' he asked, his voice low.

'I'd agree, but… I'm not looking for romance, just so you know. I'm not looking for a relationship. I don't do those—'

'Neither do I.'

'But…'

'But?' He was staring intently at her, his bright sparkly eyes now dark and dangerous.

'What do you think to the idea of a kiss? A kiss between two relative strangers who've met on a hill beneath the stars, in a one-time-only deal?'

'A kiss?' His voice had changed. Grown more husky. She liked it. She liked it a lot.

'A kiss. Nothing more.' She smiled at him, wondering what he might taste like, this boy she had once known, yet forgotten about. This boy she had dissected a frog with. This boy who had grown into a fine, handsome figure of a man, who she knew liked her a lot. Someone she suddenly wanted to play with.

Why not do something crazy? She'd always stuck to the rules! Always behaved! And look how that had worked out for her. She'd done what was expected and had had it thrown in her face. Why not do the unexpected? Why not be crazy? Just this once? Kiss him as if she knew him, knowing she'd never have to see him ever again? There was no way she could stay in Burndale. She was here on reprieve. For a few months. Nothing more. What was the risk? It was fun. Just fun. And it had been a long time since she'd had any fun. It might make her time here in Burndale bearable. If she saw him. In the street. A fleeting glance.

The memory of what they'd done up here… A secret. Just between the two of them…

'Just one kiss…' he said, as if taking his time with the idea, as if he, too, was looking for the dangers of it. As if he, too, was wondering about how crazy it would be to do something so random and out of character? Not that she could know if this was out of character for him, but she hoped it would be, because if it was a rare thing, then he'd always remember it, wouldn't he? As *she'd* remember this night. Because she would.

I'll make sure to always remember Archer Forde from now on.

She leaned in towards him, smiling, almost laughing, watching the play of emotions cross his face, their lips inches apart. He smelt good.

He wanted it. He wanted her. But there was fear. Hesitation.

And she liked that. It made her want it even more. To touch him. Taste him. To be the one with the power. The one with the control.

One kiss and then, like a fairy-tale princess, she could disappear back to her farm and never see the handsome prince ever again.

She could do that. She knew she could. She'd had years to train herself to not get attached to guys. Years to not let her silly romantic heart run away with ideas of happy ever afters and all that nonsense, because she knew now. Knew they didn't exist. Knew they'd never existed! They were a fallacy. A trick. A trap she'd fallen into believing before and would never do so again.

But a little bit of lust? A little bit of daring and temptation? That she could deal with. Because she was making the rules and there was no way this could go wrong.

And as his lips came closer to hers, she fully believed that. Smiling, feeling as though she had won, as his mouth neared hers. And then he stopped. Millimetres away.

'You're sure about this?' he whispered.

She nodded. 'If you can keep it a secret. Can you?'

'I can. Can you?'

'Absolutely.' She moved closer. 'Why don't you kiss me, Archer? Kiss me like you've never kissed a woman before.'

And so he did and the second it began, she knew, almost at once, that it was never going to be just one kiss. Because kissing Archer made her feel as if the Earth had stopped revolving. That there was nothing else in the universe but them. On this solitary hill alone, beneath the ancient stars. That all that mattered was them.

And how he was making her feel.

Because she realised, far, far too late, that she never wanted this feeling to stop.

Two weeks had passed since the night on Rookery Point and Archer couldn't get it out of his mind. Two weeks since a kiss had become something *much more*. They'd left each other breathless and shocked and fastening their clothes, and though he'd wanted to call her to make sure she'd got back home all right, he'd refrained from doing so.

Nothing more can come from this, Archer. It was just this night, okay? What happened, happened. But that's all it will ever be.

'The one perfect night,' he'd said with a slow smile.

'One perfect night,' she'd agreed. 'Nothing more. No phone calls. No responsibility. No relationship. No falling in love.'

'No. Definitely none of that. I don't do that.'

He'd almost taken a step back towards her, but then she'd spoken again.

'Nor me.'

'Then we're okay?' He'd pulled his car keys from his pocket.

'We're okay.'

'Good.'

He'd helped her dress and, somehow, putting her clothes back on her had been just as erotic as taking them off! Sliding her jeans back up her legs, kissing her thighs as he'd done so. Pressing his lips to her belly, before the tee shirt had slid back down. Getting to his feet and stroking her cheek and planting one last kiss on her lips, before grabbing his telescope and heading back to his car.

He'd wanted to look back. Take one last glance. Absorb her in full, before he left, knowing this was his only moment with her. A crazy moment he'd cherish for ever. Only he didn't look back, because by then he was steeling himself. He'd got everything he'd ever dreamed of, but now it was over. They'd both agreed. Neither of them were looking for love. Neither of them were looking for something permanent. It could never happen. He'd been burned before. By her, even though she'd never known it and it had taken him a long time to get over the fact that she'd gone and left Burndale behind for good. There'd been one other woman. One other woman who he'd allowed to get close and he'd got hurt there, too. It just wasn't worth the pain.

At work, he got to his computer and called up the screen that showed the daily appointments to get a handle on what his day might be like. Letting his gaze scan the names and the pets and the…

Halley Campbell.

She was coming here? He clicked on the note beside her name. Saw that she was bringing in a trio of elderly guinea pigs for their annual check-up.

He licked his lips, trying to decide whether he should give her to Jenny, his new vet, instead? Let her handle her? But he didn't want to seem petulant, or childish, when he was a grown man and he ought to be able to handle one vet appointment. What would it be? Twenty minutes at the most? He could keep it professional. If she'd booked in with him and then she got here and found out she'd been handed over to Jenny, she might think he was ashamed of what they'd done, or was avoiding her after getting what he'd wanted, and he didn't want her to think that. Because it wasn't true. And besides, it would be an opportunity to make sure she was doing okay herself. Find out how everything was going on the farm. How her mother was doing.

See? Plenty of things for me to talk about.

Plus, it would give him a chance to look her in the eye. See her in the daylight. Become her friend as well as her vet. Technically, he had no doubt that she could do the annual health checks herself, what with her being a veterinary nurse, but the farm was a public farm.

It allowed children in to handle the animals and there were various rules and regulations that needed following and that meant getting a trained vet to assess the animals annually for temperament, diseases and health, to protect everyone involved. And they needed to be signed off by a third party. Not a family member.

Halley wouldn't be here until midday, so he could relax for a bit. He'd even get his morning break before she arrived, so that was good. He could check on how Jenny was settling in. He knew Jenny. Liked her. They'd met at college and become good friends after discovering they both were fans of James Herriot and watched all the shows and read all the books. It shouldn't have been a surprise to find another person who aspired to be the best vet in Yorkshire, but they'd laughed over a few drinks together in college and stayed in touch ever since. So when Max, the senior partner, had declared he was ready to retire and move to Portugal with his wife, Archer had advertised and Jenny had been one of the first to reply.

It had made sense to take on his friend. He'd felt as if he'd lost a surrogate father when Max said he was leaving to emigrate. So it was good to feel as if he was gaining back someone who he felt close to. Who he knew he could work with.

'We've got an emergency coming in,' said Barb, one of the receptionists, catching his attention.

'What is it?'

'Mrs Timball's cat, Felix. She thinks he's been run over by a car. She found him in the garden this morning and says he can't move his back legs. Feels cold.'

He nodded. 'When she gets here, send them straight through.'

'Will do.'

By the time Mrs Timball arrived just a few minutes later, he was ready with warming blankets and he quickly assessed the brown tabby. The cat was cold and a little wet from the morning dew of the grass, but it didn't feel as if he had any broken bones. All the joints and hind limbs worked fine upon manipulation. It was just that the cat couldn't move them himself, dragging them behind him like a puppet with its strings cut. Maybe this was a stroke?

'I need to do an X-ray, a scan, some bloods. Why don't you sit in the waiting room and I'll fetch you when I know more?' he suggested to Mrs Timball, who tearfully nodded, dabbing at her eyes with a white handkerchief as she returned to the waiting room.

Archer rushed the cat into the back room where the veterinary nurses were waiting and quickly and gently ran the cat through a battery of tests. X-ray. Ultrasound. Bloods. They gave Felix a shot of painkiller, just in case he was in any discomfort, but he didn't fight them at all. He seemed, if anything, resigned to his fate. He was eleven years old. A senior cat. But not so old that there was no point in seeing if there was anything they could do.

During the examination, poor Felix soiled himself and lost his pulses in his groin. With the scan results and imaging, Archer quickly had an answer to poor Felix's condition. He called Mrs Timball back into the examination room, where he had Felix lying on a warm, padded mat for comfort.

'I'm afraid it looks like Felix has a spinal embolism. In cats it's called fibrocartilaginous embolic myelopathy. On the imaging, we were able to spot a swelling and blockage in his spinal cord, causing Felix to lose control of his rear end. He's cold because he is losing blood flow to his rear end and there is evidence of progressive spinal damage.'

'So what do we do?'

'I'm afraid, in these cases, euthanasia is the kindest thing.'

'No!' Mrs Timball began to cry, hunkering down to place her face next to her cat's, stroking him and saying sorry and how much she loved him. She pressed her forehead to his and Felix softly closed his eyes and tried to purr. 'Are you sure there's nothing we can do?'

'I'm sorry. I can give you some time with him if you wish. He's on painkillers, so he should be comfortable if you want to call any family to say goodbye.'

'No. It's just me. And it wouldn't be fair to keep him hanging on. When will you do it?'

'We can do it straight away.'

She nodded. 'Okay.'

'Do you want to stay in the room? You don't have to, if you don't want.'

'This cat has been by my side for everything. When I lost my husband. When I got Covid. Everything. It's only right I stay by his side when he needs me, too.'

'All right.'

Archer gathered the medications he would need. 'This is pentobarbital. It will render Felix unconscious and then his heart will stop. It won't hurt him…it'll be like going to sleep.'

Mrs Timball nodded, tears dripping down

her face as she stroked Felix, not taking her eyes from him.

'Are you ready?'

'Yes.' Mrs Timball leant down and whispered, 'I love you, Felix.'

Once he was sure she had said everything she needed to say, he slowly injected the drug. It took less than a minute. Felix's head lay on the table and his eyes stopped focusing. Archer picked up his stethoscope and checked the heart, but it had stopped. 'It's done. He's passed.'

Mrs Timball's crying began anew and she began to tremble and shake and so he stepped around the table and draped an arm around her shoulder. 'Can I call anyone for you?'

She shook her head. 'No, love. There's nobody. I'm all alone.'

'What about a friend?'

'No. I'm all right. I'll be all right. Can I have him cremated? Get his ashes back?'

'Of course. I'll make the arrangements. Would you like to sit with him for a bit?'

She stared at her cat. 'No. Let him go. I ought to be getting back and, besides, you have a full clinic out there, you need to use the room.'

Mrs Timball wiped her nose and eyes with her tissue, sucked in a deep, steadying breath and gave him a quick smile. 'I'll go. You'll look after my boy, won't you? Make sure he's treated with respect?'

'Of course. As if he's my own.' Archer did have his own cat. Jinx. She was a rescue moggy. Pure black, with green eyes. Black cats were often the ones left behind in rescues or rehoming centres as some people were superstitious, even today. He knew she'd been mistreated at a previous home and he'd got her when she was seven years old. After she'd sat in the rescue centre for six years, being passed by every time. Well, he couldn't pass by, and she was the best cat. Affectionate, despite her past. A lap cat. With the loudest purr he'd ever heard.

He would treat Felix as he would treat Jinx. As he would treat any animal. With the respect it deserved. Each animal, each pet he saw in this practice was loved and beloved by its owners. They were family members and nothing less than that. They weren't just animals.

When Mrs Timball had gone, Archer took a moment to gather himself before his next patient. He'd always known that euthanising an animal was going to be the hardest part of his job and, though he'd grown used to steeling himself so he could deal with his patient's owner's grief, he still always needed a minute after, to gather himself and shake off the pain and upset that he had witnessed.

This was the hard part of love. The hardest part. Saying goodbye. Love was pain. He saw it every day. He experienced it every day. Loving someone who couldn't love you back? That hurt. Being left behind hurt. It was why he'd decided it was easier to not get involved. To stop giving his heart away for free, because every time he did, he suffered because of it and he didn't want to do that any more. His love had never seemed enough.

And yet still, despite hardening his heart, he felt it. Every loss. Losing an animal was hard. Losing a beloved pet was difficult and he saw the love the owners had for that animal. Witnessing their pain reminded him of his own and what was waiting for him when it was Jinx's time. He'd not wanted to get a pet because of it. Why put himself through that?

But he hated living alone and it was nice to have someone to come back home to at the end of a difficult day and animals were easier to love than people. They didn't hurt you deliberately. They loved you. Adored you. Wanted nothing more from you than what they gave themselves. They didn't fall out with you, or cheat on you, or deliberately go out of their way to lie to you or make you feel as if you were nothing. Or not good enough. Animals loved you for who you were and that was that. It was simple and Archer liked simple.

He scanned his list to see what was coming next. A dog with a mystery lump.

He hoped it was a simple fatty lump and nothing more.

He wasn't sure he could deal with any more heartbreak today.

Halley sat feeling nervous in the waiting room with her box of three guinea pigs—Milly, Molly and Moo—hoping that this visit would be simple. Easy. No making eye contact with anyone. Say hello. Get the three girls their clean bill of health. Say goodbye. Smile and go.

Why on earth did I sleep with the village vet? Of all the people I could have chosen, I choose the vet when I'm going to be working on the farm!

She knew she should have thought ahead about the practicalities of such a tryst but, to be fair, her brain hadn't been thinking of sensible things after lying on a blanket beneath the stars with Archer. She'd been thinking of other things. About how his hands looked adjusting the telescope. How square and strong they looked. How deftly he moved his fingers.

His biceps and how pronounced they were. The way his bottom looked in his jeans when he stood up to stretch. He was hot. Archer Forde was *delectable*. No two ways about it!

And she was a woman who hadn't been with a man for a long, long time and there was a need she'd felt to do something about that! And they were there. Together. Alone, under the stars. And it wasn't as if they were strangers, was it? She'd known him. Once, a long, long, time ago, and yes, maybe she hadn't noticed him, because back then he'd not been in her friendship group, but he was *gorgeous*, and she was a hot-blooded woman, and women had needs too, and…

You did it. It's fine. It was allowed.

It would be fine. They'd both set boundaries. A one-night-only deal and they'd stuck to that. She'd not heard a peep from him in the last two weeks since it had happened. No annoying phone calls bothering her asking for more. No awkward texts. No emails. No gossip whizzing around the village like wildfire. Clearly he'd got what he'd wanted from such an interlude, just as she had, and that was fine.

Even if it was the best sex I've ever had in my life.

Maybe it only felt like the best sex she'd ever had because they'd known it would only be the once? And so they'd both gone full out? Nobody normal had sex like that all the time, right?

She sighed and glanced upward at the clock in the waiting room. Each number was an animal. Twelve was a rooster, of course. One was a green snake, two was a chicken, three was a sloth, four a dog, five a starfish and so on and so on. Of course they'd have an animal-themed clock in here. Everything in here had an animal on it. The posters on the walls. The information leaflets. The stand in the corner selling dog and cat toys, treats and food.

Opposite her was Mr Knight. He'd been her headmaster at junior school. He looked old now. Silver-haired. Tired. But there was still that twinkle of mirth in his eyes as he looked down at his Jack Russell dog that lay at his feet, panting, quivering and shaking. Clearly the dog was no fan of being at the vet, either. Knight hadn't noticed her. Or recognised her, anyway, so that was something to be grateful for. Probably something to do with the sunglasses she had on, along with the floppy hat.

She'd hoped Hillary could have brought the guinea pigs. In fact, she'd promised to. But then one of the twins had been up all night with a fever and she'd rung first thing to say she couldn't make it over and that Halley would have to do it instead. She'd forgotten the time of the appointment and so Halley had rung to double-check and let them know that she was bringing in the guinea pigs instead. Maybe she wouldn't even get Archer? There was a new vet that had started, apparently, or so she'd heard. Maybe she'd get her?

But then the door opened and there he stood. Looking just as handsome as he had that night. Maybe even more so, because now she could see that his eyes were a rich hazel colour and, in his pale green scrubs, he looked even more attractive than she remembered.

Her heart pounded in her chest and she felt her mouth go dry in anticipation and so she looked away from him, not wanting to let him know just how he was affecting her, because she hadn't been expecting that.

I mean, maybe a little, because of how hot that night was, but this?

She tried to nonchalantly gaze out of the window to the street outside, but it was as if she could feel his gaze upon her and all she could think about was how his hot gaze had travelled over her semi-naked body that night and how he'd whispered against her neck how beautiful she was and she'd shivered and—

'Miss Campbell?'

She closed her eyes. He'd said her name. She

wasn't getting the lady vet. She was getting *him*. Archer. A guy she'd pinned to the ground as she'd straddled him and moved faster and faster until she was crying out as literal celestial rocks grazed the surface of the sky, creating fireworks.

She gave him a curt smile, nodded, and picked up the box with the guinea pigs and strode primly past him into the examination room, glad to be away from any prying eyes in the waiting room, placing the box onto the table that she could see was still damp from antiseptic spray.

Behind her the door closed. 'Good morning.'

The sound of his voice sent literal trembles down her spine. 'Morning.' She removed the sunglasses. Perched them on top of the hat.

'Milly, Molly and… Moo?' He smiled.

Grudgingly, she nodded. 'I didn't name them. They were nothing to do with me.' She laughed, not wanting him to think she was some kind of simpleton. Her mum had named them. Not that her mother was a simpleton, either, she just picked names that she thought children would like. If children liked the names, then they felt closer to the animals. Liked them more. Wanted to adopt them. It was a business decision. Sensible even. They made a decent sideline in animal adoptions.

'And how are they? Have you noticed any issues?' He stood in front of her now, looking at her, but she felt unable to meet his gaze. She kept staring down at the box the animals were in.

'Er…no. I think they're fine. They just need their annual check-up.'

'Okay.'

She tried to focus on his hands again as they opened the box. Inside, the guineas were huddled together in one corner.

'And can you tell me which is which?' He picked up the tortoiseshell one, with all the mad tufts of fur going in different directions.

'That's Moo.'

'Okay, Moo, let's take a look at you.'

As he bent down to examine the guinea pig, it gave her a moment to look at him unwatched. Unnoticed. He was tanned. As if he'd been away recently and caught the sun. He had a tiny brown mole on his clavicle, muscular forearms, and he handled the guinea pig gently and calmly, listening to its chest and lungs with his stethoscope, after examining its eyes, teeth and ears. 'Everything seems good here. How old is she now?'

'Erm…five years old. They're all five, I think.'

'Old enough for retirement?' He looked up at her, made eye contact and smiled and it was like being punched in the gut. She felt breathless. Unsteady. She placed a hand on the examining table and tried to breathe steadily.

'Yeah, Mum doesn't like these ones to get handled so much now. It's a young guinea pigs' game, apparently.'

He smiled and began his examination of the other two.

Halley was beginning to think she could relax. He wasn't going to say anything about that night, was he? And that was good. Because she didn't need him to. It was easier not saying anything. It would make the next time they met even easier. If there was a next time, but she lived on a farm, with lots of animals, so the likelihood was high.

But weirdly, she was also disappointed that he hadn't said anything. Now why was *that*? she asked herself. Did she want him to want her? Did she want to think that he'd been so affected by their meeting that he couldn't get her out of his mind and wanted more? As if she were some sort of drug? A mind-altering substance that he still craved? Because that would be a bonus for her ego, right?

That's all this is. Ego. I need to know that he was affected by that night as much as I was.

But that was all it was. Being *affected*.

It wasn't anything else. Because something that good *would* affect you. Wouldn't it?

'Well, they're all good. Milly could do with a nail trim, so shall I do that? Or are you able to do that back at the farm?'

'Oh. I can do that, that's no problem.'

'Good! Okay. Then we're done.'

'Okay.' She felt as if she ought to say something though. An acknowledgement? A reference to that night? Or just act as if it *hadn't* happened? 'Maybe I'll see you around?'

'Maybe.' He smiled and began tapping his fingers against the keyboard to input his findings into the animals' files on his computer.

'Okay. Bye, then.'

A quick glance. A quicker smile. 'Bye.'

And he continued to type.

The message couldn't be clearer. It really had just been one night.

Just as she'd requested.

Just as he'd insisted.

So why did she feel a little disappointed?

When it was exactly what they'd *both* wanted?

CHAPTER TWO

HE COULD BREATHE again after she left. How he'd managed to hold it together whilst she was here, he didn't know. He'd felt his hands trembling. Had she noticed? Thankfully the guinea pigs hadn't and animals were usually good at noticing nervous handlers. Maybe they sensed he wasn't nervous of them, but her?

She was even more beautiful in daylight. Her hair was golden. Honey-blonde and falling about her face in soft waves from beneath that crazy hat she'd been wearing, that he'd wanted to reach out and touch. Her eyes were beautiful. Her skin creamy, with a hint of pink in her cheeks. Her lips...*dear God, her lips*...were full and the most dangerous thing about them was that he knew how they felt upon his body.

But it was more than her looks. He'd always thought she was beautiful, but that beauty wasn't just on the outside. That night up on Rookery Point, they'd talked. Before and after.

She was funny. Kind. Thoughtful. They said never meet your idols and there had always been a part of him as a child that had told him that she probably wasn't as great as he imagined her to be, but she *was* and that blew his mind. There was nothing wrong with her.

Except for the fact that she was a woman who could hurt him again and, despite her being a goddess, he couldn't take the chance even with her. Besides, she didn't want a relationship either, so there it was, right there. She didn't want a relationship. She wasn't cut out for those. She'd told him, just as he'd told her the exact same thing, even though deep down he wanted something more. They were both done with all that, they'd said. They'd been there. Done that. Been scorched by flying too close to the sun. Burned.

And burns hurt.

Deeper burns seared away all those nerves and left you numb and unable to feel and that was how it was with him.

He'd tried to fly high and crashed and burned.

He would never try to do so again. Amy had seen to that.

But he didn't want to think about Amy. Right now, he just wanted to acknowledge the fact that he'd seen Halley again and that they'd got through it, without it being awkward, and she hadn't gone back on her word and asked him for anything he was incapable of giving her. Not his phone number. Not if he wanted to meet for coffee. Not any of that dating stuff.

They'd shared one hot night and it would be something he treasured for ever, but that was all it could ever be. He'd spent a night with the girl of his dreams, beneath the stars, and it couldn't have been more perfect and that had to be enough. It was enough.

It was...enough.

From now on, they would just be friends. Clients, if he had to go to the farm, or she had to come here with an animal. Nothing more.

Nothing more at all.

Halley hefted a bale of straw and dumped it down beside the others, cutting the twine and pulling it loose, so she could begin to cover the floor of the pen for the pygmy goats that she'd just cleared out.

This was hard work. Tough, back-breaking work and she wondered, once again, how her mother managed it. Her mother was much older, but she did this every day. Yes, there were farm helpers and all of that, but she knew her mum was very much a hands-on boss, who wasn't afraid of getting her hands dirty. She wasn't one of those bosses who sat in the office, punching numbers into a calculator and shouting orders at her underlings.

Halley had been here two weeks and already her back hurt and her muscles were sore and every night she fell into bed she was stiff, tired and exhausted. Sure that she'd have no energy the next day to get through anything, but somehow finding it.

Today was no exception.

However, it was fun and different from her usual work in a veterinary surgery. Back at Downlands Surgery, in Edinburgh, where she usually worked, she would either be sitting on Reception taking calls, or assisting in a surgery, or seeing patients of her own for six-monthly checks, or what have you. She'd always liked the practical nature of her job. That she wasn't sitting at a desk every day, that every patient was different and some of them were absolute mysteries until they could work out, like detectives, what was wrong and how an animal might be made better, if possible.

But being at the farm was good too. It was nice to be home, strangely. She wasn't in the village having everyone look at her with pity in their eyes, she was here. With the animals, and animals didn't judge you at all. Except to decide if they could trust you. And almost all of the animals here, with maybe the exception of Ivan the alpaca, seemed to trust her. They were used to human beings. They were used to being around them. Being petted. Being fed. Being looked after. A relationship with animals was more honest than any relationship she'd ever had with a human. It was simpler and she liked simpler. There was no subterfuge. No lies. No hiding. What you saw was what you got.

'There you go.' She opened up the metal gate that allowed the pygmy goats back in. They were Southern Sudan Goats and Mum had reared a fair number of them now. They had seventeen at last count and two of the females were pregnant, both of them with sets of twins, so that would take their total up to twenty-one, and Mum said when they reached twenty she'd swap some stock with another children's farm over in Cumbria, just to keep the breeding lines clean.

The goats tottered in, bleating, looking around before going over to the buckets that had their feed in on the far side.

Checking her watch, she realised it was breakfast time and she'd not eaten yet. She'd wanted to get these pens clean before opening and, now that it was done, she had half an hour before the farm opened up to the public at nine o clock.

Her stomach gurgled as if to remind her that she was, in fact, starving. She stepped through the metal gate, closing it behind her, then went over to the hand-washing station. One of many that were set up all over the farm, for kids to wash their hands. It meant bending quite low and she felt the strain in her back muscles, after hauling all of that straw.

But inside, she kicked off her boots and pulled off her navy overalls and headed into the kitchen to make Mum and herself breakfast. 'What do you fancy this morning, Mum?' Before Halley came home to help, Hillary had arranged for a bed to be set up downstairs, so their mum didn't have to manage the stairs. That wasn't needed now. Mum could make it up the stairs, if she took her time. She just needed to build up her strength.

'Eggs.'

'Okay. Scrambled? Poached? Fried?'

'Scrambled, please, love. On toast. One slice though, for me.'

'You'll have two. Keep your strength up. You've got that physio appointment this afternoon, remember?'

'All right, two, then.'

Halley smiled. Mum could sometimes be a

stubborn patient and Hillary said they'd had one or two fallings out since she'd come home from the hospital, but that was only because her mum didn't like giving up control of the farm and wanted to do everything herself.

'Everything okay out there?'

'Yes. Absolutely fine. Just as it was yesterday and the day before that.'

'And you know you've got the vet coming over late this evening to check on Bubbles?'

Halley paused mid-stride to turn and face her mum. 'What? What's wrong with Bubbles?' Bubbles was the miniature Shetland pony that they'd taken on as a rescue.

'Hillary thought she needed a check-up.'

'Wh-why?' She didn't want Archer to come here. She'd seen him only yesterday! He might think she was deliberately trying to see him again.

'Said she noticed she was lying down a lot yesterday and she's worried the laminitis issue might be back.'

'Well, I could check for that! We don't need the vet.'

'Well, I booked it already. I called them yesterday afternoon.'

Halley stared morosely at her mother. 'Which vet? The new one or the old one?'

Her mother shrugged. 'I don't know, love.

I didn't ask. Though it would be nice if it was Archer, I know him. Have you met the new one? Pretty thing, apparently. Was she there yesterday when you took in Milly, Molly and Moo?'

She shook her head. 'No, I only saw Archer.'

'Oh. Though thinking about it, it might be nice to meet the new one. Introduce ourselves. After all, we'll be working with them a lot.'

Halley slammed a cupboard shut after getting the bread out, and cracked the eggs into the pan, bursting the yolks and angrily giving them a stir. She added a splash of milk, a knob of butter and turned up the heat as the bread toasted. Her own appetite was diminishing by the second at the news of a vet visit. It seemed a complete waste of time! An expensive waste of time! She was a trained veterinary nurse. She'd be able to tell if Bubbles had laminitis. After breakfast, she'd open up and then go check that pony herself and when she discovered that she didn't have it and was absolutely fine, then she could cancel the visit.

Damn Hillary and her belief that what Halley did for a living wasn't a real job. Her older sister was a solicitor and felt as if she were the only one that had trained and studied hard for her living. To Hillary, Halley was nothing more than a glorified healthcare assistant. Something anyone could do. Well, she was wrong!

The toast popped out of the toaster and she placed it on two plates, spread butter on, then added the now scrambled eggs on top. She took the two plates over to where her mother sat, then she went to sit at the table to eat her own breakfast, but, even though she'd been starving earlier and looking forward to something to eat, the eggs tasted awful. Metallic. And the smell was beginning to turn her stomach.

Damn Hillary and her interfering!

This was her fault.

Archer pulled up at Campbell's Children's Farm, parking in the main car park beside the barn. He'd been here a couple of times, usually called over by Halley's mother. He liked Sylvie. She was a good woman, who ran a damned fine farm, educating children and their parents on farm life, animals and maintaining a healthy environment for all. He'd always enjoyed his previous visits, chatting with Sylvie. He wondered if she was up and about enough to speak with him today, or whether he'd get one of the daughters.

Whether it would be Halley.

Her visit to the surgery the other day had

felt a little awkward, but it had gone without event, which was good. That first meeting after having shared what they had was always going to be weird. But now he might see her again. Would it ever get easier? Would it ever be *comfortable* with her?

He killed the lights and turned off his engine and looked out to his right, where he could see a figure working in the barn. He instantly saw it was her filling up water troughs with a hose. Her golden hair gleaming in the lamplight. She glanced briefly in his direction then turned away again. He felt his heart rate accelerate and he turned away to take a breath, to tell himself to calm the hell down.

It's all going to be fine.

He walked to the rear of his vehicle, donned his wellies, grabbed his go-bag, squared his shoulders and then began to walk towards the barn, his gaze on her, taking in what he could before she turned. She wore fitted blue jeans, scuffed with mud, aged black boots, a tee shirt with a flannel shirt over the top. Her hair had been twisted up into a messy bun and strands of gold fell down beside her face, which, now he was closer, he could see had a smear of dirt across her cheek. 'Hey, good evening.'

She glanced at him. 'Hi. We must stop meeting like this.' She went over to a tap and turned it off, draping the hose over a hook on the wall.

He smiled, hoping she was just joking. 'These things happen.'

'I don't know why my mum called you. I was able to check the pony myself.'

'And what were your findings?'

She stared at him as if she were struggling to admit them. 'Laminitis. The pony's had it before, I believe.'

She had. He'd checked the file before leaving. 'Once before, yes. Want me to take a look, just to confirm?'

'Knock yourself out. If I'd had any spare anti-inflammatories from before I wouldn't have called you out at all.'

'Understandable.' He was beginning to get the feeling that she didn't want him here. Which hurt, but was fine. These visits here for him were difficult too. He'd made love to this woman on a hilltop. This woman he'd loved for years, ever since he was a little boy. Being with her was like fulfilling a lifelong dream and now she was talking to him as if he was an inconvenience? 'Where's Bubbles at right now?'

'I've got her in the stable. Follow me.'

Archer hated being made to feel as though he was an inconvenience. He'd had that his entire childhood. His mother had made him feel as though he and Axle were mistakes she'd made with their father. That she'd been left with the burden of raising them, after their dad abandoned them all, and she resented their existence, barely finding the energy to interact with them if the TV was on. He'd felt desperate for a smidgen of her love, which she'd given rarely and only when she was on her full meds and got straight.

But most of the time? He'd lived without it. Without his mother's love. Taking responsibility for his younger brother and making sure that *he* didn't feel as if no one loved him. His mother had made him feel as if her life would have been a whole lot easier without him around. Exactly how Halley was making him feel right now. As if she'd made a terrible mistake and regretted it. He was sensitive to feelings such as those. Maybe too sensitive? He tried to shrug it off. He was here to do a job.

Halley led him to one of the stables, where the pony, Bubbles, waited. She was lying down on the wood shavings as they entered.

'It seems to be mostly in her front hooves.'

'Okay. I'll take a look.'

He concentrated on the pony. He would show Halley that she might not want him there, she might regret that he was there, but he would prove that it was *important* for him to be there. He knelt to check the pony's hooves, gently examining them all, to see which were affected, which were worse, and Halley was right. The two front hooves were hot and tender.

'I've put her in here with a deeper bed of wood chips to help.'

'That's good.'

'And when I muck her out I put her in a bay with a rubber mat.'

'Sounds like you're doing everything you can.'

'I'm trying. But if you could just prescribe some more anti-inflammatories, that'd be great, and I'll get her started on them right away.'

She was trying to hurry this thing along. Get rid of him. He looked up at her and raised an eyebrow. 'Let me do a complete examination first. I'm here, might as well get the most out of me.'

She smiled, but it didn't reach her eyes. And it was brief. Too brief. There, then gone in an instant. Clearly he was making her uncomfortable. She seemed angry, almost. Should he be pleased at that? That their night together had had some sort of impact on her? Or should he be upset? Normally he'd like to think that if he'd been with a girl and she'd enjoyed herself, she'd be pleased to see him again, so why was Halley being like this? They'd had a great time. An amazing time!

'Does she need an X-ray?'

'Let's try the medications first and if that doesn't help, then maybe we should. Also it might be worth you calling the farrier to trim the hooves often.'

'He's coming tomorrow.'

'Well, then, you're doing everything you can. She's not overweight, so that's good. You don't have to worry about slimming her down. Let her rest. Maybe keep her away from the kids until she's better. And I've brought some anti-inflammatories with me, just in case, so I'll give you those so she can get started on them right away.'

'Thank you.' She sounded relieved now. Relieved the appointment was over?

He decided he needed to address the elephant in the room. He did that now. He'd been silenced so much as a child, as an adult, he liked to address problems and have his say. 'You know…we can be civil to one another.'

She looked at him. 'How do you mean?'

'I rather get the feeling you don't want me here. After what happened between us.'

She seemed uncomfortable at him mentioning it. 'Nothing happened.'

'But it did. We slept together. Unexpectedly, yes, but I'm not going to regret it. I, for one, thought it was rather beautiful and I will cherish the memory of that night, but you're making it difficult for me to enjoy it.'

'How do you mean?'

'Well, you can barely meet my eye, and you're making me feel like *you'll* feel a whole lot better if I just left.'

'I just… I don't do that sort of thing. Sleep with a guy I barely know. I try to get to know him a bit before I…' She seemed to colour. Blush.

He found it adorable. 'We got to know one another a little.'

'I know, it was just…impulsive and out of character for me and… I just don't want to make any more mistakes with my life, you know?'

'You're saying I was a mistake?' That hurt. His mum had once told him that he and Axle were both mistakes. Mistakes she regretted. It had taken him a long time to get over that admission from her, so he most certainly did not need to hear that from Halley, too. Not about something that he'd thought was so beautiful, because how could something so wonderful as their liaison be anything but?

She stared back at him. 'Yes.'

'Then I'm sorry you feel that way.' He marched away, unable to believe that she would say such a thing. He had feelings, he wasn't a rock. That night, however unexpected, however surprising, however brief, had meant something to him. And no matter what *she* said, he would cherish it and not let her cheapen it by calling their union a mistake.

It could never be a mistake.

Not with *her*.

Halley felt bad after he left. It left a sour feeling in her stomach. She'd not meant to say he was a mistake, but now he'd gone thinking that she thought of him with regret. It wouldn't do wonders for his masculinity, but what could she do? Tell him the truth? Tell him that, in moments of quiet, her mind kept returning to that night and dreaming of how he'd made her feel? And how she'd love to feel that way again? How in a perfect world she would return here to Burndale and maybe they might be able to have a chance, if she was brave enough?

Archer had treated her body and her soul

with reverence. That night had not been a passionate quickie under the stars, it had been more than that. Much more. It had been as if…as if she'd known him for years. He had touched her as if he loved her. As if he adored her. As if she were precious and he were going to savour every infinite moment with her. She'd felt special. He'd made her feel that way, that she was the centre of his universe, and she'd never been made to feel that way before with a man. Not even with Piotr. No wonder she still craved it!

What she hated was the fact that he had left an impression on her. Archer had left her wanting to feel more of that. Craving more of that. He'd intrigued her and left her thinking of him all the time and she didn't want that. It terrified her what that meant. Because the last time she'd felt that way about a guy—about Piotr—she'd been left with pie on her face. Jilted at an altar. The subject of ridicule and village gossip and pity. And she *refused* to feel that way again. Her whole love life had been exposed to the village of Burndale and they'd witnessed her fall. Her humiliation. And she would not embarrass herself again, in front of them, with the village veterinary surgeon!

'Was it laminitis?' her mother asked as Halley came in, pulling off her wellington boots.

'Yes.'

'Poor thing. Did he give you medicine?'

'Yes.' She shrugged off her jacket and hung it up on the hooks by the front door and dropped into a sofa, filled with cushions.

'You look tired, love.'

'I am. I'm exhausted.'

'What's for dinner?'

Dinner. Now she had to cook dinner? No wonder Hillary couldn't keep up with this. Running a farm and being a carer. 'I don't know. Something quick. Pasta?'

Her mother nodded and picked up her book. Some romantic saga she was reading. Not Halley's thing. It looked a thick book. Maybe five hundred pages? 'Whenever you're ready.'

'I might just close my eyes for five minutes.'

Her mother glanced at her. 'Not too long though, love.'

'No. Not too long.' She allowed her eyes to close and fell into a deep sleep, almost instantly. She dreamed of Archer, of course. Him and her, back on Rookery Point, beneath the stars and she was holding his hand, staring up at the sky. Neither of them saying anything. Just being together and it being enough. And she turned to look at him as he said, 'Halley, I need you to wake up now. Halley!'

And she jumped, because it wasn't his voice, but her mother's, and when she blinked her eyes open, her mother was staring at her, frowning.

'I'm sorry…what?'

'I'm starving, love. I'd do it, but you'd tell me off, so… Can you make us something to eat?'

'Sure. Sure.' She scrambled to her feet, trying to feel awake as she stood.

'You talk in your sleep, you know.'

Halley turned around in the kitchen doorway. 'Do I? Did I say anything vaguely sensible?'

'You were muttering about the vet, I think. You kept saying Archer.'

'Oh.'

'You must have been worrying about Bubbles way more than you thought!'

Halley smiled. 'Yes. That must be it.'

Her mother smiled back. 'Bless your heart.'

She thought he'd been a mistake. Well, that hurt, because he would never think of what they had done as a mistake. Even though he'd known, at the time, that it was something that would never be repeated, because they'd both stated that quite clearly. Neither of them wanted anything to come of their…interaction. But he would never call what they did a mistake.

To him, it had been a beautiful thing. Something he would cherish for ever. He would never think of Halley Campbell as a mistake, even if she regretted their association.

His brother, Axle, deliberately stepped in front of him to get his attention. ‘Hey, are you even listening to me?’

Archer blinked and nodded, smiling. ‘Of course!’

‘Then what did I just say?’

‘Er…you were talking about Joanne.’

‘And?’

Archer grimaced. ‘Sorry. You’re right. I got distracted. What did Joanne have to say when you last spoke to her?’

Axle frowned. ‘That she’d been offered a promotion in her job and it would mean longer hours and she couldn’t see herself coming back to Burndale or even Yorkshire any time soon.’

‘So when do you get to see the kids?’ Axle had had two kids with Joanne, but their relationship had been problematic from the get-go, with issues over jealousy and lying, and they’d had an on-again, off-again relationship for a couple of years, before Joanne had upped sticks and moved to Cardiff, taking Axle's two sons with her. He'd barely seen them since.

'She said not any time soon.'

'But you can visit them?'

'You know what she's like, though. She agrees to let me see them, then I travel all that way for my appointed time and she goes out, or she refuses! The last time she slammed the door in my face.'

'You did turn up slightly drunk.'

'I needed a drink before seeing her. You know how she pushes all my buttons. I just wanted to spend some time with my kids, you know, is that so bad?'

'Of course not. You want to be a good dad. But, Ax, turning up drunk isn't going to get you that. You need to lay off having a pint with the lads before you go there. If she gives you a time to see the boys, then get there for that time, and if she mucks you around, stay calm and ask for another time to see them. Be calm and assertive, not aggressive.'

'I miss my kids, Archie. I don't want them growing up thinking they haven't got a dad, like we did. Or that they have a parent that doesn't care.'

'I know.' He laid a reassuring hand on his brother's shoulder. 'Has she said you can visit?'

'This weekend I'm going down to Cardiff.'

'Okay. Well, maybe this time it'll work out.'

'You said that last time. And the time before that. Do you think I'm going to have to take her to court just to see my kids?'

'I hope not. I hope you can work it out between yourselves.'

'Yeah. Me too.'

'You been speaking to the boys on the phone, though?'

'Not since last time. She won't put them on the phone and they're too young to have mobiles of their own, so I always have to go through her. Do you know how hard it is, Arch, to want to be with someone so badly and they just won't let you?'

Archer nodded.

'It drives me crazy! I should never have got involved with Joanne. She was a big mistake! I should have picked someone like me. Who wanted the same things as me.'

'You did what you thought was right at the time.'

'But it was never enough.'

Archer didn't know what to say. His brother was hurting, and he couldn't imagine being in a similar situation if he were to ever make the mistake of having kids. He'd told himself long ago he'd never have them, and it was hearing stuff like this that told him he'd made the right decision.

CHAPTER THREE

HALLEY WOKE FEELING EXHAUSTED, despite having an early night and sleeping for ten hours straight.

Maybe I've had too much sleep?

She'd read that once. That too much sleep could be as bad, if not worse, than too little.

Maybe it was all down to the physical work she was doing, not just on the farm, but also in looking after her mum.

She grabbed her robe and ambled down the stairs, frowning when she heard noises and music coming from the kitchen. 'Hello?'

She turned the corner at the bottom of the stairs and saw her mum, already on the couch reading a magazine, and in the kitchen, stirring a pan, was Hillary, her sister.

'Afternoon, sleepyhead,' said Hills, with a raised eyebrow.

Halley looked at her wristwatch. It was only eight-thirty. 'It's still morning.'

'And Mum needed her pain meds at eight. She had to call me to come over to give them to her, because she couldn't reach them from the high cupboard in the kitchen.'

Halley frowned and looked at her mum. 'You could have called me.'

'I did. You didn't answer. I got worried and called your sister.'

'Luckily, I'm not in court until this afternoon and I'd already dropped the twins off at breakfast club, so I could come over. I checked you were still breathing and then gave Mum her meds. I'm just doing her porridge, now.'

'Oh, well, thanks. I'm sorry I didn't hear you, Mum. I must have been well tired.'

Hillary tilted her head to look at her. 'You do look a little peaky.'

'I always look like this first thing.'

'Well, thank God you don't have a boyfriend, then—he'd run a…' She stopped. Grimaced. 'Sorry.'

'No. It's fine.' Halley activated the camera on her mobile phone and glanced at her appearance. Hills was right. She did look a little pale. 'Ugh.'

'You feeling okay?'

'Tired.'

'It's hard work, isn't it? Do you see now, why I asked you to come back and help me?

I've been doing this, the farm, Mum, looking after the twins and trying to be a solicitor! It's your turn, now.'

'I know, I know. Thank you for all you've done. You're Superwoman, Hills.'

Her sister smiled and bit into a piece of toast. 'I've put on enough porridge for you, too, if you want some?'

'Sure.' Halley settled down onto a seat in the kitchen as Hillary poured some porridge into bowls and set one down in front of her. Halley sprinkled some sugar on the top and then ate a mouthful, grimacing at the heat and the taste.

'Something wrong with it?'

'What have you put in it?'

'Nothing. Oats. Mum likes it plain.'

'It tastes…awful!'

'Well, thank you. You're very welcome,' Hills said sourly.

'Tastes fine to me, love,' said their mum, from the couch.

'Perhaps there's something wrong with your tastebuds then, because this tastes like…' She trailed off as she had a sudden rush of nausea in her stomach. It came over her like a wave and was then gone again, almost as quickly as it came. Halley pushed the bowl away. 'Ugh… I think I'll just have some toast, or something.'

'Ingrate.' Hillary took their mother a glass of orange juice. 'Right, now your actual slave has crawled out of her pit, I'll be on my way.' She turned to Halley. 'Don't forget to open up!' And then she was gone. The whirlwind that she was, out of the door and gone.

Halley stared at the toaster, waiting for her second choice of breakfast.

Why do I feel like crawling back into bed?

Lunchtime and Archer had popped into the local shop to pick up a sandwich or something. It had been a busy morning. A full clinic of yearly boosters, general check-ups and he'd even managed to spay two cats. He enjoyed doing surgeries. He liked the calm and the peace that came over him when he had to wield a scalpel. The operating room was like a different world from the real one. Where time slowed down and all that mattered in the world was the animal on the table and his own skill. It gave him a nice healthy appetite when surgeries and clinic went well. And after his visit from Axle, he'd needed a calming day. A good day. Because he'd been feeling out of sorts since meeting Halley on Rookery Point and hated that they'd had a little disagreement last night. But he'd needed to say something.

He'd picked up a basket and was browsing

the refrigerators and the sandwich selection, trying to decide between a BLT or a chicken Caesar, when the bell over the door rang, admitting a new customer.

His first glance told him it was none other than Halley Campbell, the girl who thought of him and their tryst as a mistake. The second glance took in the fact that she looked tired and a little pale. Two small spots of pink on her cheeks.

She didn't see him as she went straight over to the shelves where the medicines were. Painkillers, sore-throat lozenges, that kind of thing.

Archer selected the BLT and grabbed himself a drink, trying to steady the rapid beating of his heart. When he'd asked her to be more civil when talking to him, he'd truly asked it as a simple request. He'd not said it in a mean tone, or an accusatory one. But he hated that he'd had to say it at all. He wanted relations between them to be good. Especially after what they'd shared. Two people who could be that good together sexually ought to be decent.

'Do you have any antacids?' he heard her ask Ruth, the shopkeeper.

'Bottom shelf, love.'

'Oh, yeah. Thanks.'

He came up behind her as she went to pay

for them, standing there with his basket, waiting for her to be served.

'Five fifty.'

Halley reached into her coat pocket for her purse, but then stopped, pausing, closing her eyes to shake her head and groan.

Archer frowned, instantly concerned. 'Are you okay?'

'I'm fine. I'm just…' She reached out to put a hand on the counter as if to steady herself.

Archer put his basket down and stepped forward, reaching out to help steady her. 'Do you need to sit down? Ruth, can you get her a chair?'

She shrugged him off. 'No! No, I'm fine. I just felt a little weird, is all.'

'Maybe you need to see a doctor?'

She turned to glare at him, her cheeks flushing with anger. 'I don't need to see a doctor! I just didn't have breakfast this morning, that's all.'

He turned and reached for a chocolate bar off the shelf, ripped open the wrapper and passed it to her. 'Then eat this. Now. Ruth, you can add it to my bill in a minute.'

'I don't want chocolate.'

'Tough. If you've not eaten breakfast and you're light-headed enough to almost pass out in the village shop, then your blood sugar is low and chocolate is the quickest thing to raise those levels.'

She held the chocolate bar and stared hard at him. 'Actually, you'd be better getting me to rub honey or jam on my gums. That'd be fastest.'

'Just eat the bar!' he said, exasperated. Why was she fighting him on this? Was it her way? To be antagonistic on everything? Or was it only him that had this effect on her? He calmed his voice. 'I'm just trying to help you.'

'I don't need your help.'

'No. You need sugar. Now eat the chocolate.'

She stared at him as if contemplating another challenge, but decided against it and sullenly took a bite. Wrinkling her nose at it.

'Something wrong?'

'I'm not a big fan of this one.'

He smiled. 'I'm so sorry. Which is your favourite? I'll remember it for the next time.'

'There won't be a next time. I don't like to almost pass out in village shops.' She glanced over at Ruth. 'Don't go telling people about this. I'm enough of a talking point already.'

Ruth made a zipping motion over her mouth and smiled.

After a couple of mouthfuls, the chocolate bar was gone.

'Better?'

Halley nodded.

'Okay. Let's pay for the antacids and I'll walk you to your car. Are you going to be okay to drive?'

'I'm fine.'

'Maybe I should follow you back to the farm, just in case?'

'Don't you have work?'

'Yes, but I'd rather make sure you got home safely.'

'Look, I don't need you babysitting me and I don't need to be responsible for your clinic running late. How about you go back to your job and I'll text you when I'm home, so you know I got back safe?'

'You don't have my number.'

She pulled out her mobile phone, opened up the contacts list and then passed it over to him. 'Put it in.'

He typed his number into her phone and passed it back. 'No cheating.'

'I don't cheat.'

'I'm glad to hear it.' He stared back at her with a smile, glad that their relationship had changed from peeved and mistaken to tolerant and challenging. It was a step forward!

Archer paid for his sandwich, drink and the chocolate bar and followed Halley out to her car parked on the road. He watched her get in, smiling all the time.

'What is wrong with you?' she wound down her window to ask him.

'What do you mean?'

'I mean no one is this happy all the time.'

'Maybe you're giving me things to be happy about.'

Halley frowned. 'Well, stop it. I don't like it.'

He had to stop himself from laughing. 'I'll try to be more glum.'

'Thank you.'

'Until I get your text and then I'll be happy again.'

'Just go to work, Archer.'

Now he did laugh. 'Yes, ma'am.' He gave her a salute and began to walk back to work.

Halley watched him go, silently cursing. What was it about him that was winding her up? That he challenged her? That he'd seen her semi-naked and vulnerable, as well as ill and vulnerable? He was always around! Or maybe that was just the problem with living in a village—you kept running into the same people. That was one of the only reasons Edinburgh was better. It was big enough to be anonymous in.

Here, in Burndale, you couldn't get anonymity if you tried. Everyone knew everything about you and, despite Ruth's assurances that she wouldn't say a word about Halley's little spell in the shop, she knew that by teatime plenty of people would have heard about it. It was the village shop and Ruth was a talker. Always had been. Always would be.

The idea that she'd be the number one topic once again did not sit well with her and so she ripped open the antacids that she'd bought and took a couple. That chocolate bar had taken away some of the nausea she'd been feeling, but it was back again. She felt hungry, too, at the same time. It was weird. The morning had been frightening too. She'd never passed out in her life! And what had that moment been? In the shop? She'd been about to faint or something…

It was down to not having eaten—it had to be that. She was doing a huge amount of physical hours now. Running the farm. Caring for her mum. Dealing with all the issues that came along with that, day after day, and not eating? Well, that was a recipe for disaster, right? And this nausea that she'd had for a couple of days? It wasn't terrible. It wasn't as if she couldn't deal with it, but it was always there. Low-level. In the background.

Maybe it's stress? I'm not used to it.

Whatever was causing it, she didn't like it. She didn't like feeling out of control. Even over her own body. Halley controlled every aspect of her life for a reason. So that she didn't get hurt again. So that she never had to go through something so publicly again. And could she do that if she was going to pass out all over the place?

Maybe I ought to get checked out.

It seemed the sensible, logical thing to do. Prevention was better than cure, or so they said. So, instead of driving home, Halley made the short drive to the Burndale Doctor's Surgery and made an appointment. She was lucky. There was an appointment for first thing the next morning. She'd go after opening up.

She'd probably feel better by then anyways.

He dealt with an ear infection in a spaniel dog before Halley's text popped into his phone confirming she was home safe. There was even a picture of her standing by the farm sign, smiling sarcastically at him.

He couldn't help but smile back and saved her details in his contact list. Another guy might consider this progress—getting a girl's number—but he didn't need it. It wasn't as if they were in a relationship or anything.

She was just going to be a friend. A reluctant friend, maybe, but a friend, nonetheless.

He texted back.

Now go put your feet up.

I've got too much to do.

When you're finished. Put your feet up. Or do I have to come round there to make sure that you do?

He added a couple of smiley faces and waited for her reply. Nothing came for a while and he was about to put his phone away and call in his next patient, when his phone beeped a reply.

Fine. I'll rest.

And she put a smiley face, too.

Archer put his phone away, feeling much better. Their relationship was in a better place than before, yet again, and all it took was a little mild chiding and a show of concern. Maybe she did let people in, after all. And maybe he did care, but so what? He was just being a friend.

He called in his next patient. 'Mango?'

Sarah Chalmers stood up and carried in her Yorkshire terrier, giving him a nice smile as she passed him by. ‘Hello, Archer.’

‘Hi. What seems to be the problem?’ He closed the door to the consulting room behind them and came around the examining table that Mango was now standing on.

‘Well, I’ve noticed she has this weird cough and seems to gag a lot. I’m afraid she does chew a lot of sticks and I’m worried she’s got something stuck in her throat.’

‘Okay, and how long has this been going on for?’

Sarah shrugged. ‘A few weeks. I would have brought her earlier, but I’ve not been well myself.’

‘I’m sorry to hear that. Are you better now?’

‘Much. I had a chest infection and had to go on antibiotics.’ She paused. ‘I’ve not given it to my dog, have I?’ she asked with real concern.

‘Not likely. Let me examine her and we’ll go from there. I’ll just do her general observations first and then look in her mouth.’

He checked the dog over and found nothing of concern. It didn’t have a temperature… its stomach was soft. Heart was good. Eyes clear and bright. But he could hear a rasping noise and when he looked in the dog’s mouth, he couldn’t see a blockage trapped there anywhere. 'Do you have anything in your home like scented candles? Or do you smoke yourself?'

'I don't smoke and do occasionally have a scented candle when I'm in the bath, but not often.'

'And I see you have a lead on a neck collar. Does she pull on walks?'

'She does, actually. Quite a lot. She hates big vehicles driving past and gets scared and she's always pulling to get back home.'

'Okay. Well, little dogs like these can sometimes have issues with their trachea, that can be exacerbated by neck collars. It's best to use a body harness, rather than something that can pull on their throat, especially if they're a puller.'

'Really? I never knew that. Is that what you think this is?'

'We'll need to do some bloods and maybe an X-ray just to confirm there's nothing in her throat that shouldn't be there. But I can give her some anti-inflammatories for now, just in case it's anything else.'

'And when would you do the bloods and X-ray?'

'Bloods we can do tomorrow, first thing. X-ray would be later on that morning. Could you bring her in first thing tomorrow and then we'll give you a call when it's all done?'

'Sure. Thank you.'

'No problem. In the meantime, why not try adding a little bit of organic honey to her food? It should help calm any coughing she's doing.'

'Okay, thank you, Archer.'

'No problem. We'll see you both tomorrow.'

She thanked him as she left and he closed the door to type up his notes to add to Mango's file.

Halley hated doctors' surgeries. More specifically, she hated doctors' surgery waiting rooms. Especially here, in Burndale.

The room was full of waiting patients, all of whom knew each other. All of whom knew *her*. So when she walked in, she felt all eyes turn to her, a couple widening briefly. Then there was whispering and she knew, yet again, that at least by lunchtime half the village would know that she had been at the doctor's that morning.

She sat in a corner seat and picked up a magazine to hide behind. It wasn't even a good magazine! It was one she associated with being aimed at older women. Filled with recipes, health advice and short stories. She tried to concentrate hard on some story about a woman who couldn't sing, but who got asked to join a church choir and found love on the way, but it was difficult when Halley heard her name whispered over to her right.

Her cheeks flushed and she raised the magazine higher. What a highlight it must be for these women! Halley Campbell, jilted at the altar, back home in Burndale! She bet they knew why she was back. Her mum's fall at the farm and her subsequent broken hip was old news. But Halley herself?

'Halley, love…how's your mother doing?'

She lowered the magazine to peer at an old woman she wasn't sure she recognised. But she was sitting next to Mrs Grigson, who was one of the nosiest people in Yorkshire! 'She's doing fine, thanks.'

'You and Hillary helping out at the farm?'

'We're trying.' She was trying to be polite, too.

'You were in Edinburgh, weren't you?'

'That's right.'

'Settled in nicely up there, have you?'

'Yes, wonderfully so.' She wasn't going to tell Mrs Grigson the truth.

'Oh, I am glad. After all that business with that man…'

Piotr. She meant Piotr.

'You're happy now?'

'Very happy.'

'Must be difficult for a young woman living alone in such a big city...?'

She was prying. Trying to find out if there was anyone new in her life. 'Not really.'

'I could never do it...oh, no. But then I don't have to. I've got my Duncan by my side and he looks after me wonderfully.'

Duncan Grigson was her husband of many years. 'I'm glad to hear it.'

Mrs Grigson leaned in with a smile. 'Have you managed to find yourself a nice young man? Pretty thing like you?'

Halley had to hold back from saying something startling and astonishing like, *Well, I screwed the vet on top of that hill a couple of weeks ago...he was nice.* But she chose not to. It might be nice to see the shock on the old ladies' faces, but after that it would just get ugly and more and more difficult for her, so she chose to give them nothing. 'That's very kind of you to say, Mrs Grigson.'

'Halley Campbell?' A young lady stood in the doorway that led to the consulting rooms. She wore an NHS ID badge at her waist and had a stethoscope draped around her neck.

This must be the locum she'd been booked in with.

'Excuse me,' she said to Mrs Grigson and her companion, smiling as she placed the magazine down, before walking away, glad to be out of the viper's pit.

The locum smiled. 'We're at the end of the corridor, I'm afraid.'

'That's fine. Gets me my steps for the day.'

The doctor opened the door to the consulting room and led her in. 'I'm Dr Meacham. Why don't you tell me what brought you in today?' She sat down by her desk and indicated the seat that Halley should sit in.

'Er…well, I'm not sure. I think I might be deficient in something. Maybe my iron levels? I'm so tired. Exhausted all the time and yesterday I nearly passed out in the village shop.'

Dr Meacham nodded. 'Okay, and how long have you been feeling like this?'

'I've not felt right for a few days, but I've been iron deficient before and it kind of feels like that.'

The doctor smiled. 'Well, as you're a temporary patient we don't have your medical records here for me to check.'

'Oh, that's right, yes. I had to fill in a form yesterday. Did my surgery not send over my files?'

'We don't appear to have them yet, I'm afraid. So, before when you felt like this, how did they treat it?'

'Iron pills for about three months, I think it was.'

'Okay, and otherwise, you're fit and well?'

'Yes.'

'No chance you could be pregnant?'

Halley smiled, thinking of the night she'd spent with Archer. They'd used a condom. 'No.'

'Okay. You're sure?'

'Absolutely.'

'Are you sexually active?'

She blushed. 'I have been, yes, but we used protection.'

'What kind? Are you on the pill?'

'No, we used a condom.'

'All right, and are you under any stress at the moment? Has anything changed in your life recently?'

'I'm here looking after my mother. She broke her hip, so I'm caring for her and helping run the farm.'

'That's a lot of work! No wonder you're tired. Okay, what we're going to do, if it's okay with you, is that I'll do a basic set of obs, then we'll get a sample of your blood to send off and see if you're deficient in anything at all. And we'll put in an hCG anyway, just in case, to make sure you're not pregnant because, even though protection is great, nothing is one hundred per cent effective, okay? How does that sound?'

'Fine. Could you do the bloods now? It's just a bit of a palaver if I have to come back for another appointment, what with looking after Mum and needing to be at the farm.'

'I'll do it now.'

Dr Meacham got out the equipment she would need and examined both of Halley's arms. 'Nothing obvious.'

'Yeah, people always struggle to get my blood.'

'Challenge accepted.' The doctor smiled, palpating her arms to find good veins. When she thought she'd got one, she stuck in the needle, but couldn't get anything out at all. She tried a second time. Still nothing. 'Huh. Maybe you were right. Let me see if one of the nurses is free.'

'Okay.'

Halley sat in the room on her own for a moment and then Dr Meacham reappeared, followed by Chloe, the nurse. A familiar face.

'This is Chloe. She's our nurse practitioner. She's going to have a try, is that all right?'

'Fine. Hi, Chlo, how are you doing?'

Chloe smiled at her. 'Not too bad. How are you? I'd heard you were back to look after your mum. How's that going?'

'Exhausting.'

Chloe nodded. 'I know the feeling. I'm doing the same thing.'

'Is your mum not very well?'

She grimaced. 'Parkinson's.'

'I'm sorry, that must be hard.'

'It is, but… I don't mind. It's my mum, you know?'

Halley nodded. She felt the same way. It had been hard to come back here, to a place she'd always wanted to escape from, but her mother had needed her and it was the right thing to do.

'Okay, so I won't stick unless I'm absolutely sure, because you've had two attempts already.'

Halley liked Chloe. She was pretty. Blonde-haired. She had a kind face. The kind of person you could imagine being wonderful with young kids, old-age pensioners and animals. If she were a cartoon character, bluebirds would encircle her and do her household chores.

'There you go.'

Halley looked down. Chloe had got the sample. She pressed a cotton-wool ball down in the crease of her elbow and asked Halley to press on it, before she applied a strip of tape.

'Thank you.'

'You're welcome. Maybe I'll see you around? Or we should get together and have a drink one day?'

'Sure. I'd like that.'

Chloe smiled and left the room.

'How long till I get the results?'

'A day or two. But in the meantime, I'm going to prescribe you some iron tablets, just in case. Take them every day, preferably with orange juice to help their absorption. We'll text the results to your phone—let me just check the number with you.' Dr Meacham read out the number she'd given them.

'Perfect.'

'And if anything comes back that's a little worrying, I'll give you a call.'

'Great. Thank you for seeing me.'

'No problem. In the meantime, look after yourself. Take frequent breaks, if you can, and make sure you're eating healthily.'

'Thank you, Dr Meacham. It was a pleasure to meet you.'

'You too.'

And Halley left the surgery feeling optimistic and bright. She had no doubt that it would come back as iron-deficiency anaemia, and she could take care of that with a pill every day. And then she could go back to feeling better and less tired.

And life could go back to normal.

Exactly as she liked it.

CHAPTER FOUR

I'm going up to Rookery Point again tomorrow night. Skies are meant to be clear. We should be able to see Jupiter.

He typed out the message on his phone, his thumb hovering over 'Send'.

He felt it only fair to warn her that he would be there. Clearly she liked gazing at the stars too, and if she was going to go, he didn't want to just show up and make her think that he was stalking her or something. Telling her his intention ahead of time would absolve him of any blame and, worded like that, it didn't come across as an invitation.

Or did it?

We should be able to see Jupiter.

'We' meant stargazers in general. The world. Not the two of them. But he could see it might

be ambiguous and she might take it the wrong way. He wasn't asking to see her again, or repeat what had happened the last time they were up on Rookery Point. Not that he'd say no, but…

Did you hear that Jupiter should be visible tomorrow night? I'm going up to Rookery Point to check it out.

He grimaced. It still sounded like an invitation. He deleted the message and typed another one.

Fair warning… I'm going to be at Rookery Point tomorrow night to see Jupiter.

Better. He pressed 'Send' and heard the whoop noise as the message got sent into the ether.

Fair warning—it sounded as if he was just giving her the heads up that he was going to be there, so that she could pick another place if she wanted to. He didn't need her there, whilst at the same time he was letting her know about Jupiter, in case she didn't know. Giving her a chance to see it, too. Though not with him.

Even if he would be happy to share that experience with her again. Even just sitting chatting to her might be nice. He'd enjoyed talking to her. She was easy to chat to. Easy on the eye, as well, and now that he knew her more intimately…

No. Stop it. That can't happen again. I will not allow myself to think anything more for Halley Campbell.

It was a dangerous road to walk down and if he did, he'd only get wrecked all over again. Halley was here temporarily. Her life was in Scotland these days. His was in Yorkshire. He had a business here! His entire life! Only being her friend was practical and logical.

And safer for everyone involved.

But to sit beneath the stars with her again would be…simply magical.

As a young boy he'd had all the various teenage-crush ideas. Kissing her. Holding her hand. Having everyone know that she was his girl and them being amazed.

Halley Campbell and Archer Forde? Are you kidding me?

All the other boys would be jealous and all the girls would be confused, because they'd think Halley could have had anyone. Why pick sad little Archer Forde?

He'd imagined having picnics with her, or walking by the river. He'd imagined one day getting down on one knee and proposing to her. She would gasp with surprise, or cry, but ultimately say yes and then he would pick her up and swing her around…

And the knowledge that that would never happen was sad, yes, but…he liked that things were different between them now. He wasn't the Archer Forde he used to be. He'd filled out. Grown. He wasn't a sad, pathetic figure any more. He was a businessman. A trained veterinary surgeon with a thriving practice. He'd once heard someone refer to him as Burndale's most eligible bachelor!

Now things were different. He and Halley were friends. She knew him. She would never forget him now. And they would always have that one, hot night.

Could he possibly ask for anything more?

As promised by the weatherman on TV, the skies were clear and Archer was settled on Rookery Point, with his telescope pointed at the sky, staring at Jupiter. After the moon and Venus, Jupiter was often the third brightest point at night and it looked beautiful. Looking at the planet always made him feel as if his issues, his problems in life, were so insignificant, when he thought about the vastness of the galaxy and the universe.

Human beings could get so caught up in

worrying about stuff that really they ought not to worry about! Did any of it matter? When you thought about the vastness of the cosmos? He sat back and sighed, lying down on the ground with his hands behind his head, enjoying the soft cool breeze and the sound of the trees rustling in the wind. He sensed a movement off to his left and turned to see a rabbit bolt out of sight and he smiled, then frowned as he saw headlights coming up the hill road towards Rookery Point.

Was it Halley after all?

Or was it some other stargazer?

Or maybe just someone looking for a quiet spot to park up?

It could be anyone and he didn't want to get his hopes up. If it *was* Halley, then what would that mean? That she was just here because it was the best place in Burndale to view Jupiter, or that she was here because she wanted to spend some more time with him? The latter would be good, but they'd both agreed they were only friends. Friends with benefits?

The vehicle stopped at the car park and he heard a car door open and then slam shut. Then footsteps. Quiet footsteps that crunched gently over gravel. Stopping briefly, as if the person was having second thoughts about continuing on, and then starting again.

The figure appeared from the shadows and he turned to say hello, not expecting he would be lucky enough to see Halley, only to see that it was, indeed, Halley.

A smile lit up his face, falling slightly only when he noticed that she didn't look happy at all. She looked upset. And she didn't have a telescope with her or anything, so she didn't look as if she was here to stare at planets in the solar system. So what was she here for? 'Hey, you okay?'

'No. No, I'm not okay.'

She seemed really upset. As if she was on the verge of crying. His concern for her washed over him like a wave. 'Is it your mum?'

Halley frowned and shook her head. 'No. No, it's not her.'

So if it wasn't her mum, then what was it? 'Come here. Take a seat.' He indicated the ground next to him, laying out his jacket so she didn't have to sit on the grass.

'I'll stand, thanks.'

'Okay.' So he stood, too. Waiting.

He saw her swallow. Saw her look around them. Down at his telescope. Up at the sky. Saw that she was gathering herself to tell him something that had to be momentous.

'Two days ago, in the shop after I…'

'After you got dizzy?'

She nodded. 'I...er...went to the doctor's. Just in case. I've been feeling...odd, lately, and she examined me and took bloods and all that jazz.'

'Okay.' He couldn't read her. She wouldn't look him in the eye. 'Oh, God, are you sick?' If she had something terrible, like cancer or anything, he wasn't sure he'd be able to bear it!

'No, I'm not sick, Archer. I'm pregnant. Pregnant with your baby and I know it's your baby because you're the only person I've had sex with in months! And yes, I know we used a condom, but those things are only like ninety-seven per cent effective and it looks like we are in that three per cent that it didn't work for.' Now she looked at him, to gauge *his* reaction.

Pregnant.

Pregnant!

He opened his mouth to say something, but nothing came out as the import of her words sank into him like punches. Pregnant. A baby. There was a baby. His baby. In Halley. They'd made a baby. Accidentally, but still. So what the hell were they meant to do?

'I don't know what to say.'

'Then that makes two of us. I just got the blood results back late this afternoon and I knew I had to tell you. I shouldn't have to struggle with this on my own.'

'No.'

Pregnant! What the hell were they going to do now? All these years he'd told himself he would not get into a serious relationship ever again and now he was going to be a father? Could there ever be a more important relationship in life? To parent a child?

'I don't know what to say.'

'You said that already.'

'I know! But…are you keeping it?'

'I don't know. I think so. I can't ever imagine having a… I don't know. This isn't a good time to be having a baby! I mean, I have the farm and Mum and my life back in Edinburgh and it's not like we're in a committed relationship and… I never planned on this happening! I've never wanted this!'

As she grew upset, he reached out and pulled her close, wrapping his arms around her, sharing her distress and confusion. They were both in the same boat here. 'We'll get through this together,' he muttered into her hair, not entirely sure how they would actually achieve that. Her hair smelt like flowers. How could they get through this together, if he couldn't concentrate when she stood so close?

'How?'

That's the million-dollar question, Halley.

'Somehow. We'll figure it out. We're grown-ups...we can handle this.'

'I don't want to be known as a failure in this village again, Archer. I can't be!'

'You're not going to fail. *We're* not going to fail.'

'That's easy for you to say. Society always looks down on women more than men. They'll see this as my fault. She couldn't find a guy to marry her in a church without discovering he's a lying bigamist and now look at her. Pregnant and alone. Couldn't even find a guy to be her baby's daddy!'

'Hey...you're not alone.'

'Aren't I?' She pulled away to look up at him. 'We're not in a relationship and I'll be the one left holding the baby and looking after it all the time, except on what? You'll have it weekends? What kind of life will that be?'

'We'll find a way to make it work.' He wasn't sure how at all. Halley's concerns were real and viable. If this went all the way and they weren't in a committed relationship, then how often would he get to see his child? How much would be enough? He'd never planned on becoming a father but, now that was a real possibility, he couldn't imagine not knowing his child! He'd grown up without his own father around and always promised himself he would never do that to a kid of his own.

'Look, we're both in shock. Let's take some time to let this settle in. Think about it. We're both just blindly reacting right now. We need time to absorb this news and then think about what we will do.'

'Well, the clock's ticking, Archer.' She stared at him.

He stared back. His gaze dropped once to her belly and then he was unable to look away.

It most certainly was.

Her mother was asleep when Halley got back from Rookery Point. She was glad of it, but knew she would have to tell her mum the news sooner rather than later.

Oh, God! I'm going to have to tell Hillary, too!

Hillary would no doubt laugh, or be smug. She'd always thought she was the better sister. The one that had done well for herself. The one who'd found a decent husband and had her babies in wedlock.

Hillary has twins. Twins! What if that runs in the family and I'm carrying two babies, as well?

Halley slipped into the kitchen and grabbed a biscuit to calm her stomach and nerves. Archer had taken the news better than she'd thought. He'd been pretty calm, though his eyes had looked panicked for a little while. She couldn't blame him. She felt the same way.

A baby!

As a little girl she'd often dreamed of finding her prince. Her knight on a white horse, who would make her swoon and fall in love. Who would place a ring on her finger and make her the happiest woman in the world. And she would bear his children and they would make everyone else jealous with how perfect their little family was.

She'd been in love with love. In love with the idea of a perfect romance. What little girl wasn't? And she'd been so sure that that ideal would fall into her lap one day.

It was why she'd made such a mistake with Piotr. Because their love story had been perfect. Too good to be true. A holiday romance that had become something deeper. Or so she'd thought. But Piotr had been a conman. A swindler. Who'd preyed on her naivety. But thank God she'd found out the truth before that ring ended up on her finger. Before she'd got pregnant with his child, because he'd mentioned that a lot. About how happy he would be to be a father and how they would start trying on their honeymoon. And she'd loved him so much she'd agreed to it!

Let's meet for coffee tomorrow. I have the afternoon free. Let me know a time that's good for you. Or I could come to the farm, if that's better. A x

She stared at the text. Appreciating that Archer hadn't run for the hills the second she'd told him, or offered to pay for an abortion, or anything like that. Of course they needed to talk about it. There was so much to discuss!

But even though this had never been in her plan, she knew, deep down, that she would be keeping this baby. Hopefully Burndale wouldn't notice she was carrying until she felt it was the right time to tell anyone and she and Archer could come to some arrangement regarding visiting. Because she had no idea where she was going to live now. Edinburgh had always been a bolt-hole, but she'd begun to hate it there and here there was family and…

Archer was here. The baby's father.

But he'd told her he didn't do relationships. That night on Rookery Point, the first night they'd met, he'd told her he wasn't looking for a serious relationship and never would be. He wanted to remain free to live his own life uncomplicated by anyone else's.

She'd naively said the same thing too, as if this were something they could control.

But life had a way of throwing a spanner in the works and if her life had to change?

Then so did his.

She'd agreed to meet him in the local café. He was glad of that. A public space, where neither of them could lose their composure. Where both of them would be civil. At first she'd argued against it. Not wanting to be seen in public with him, in case it got the gossip mill going anyway, but he reminded her that people were already discussing her near-fainting episode in the shop and they could explain their chat in the coffee shop as one person simply checking to make sure the other one was all right.

'The less we hide, the less they'll talk. Make this a big secret and we've no chance.'

Thankfully, she'd agreed.

He understood her reticence. She'd disappeared from Burndale after her wedding disaster, but he'd been here and he knew how the rumour mill had leapt into action. For *weeks*. People were discussing Halley for far too long and he'd hated it, on her behalf. And he'd experienced something similar when Amy had died and he'd endured weeks of pitying looks.

Gossip was a commodity in a place such as Burndale, where so little happened. It didn't have a high crime rate, the kids were mostly good, the only thing to talk about was each other and if that meant discussing something as simple as number sixty-seven putting in a new kitchen, or the local vet losing his girlfriend to brain cancer? They were both fair game.

He sat nursing a coffee and waited for her to arrive. He'd chosen a booth at the back, away from the window, that gave them the most privacy, and kept checking his watch as the time they'd agreed upon came and went.

Was she not going to show?

The bell above the door tinkled announcing a new arrival and he looked up and saw her come in, her eyes scanning the tables, until her gaze met his and she nodded, before heading over, sliding into the booth.

'Hey.'

'Hi. Can I get you anything? Tea? Coffee?'

'Tea, please, and maybe a slice of cake if they've got any?'

'Sweet tooth?'

'Nausea. Strangely, eating helps.'

'Oh. Right.' He got up and ordered for her,

choosing a slice of Madeira, which he thought would be the most plain, figuring she wouldn't want anything chocolatey or creamy. But then chose a slice of lemon meringue for himself, in case he was wrong and she'd want his instead.

Who knew?

He brought the tea and the cake over to the table and settled opposite her. 'There you go.'

'Thanks. That's perfect.'

He watched her add sugar and milk to her tea. Stir it. Take a sip. Then she looked up at him and sighed.

'So?'

'So...'

'Have you told anyone?' she asked in a low voice, looking around them.

'No. Have you?'

'I told Mum. Figured she'd need to know. She already wants to hire some extra lads from the village to *"take on the heavy lifting"*, just in case.' Halley did the speech quotes thing with her fingers. 'I'll tell Hillary later.'

He nodded. Thinking of Hillary in her swish car with leather seats, her power suits and her twin children. 'Do twins run in the family?'

Halley met his gaze and laughed. 'God, I hope not. Hills is the only one that I know, so maybe it was a freak occurrence or something? Why? Twins scare you?'

'Does it not scare you?'

'I'm *terrified*. One baby is a bombshell. Two of them?' She shook her head in wonder. 'Hills coped because she got a nanny in full time, but, even then, I still remember how she used to look in those early days. Exhausted. Confused. Sleep-deprived.'

'You can look that way with one,' he said, remembering how Axle had looked in the early days when he'd still been with Joanne.

'So what are we going to do? How are we going to manage this situation that we find ourselves in? I mean, it's hardly ideal, is it? We don't live together. We're not in a relationship. We hadn't planned this.'

No, it wasn't ideal. But that didn't mean they couldn't find a way to make it work. 'I'll be honest with you, Halley. I've never wanted kids, but I knew the second you told me that there was going to be one and that I was going to be a father—I knew instantly that I was never going to let my child feel the way I felt when I grew up.'

'And how was that?'

'Abandoned. Alone. Fatherless. A burden. I won't do that to my child. I'm going to be in its life as much as I can.'

'But how? You live here. Your business is here and my life is up in Scotland.'

'Then one of us agrees to move.'

She raised an eyebrow. 'I suppose you mean me? Come back here? To be gossip fodder? Halley Campbell? Single mother, as well as jilted bride?'

'You wouldn't be a single mother. We'll find a way to co-parent.'

Halley laughed. 'Oh, just what I always wanted.' She stabbed her fork into her Madeira and ate a bite.

'Well, then I'll move. I'll leave here. Find a veterinary posting in Edinburgh. Maybe locum for a while, if I have to.' He didn't want to. Not really. But this wasn't about just him any more. If he was going to become a father, then he was willing to make sacrifices. Compromises. And if Halley wanted to stay in Edinburgh, then he'd move there, too.

She stared at him. 'You'd do that for me?'

He shook his head. 'No. I'd do that for my baby.'

They were hardly the most romantic words she'd ever heard in her life, but romance wasn't what she was after here. He was offering to up sticks and move his life up north, to be with his child, so that they could parent this child together.

She was grateful for the offer.

'You don't have to do that.'

'But I will if I have to.'

'You don't.'

'But—'

'Archer, no. You don't have to move across the country to be up there when…when I'm not even sure if I'm happy up there anyway.'

'Oh.'

'I've hated Burndale. Believe me, I've hated this place and what it can do to you when you've been treated badly, but…up in Edinburgh hasn't been a picnic for me either.'

'How do you mean?'

'Anonymity is great for a while, but at the end of the day I sit in my flat and I'm all alone. I don't have family around me. I don't have any friends I've known my whole life and I can't imagine wanting to parent in a place where I don't have any support.'

'It takes a village.'

'What?' She frowned.

'It's what they say, isn't it? It takes a village to raise a child.'

She nodded. 'Perhaps they're right? That it's not something you can do alone. Well, you can, but it's going to be difficult for you. I fought coming back to Burndale so much, but maybe it's the right thing here. You'd still have your job and your brother and I'd have my family. The farm. Hills, for goodness' sake!'

'So...you're staying here? Is that what you're agreeing to?'

She nodded. 'I think I am.'

He let out a long breath. Smiled. 'Okay. So we've made a start. On deciding the best thing for our child. You see? We can do this. We can find a way.'

'Agreed.' She smiled. But she still felt sad inside. This wasn't what she'd imagined for herself when she was a little girl. She'd always imagined having a family and being happily married and in love with an amazing guy. Instead, she was getting this deal. Co-parenting. Agreeing to stay in Burndale, a place she'd always felt the need to run away from. Was she making a big mistake?

'You look sad, though.'

She smiled. Even though he was right. She felt sad. This wasn't the way life was supposed to happen! And even though Archer was a great guy, they were hardly in a relationship with great foundations, were they? They weren't madly in love, even if she did think he was hot. Damn it, he was probably the most eligible bachelor in the village! 'It's just not what I'd imagined for myself, that's all. I don't want to do things in life because I have to. I want to do them because I want to. Because I'd love to.'

'I get that. I kind of feel that way, too. Look, I know this is probably way out there and everything and we've barely discussed the basics, but why don't we agree to meet every day? Get to know one another a little more. We're going to raise a child together, so we need to know one another inside out.'

'And how do you propose we do that?'

'We meet. We talk. We share dinners or lunches. We get to know one another. I could introduce you to Axle.'

'Sounds like dating and I think we've established that neither of us wants that complication. It's complicated enough.'

'Then they won't be dates. Let's call them meetings. Strategic planning meetings.'

Halley laughed. 'Sounds like we might need a secretary to take the minutes.'

'We'll take our own minutes.' He reached across the table and took up her fingers in his. 'Let's get to know one another properly, Halley Campbell. Let's get this right for our child from the very beginning.'

It sounded like the best she could have hoped for. Archer seemed keen. He wasn't running away…he wasn't absolving himself of all responsibility. It sounded as if he cared a great deal as to how his child would feel and he wanted to be around. Could she have asked for a better reaction?

'Then why not come to mine for dinner tonight? Meet Mum and Hills. Become part of the family.'

He looked surprised.

'Too much?' she asked.

'No. No, it's not too much to ask. Fine. What time is dinner?'

She smiled. 'Our first strategic planning meeting will be at six p.m. How does that sound?'

He smiled and nodded. 'Then I second and carry that motion.'

CHAPTER FIVE

HE FELT NERVOUS about going around to Halley's for dinner with her mum and sister. He wasn't used to meeting parents and officially declaring himself in a relationship with someone, apart from Amy's parents, and even now it wasn't because he and Halley were in a romantic relationship.

This was something else.

They were going to bring a child into the world. Maybe it was still too soon to be announcing this to everyone, but he could understand Halley being scared by this and needing to tell people. She already had so much on her plate, what with the farm and looking after her mum. And now this bombshell that she'd probably stay in Burndale to live!

He had to admit to being incredibly happy that she wasn't going to be leaving and taking his child away! That would have been horrible for him to deal with. The guilt itself would be incredible. And the idea that he might have had to up sticks and go to Edinburgh had been worrying. Leave everything behind? Leave Axle? He and his brother were so close, he couldn't imagine not being able to just pop round to see him whenever he felt like it.

But if she was going to stay, then where would she live? On the farm? Or would she look for somewhere in the village?

He parked by the house, grabbed the bunch of flowers he'd bought at the shop on the way over and got out of his car, knocking on the front door.

Presently, the door opened and there stood Halley, smiling and looking at the flowers in wonder. 'Oh, they're beautiful! Thank you!'

He maintained his smile. 'Ah. This is awkward. They're actually for your mum.'

'Oh!' She laughed and stepped back. 'Not awkward at all. Come on in. Please excuse the mess. Everything's all over the place.'

'Don't worry about it.' He followed her down the small hall and into the living area. Sylvie was sitting in one of the armchairs, propped up with plenty of pillows.

'Excuse me if I don't get up, Archer,' Sylvie said, smiling at him warmly.

'How are you doing?' He leaned down to

drop a kiss on her cheek and presented her with the flowers.

'Oh, they're gorgeous, love! You shouldn't have!'

'My mum didn't teach me much, but I did learn that you never arrive at someone's house for a meal without taking some sort of gift.'

'Well, it's not me doing all the cooking. These flowers should be for Halley. She's doing all the work.'

'We'll both enjoy them,' Halley said, taking them from him. He watched her go into the kitchen and rummage in a cupboard for a vase, finding one and filling it with water.

'How are you getting along after your surgery?'

'Much better. A lot of the stiffness has gone and I've been given all this physio to do, but I should be more like myself soon.'

'She's trying to run before she can walk,' Halley called from the kitchen. 'I caught her trying to do the stairs earlier on her own.'

'I can do the stairs, love,' Sylvie insisted.

'But only if you've had your painkillers. Take a seat, Archer. Can I get you a drink?'

'Whatever you're having is fine. Hillary not here yet?'

'She's coming over later. Her court case has

run over time and she's stuck in traffic from Ripon.'

'Oh. Okay. Do you need any help in the kitchen?'

'Er… Can you rinse the rice for me?'

'Sure.'

He set to work in the kitchen, rinsing the uncooked rice in cold water first before it was cooked. 'Something smells good.'

'Chicken tagine. Ever had it?'

'I don't think I've ever had Moroccan food.'

'Then you're in for a treat,' Sylvie said. 'Halley's tagine is to die for.'

'Mum! You don't need to sell Archer on what a great little cook I am.'

'Don't I? He might want to know that the mother of his child can cook a decent meal.'

Archer paused. It was the first time someone other than he and Halley had referred to *their* baby. 'I'm sure the tagine will be great,' he replied diplomatically.

'Do you cook, Archer, love?' asked Halley's mum.

'I do. I love to cook, actually.'

'So you're not one of these men that lives on take-outs and meal deals?'

He smiled politely. 'No.'

'Good.'

Halley turned to him in the kitchen and mouthed the words *I'm sorry.*

'Hey, if this is the limit of the inquisition, then tonight is going to go just fine,' he whispered back.

'You'll be lucky.'

'What are you two whispering about?' Sylvie called.

'Cooking instructions, Mum!'

'Oh. Well, come in here when you have a spare moment. I think we have a lot more important things to talk about tonight.'

'She's right,' Archer said.

'Well, don't say that out loud. We'll never hear the end of it.'

He laughed. 'Anything else I can help with?'

'No. Now that the rice is on, we've got about eight minutes of interrogation. You ready?'

'Absolutely.'

'Okay, let's get this easy round done. Hills might be a lot worse.'

'So…a baby. That's a big life-change for the both of you.'

Halley gave Archer a small, supportive smile. 'Yes, it is.'

'How are you going to deal with it? Because if everything goes well, in a few months all our lives will change and I need to know if

I'm going to be on babysitting duty up in Edinburgh. Because if I am, I'll need to arrange someone permanent to manage the farm.'

Halley hadn't thought about how a baby arriving might affect her mum. 'I've decided that I'm most likely going to return to live in Burndale, Mum.'

'Really, love? I thought you couldn't wait to leave?'

'Well, things have changed, and Edinburgh is amazing in many ways and all, but it doesn't have family and I think I would like my child to know its family. Grandparents, aunts and uncles and all.'

'Oh. I suppose your mum feels the same way, Archer?'

Halley grimaced.

'I haven't told my mum about the baby yet.'

'Why not?'

'We're not that close.'

'That might change with a grandchild on the way.'

'She could barely be there for me, I don't think she's going to be all that interested, to be honest with you.'

'Well, I'm sorry to hear that,' her mum said. 'But I do like the idea of you coming back to Burndale, Halley. It's not been the same with you so far away and not seeing you very often. Have you looked for places? What sort of thing are you looking for?'

Halley shrugged. 'I don't know. I haven't looked at anything. I only pretty much decided today.'

'Will you be going back to Edinburgh to work your notice?'

'I don't know.'

Her mum nodded. 'Maybe you could help her look for a place, Archer?'

'Er, sure! When I'm not working, of course.'

'Fantastic. It is something you should decide together, because wherever she picks is going to be the place she raises your child, so you'll want somewhere nice and suitable.'

He nodded. 'Of course.'

Halley wondered if he was always this polite. Her mum was kind of leading this conversation for them. Maybe if they got it all out of the way now, when Hillary arrived there'd be nothing left to sort out! 'There's a lot for us to decide, Mum, we know that. We're still getting used to the idea that we might be parents. Give us some time.'

'God willing, everything will be fine, but, believe you me, I'm talking from experience and Hillary will say the same thing, but these next few months will go by so fast for you.

You need to make decisions and get everything in place sooner, rather than later.'

'You're right, Mrs Campbell.'

'Call me Sylvie, Archer.'

Dinner went well, even if Hillary didn't arrive until after they'd finished eating. The chicken tagine had settled in her stomach well, for which she was grateful. She'd found out to her cost that some things she craved just wouldn't stay down for that long, so Halley was always hesitant when she did eat. She made sure not to overload herself. Eating little and often seemed to be the key to fighting the nausea.

And Hillary was as judgmental as Halley had imagined she would be, grilling Archer over his intentions and making conversation difficult.

'This must be a shock for you, Archer? I don't know many eligible bachelors who take the news of fatherhood so calmly. Are you just making all the right noises to placate us?'

Archer had not looked away from Hillary. 'I'm making all the right noises because they are the right ones to make. Yes, this was a shock to us both and, no, it wasn't planned. But it is happening. and I think you'll find that I'm a man who takes responsibility for his actions. I'm going to be there for your sister and the baby.'

Hillary stared back at him, hard. 'You'll go to all the appointments? Have your name put on the birth certificate?'

'Absolutely.'

'You make the decision to be a father so easily, considering you told her that you never wanted kids. Didn't you do the same thing with Amy?'

Halley frowned.

So did Archer. 'That was different.'

'How so?'

'The situation was completely different. Amy was about to undergo cancer treatment. Her eggs would freeze better if they were fertilised.'

'But you'd not even discussed having kids with her at that point, had you? Her mum told me.'

Archer let out a low breath. 'I'm not on the stand, Hillary. You don't have to like me, but if you want to judge me, then judge me by my actions and my words as I present them to you. I am a good man, who is kind and considerate of people. No, I hadn't discussed having kids with Amy, but if she were to survive I wanted her to have that option in the future. But she died. I lost her and I thought I'd never have kids ever. But now there is going to be a baby. Our baby. And I am going to love it and be there for it, every single day. The second I'm not? You can stand before me then and tell the world "I told you so", but, believe you me, you will never get to say those words!'

Hillary didn't say much after that.

The evening drew to a natural close and Halley offered to walk Archer out to his car. She felt proud of him. Not many people were capable of standing up to her sister when she was in full flow, drilling them with questions. She kind of liked that Archer had silenced her. It was good. It meant that he was strong, as well as polite, and it had also kind of been a bit of a turn-on to hear him stand up for not only himself but the situation they both found themselves in.

'I'm sorry my sister was so rough.'

He smiled. 'That's okay. She was looking out for you. It's what siblings do.'

'Yes, well, she got her solicitor head on and drilled you like you were in court having sworn to tell the truth, the whole truth and nothing but the truth.'

'She's worried for you.'

'I'm worried for me. She just needs to support me. That's all I need from her.'

'They were both right, though. This time

will go fast and we need to know how we're going to do this. Finding a place for you to live, for example. I'll help, like I promised.'

She nodded. 'And I will inform my old job that I'm not coming back.'

'You're absolutely sure?'

'Yes. I am. They'll be fine about it. Then I'll just need to find something to do here. Any jobs at your place?' She laughed.

He shook his head, sadly. 'Not at the moment. But your mum's paying you for running the farm, right? You can keep doing that whilst you keep an eye out for veterinary nursing jobs.'

'I guess. Well, thank you for coming over and remaining graceful under my family's onslaught of questions.' She truly was grateful. Not many men would have done so. And strangely, sitting listening to him answer, she felt as though she could trust his answers, even though she hadn't known him that long. Because even though she didn't know him well, her mum did, and she'd know if he was lying about anything. She'd lived here all her life, same as him.

And Archer hadn't tried to evade anything. He'd even told them all about how strained the relationship was with his mum. And knowing that this situation wasn't something that he'd wanted, she was grateful and proud that he had sat there and answered every question as truthfully as he could.

He wanted to be there for the baby. That much was clear.

And knowing that she wouldn't be alone? Meant a great deal, indeed.

'You were great tonight.'

He met her gaze. 'So were you.'

'You think success is written in our stars?' she asked.

Archer looked up at the night sky above them. 'I hope so. I really hope so.' He pulled his gaze back to her. 'But I'd like to think that we both know how to keep our feet on the ground. And step one of that is finding you a place to live.'

She nodded. Her mum had offered to let her stay at the farm, but Halley was used to being independent now. She didn't want to take a step backwards and move back in with her mum. 'I'll get the local paper tomorrow. Start looking.'

'Make any viewing appointments for the weekend. I'll come with you.'

'All right. So we're doing this?'

'We are doing this.' He leaned in towards her and dropped a kiss on her cheek. His beard brushed against her cheek and she felt a surge of lust as she remembered that night on Rookery Point.

Did he linger? Was she imagining that? What she did know was that she yearned to feel his lips brush against her skin again.

And then he was sliding into the driver's seat and starting the engine. He wound down the window and gave her a little wave, before reversing out and then disappearing down the lane.

She watched his tail lights all the way, until they disappeared.

Was she being a fool for putting her trust in him? She'd thought she'd known Piotr and she'd been wrong. Was she relying too much on a man who'd told her at the very beginning of their relationship that he would never commit to another woman ever again?

Well, he's not committing to me. He's committing to his child and that will have to be enough. It's not like I'm giving him my heart, either.

When he'd told Axle about his impending fatherhood, his brother had been initially happy, then concerned when he'd learned that he and Halley were not in a relationship.

'I hope it goes well for you, Archie. Make

sure she knows your rights. Get your name on the birth certificate, everything.'

He'd promised he was going to do everything he could to stay in his child's life.

'And this Halley…she seems like she'll play fair with you? Give you access?'

'Yes.'

'I hope so, bro. For your sake, I hope so. I don't ever want you to go through what I am. You sure there isn't anything between the two of you? I mean, you hooked up to make a baby, there must be *something*.'

How could he tell Axle that this had been the girl of his dreams when he was younger? He'd just get excited and tell him to go for it and forget what happened before, but it was easier said than done.

Yes, he had feelings for Halley. How could he not? But it was so hard keeping them under control when clearly all Halley wanted was for him to be involved with their child. She'd not asked him for anything else, for any other type of commitment, and he understood why. She didn't want to be left behind again. She didn't want to be abandoned if anything went wrong. Why put herself through any more heartache? He got that. He didn't want heartache, either.

It was safer for the both of them if they kept this simple between them.

This was all for the baby.

He tried to keep telling himself that as he got ready to go and pick Halley up so they could drive around Burndale and look at the two properties that she'd arranged appointments for. Over the phone she'd told him the first property she'd found was a two-bedroomed flat above a shop. The second one was a small two-bedroomed cottage on the outskirts of the village. They both sounded fine and he was hoping that finding a place for her to have the baby in would be easy, because if they could cross something so major off the list, then they'd be well on their way. Once Halley had a place, they could move her in, get her settled, fix anything that needed fixing and then all she had to do was grow their child.

Simple.

But he couldn't help but feel that something was missing and he couldn't figure out what that was. He felt uneasy. Afraid. That no matter what he did to try and protect his child, he was somehow going to fail. He would somehow let it down, or hurt it, or be a bad father from the get-go and he couldn't allow himself to imagine how that might feel. He'd made a hell of a vow to Halley and her cautious sister, Hillary. And if he did make a mistake, if he wasn't the father he hoped he could be, would Halley do to him what Joanne had done to Axle?

When he knocked at the farm door, he heard Sylvie call from inside that the door was unlocked and to let himself in. He did so, uncertainly, calling out hello as soon as he stepped inside.

'She's upstairs in the bathroom, love. Morning sickness is bad today.'

He felt bad for her. 'Should I go see if she's all right?'

'I'm not sure she'd want to let you see her like that.'

'What caused it? Was it food, or…?'

'She put honey on her porridge and apparently that wasn't the best idea.'

'I'll go up. See if she needs any help.' He wanted to be there for her. He'd got her into this situation, after all. 'Is that okay?'

'Be my guest, then.'

He smiled at Sylvie and began to make his way up the stairs and followed the sounds of retching to a door. He knocked gently. 'Halley, you okay?'

There was a groan and then the flush of the toilet. 'Marvellous. Never felt better.'

The bathroom door opened and Halley stood there, looking pale and ashy. His heart melted in that moment, and he reached past her to the sink where there was a small basket of face flannels all rolled up. He took one, rinsed it under cold water and wrung it dry, before using it to pat her face.

She looked at him the entire time. 'Do I look a state?'

'You look beautiful.'

'You have to say that—I'm the mother of your child.'

'I don't say anything I don't mean. We don't have to do this today, if you're feeling rough.'

She laughed. 'Are you kidding me? I always start the morning this way. There's nothing that gets the blood pumping faster in the morning than twenty minutes' worth of retching before work.'

He put the flannel down on the side of the sink. 'You're okay?' She'd never looked more beautiful.

'I'm okay.' She smiled. 'Besides, if I'm going to be like this for a while, I can't put stuff off. We've got to get sorted. Time's a ticking.'

He nodded. 'Well, only if you're sure?'

'I'm sure, but thank you for trying to take care of me.'

In the small, confined space of the bathroom they were quite close. The proximity was disconcerting for Archer. He itched to reach up and tuck a strand of her golden hair behind her ear. He longed to touch her in some way. Just to let her know that he cared about her and that he didn't like that she was suffering with morning sickness. And perhaps he ought to say something? Because right now, standing here like this? Facing one another. Inches apart. Staring into her eyes? It was getting weird.

'I'm sure it will pass soon. When you get to three months, isn't that what they say?' It felt important to him to try and see the positives. Most pregnant women only suffered with this for a couple of months, even though he knew there were cases that lasted longer. Sometimes all the way to the day of delivery.

She nodded. 'Fingers crossed.'

The hopeful smile she gave him was sweet and he pushed down the urge to kiss her. Now was not the time, nor the place. And he wasn't sure if she'd give him a slap for trying.

The flat above the shop was situated over the local newsagent's. The door was at the back, in a small, cramped alley, and she looked at Archer in question. 'Think I'd be able to get a buggy through here?' There were large bins back here. One filled with cardboard, another filled with rubbish, and when the agent let them in, there was a narrow flight of stairs that took them up to the flat itself.

Halley tried to imagine herself coming back with a baby, having done a supermarket shop. 'Might be hard trying to get shopping and everything up these stairs. There's nowhere close to park my car, either, so if I had to carry a lot of stuff, back and forth, if I were on my own? I can't see how that would work.'

The agent, a young man from an estate agent that she didn't know, simply smiled. 'I believe the current owner arranges for a delivery from a supermarket and they carry it up into the flat for him.'

'Oh, I see.' She smiled, to be polite, as if the estate agent's answer were perfect and how had she not thought of that?

When the door to the flat was opened, they followed the agent inside. Archer wasn't saying much. She wondered what he was thinking. She needed a sign from him. Something.

'This room here, to the left, is the main living area with a front aspect that overlooks the village green.' The agent stood by the window and smiled as she and Archer stepped into the space. It was a decent-sized room. Painted white, with green curtains hanging. There was room for a three-seater sofa and another two-seater, a low coffee table and an entertainment unit. The TV was mounted on one wall. There wasn't much character to the place. It was just functional and so she tried to imagine sprucing the place up. Adding some colour. Her own furniture. Some plants. But then she'd also need room for baby stuff, too. What exactly did babies need? Judging by Hillary's house, they needed everything, but then she'd had to have double the amount what with having twins.

Oh, please don't let me be carrying twins.

A place for a cot, for sure. A Moses basket? A changing station? Though she guessed she could do that on a mat on the floor. Halley looked down at the current carpet and grimaced. It wasn't exactly in good condition. It looked old. Stained in places. It would need ripping out and replacing, which was going to add to any expense. Though she briefly wondered if there were any decent floorboards underneath it.

'Want to see the kitchen? The current owner has recently updated it and I think you'll find it's quite appealing.' The agent led them from the room and back into the hall. The next door on the left led to a small kitchen in bright white. It really was quite modern.

'There's not much surface space, is there?'

The agent beamed. 'Not as it stands, but

try to imagine it without that coffee machine taking up space, or the microwave. But there's plenty of storage.' He indicated the cupboards above by opening them and showing the interiors. 'And there's a concealed dishwasher just here.'

'Where's the washing machine?' Archer asked. 'Is there a separate utility room?'

'Er...no. I believe the owner uses a launderette in town.'

Archer raised an eyebrow at her. It told her everything he was thinking. That this place wasn't going to be suitable. Babies created a lot of laundry. She'd need a home with space for a washing machine!

'Let me show you the bathroom. Again, the owner has recently modernised it and, though there isn't a bath, there is a brand-new double shower, which is exquisitely tiled, if I do say so myself.'

Dutifully, they followed the agent around, though she strongly felt, and sensed Archer did too, that this place wasn't for them. The bathroom was fine and, yes, it had been done nicely, but it wasn't enough to sell it to her. The main bedroom was a fair size, but the second room was very small and certainly not big enough for all the things a baby would need. Halley wasn't an expert, but she knew this, at least.

'I'm not sure this is right for us,' Halley ventured.

'I agree with Halley. This isn't the one. Plus, it's above a newsagent's, so she'd be woken early every morning by the papers arriving.'

She'd not even thought of that. 'Can we go and view the cottage, instead?'

The agent clearly realised that this was not going to result in a sale. They had made up their minds. 'Of course. I'll meet you there in…' he checked his mobile phone '…half an hour?'

'Yes. Thank you.'

Halley and Archer headed back to the car and sank into the seats gratefully.

'How are you holding up? Do you need anything? Want to grab a coffee?'

'Ugh, coffee…you know what I really fancy?'

'What?'

'A strawberry milkshake. Extra thick.'

He laughed. 'Really?'

'The baby wants what it wants.'

'We'll pass by the café. Pick one up for you.'

'Great, thanks. I hope we have better luck with the next property. I'd viewed the photos of that flat online and it had all looked good.

It's amazing what they can hide with photography, huh?'

'I know. I think that flat will be good for someone without kids. Who's got some extra income to modernise the other rooms and replace the flooring and find some way to plumb in a washing machine, but it definitely wasn't right for us.'

'Us?' She looked at him and smiled.

'For you and the baby.' He smiled back and started the engine.

She'd known what he'd meant, but when he clarified his statement, *'for you and the baby'*, it made it seem as if she was on her own with this. That he was helping, but at the end of the day it would just be her and their child alone at home. Because he would get to drive away and leave them there. To carry on with the rest of his life.

Suddenly the extra-thick strawberry milkshake didn't feel all that appealing and so when he bounded out of the café carrying one and passed it to her, she could barely raise a smile of thanks.

They drove to the next property, the two-bed cottage on the edge of the village, but once again the details and the photography had been presented in such a way that just the sight of the property was disappointing before they'd even got inside. The only thing nice about it was the small garden out front. Neat lawns with a couple of shrubs. But the garden itself backed onto the road that edged their village and they both knew that traffic could be fast there, barrelling down the lane at high speeds. That wouldn't be safe for a young child. Not safe at all.

Once again, the estate agent did his best to try and sell them on the positives—a large cottage kitchen, an inglenook fireplace, a traditional range in the kitchen and two large bedrooms. But nothing could overshadow the facts that there was a large fishpond in the rear garden, damp climbing up the walls in the outhouse attached to the cottage and the property was single-glazed throughout and had a thatched roof that would need replacing within the next year.

It was all too much. Halley and the baby would need a place that was ready to move into. That needed the minimum of work doing to it, so that she could settle in with her growing bump and happily wait for her baby to be born, without worrying if the damp was getting worse, or if the roof was going to have to come off and be replaced.

The estate agent gave them his card and told

them to ring him if they had any questions and he sped away in his car.

Halley turned to Archer. 'I think this is going to be harder than we realised.'

'Yeah, stressful too. But, you know, that's just a couple of places, there's bound to be others and we still have time.'

She nodded and took a swallow of her milkshake. It had melted slightly, but tasted wonderful, settling in her poor, troubled stomach nicely. 'Well, thanks for coming with me.'

'I wouldn't have it any other way. Want me to drive you home?'

No. She didn't. Not yet. Despite the disappointing properties, she'd enjoyed being out and about with him and there was nothing pressing at home. Hillary was there looking after Mum. 'Could you not? I just want to… I don't know, have a break. Can we do that, or do you have to get back, or…?'

'It's no problem. Where do you want to go?'

She shrugged. 'Somewhere nice. Where we don't have to think about houses, or the fact that I'm pregnant and my life is about to change big time. I just want to be normal. I just want to not have to think. Is that okay? Know any place like that?'

He smiled as he gazed at her. 'I think that I do. There's a place that I go when I want peace and quiet and calm and I think it will be perfect.'

'Where is it?'

'You'll see it when we get there,' he answered enigmatically, starting the engine.

Halley smiled. She liked that he was keeping it a mystery. She liked that he was willing to spend time with her. That he wanted to help her find some peace.

He was a good man. He was being a good man. Had one been here, right before her eyes, ever since she was a little girl and she hadn't noticed? And she hadn't noticed because back when she was younger she'd been incredibly shallow and only noticed the boys who were captains of the rugby team. Boys who got the lead in school plays. Boys who had the most friends and were deemed cool.

She'd certainly not paid any heed to the guy who had sat quietly on the sidelines and watched her dissect a frog. That boy, back then, had seemed small. Weedy. Pale. He'd worn glasses that weren't trendy and, if she remembered correctly, he'd always seemed a bit...scruffy. A bit neglected. Which of course he had been. He'd told her so. And that just made her feel incredibly guilty. Because he didn't look that way now, and now she noticed him.

'Did I ignore you?'

He glanced over at her. Frowned. 'What?'

'At school? Was I even worse than that? Was I mean?'

'No! No, you were…perfect. You were… amazing.'

'I didn't speak to you. I didn't notice you.'

'Who did? Look, don't beat yourself up about something that happened when we were kids. It's a different life. You have different rules for yourself. In school, you do your best to be like everyone else. To fit in. To be the same. It's only when you're an adult do you realise how important it is to just be you and, no, you may not have noticed me, but you weren't mean. You were still you.'

'I think you're just being gracious and kind.'

He laughed. 'Well, that's me.'

'You're sweet. I should have noticed that, at least.'

'It's a bit hard to notice when I hardly spoke as you wielded a scalpel.'

'I should have noticed you, Archer. I should have made the attempt to get to know you.'

'Do you notice me now?' They had stopped at a red light and he was looking at her intently.

He was gorgeous. Manly. Cool and a little edgy. Intelligent and kind and he was going to be the father to her baby. In her life, for the rest of eternity, in some capacity. 'I do. Very much so and I'm glad of it,' she answered earnestly.

'Then everything worked out well, didn't it?'

Archer parked up in a car park near Ripon high street and led her to what looked, on the outside, like a normal run-of-the-mill bookshop called Many Worlds.

'Books?'

'And cake. Lots and lots of cake. Come on!' He was smiling. Happy as he pulled open the door and she stepped inside, straight into a magical mystery world, unlike any bookstore she had ever been in.

The interior looked like a forest and all the shelves were branches of trees, lined with books. But there wasn't any women's fiction here. No romance. No crime. All the books were fantasy, or science fiction or even horror. There were nooks to sit and read, filled with comfy chairs or bean bags. There were models and figurines of creatures that looked like dragons and elves or swamp monsters. In one corner, there was a huge screen, playing the latest fantasy blockbuster with a group of people sitting in front of it, watching intently.

She turned to look at Archer, surprised. 'Tell me the truth. Are you a secret geek?'

He smiled. 'I am. And our child will be too, so get used to it. I shall introduce him or her to the possibilities of dragons, vampires, werewolves and wizards. So get used to the idea right now.'

She laughed. 'I don't have to!'

He raised an eyebrow. 'Are you going to fight me on this?'

'Why would I? When I'm a geek, too? I love this place!' And she walked forward to a shelf lined with dark books, saturated with reds and purples and gothic fonts. They gleamed. They glowed. The typography was gorgeous, the artwork striking, drawing her in, making her slide one book out from the shelf after another, to read the blurbs on the back. Her pregnancy was forgotten. House-hunting forgotten. Feeling bad about her schooldays was over. Just being here, in this wonderful place, this magical world, was more than she could ever have hoped for! 'How didn't I know of this place?'

'You've been away. It opened up three years ago now, I believe. There's an upstairs you haven't seen yet, it's like a treehouse, with even more books and a café, filled with cakes and delicious pastries that you just know you shouldn't eat, but have to, because they look so amazing.'

She beamed a happy smile, feeling hungry for a change. 'We'll get up there in a moment. I want a proper look down here first. Ooh, that looks good!' She reached for a book. A thick one, a good five hundred pages, with a metallic green serpent on the cover, wrapped in and around the letters of the title, written in gold.

I could spend a fortune in here!

They passed a section that was all graphic novels and, though she'd never read one in her life, seeing them all face out like that intrigued her and she went in to browse them, picking up one or two that sounded interesting.

'You big into those?' Archer asked, smiling at her, enjoying her joy.

'Never read one in my life.'

He laughed and she liked the sound.

She smiled at him, noticing that he'd picked up a couple of books that he was carrying around, too. 'Show me.'

He'd picked up a book that was the third one in a trilogy that he'd been reading about a demon horde and the other title was a standalone that looked like a gothic thriller, judging by the creepy house on the cover. 'You can borrow them, if you like?'

'Thanks. I just might.' So they both liked

stargazing. Both loved animals and caring for them. Were both into fantasy and horror novels. And were both scared about getting into a full-time relationship. What else were they matching on? Apart from the fact that they were going to bring a child into the world together.

Maybe this could work? Maybe they were more similar than they realised? If they had the same beliefs and the same likes…then why couldn't this work out?

But as soon as she allowed herself to hope about the possibility, she instantly got scared. Because what if it all went wrong? In front of the whole village yet again? Imagine if they got together and set up a home together and had their baby and then it all fell apart? What would people say then? Could she fail in front of them again? Could she fail herself? She'd set herself these rules for a reason—to keep herself safe—and if she stuck to them and stuck to them hard, then she wouldn't be in danger at all, would she?

'Ready to see upstairs?' He proffered his hand.

She took it. 'Sure.'

There was an escalator that took them to the next floor and as they rose, they passed a tremendous mural on the wall of a castle perched high on a mountaintop and all around in the sky and sitting on the castle turrets were dragons of all colours and sizes. There was a dark forest and, if she looked carefully, as they rose higher and higher she saw little candle lights in the darkness and sitting around them were elves and goblins and pixies. All the things that made her heart sing. 'I think I know how I want to decorate the nursery,' she said, turning to smile at him standing behind her.

Archer laughed. 'Absolutely.'

When they reached the top, the smell of coffee and cake reached her nostrils, making her salivate.

The bookshop café was perfect. Lit by wall sconces as if you'd reached the top of the tower, the walls were painted grey and had all these nooks and crannies built into them and in each one lurked a creature, backlit by a glowing coloured light. The floor was painted as if it were exposed wood and in the gaps between the wooden slats you could see a magical land far below, through the clouds.

There were more bookshelves, filled with books that were highlighted as the bookseller's choice of the week, or there was a table with a large pile listed as being written by a local author. Each of them adorned with a golden sticker that indicated it was a signed copy. On one wall was a large glass case, filled with cakes and pastries, just as promised. It was a delight for the eyes, as well as the nose, and Halley had difficulty choosing what she wanted. In the end she went for a cake called the Dragon's Eye—a coconut macaroon with a pool of yellow jelly in the centre.

'This is amazing,' she said as they sat at a table. 'This was perfect. Just what I needed.'

'I did think about taking you to the observatory, but it's best to prebook.'

'That would have been amazing, too. Mum's going to be annoyed that I've bought a load of books, instead of buying a place to live, but…'

'You're allowed to treat yourself. And you're still you, with your own identity. You don't lose that just because you've become a mother.'

'Or a father,' she said. 'Do you think that'll happen? That we'll lose who we are?'

'I hope not.'

'Hillary talks about her children all the time. Them or her work. I'm not sure I know who she is any more.'

'She's your sister. She always will be.'

'I know, but she used to be into music big time. She could sing, you know? She had this amazing voice and I used to tell her to go on one of those TV shows and audition, because she'd be able to make it through, but I don't even hear her sing any more. Will we lose this? This interest in reading fantasy? Or not have the time to do what we love? Will we lose our interest in looking up at the stars? Will we lose ourselves when we become Mum and Dad?'

'I'll make sure that we don't. I'll ensure that we make time to each do our own thing.'

'How though? How are we going to do that? You'll live in your place. I'll live in mine. You'll be working. I'll be raising the baby. We could get lost in all of that.'

'We'll find a way.' He looked determined.

'You keep saying that, but *how*? You make all these promises and they're great, they really are, but when reality hits?'

'You think I'm not going to stay committed?'

'No. But I think we'll be separate. I'll have the baby most of the time, then you'll come over to pick up the baby to have for the weekend or whatever and you'll go off and do that alone and I'll be alone waiting for the baby to come back and…' She shrugged. 'That's not how I want this to be.'

'What do you want?' he asked softly, leaning forward, his eyes intense in the darkness of the café. She wanted to stare into his eyes for evermore. She wanted to lean forward and kiss him and taste him once again to remind herself that this was real. That he was real. That she was safe.

She wanted a relationship. She wanted them to have an equal share. She wanted to be a person in a loving and committed relationship if she was going to have a child. Not someone who treated their child like a timeshare apartment. But she was afraid to say it. Afraid to say what she really wanted, because if she did? And that wasn't what he wanted? Where would that leave her? 'I don't know,' she said softly, knowing that she was lying, but fear held her back from the truth.

She liked Archer. She thought that he was one of the good guys. He'd already shown her that he truly cared and would help her out as much as he could. But did he want love? Could he ever love again?

'Tell me about Amy.'

Archer blinked. 'What? Where did that come from?'

'Hillary brought it up—I thought we should talk about it. It's a significant part of your past.'

He looked about them and she could see he was trying to work out how he was going to tell this story. 'Amy was my girlfriend. She didn't come from Burndale. She was from Yorkshire, though. Worked as a drug rep and came into the surgery one day to argue with me about what the best anti-inflammatory was. I thought she was cheeky. Daring. She had this smile that brightened up the room, so I asked her for a drink and our relationship developed from there.'

'You loved her?'

Archer grimaced. 'I don't know. Probably. I was infatuated with her. She reminded me of…' He laughed. 'She knew her own mind. Knew what she wanted from life. Marriage and kids, the whole shebang. I wasn't ready. I wasn't sure I wanted to fully commit and then we found out that the headaches she'd been having a lot of were actually caused by a brain tumour.'

'Cancer?'

He nodded. 'A glioma. She was scheduled for chemotherapy, but because of her age they suggested that beforehand she use drugs to make her ovaries create a lot of eggs so they could be frozen for when she was better. The doctors said that the eggs would stand a better chance if they were fertilised and, because I was her boyfriend, her family turned to me.'

'What did you do?'

'What was I supposed to do? I couldn't walk

away. So I did what I had to do and they managed to freeze four healthy embryos. But Amy didn't respond to the chemotherapy. Nor the radiation. Her cancer was fast and aggressive and she died.'

'I'm so sorry.'

'Her family grieved, but after a time they got this idea that they could use the embryos in a surrogate, so they could still have a piece of their daughter. I think this is what Hillary was referring to. I didn't know what to do. What to say. I couldn't imagine it. I'd fertilised those eggs to give Amy a future, but she wasn't there any more and I'd been left in a difficult situation. I didn't want to have a child like that. Out in the world, without me. But thankfully, they changed their minds.'

'Really?'

He nodded. 'They were planning on leaving Yorkshire, emigrating to Australia, and they wanted to take the embryos with them, but I didn't give consent for them to do that. I didn't want a child of mine being raised halfway around the world with no contact and I also didn't think they should have pushed to have grandchildren, just so they could somehow hold onto Amy. That's not what she would have wanted and, in the end, they agreed with me.'

'Did you ever want a child?'

'Honestly? I never envisaged it. But it's happening and it's here. It's not me and Amy, it's me and you and we're a whole different kettle of fish. You're staying here in Burndale. We're going to be close and I'm going to be damned sure that I'm in the life of my child, so that it knows it has a loving father, who will be there for it, for the rest of its days.'

He paused. 'Listen…my childhood wasn't the greatest. I had no father. My mother was distant and unwell. I was made to feel like a burden and I swore I would never let any child of mine, if I had them, feel the same way. That's why I was against the idea of kids. But because my childhood was rubbish, doesn't mean my baby's childhood will be the same way. Children give us the opportunity to be better. To not repeat the same mistakes. Babies are a clean slate. A fresh start. A chance for us to be different, so that history doesn't repeat itself. I'm not going to let history repeat, Halley. I'm going to be present. I'm going to be loving. I'm going to be the best dad I can be, because my child deserves more than what I had.'

She could see the passion in his eyes. He meant every word and she reached for his hand without thinking. And that soothed her soul for a little while.

Archer Forde would not leave her to deal with this alone.

He would find a way to make this work.

She believed in him.

She believed in *them*.

CHAPTER SIX

HE WAS GLAD the subject came up. He was glad that she'd raised it, that Hillary had raised it at the dinner, too, because he'd not wanted to hide it and hadn't been able to think of a way in which to explain what had happened.

How could he have raised that? How could he have just dropped that into conversation? He'd never intended to have a family with Amy. She was fun. She'd been great. But had he ever viewed her as someone he wanted to be with for ever? And fertilising her eggs had been something he'd felt he had to do. He'd cared for her deeply and he'd wanted her to have the opportunity to have children in the future, in case her cancer treatment left her infertile, and embryos froze better than eggs.

He'd never thought she would die. He'd never thought she would be infertile, after the treatment, that was just something they warned you about as a possibility. And there *had been* a chance that he and she could work out. That they'd be together for ever. Nothing else had been on the horizon for him, so he'd thought he could make it work. He'd believed she'd get better. He'd been optimistic still, back then.

Losing Amy had been hard. One of the most difficult things he'd ever had to go through. Allowing himself to get attached, to develop feelings for her, to believe that he might have kids, that his future was more than likely tied into hers, had only made everything hurt the more when she'd died. Having hope taken away had been just as difficult to deal with as her death. He'd had to say goodbye to that idea.

Archer had thought that his mother's inability to love him and Axle had been horrible. To not have the love of someone who should love you… To have spent years craving his mother's favour… For her to just one time tell him that he was a good boy, that she was proud… He'd got used to yearning for love and so it had been easy to turn his affections to Halley at school and yearn for her from afar. She'd become his idea of perfection. He'd decided that if she ever were with him, then their love would be perfect. But he'd never been brave enough to speak up. To stand close. To engage with her, because he'd been too afraid of her rejecting him, too. Worse than that, what if she'd laughed at him? It was bad enough his own mother couldn't love him properly, if Halley rejected him as well, then his one iota of happiness that he nurtured secretly in his heart would die.

To lose a love he'd actually pursued? He'd got brave with Amy. She'd seemed safe. Less likely to hurt him. She was a love that he had allowed to creep in and wrap its tendrils around his heart and when those connections had broken apart with her death, those tendrils had torn him in two. Losing Amy had hurt so badly that he'd vowed to never love deeply again. Just so he never had to face such terrible pain again. Living in a state of numbness worked better.

But now there was Halley.

Now there was the baby.

And he knew he would fall in love with this baby and that would put him at risk for ever. What if it got hurt? What if it got sick, like Amy? Something serious? What if they lost it before it even got born? He couldn't imagine how that would feel.

As he drove her home, he must have been quiet in the car.

'Everything okay? You haven't said much.'

He smiled to reassure her. 'Just thinking.'

'What about?'

'Life. How you're never in control of it, even though you think you are.'

'Tell me about it.' She rubbed at her belly.

'Do you need anything?' He wanted to help her. Wanted to give her anything that she might need. If he could be her person strongly enough, then maybe he might feel a smidgen of what he needed himself.

She sighed. 'I need lots of things. I'm never going to get them though.'

He smiled, indicating to take the left turn that would take them back to the farm. As he drove towards it, he wondered if it would always be like this. Him spending a few hours with her, but then both of them going back to their own homes. Together, but *not* together. It would be the same when the baby was here. How much of his child's life would he miss because they didn't live together? Would he miss his baby's first word? The first time it sat up? The first time it slept through the night? Suddenly, he knew he couldn't live like that. He couldn't live another life missing out on the love he would feel for his child.

'I don't want to miss anything, Halley.'

'What?'

'I don't want to miss anything. I want to

be there for the milestones. The first nappy change. The first solids. The first sleeping through the night. I want to have to pace the floor of the nursery because the baby won't settle. I want to complain of being sleep-deprived. I want to be there for everything.'

She didn't say anything. If anything, she frowned, as if trying to think. Trying to find a solution.

'Maybe you should move in with me?' The words were out of his mouth before he could even think about what he was saying.

'What?'

'Maybe you should move in with me? When your mum is better and up and about and able to do things again. I have a nice three-bedroomed cottage. It's double-glazed, it doesn't have damp, there's no pool or pond in the back garden. I use one room as an office, but we could make that your room, so you have your own space, but we'd be together. We'd share everything equally. The garden is mostly lawn, so plenty of places to put up a Wendy house or a treehouse or whatever our kid wants. I have a washing machine. All mod cons. We could each be who we need to be, but, most importantly, we'd be there for our baby together.'

She stared at him in mute shock and surprise.

It was a crazy suggestion, he knew, but one that seemed to make sense. He had the room, and this way he could be there for everything and so could she. Neither of them would have to miss a thing.

'You mean that?' she asked after an inordinately uncomfortable amount of time.

'I do. It might be a little unconventional, but we could make it work. We get along. We like a lot of the same things, but this way we'd each still have our independence, whilst at the same time share the responsibility and care. Do you really want to be a part-time parent, Halley? Because I don't want to be. If I'm having a baby, then I want to be there for it. Always.'

She let out a laugh. 'It's a crazy idea!'

No. He didn't want her to think it was crazy. Or that he was joking. He meant this. 'Just think about it. I think it could work.' He pulled up at the farm and watched as she pushed open the door and got out. The soft breeze whipped at her hair, drifting across her face, and she had to tuck it behind her ear.

She stood there for a moment. 'When would you want this to happen?'

'Before the baby's born. That gives your mum plenty of time to recover.'

'But if we lived together, don't you think

that might be a little weird? I mean…what if you wanted to go out on a date?'

He frowned. 'I don't think either of us is going to have much time to go out on dates.'

Halley laughed. 'Maybe not. Hmm… Let me think about it, okay?'

'Okay, but just promise me you'll consider it carefully. I really think this could be the answer to our worries.'

She nodded. 'I promise.'

'Okay. I'll call you tomorrow.'

When she got in, her mum was halfway up the stairs.

'What are you doing?' She rushed over to help her sit back down onto the chair.

'My physio exercises! I need to do them at least three times a day.'

'But only when I'm home! What if you'd fallen over? Where's Hillary?'

'One of the lads said he thought that one of the pygmy goats was in labour, so she went out to check. She's been gone for some time, so I can only guess we have kids on the way. Or already here.' She sighed as she sat back in the chair. 'How did the house-hunting go?'

'Not great. Neither property was suitable.'

'Oh. Well, that's a shame. You were out for

some time, though. Did you go on to somewhere nice?'

'A bookshop in Ripon.' She pointed at the bag she'd placed on the table. 'Archer bought me some books.'

'And what did he think to your choice in reading material?'

She smiled. 'Actually, Mum, he likes the same things.'

'Really? Well, that's interesting.'

'Why?'

'I don't know…it's just two young attractive people like yourselves, both into animals, both into astronomy, both into elves and magic… having a baby together. It's just surprising that neither of you can see what's right in front of you.'

Halley tilted her head to one side. 'And what is that exactly?'

'That you're perfect for one another.'

'I think it takes more than stars and magic to make two people fall in love, Mum.'

Her mum smiled her knowing smile. 'Oh, I don't know about that. I think stars and magic are just perfect.'

'Do you want some tea?'

'That'd be lovely, thanks.'

As Halley brewed a cuppa in the kitchen, her mind whirled with Archer's suggestion about moving in with him. About Mum's comments about how similar she and Archer were. How suited they were for each other. 'Mum… how did you know that Dad was the right man for you? How did you know he was the person you wanted to live the rest of your life with?'

Her mum looked at her oddly. 'Well, he was so lovely. So kind and thoughtful. He was always looking out for me. Always trying to make me smile or laugh. I just knew he would make a good husband. A good father.'

'And when he asked you to marry him, was there any hesitation?'

'None at all. I couldn't imagine saying no. Why? Has Archer asked you to marry him, love?' she asked, her voice rising in surprise.

'No! No, he hasn't. But he has suggested we live together at his place. He's a great guy, but I have all these reservations. Whereas with Piotr I had none, and look how that turned out!'

'You were very young when you met Piotr. Just turned twenty. You've had more life experience now. You know how things hurt, of course you're having reservations.'

'It's not love, or anything. He simply suggested it for the practical arrangements. He really wants to be there for his baby and not miss anything and he has a three-bedroomed cottage, so I'd have my own room.'

'I see. What's your gut reaction?'

'If he wants a relationship with his baby, then it's perfect. But if I move into his place, will I lose my own autonomy? Will everything be his rules because it's his place?'

'If you're worried about that, agree to it only on certain conditions, then.'

'I guess…'

'What sort of rules do you want in place?'

'I don't know. He's only just asked me as he was dropping me off. I haven't had time to think about it. It was such a surprise.'

'I've known Archer a long time, Halley. He's been coming here and caring for the farm animals for many years. He's been through a lot himself. He lost the love of his life, too. You're not the only one hurting here. I'd also bet you're not the only one feeling cautious and wanting to establish some ground rules. But he's a good guy, so just talk to him. Talk about what he's suggested and see if it could work.'

'He says we wouldn't have to do it until you were back on your feet again.'

'Considerate, see? But I'm getting stronger every day. I can manage the stairs. Slowly, but I can manage. And I'm walking more. You girls don't need to hover over me so much.'

'So you think I should do it?'

'I can't make that decision for you. But if you're not able to find a suitable place before the baby is born, it might just be the answer to your prayers. He's offered you your own space, so he's not presuming anything about the relationship.'

'No, he's not.'

Her mum looked at her strangely. 'Do you want something more from him?'

Halley met her gaze. 'I like him. I do. A lot. But I'm scared to think that anything could happen between us. And if we're in a forced proximity… I just don't want to make a huge mistake.'

'Moving in and allowing yourself to fall in love in case it all goes wrong?'

She nodded.

'You can't live like that, love. Look at how long you've been on your own. How happy have you truly been?'

'I've been fine!'

'But what if you could be more than fine?'

Halley didn't have an answer.

Archer's next patient was Sanjay Singh, bringing in his cat, Jess, because it had been injured during a fight with another cat.

Jess was a beautiful Siamese cat, chocolate

point, long and slender, but had a nasty bite mark on its side that looked as if it was turning into a bit of an abscess.

'Neighbourhood cat?' Archer asked.

'No. This was our fault. We went to the cat rescue place. My wife has always wanted to rescue an older cat and so we went and picked up this old codger. Big fella he is. Called Badger. We brought him in a couple of weeks ago. Saw Max. Just to get him checked over, you know? We tried doing slow introductions—you know, the way you're meant to—but then one of the kids left a door open and there was this big fight and this happened.'

'How did Badger come out of it?'

'Not a scratch. But he's this big fluffy Persian cat and I think his fur protected him from Jess's claws and teeth.'

'Lucky guy. Okay, Jess, let's have a proper look at this, shall we?'

He gave Jess a thorough examination, finding a couple of clean scratches on her ears and beneath her eye. The bite on the neck and shoulder area seemed to be the worst of it and he had to shave off some of her fur to get a decent look at the abscess that was forming. Her temperature was slightly raised, indicating the infection. 'Okay, so what we need to do is give Jess some antibiotics to help rid her of the infection. I could give her a painkiller as well, if you wanted, but she seems to be moving pretty well and isn't restricted in her movements. You say she's getting around the house normally?'

'Yes. Jumping all over the place. Getting on top of the fridge. My wife hates that.'

'Eating and drinking normally?'

'Yeah…yeah.'

'Toileting okay?'

'I think so. But she goes outside, so I can't be sure.'

'And she's washing and cleaning herself normally?'

'Yeah.'

'Okay. Well, I'll give you the meds and see how she goes. But if you have any concerns or anything, then just give the reception team a bell and we'll fit you in.'

'Okay, great, thanks.'

He waved Sanjay and Jess goodbye and inputted the consultation into the computer. Unfortunately cat bites were something he saw a lot in his job. Introducing two animals that didn't know each other into the same space was always going to be fraught with problems, especially if they were two adult cats that had already lived a bit of life. Were stuck in their ways and knew how they wanted their life to be. He supposed there were teething problems with anyone moving in together.

Would he and Halley have issues if she took him up on his offer to move into his place?

Part of him still couldn't believe he'd even asked it out loud! Another part of him told him it was the most sensible solution to all their problems. They were struggling to find Halley a place. It made simple economic and emotional sense. It would be beneficial to both their finances. They'd both be there to raise their child. They'd be able to make decisions together and they could each still live their own life.

It was sensible. And if they established ground rules between them, as well, so they each knew the other's expectations and limitations…then he couldn't see any reason why it wouldn't work.

Of course, it would be strange to actually live with Halley. He'd never lived with another woman before. He and Amy had been going out, but they'd not moved in together ever, even if he had felt as if he'd slept over a lot when she'd had chemo and he'd wanted to be there for her, in case she'd needed help in the night. But he'd still had his own place. His own bolt-hole. His own escape, for when it all became too much. That was why he'd told Halley they'd each have their own space. Their own room. They'd need that, because if she accepted, both their lives would be pretty much full on. And he felt sure he'd be able to separate his emotions if this happened. Liking Halley and loving Halley, living under the same roof…with rules in place, there was no chance he'd do something silly and risk it all.

Would he?

Because he knew he could never take that chance and ruin everything. He needed to be there for his kid and that was a strong enough reason not to risk pursuing anything physical or emotional with her.

A quick knock on his door behind him and Jenny, his new partner, popped her head in. 'Ready for a cuppa?'

He nodded. 'Absolutely! Sounds a great idea. I think we've got some chocolate biscuits lurking in the staff room, too.'

Halley had been scanning estate agents' websites and there simply wasn't anything suitable that came up. The only property that did was way out of her price range and so Archer's suggestion was seeming a more sensible idea with every second that passed.

When Archer texted to see how she was doing that morning, she sent him a text back and asked if she could meet him midday for lunch and a chat.

He suggested twelve-thirty in the village and she agreed to meet him then, saying she'd bring lunch and she'd meet him outside in the car.

When lunchtime rolled around, she saw him stride out of his practice and towards her car, giving her a quick wave.

She smiled in return and admired him as he grew closer. He really was a very attractive man and she almost had to pinch herself to tell herself that this was real. She was having a baby with this man!

'Hi. How are you doing?' He got in the car and leaned in to drop a peck on her cheek in greeting. She tried to ignore the fluttering of her heart and instead smiled and passed him a container.

'Great. Haslet and pickle sandwiches. That all right?'

He raised an eyebrow. 'Craving food?'

She laughed. 'Craving food. We can stop off and get you something different, if you'd like?'

'No, it'll be fine. Where do you want to go and eat?'

'The benches at the back of the village green? I noticed it was in the sun as I came past. It should be nice.'

'Sounds perfect. Not worried about people seeing us out and about together?'

'That ship has sailed. Mum told me that Mrs Grigson called her the other day to say they'd not only seen us in the café together, but that apparently we'd been seen in Ripon together, too.'

Archer laughed in amazement. 'That woman does better research than a private eye. I wonder who spotted us in Ripon.'

'Who knows?'

'It's kind of sweet, though.'

She looked at him, surprised. 'You think so?'

'They may gossip, but isn't it good, too, to know that people are looking out for you?'

'You mean that they care?'

'Possibly. That they're keeping an eye out for you. I mean, if you were in danger, someone would step in. To have someone care about you, no matter their reason, is much better than having no one care, or no one noticing.'

'I guess I never thought about it like that.' He really was amazing, she thought. The way he considered things. But having learned more about his childhood, the way he and Axle were raised, she ought not to be surprised. His upbringing could have made him bitter, or angry. But he was neither of these things and his overt goodness, despite his past, made him very attractive indeed.

She drove them round to the green, parking up in a space by the village post office, and then they got out and found their bench, settling down and immediately being surrounded by hopeful birds. Sparrows. A random seagull that seemed huge enough to be an albatross. Starlings. A robin. 'I've been thinking about your offer.'

'Oh. Okay. What did you conclude?'

She sighed. 'I concluded that you may be right. I can't afford anything decent in this village. Prices have risen sharply since the pandemic and I'm not sure if you're aware but unemployed veterinary nurses don't have a steady wage.'

'Your mum's paying you, though, right?'

'Yes, but it's not much and it's not permanent. I need to be realistic.'

'Fair enough. So…?'

Haley sucked in a big gulp of air. 'So…it looks like I'll be taking you up on your offer to move in. I'll need to look at the place first, though. Make sure it's right for us all.'

'Wow. Okay.' He seemed happy and that warmed her heart. He wasn't doing this because it was simply practical, he really seemed to want her there.

It was scary. A huge decision and she still felt hesitant. She'd put herself out there once before and it had drastically backfired. If they took their time, did this slowly, then any kinks could be worked out before they became huge issues.

'But I won't move in just yet. Not until Mum is fully back on her feet.'

'Great.'

'But I do think we should establish some ground rules between us.'

'Agreed.'

'I contribute fairly with rent and bills.'

He nodded, listening, and took a bite of his sandwich.

'Before I move in, I get to prepare my room. I want to be able to move in and not have anything to do.'

'You mean decorate it?'

'If that's okay?' If he was going to get upset about something as simple as that, then maybe this wouldn't be a good idea.

But he simply nodded and smiled as he chewed.

'And I also guess we ought to decorate the nursery, too.'

'We'll do it together.'

'Okay. When can I come round to see it?'

'When are you free?'

'Hillary's coming over tonight with the twins to see their grandma. I could come round then?'

He gave a nod. 'Sounds good to me.'

'And one last rule.'

'What's that?'

'No flirting. No trying to make this more than it is. We don't need to make this complicated. We don't need to ruin something that could be really good,' she said, hoping on some level that he would be upset about that, or gasp and say, *Absolutely not!*

He smiled at her. 'I'll do my best.'

She forced a smile back at him. 'Good.' Feeling it wasn't that good at all.

He'd done what he could to smarten up the place before she came round. Not that he made much mess as a single guy. Archer considered himself to be quite good at keeping neat. He blamed it on the fact that when he was growing up, his mum didn't really pay attention to cleaning and so he needed to and he prided himself on picking up after him and Axle. It became a habit. Not to make mess. To wash dishes after cooking. To put dirty laundry in the wash. To hang it immediately out to dry, so that it didn't crease too much, because he hated ironing. And he'd learned over the years how to make a home. Houseplants were good.

Lots of greenery. Some decent art on the walls. Candles looked good. A throw over the sofa. He'd kept colours quite neutral. White, cream, taupe. His statement pieces added the colour.

The room that he hoped would be Halley's he'd been using as a bit of an office, but if she moved in, that was okay. He could move his desk and chair into his bedroom, put up some shelves for his files and books, and the nursery was just being used for random stuff that had no actual place in the cottage yet. He stored his bike in there, but he could buy a storage shed for it and put it in the garden. There were some old boxes with his childhood stuff contained within, but he could go through that, or put it in storage beneath his bed or in the back of his wardrobe.

He was willing to make room for Halley and the baby. Willing to make room for them so that they could feel at home. So that he could be there at all times for his child. Having Halley there too would be a wonderful bonus and she'd made it clear that there couldn't be any flirting, so that was good, they both knew where they stood.

No flirting…that was going to be hard. He'd slept with this woman. Knew how she felt. Knew where to touch her to make her gasp, to make her purr with pleasure, and he'd be thrilled to hear those noises again. To make her happy, to make her forget the world, if just for a little while, whilst she lay in his arms.

Could he do that?

When his doorbell rang at seven o clock on the dot, he knew it was her. He'd showered and changed after coming home from work and put on some jeans and a tee. His hair was still a little wet from the shower, but he figured he still looked presentable.

'Hey, welcome to your possible future abode!' he said, opening the door wide and inviting her in.

As she walked in, he stooped to kiss her cheek in greeting.

She blushed, which was cute. Watching her face develop rosy spots. 'Something smells nice.'

'Oh! Yeah, I'm baking some lemon twists for Barb.'

'Who's Barb?'

'One of the receptionists at work. It's her birthday tomorrow and she loves my lemon twists, so I make them for her every year. I'll let you try one when they're out of the oven.'

'Sounds great, thanks.'

'No problem. So, do you need a drink first, or do you want to get straight on down to business?' That sounded odd, so he cracked a grin, to show he was joking.

Halley smiled. 'Tea would be great, if you have any?'

He smiled back. 'I have plenty of tea. Decaf or normal?'

'Er, decaf, please.'

'Milk and sugar?'

'Milk, one sugar.'

'Coming right up.' He started to walk down the hallway and then stopped. 'Guess I can start some of the tour here. This is the hall, as you can see. Probably wide enough to get a buggy in, wouldn't you think?'

She nodded, looking about her. 'It's very light.'

'It's the mirrors. I saw it on a show once.' He paused in a doorway to his right. 'This is the lounge. Kitchen's at the end at the back of the house.' He watched her step into the lounge and take a look around. Saw her gaze land on his film poster, then drift on over to his bookshelves. A small smile lit her face as she went over and perused the titles on them.

'You weren't kidding about liking fantasy.'

'I never kid about my fantasies.' Oops. He was doing it again. But he was nervous! Couldn't help it. He wanted this to go right. 'Sorry, I meant...'

She laughed and waved it away as if it were nothing, then turned away to look at the rest of the room. 'Open fireplace.'

'Yep. But we could put a safety guard in front, you know, for when baby starts crawling and walking on its own. And this cottage is usually pretty warm, so I only tend to really use the fire when winter hits hard.'

'That must be nice? A real fire.'

'It can be. Would be nicer to share it with someone.'

Another smile.

'Want to see the kitchen?'

'Mmm-hmm.'

He led her back into the hallway and to the kitchen. When he'd first moved in, it had been much smaller, but he'd knocked a wall through into an old outhouse and really opened it up, with skylights and bifold doors that led out to the garden. Then he'd ripped out the old wood-effect kitchen and installed a new one that was glossy white with marbled surfaces.

'Wow. Looks amazing. No wonder you love to cook in here.'

He laughed. 'I dabble when I can.' He flicked the switch on the kettle and got out a couple of mugs and began to make tea. When he turned to glance at her to see what she might be thinking, he was surprised to see such a concerned look on her face. 'What's wrong?'

She paused before answering. 'Nothing.'

'No. There's something. What is it?' He went to her. Stood in front of her, trying to work out what was wrong and if he could help.

'It's just…this all seems so grown up, doesn't it? Moving in with someone? Sharing their living space. Do you think we might be rushing into something we might both regret?'

'Do I think we're making a mistake in coming together to raise this baby? No. I don't.'

'You don't have any doubts whatsoever?'

His only doubt was whether he'd be able to stop thinking about Halley in ways she'd plainly told him she didn't want. Halley had been the girl of his dreams for years as a child and now she was back in his life. More beautiful than ever and carrying his baby. He knew what it was like to be with her physically. To be with her in other ways? Mentally? Emotionally? Yeah, that was going to be an adjustment. 'Living with someone is always going to be weird, when you first do it. Our situation, though unique, is not strange. I think it's something that we have decided to do after thinking of all the alternatives, because the alternatives of raising this baby in separate homes isn't something either of us want. We want more for our child. We're on the same page, for our child, and that means something. We want…' he smiled '…we want our child to have everything that we didn't and we're both committed to making that happen. I've never shared my space with anyone before and I've always been protective of my home space. It's just for me. But now my world isn't just about me any more. It's about you and our baby. So I want to share it, because I feel safe here and I know that you could feel the same way. That our child could feel the same way. So no. I don't have any doubts about *that*. Do you?'

Were there tears in her eyes? Yes. There were.

'Not when you put it like that, no.'

He passed her her tea. 'Want to see your room?'

She took a sip, then nodded. 'I'd like that.'

Her bedroom-to-be was a good size. As big as his, it seemed, and yes, it had felt strange to peer into his bedroom and know that she had been intimate with this man and she was now standing over his bed.

She'd not known what to expect on entering his home. Would he have the typical bachelor pad? Would it be bare and sparse, the fridge empty of any real food and a gaming console sitting in front of the TV in a mass of cables and wires?

But there'd not been any of that. There'd been thought put into the decor. It looked comfy. There were throws and pillows on the couch. No gaming console to be seen, but there'd been lots of bookshelves and even a guitar, on a stand, that hung on the wall. He had art and lots of lots of green, trailing house-plants. It was clean, and properly clean, too. He'd clearly not quickly whizzed around the cottage with a hoover and duster, but done it properly, and there were diffusers in each room and lots of lights. The kitchen had been modern and minimalist, his only clutter on show a mass of fresh herbs growing on the windowsill and a spice rack filled with pots and flavours of all kinds. He'd told her he liked to cook and he clearly did. He was even baking right now for one of his staff at the surgery!

Upstairs, his room had the clean, minimalist look, too. His bedspread was spotless, his pillows fluffy and he had this amazingly soft-looking bed runner and she'd itched to reach out with her hand to stroke it. But she'd stopped herself. What would it look like if she stroked his bed? Wouldn't that send the wrong message? Pregnant with his baby and looking as if she was longing to rip back the sheets and lie down?

Her room-to-be was tidy, but filled with random things. A desk. A chair. Lots of box folders stacked against a wall. But it had a good-sized window and plenty of floor space if it was emptied out. She'd easily fit a double bed in here. A wardrobe. A dressing table. A cot, if she had the baby in with her to begin with. Hillary had told her she might want to do that in the early days when she was still breastfeeding.

'It just makes it easier.'

'You could do whatever you wanted to make this home for yourself. Paint it. Wallpaper it. I could help you, if you want? I'm a pretty dab hand at all of that.'

'You're good at DIY, too?' she asked.

'When you grew up the way I did, you learned how to do a lot of things for yourself.'

'All right. Thanks. I might take you up on that offer.'

'Do. I'd rather you didn't start climbing ladders and balancing on them, whilst you're pregnant.'

He was being protective. She liked that. And to be honest? She'd never been good at painting or wallpapering. She'd tried it in her flat in Edinburgh and she'd made a good hash of it, wishing afterwards that she'd had the money to pay a proper painter and decorator.

'Let me show you where we could have the nursery.'

She followed him through to the next room, that was much smaller. Almost a box room. But it looked out over the rear aspect of the property, over the garden, and right next to the window, on the left-hand side, was a beautiful cherry tree. 'That must look lovely in spring.'

'It is, when it blossoms. Plenty of fruit on it right now. Actually, I just picked a lot of it, if you want to take some home to eat, or make a cherry pie?'

'Mum loves cherry pie.'

'I'll make sure I give you some, then. So what do you think? Big enough? It could fit a cot, a changing station, and I thought we could even fit in one of those rocking chairs with a footstool, to make any night feeds easy.'

'You've thought this through.'

'Haven't you?'

'Yes. I have.' But it was nice to know that he had, too. He was making a grand gesture and putting in a lot of effort. Opening up his home to her, sharing his space, so that they could do this together. Plus, living with him would protect her reputation in the village. Everyone would think them a couple and that was fine by her. No one would have to know the truth of their situation. Even if she did yearn for it to be different and exactly what the village thought it was.

'There's a big DIY store out at the industrial estate past Ripon. We could go there when you're next free and pick out paint, or wall-paper.'

She nodded, looking around at the room, imagining herself in here with a baby. 'Sure. I guess we ought to wait past the first trimes-ter before we do anything. After we've seen the first scan and know everything's all right.'

'Have you got a date for that?'

'I'm still waiting to hear, but it should be soon, my doctor said.'

'Are you taking your folic acid?'

She smiled. 'I am.'

'That's great. Good.'

'And what colour were you thinking for in here? Do you have any ideas?'

'I guess it depends on whether we want to find out the sex. Or we stick to classic neutrals and not find out at all. Or we could go crazy and paint a fantastical mural on the walls, like in that shop?'

'I think I'd want to find out what we're having first. What about you?'

'I think I'd want that too.' He smiled at her for a long time and she was struck by the urge to go over to him and kiss him. To stand before him, lay her hand gently against his chest and then just kiss him.

But she fought the urge, pushing it away hard, because this was complicated enough without them making it into something else it wasn't ready for. That she wasn't ready for, even though every part of her was screaming at her to go to him. 'Then we're agreed?'

'We are.'

Okay, standing here in this small room, with him so close to me looking all sexy with his damp hair and his gorgeous brown eyes is simply too much!

'Sorry, I…er…need the bathroom. Just excuse me, would you?'

'Sure! I'll meet you back downstairs. I need to take those lemon twists out of the oven.'

'Great!' She fled to the bathroom, locking the door behind her and letting out a big sigh. Her feelings for Archer Forde were getting a little out of control. Maybe it was hormones or something? A deep-seated biological drive to stay with the father of your child for protection whilst the female was vulnerable? Feeling attracted to him to offer him sex and keep him interested? It had to do with something stupid, like her lizard brain, but she simply couldn't have it!

If she slipped up and kissed Archer Forde, it would put all of this at terrible risk and then where would she be?

The lemon twists were slightly more brown than he would have liked, but he'd forgotten all about them whilst showing Halley the house and the bedrooms and then, when they'd stood discussing the baby, about finding out the sex and she'd looked at him, all warm and smiley? Her beautiful blue eyes staring into his? He'd felt something pass between them that had scared the living daylights out of him!

I wanted to kiss her! Imagine how I would have ruined everything if I'd done that!

She'd just agreed to move in. She'd not agreed to him making a move on her. That sort of thing would have scared her off, for sure!

Thank God she went to the bathroom, so I could breathe again.

He heard her footsteps behind him as he was transferring the twists onto a cooling rack.

'Smells great.'

'Want to try one?'

'Maybe when they've cooled down.'

'Okay.' He turned and pressed himself back against the kitchen units to stay as far away from her as possible. Perhaps avoiding temptation from the get-go was the best thing and now that he was aware that his attraction for her was still there, it was best to take steps to avoid it.

'Archer, we do need to talk about what it will be like for us. Living together, I mean. What rules we need in place.'

'We've already agreed to no flirting.'

She smiled. 'Yeah. I don't want to ruin this situation by anything happening between us. You understand, don't you?' she asked with imploring eyes.

She really meant this—he could tell. She couldn't risk anything happening between them, either.

'I do. I very much do. We're both singing from the same hymn sheet, don't you worry,' he agreed. Of course he agreed. But he still wasn't prepared for the wave of sadness that washed over him as he realised that, by agreeing to that, he would never get to be with Halley the way he'd always wanted. It was like being surrounded by the ocean, with nothing to drink. She was there. She was with him. But she wasn't his.

And never could be.

Not if they wanted this living situation to work.

CHAPTER SEVEN

THE SMELL OF paint was making her feel nauseated, so Archer told her to go and put her feet up in the garden and he'd carry on with painting her bedroom-to-be. She'd fallen in love with a soft grey colour and had found a ridiculous fluffy lavender lamp that she'd decided to work her colour scheme around. It looked as if it had ostrich feathers on it, but she'd fallen in love with it and, after that, any other colour just hadn't seemed right.

Archer had covered the carpet with plastic sheets, moved out all the office stuff he'd had in there, as well as his bike, and emptied it completely for when she wanted to bring over furniture. But right now, he was using a roller to paint the walls. To start with, she'd assisted, offering to go around the edges of the windows and doors and to paint the corners where the walls met, but the aroma of paint had become too much for her still sensitive stomach to handle and so now she sat in the garden, on a sun lounger, beneath the morning sun, pretending to read one of the new fantasy books that Archer had bought her.

Instead, she was watching him through the window. He was wearing some old jeans and a tight white tee that he'd clearly used for decorating before as it was already covered in splashes and old fingerprint smears in white and taupe. From here, she could see the muscles in his arms as he pushed the roller up and then pulled it down again and she had to admit he was a fine figure of a man.

She felt herself stir and feel a yearning for him. Someone she couldn't have. Her hormones were driving her crazy. Sick she might be feeling, but her sex drive was still on full power! It was driving her crazy! From the open window, she heard him receive a phone call on his mobile.

'Oh, hi, Jenny. What's up?'

She watched him listen as he spoke to one of his partners at the practice. Halley liked Jenny and she could see why he and Jenny were friends. And now there was another old college friend that had appeared on the scene. James. James was another new vet at the practice, after Jenny had to go part time to help look after her mum with dementia.

'And what were the findings on the X-ray? Okay. Okay.' His voice dropped and he went solemn. 'Well, if they're able to wait I can pop in and have a chat with them. Sure. Okay. See you in ten.' He ended the call and looked out of the window to her. 'I've got to pop to the surgery. Will you be all right here on your own?'

'Problem?'

'A client who wants my opinion on a case. They know me, they're not used to Jenny.'

'I could tag along?'

He smiled. 'Okay. Five mins. I just need to change.'

'Okay.'

She swallowed hard as he walked away, pulling off his tee shirt. She got a too-brief glimpse of his muscular back and she groaned quietly. 'Seriously?' she muttered, getting to her feet and ambling back into the house.

She pottered about in the kitchen, rinsing the cups they'd used for tea earlier, and then Archer was there, in a new shirt and fresh jeans and smelling delicious, and she forced a smile. 'So, what's the case?'

'I'll fill you in on the way.'

It was a sad case, and one that Archer had been dealing with for a few years. The Taylor family had rescued a dog they'd found on holiday in Cyprus many years ago. They'd been at an outdoor restaurant and this mangy old hound had crept up to their table and begged for food. Tex, as they'd named him, had been skin and bone. His ribs visible, his face full of scars from fights and one or two scars on his body and hind quarters that Archer had identified as possible cigarette burns.

They'd discovered that Tex was probably still a young dog when they'd got him, about three years of age, and slowly, but surely, they'd brought him back to health. Tex was a great dog, and when his fur grew back they could see he was some kind of Labrador mix. But when Tex was five, Archer had diagnosed him with alimentary lymphoma. He'd become weak. Had developed sickness and diarrhoea on occasion. Was beginning to lose weight. The Taylors had decided they wanted to help Tex fight for his life as he was still a young dog and so they put him on chemotherapy.

Tex did well with the chemo. He didn't suffer too badly with any side effects and it had seemed as if his treatment was working. Only that morning, the Taylors had brought him back in, after noticing he was losing weight again and there was a lump on his chest, and when Jenny had taken an X-ray, she had discovered multiple tumours in his lungs and chest wall. The signs were not good and Jenny was recommending euthanasia, as signs were that Tex was in a great deal of discomfort and pain. The lymphoma had clearly come back and must have been metastasising quietly.

The Taylors wanted to talk to Archer. He'd kept Tex alive for them all these years and they wanted his opinion.

As he spoke to the owners, Halley offered to go out back and see Tex herself.

'I think the day has come where we need to make a careful decision,' Archer said to Jane and Kevin Taylor, knowing and hating the impact of his words. 'Tex has clearly had some advancement in his disease and we need to decide what is the best treatment for him going forward.'

Kevin looked quite pale. Jane was red-eyed from crying.

'He's only seven years old, Archer! It's too soon!'

He swallowed hard. He felt their pain. He'd hoped, too. He'd wanted this dog to beat the cancer. To reach a time they could say he was in remission and celebrate. But it had already been a long slog. Tex had fought for so long and now he was tired.

Archer had seen the same thing when he was with Amy. She'd fought as long as she could, but there just came a day when you had to say enough and accept the decision to stop. Animals were lucky. Their owners could pick a time for them and allow that time to be peaceful. Like going to sleep, without watching them suffer as the cancer or whatever disease it was ravaged their body. Amy had never had that choice, though he could remember her discussing going to that clinic in Switzerland.

'I know this is probably going to be one of the hardest things you'll ever have to do. But I've looked at the X-ray imaging myself and I have to say that I agree with my colleague.'

He waited for his words to sink in, struggling to maintain his own composure, but fighting for it. He liked Tex. He was a good dog. Good-natured. Friendly. A wonderful patient.

'But he's a fighter! Let's give him a chance to fight!' begged Jane.

He nodded. 'We have. He's been fighting for two years, but we have to look at the evidence. He has eight new tumours growing in his lungs and pleura. He has one tumour invading his abdomen, into his liver. He's losing weight and is clearly in great discomfort. I could continue to give him painkillers, but he would still be in discomfort and his quality of life would not be what you would wish for him.' He paused to let his words sink in. 'You have given him a good life. You saved him, more than once, and you love him dearly. But the best thing for him, the kindest thing for him, in my opinion, is to let him go now.'

His voice broke slightly and he had to clear his throat to regain control as Jane sank into her husband's arms and began to sob.

Kevin's eyes welled with tears. 'Can we spend some time with him before we...?'

Archer nodded. 'Of course. I'll bring him through.' He stepped out of the consulting room and into the back where they kept the animals that were inpatients. Halley was kneeling on the floor, scratching Tex's belly. He gave her a weak smile and knelt down beside her to give Tex a little scratch under his chin. As he knelt, Tex's tail thwacked against the floor in greeting.

'How's it going?' Halley asked.

'We're going to do the kindest thing,' he said, his voice soft, looking at this wonderful dog, who'd done nothing wrong and yet was having to have his life cut cruelly short. He felt his tears well up in his eyes and then Halley laid her hand upon his arm, then her head upon his shoulder.

'It's okay. It's for the best. You would never do this otherwise.'

He nodded, unable to meet her gaze, but grateful for her comforting touch. 'They want to spend a few moments with him. Could you bring him through?'

'Sure. But do you need a moment first? To say goodbye?' She looked up into his face and the care and concern she had for him was plainly there on her face and it all became too much.

The tears came then. He didn't often cry when he had to euthanise a pet, but there were some animals that just brought it out in him. Pets he'd known all their lives. Pets, like Tex, that had fought bravely against a cruel disease. Cases of animal cruelty where his tears came from a source of anger and frustration at what a human had done. Halley draped her arm around him and laid her head upon his shoulder again and he sank against her as he stroked Tex and rubbed his ears and told him what a good boy he was. The best. Then he sucked in a breath and stood up, squaring his shoulders, wiping at his eyes. Halley stood too and held his hand, passing him a tissue from a box on the side.

'Okay?'

'Yeah. I'm good.'

'You can do this.' She stroked his arm, her eyes full of compassion.

'I know. Okay, let's go.' He opened the door back into the consulting room and let Halley walk Tex through.

Tex stumbled a little, but his tail wagged furiously at seeing his mum and dad again and they sank to cuddle and kiss him.

'We'll be back in about ten minutes,' he said.

Halley took his hand and stepped out of the room with him.

Her heart ached for Archer. Seeing him so upset. So distraught. It was the hardest part of their job, having to do something like this. Halley hated having to be in the room when it was done, but she did it if the owners didn't feel strong enough to be there for the end. She would offer to go in and stroke the pet, so it wasn't alone. It was a privileged position to be in. To be able to confirm to the owners that their beloved fur baby had passed peacefully and without pain.

Tex had clearly meant a lot to Archer and now they were in the staff room at the back of the surgery, she made them both a strong cup of tea and sat him down on the couch. She sat next to him and held his hand.

It was meant to be a purely comforting thing. An *I'm with you* gesture. *You're not alone.* But as they sat there, she began to realise how much she didn't want it to stop. She liked holding his hand. Being this close to him. She liked that he wasn't pulling away from her. That he seemed to be drawing comfort from it and, weirdly, she realised how strong she felt, holding his hand.

Their teas sat on the low table, slowly going cold.

'It's times like this that make me second-guess having Jinx.'

His cat. His rescue cat. Jinx never seemed to be at the cottage when she called. She'd seen her once. Curled up on the sofa. 'Because you're worried about the day you'll lose her?'

He nodded. 'Their lives seem so fleeting sometimes and losing them hits us hard. They become such a strong part of our lives, our family. Why do we do it to ourselves?'

'Love. Companionship. Some people find it easier to be with animals than people.'

'I think it's that unconditional love. We can be whoever we want to be, act however we want to and a pet just won't judge us. They accept us. Love us back. No matter what. Who else in our lives gets that excited when we come home? Love that is unconditional is rare, don't you think? Humans don't love unconditionally. What a world it would be if we did.'

She nodded and squeezed his hand in hers. 'Animals don't get angry with us. They don't lie to us. They don't cheat. They don't abandon us at altars.' She smiled ruefully. 'They love to spend time with us. They think we're great. All the time. Even if we have just accidentally stepped on their paw, or told them off for doing their toilet in the house. They're innocent, aren't they? Not guilty of anything.'

'They just ask to be loved. That's all they want.'

'Isn't that what any of us want?'

He looked at her. Pondering her words, the tone she'd used. She'd sounded as though she was talking about herself. That she was saying she yearned for his love.

Halley blushed and reached for her cooling tea, taking a sip. It wasn't too bad. But she couldn't believe that that had slipped out. She wasn't asking him to love her. Even if sometimes she did dream of what real love, true love, felt like.

Archer let go of her hand as if electrocuted and stood up. 'I ought to go and do the deed. Not let it drag out. Have they had long enough alone, do you think?'

She glanced at the clock on the wall, grateful for the change in subject. 'It will never be enough time.'

'Would you come with me?'

She stared at him. Pleased that he wanted her there as his support. 'Of course. If you want me,' she added in a low voice.

'I do.'

Halley nodded and followed him through to the room where the Taylors and Tex waited.

Her mum was up and about in the kitchen, making herself a cup of tea. 'I've been thinking, love.'

'Oh, God, alert the media!' said Halley as she came through the front door, kicking off her work boots. She'd just spent two hours cleaning out the barn and she was exhausted.

Her mum gave her a look. 'I'm back on my feet now. I can do some things for myself and I don't want you out there lifting and carrying in your condition any more.'

'Well, you can't do it.'

'I know, so I've actually done more than just thinking. I've made a few phone calls.'

'To?'

'An employment agency. I've asked them to advertise for some farmhands and a temporary manager to take your place, until I'm fully fit again.'

'We've already got Paul and Will.'

'And they're great, but we need more help,

especially as we head towards autumn. Farms are great in the summer, but the colder months are much harder to get staff, you know that.'

'Okay.'

'You're happy with that?'

'It sounds sensible. I did think you were taking on too much and it will be a while until you're at full strength.'

'Good, and when the new staff start I want you to move in with Archer. Get settled into your new home and look after my precious grandchild.'

'There's plenty of time for that. Besides, we're still decorating.'

'And it will be done by the time I've got the new staff up and running. So, you can go.'

'You sound like you're trying to get rid of me.'

'Oh, love. I could never do that. But for a long time now I've been worried about you. Alone and up in Edinburgh. But now you're back and you're staying. And I have a chance to see my new grandchild whenever I want. But more than that...you have a chance to be happy and settled and not alone. With Archer.'

'It's not like that between us,' she said, knowing that it felt everything but.

'Isn't it? You made a baby.'

'We weren't trying to.'

'Maybe so, but you have and you're planning on raising that baby together and I so want you to be happy. After Piotr, I thought you'd never be happy again.'

'We're just friends,' she said, knowing that, in her heart, she felt so much more for him.

'And from friendships great loves are often born. How many couples do you hear say that they were friends first?'

'Archer's not looking for a romantic relationship, Mum.'

'Are you?'

It was hard to stand there under her mum's questioning stare, because the truth was that she craved to be loved. Craved to be adored and made to feel as though she was the only woman that any man could love. To be treated like a precious jewel. To be thought of when she wasn't there. To be missed, desperately. To be someone's whole world. She thought that maybe Archer might love a woman that way. 'I'm scared.'

'You can't live your life in fear, love. That's no way to live.'

'But what if I make a mistake?'

'We're human. We make mistakes. No one in this village, this world, is perfect. What matters is how we deal with the cards we're dealt. I understand why you retreated after

Piotr's wife appeared, but all these years you've been alone and I've felt so sad for you. You weren't living, love, you were existing! And now you have a rare chance. Archer's a good man and he loves deeply. You weren't here when he lost Amy, but I saw it in him. The way he took care of that girl when she was sick… He's been grieving a long time. Same as you. But together? I think you two could be something amazing. You just need to be brave enough to see it.'

Halley hugged her mum. She could see it. That was what scared her. She really appreciated everything her mum was saying. It meant a lot. But words were sometimes easy to say. Actions could sometimes be harder.

What if she took that chance and opened up her heart to Archer and he rejected it? What if he was still hurting and wasn't ready for the onslaught of her feelings? She knew she could be pretty full on sometimes and some guys might think it a bit much. Because when Halley fell in love, she went in all guns firing.

She wanted things to be good between her and Archer. That way, her baby would have its father around all the time. But if she scared him off before this baby got here…? Then losing him would be all her own fault. And she wasn't sure she wanted to carry that guilt. Archer had said nothing to her about his feelings for her. But he had said plenty of what he wanted for their baby. So she wasn't sure what he felt and she wasn't ready to take a chance on exposing her vulnerable heart to someone she still wasn't sure of.

It just seemed a terribly deadly mistake to make.

CHAPTER EIGHT

TWO LOVELY YOUNG girls responded to the employment agency advert and had begun working at the farm and a new part-time manager was learning the ropes, earning Halley a lie-in most mornings, for which she was eternally grateful. Now, in the mornings, she could take her time getting up. There was no need to get up at four a.m., don overalls and wellies and go out to feed the animals and muck them out, ready for the public's adoring eyes at nine.

The last few days, she'd not even bothered with an alarm clock. She'd got up when she felt like it. Stretched, donned a dressing gown and headed downstairs to get breakfast.

Her mum, an eternal lark, would already be up, and now she was able to get around much more easily and climb the stairs, as long as she took it slowly. On this morning, Halley could hear her downstairs in the kitchen, doing God only knew what, and was that the radio she could hear? It sounded like voices. Was Mum talking to someone? It was probably the new manager, Clark. He kept popping in to double-check things, so it was probably him.

Halley headed downstairs, yawning and sleepy, and stepped into the kitchen to find her mum and Archer there, sitting at the table.

'Archer! What are you doing here?'

He smiled and stood up to greet her. 'Your mum invited me over for breakfast.'

'Oh! She didn't tell me she was doing that.' She gave her mum a look that said *I know what you're up to.*

Her mum laughed. 'It's nothing like that. I'm not scheming. I just thought it might be nice for Archer to join us before work and tell you the news.'

'What news?'

'Our veterinary nurse, Anu, is leaving. She's met a guy who lives in Hull and she's upping sticks and going to live with him. She put her notice in yesterday and I thought that you might be interested in taking on the post until your maternity leave begins.'

Halley stared at him. 'You're joking?'

'No joke.' He smiled and held out her chair for her to sit down.

She sank into it, then turned to face him.

'You're serious? You want us to not only live together, but also work together?'

'It's only part time, so not a heavy workload, and this way you'd have a job waiting for you, after the baby, if you wanted it.'

'I think it'll be perfect, love. I know how independent you like to be,' said her mum. 'It would get you out of the house and earning money and, like Archer says, you'll have a real job waiting for you, if you decide you want to work afterwards. And it's only part time, so you wouldn't be away from the baby for too long.'

'Sounds like you two have got it all worked out.'

Archer shook his head. 'There's no pressure to take it. None whatsoever. I just thought I'd give you first refusal, that's all. I'm still going to advertise in *The Gazette*, if need be. So take your time and think about it.'

She nodded. 'Okay.'

'And I have news, too,' said her mum.

'Oh?'

'I'm properly back on my feet now. I'm able to look after myself. I can shower alone. I can work a little bit. I don't need you and Hillary babysitting me any more.'

Halley felt a wave of heat wash over her. 'You're evicting me?'

'No, love! You can stay here for as long as you want! But I am saying, I don't need you to stay. If you want to stay here and have the baby here, then that's fine by me. But if you wanted to move in with Archer, then I'm okay now.'

Halley glanced at Archer.

He was smiling at her, the hope in his eyes almost too much to take.

She'd known this day was coming. But it had always been this hypothetical day, far into the future, and it was easy to agree to hypotheticals, but to actually *act* on them? To move in with Archer? When she had all these feelings for him? What if she screwed everything up? Her mum was giving her the option to take a safer route. Stay here at the farm and have the baby. But if she chose to, she could take a risk and move in with Archer.

'It's a lot to take in suddenly,' said Archer, as if noticing her hesitation. 'We've spoken about it, but actually doing it is scary, right?'

She nodded, glad that he understood.

'There's no pressure from me, Halley. My home is yours and there for you, whenever you need.'

But she knew how much he wanted her there, so he could be there for his baby. And the first scan was coming up soon and she'd already imagined it in her head. Both of them leaving the house together to go to the hospital.

But from which house?

The farm?

Or Archer's?

Theirs.

Sanjay had brought Jess back in for a follow-up check on her abscess and Archer was pleased to see that the abscess was virtually undetectable and the bite wound from their resident cat, Badger, had healed and scabbed over nicely. Jess's temperature was back to normal and Sanjay reported that everything was going much better.

'We took it back a few steps with introducing them. Swapped their litter trays over so they could get used to each other's scents. Swapped toys and someone suggested giving them each other's blankets covered in a little catnip to play with before introducing them again to mellow them out a bit and it seemed to work.'

Archer laughed. 'That'll do it. And how are they now?'

'They were a little hesitant after the catnip had worn off, but they swiftly realised they wanted to be friends and last night they even washed each other a little bit.'

'That's great!'

Sanjay nodded. 'I'm so happy, I really am. I didn't want this to fail, you know? A lot was riding on this successful introduction.'

'Well, it takes animals *and* people some time to get used to living with someone new.'

'Oh, yeah! I heard Halley Campbell has moved in with you. You two are a couple. Having a baby. Congratulations!'

'Thanks.' He didn't correct Sanjay. He didn't tell him that they weren't a couple. Not really. It was just easier to let everyone assume that they were and, so far, the feedback had been positive.

'How's that going?'

'Well, it's only been two days, but, yeah, it's going great!'

'Good for you, man. I'm glad you've found some happiness.'

'Thanks. I'm glad that Jess has, too.' He pulled open the door to end the consultation and when Sanjay was gone, he closed it again and let out a breath. So the grapevine had caught up, then, and the whole village probably knew by now. He and Halley would be the high topic for a little while, but it would die down. And at least this time they were being talked about for a good reason. Yes, gossip could be a bad thing, but this was good. People were *happy* for them. That showed they cared.

Halley moving in had been both exciting and terrifying and they were both still in that stage where they were gently tiptoeing around the other person, trying not to get in each other's way, or space. But it was so hard when all he wanted to do was just sit next to her on the couch and eat popcorn whilst watching a movie together. He'd suggested it last night, but she'd got this frightened look in her eye and said she was tired and gone to bed early. That told him plenty. That even though she'd moved in with him so he could be close to his child, she was not in a relationship with him and nor did she want to be.

Which is great. Because I'm not looking for one either.

He didn't need to. He had everything—almost everything—he'd ever wanted.

But he still felt it would have been lovely to snuggle on the couch. Maybe under a blanket? As friends, if nothing more?

Would they ever get to that stage, where they felt comfortable with one another?

Or maybe I should sprinkle us both in catnip...?

* * *

'Are you ready?'

Halley nodded. 'As I'll ever be. Are you?' It was the morning of their first scan appointment at the hospital to check on their baby. Halley was thirteen weeks exactly and starting to feel the effects of the morning sickness ebbing away. Each day was getting better and she was actually starting to feel good now, instead of constantly battling endless nausea that got worse each evening.

'I'm nervous. I'm just hoping everything's all right.'

'I think everyone feels that way. I just wish I could go to the loo. My bladder is so full, but they need it for the scan imaging to be clearer. I just hope I don't pee myself when they push down on it.'

'I'm sure lots of mothers feel that way.'

'I guess they do.'

Archer opened the front door and stepped out, turning back to close the door behind her so he could lock it, but he stopped and stared at her, frowning. 'You okay?'

'What if there's something wrong? What if...they find something? Or worse, find nothing at all and there was never a baby, and I'm one of those women that has a hysterical pregnancy or—?'

'Hey.' Archer stepped back in and took hold of her upper arms. 'It's all going to be fine. We have to believe that and let's keep on believing that unless they tell us otherwise. Okay?'

She looked up at him, tearful and afraid. 'I don't know why I'm feeling like this.'

'I do.' He smiled. 'You're being a mother. A protective mother. You want your child to be healthy. You want your child to pass this first test. You've got used to the idea of being a mother and the idea that someone could take that away? That's terrifying.'

He was right. She had got used to the idea. And she'd changed her entire life around it! She'd left Edinburgh, she'd moved in with a man that she was trying her very hardest not to love, but it was difficult because he was so damned lovely all the time! Understanding and kind and thoughtful. He was perfect. And so if there was no baby…her entire life would come crashing down around her ears and she couldn't go through something like that again.

'Are you terrified, Archer? Are you scared to death that someone could take away your being a father?' She needed to know. It was important. She needed to know that she wasn't the only one stranded on a tiny raft in the middle of the ocean, here. She needed to know he was with her. That he felt the same way on this, at least. It was like standing in that church again, staring at Piotr's wife, knowing that at any moment her happiness was about to be snatched away. That it had all been pretend and never real.

But the way he was staring deeply into her eyes…the way that he was standing so close… Could she reach out? Could she pull him in tight and not let go? The urge to have him hold her, to stroke her hair, to whisper soothing words in her ear, was just so powerful!

'I am. I'm scared of it all,' he said in a low voice, his gaze going from her eyes to her lips and then back again.

And she felt it. Like a punch to the gut. That he was feeling some kind of way about her, too. This wasn't just about the baby! Maybe, just maybe, Archer had had some feelings about her, too.

And that scared her even more.

She broke the intense eye contact and took a step back, smiling awkwardly. 'We ought to get going. We don't want to be late and fail *our* first test at being parents.'

Though she felt sure the actual first test had been when the test turned positive and she'd had to tell him about the baby.

He'd passed that first test with flying colours and had continued to pass the fatherhood test ever since. She would not fail her baby by screwing that up.

She would not, *could* not, kiss Archer Forde—no matter how much she wanted to.

The waiting room was bright and cheery. White walls, with modern art in splashes of red, blue and yellow, beneath skylights that streamed in sunshine. On one wall was a vending machine filled with chocolate and crisps. Next to it, a water dispenser, with those weird polystyrene cups with pointed bottoms, so you couldn't actually put them down, but had to sit there holding them, until you were done.

It was very busy. Almost full. Filled with women of all shapes and sizes. Women like herself in the early stages, with no discernible bump yet. Those that were a bit further on, maybe midway, and those that looked ready to burst. In a far corner was a children's play area and in it a couple of toddlers played.

She and Archer found seats over by the doors to the toilets and breastfeeding room. Her nerves were running amok and her teeth even began to chatter, so Archer reached out and took her hand and held it. 'Deep breaths.'

Halley laughed nervously. 'I'm trying. But this room is making everything all so real! We're actually here because we're having a baby. A baby! And we're about to see it. The thing that's been making me ill the last couple of months.'

'The thing?' Archer smiled, raising an eyebrow.

'Don't!' She laughed. 'I'm nervous enough as it is.'

'I know. We'll be fine. You'll see.'

She loved that he had this steadfast belief that everything would be all right. He was a calm port in a storm. A rock. Where did that come from? Was it because he had to be the grown-up for his little brother when they were young? He'd told her about his mother and how she used to be. How she'd made him feel, as a child. Had he always been this sensible and level-headed?

Halley looked at the other couples. Some looked bored. Others nervous, like her. One or two looked worried. Did they have problems? If they had problems, then did that mean that she wouldn't?

Don't be ridiculous. That's not how it works.

But she wanted it to work that way. And she knew she was only hoping for that because she was scared, even if it did make her feel bad for wishing bad stuff onto other people.

I'm human. I'm not logical. Especially when it comes to protecting my own.

Maybe Archer was right and this was her motherly instinct kicking in? For such a long time after Piotr, she'd believed that she'd never get to be a mother. She'd shut down that part of her that hoped and wished for the white picket fence and the perfect husband and the two adorable children. One boy. One girl. Maybe a dog. Some chickens in the backyard. She'd told herself she'd never have it, because she didn't think she could trust any man to get close enough to get married and have kids. And yet here she was. Archer might not be in love with her and they weren't married, but they were living together and, whilst there was no white picket fence, there was a cute cottage and a privet hedge. There was room for a dog and some chickens, if they wanted.

Her full bladder ached. And she desperately wanted to go to the loo. But more than that, she so wanted to be in that room and finally have one of her life's dreams come true. To see her baby on the screen. To be told that everything was going perfectly. To hear its heartbeat. Would that happen today? Or was it too early? She'd seen women on TV or in films have it done and a few people she followed online, when they'd shared a video of having it done, and it always seemed such a magical moment.

Halley so wanted a magical moment! Happiness, just lately, had seemed like something she'd always had to chase and it was always just out of reach, almost as if the universe were teasing her. She watched as women went into the rooms and came out again about twenty minutes or half an hour later. So far, they'd all come out with smiles on their faces, clutching scan pics. Would she be one of them, too?

'Miss Halley Campbell?'

'Yes.' She stood and Archer stood with her, letting go of her hand—he'd been holding it all this time—so that she could walk ahead of him into the room.

The room was darkened. The ultrasound machine was to the left, with the two wand devices on it. One long and thin, the other looked a little like a hammerhead. Above it, the screen. Next to that, the examination couch and beside that, a chair.

'Hello, Halley, my name is Sunita and I'm going to be scanning you today. Can you confirm your date of birth for me?'

Halley told her.

'And your full address and postcode?'

Once she'd given the information, Sunita asked her to pop onto the bed. 'If you could lift your top a little and lower your trousers down a little? I'm just going to tuck this paper into the top of your underwear to protect it from the gel. It'll feel a little cold to start.'

Halley nodded and nervously got onto the bed.

'When was the date of your last period?'

Halley confirmed the date and undid her trousers and lay back nervously.

Archer sat on the chair beside the bed and held her closest hand.

She squeezed it back as the sonographer squirted very cold gel onto her belly and then turned the screen towards her. 'I'll turn this back once I confirm everything first and then I'll show you, okay?'

'Okay.'

Halley knew they did this, but still she felt scared. What if she looked and there wasn't a baby? What if there was something wrong? What would she and Archer do then? They'd talked about many things, but they'd never once talked about what they'd do if there was something wrong with the baby. Archer had always said they shouldn't worry until they got told to worry. Was that the right approach?

It seemed an age before Sunita smiled and turned the screen. 'Here you go. There's your baby.'

Halley crooked her head back to look and then her heart just melted.

There it was! A little grey blob, with something fluttering in its chest.

My baby's heart.

'Oh, my God!' whispered Archer in awe.

'Everything looks good here. I'm going to take some measurements to confirm, okay?'

Halley nodded, physically unable to speak. All she could do was stare at the screen as Sunita zoomed in on various things. Measuring from crown to rump. Thigh length.

'Now I'm going to measure the nuchal translucency, okay? This is what tells us the risk for Down's Syndrome.'

'Okay,' said Archer, squeezing Halley's fingers tightly.

And she realised, in that moment, that it didn't matter. It didn't matter if they found anything wrong, because she would love this baby, no matter what. The sickness she'd experienced was forgotten and forgiven. The cravings that had made her lose precious sleep and get up in the middle of the night knowing she needed chocolate ice cream and pickles was fine. The headaches. The bloating. The exhaustion.

None of it mattered.

All that mattered was the baby. Her baby. *Their* baby.

'Measurements are good. Nuchal translucency is in a healthy range. Want to hear the baby's heartbeat?'

Halley nodded.

Sunita pressed a button and suddenly there it was, filling the room with a steady, rhythmic sound.

'That's amazing!' said Archer.

She felt tears sting her eyes. Happy tears. How was this happening? How were all her dreams coming true? She felt as though she could lie on that bed all day and listen to that sound.

'That's it. All done. I've printed you off some pictures.' Sunita handed her a long roll of ultrasound pics as she helped wipe some of the gel off her belly.

'Thank you,' Halley managed, sitting up, then standing, to do up her trousers and gaze at the pictures.

'We'll contact you soon with the date of your next scan, okay? We usually do it around the twenty-one-weeks mark.'

'Thank you.'

The waiting room was so bright it hurt their eyes. But they left the room smiling and gazing at the pictures, pointing out features as they made it out to the car. When she got into the front passenger seat, Halley began to cry.

'Hey! What's wrong?' His arm went around her shoulders.

She looked at him, knowing she was ugly crying, but not caring, because silly little things like that didn't matter any more. 'Nothing! Nothing's wrong, I'm just…'

He pulled her as close as he could, pressed his lips to the top of her head.

'I know. You're happy.' He kissed her again. 'So am I.'

She turned to look at him. 'How did we get so lucky, Archer?'

He stared back at her. 'I don't know. But I'm glad that we are.'

Archer drove them home, feeling a lot less tense than when they'd set out that morning. The first scan had been playing on his mind a lot and so whenever Halley had started worrying about it too, he'd wanted to take that worry away from her. It was wrong that she should carry it in her heart. She had enough to do with carrying the baby. He wanted to take the burden of everything else away from her.

But then to see his baby on that screen? And look down and see Halley's face, lit by tears of happiness? The world had suddenly felt right—until they'd got back into the car and he'd been comforting her and she'd turned to him, crying.

'How did we get so lucky, Archer?' she'd asked.

He'd not known the answer, but even if he had, he wouldn't have been able to say it, because all he could think of in that moment as she'd turned to him, gazing up into his eyes, all he could think of was how much he wanted to kiss her.

It was getting ridiculous now, these feelings that he kept having for Halley. He'd tried his best. He'd tried to force them away, to tell himself that they weren't ever anything he could act upon and so he should stop feeling that way. But they kept coming back. Day after day. And they'd got stronger ever since she'd moved in.

His head kept saying, *Yeah, but wouldn't it be great if you did? Remember that night on Rookery Point? How amazing it was? You could have that again.*

And yes, maybe he could and maybe it would be amazing, but what if it went wrong? What if he lost not only Halley but their baby, too? She could move out. Take the baby with her and then he'd be back to seeing his baby part time and gazing at Halley and wondering how it had all gone wrong.

But if he didn't kiss her, then he wouldn't be risking that, would he? He'd get to keep them both, because there was no reason why this couldn't work out. What they had right now.

And so he didn't kiss her. He painfully let go of her and started the engine. Drove them home, knowing that he was in this much deeper than he had ever realised and he would do anything to keep them both safe. And if keeping them safe meant ignoring how he felt, then he'd do it.

Because he couldn't risk losing either one.

CHAPTER NINE

ARCHER HAD OFFERED to take her out to dinner, now that she was feeling better and the first scan had confirmed that everything was fine. They had a little breathing room, a little time before their next scan and he wanted to celebrate that. The local veterinary association was having a fundraising night and so he'd told her to put on her best dress, because he was taking her for dinner and dancing.

It had been a long time since she'd been able to get all dressed up and have a fancy night and now that she was feeling better, she was looking forward to it.

But she'd not brought any fancy clothes back with her from Edinburgh, figuring all she'd be doing was working on a farm, and so she'd gone out to town and bought herself a dress and some heels.

Halley wasn't used to heels. She often felt like a newborn giraffe in them and feared for her ankles if something went wrong and so she'd spent that day practising walking in them.

'I told you—you look fine.' her mum said from the kitchen table where she was sipping a cup of tea. She'd taken her mum with her to get the outfit. A bit of a girls' day out. And her mum had wanted to stay to see the full effect before she headed back to the farm. Archer was upstairs, on the phone to Axle.

'It doesn't feel fine. I'm trying to look like a woman who knows what she's doing.'

'I think that ship has sailed, love.'

Halley laughed. 'I think maybe it has. What do you think? Will I pass?'

'Let's see. Walk over there.'

Halley strode purposefully from the kitchen and down the hall, pretending she was some model on a catwalk.

'Gorgeous, love.'

'You're not just saying that?'

'No!'

'Liar.'

Her mum laughed at Halley's rueful smile. 'I'm sure Archer will think you look amazing.'

'This isn't for him. It's for me.'

'Really?'

'Yeah.'

'All right.'

'Well, what does that mean?'

'It means I know you better than you do and I know that you like him a lot. If you think you're dressing up in that dress, with those heels, just for you, then you're more delusional than I thought.'

She made a shushing motion at her mum, afraid that Archer might overhear. 'Nothing's going to happen between Archer and me,' she whispered.

Her mum laughed. 'Your womb says something different, love.'

Halley frowned and stood in front of the mirror to check her reflection. Archer would come downstairs any minute to take her out for the evening. Okay, so maybe she had picked out a dress that would look amazing on her figure and she had thought about how it accentuated her hips and breasts, but she'd just wanted to feel attractive again. She'd been in overalls and wellies for a long time and hadn't had a proper night out for ages! And as the pregnancy progressed and she got bigger and more uncomfortable, she might not have another opportunity for a night out like this for an eternity!

I am doing this for me. But if Archer likes it too? Then that might just be a bonus.

* * *

When Archer came downstairs, he was blown away by the sight of Halley waiting for him in the living room. He was very much aware that her mum was sitting there, too, watching them both, and so he tried to carefully control his facial reaction. 'Wow! You look amazing.'

'She scrubs up well, doesn't she?' said Sylvie.

'She does.' He smiled, trying to calm the rush of his heart.

'Well, you look very nice too,' Halley said, her cheeks reddening from his praise.

Her dress was amazing, clinging to her in all the right places. Red silk that looked amazing against her long blonde hair. And then, as she took a step to the table to reach for a small clutch bag, he happened to notice the side split that revealed her leg up to her mid-thigh. He must have swallowed hard, or gulped, or something, because Sylvie was laughing.

'Right, my taxi's here. I'm off. You kids have fun and…er…don't do anything I wouldn't do.' Sylvie dropped a kiss on her daughter's cheek, gave Archer a quick hug and then she was gone, the front door closing behind her with some finality.

And he was alone with Halley. All of a sudden he felt as though he didn't want to go to this fundraiser at all. He didn't want dinner and he didn't want dancing. He wanted Halley. He wanted to take her by the hand, lead her upstairs, lay her on his bed and then go exploring beneath that dress!

He gave a nervous laugh.

'What's funny?' She was looking at him curiously.

'Nothing. Nothing's funny. You're beautiful, Halley, and seeing you in that dress caused some thoughts and for my blood supply to zoom in a direction away from my brain, so I stopped thinking properly for a moment there.'

She blushed.

He held out his arm. 'Are you ready, my lady?'

Halley smiled and stepped towards him. 'I am.' And she took his arm and together they headed outside to the car.

It felt good to know she'd affected him *in that way*. If you'd asked her weeks ago if she'd wanted to provoke that reaction in him she would have fervently said no, but in the last few weeks, she had changed. On a fundamental level.

Her whole life had changed, of course, and so had she. She was pregnant now. She was going to be a mother. She had moved in with

Archer, the father of that child, and she had become more and more aware of her feelings for him. She'd not believed he felt in any way about her, so for him to react so strongly to seeing her in the dress made her feel incredibly good!

I've still got it.

She was getting used to her new body. It felt different and though she knew that the changes, physically, were probably infinitesimal at this point, she still felt different. She felt bigger. Her boobs felt rounder. Her stomach bigger. She'd noticed her jeans were getting uncomfortably tight around the waist and, at the end of the day, she couldn't wait to take everything off and put on pyjamas. Elasticated waists had become her friend. Halley went to the loo more often and her bladder felt like the size of a pea. She ached in places she hadn't known it was possible to ache. Her stomach occasionally blew a gasket and either threatened eruption or demanded strange concoctions. She'd even started eating mushrooms and Halley hated mushrooms! Her skin kept breaking out in spots. Her hair always seemed to need a wash every day, instead of every couple of days. She was changing and she felt every part of it, no matter how small, so to still look good enough to cause a sexual arousal in Archer?

She'd take it. Of course she would. It was a powerful feeling and, having felt as if she'd lost her power when the blood test had confirmed she was pregnant and that her life was ricocheting down a road she hadn't chosen, she was glad to feel as if she might be back in control, after all.

The fundraiser was taking place in an old Edwardian building that had once been the home of a duke.

They arrived to find a queue of cars, waiting to park up, and when they finally found a place it was quite the walk to get inside.

The evening had become cool, and when she shivered, Archer felt it.

'You're cold.' He shrugged off his dinner jacket and stopped to drape it around her shoulders. It was lovely and warm and smelt of him. 'Better?'

She smiled up at him. 'Better. Thank you.'

His smile was everything and Halley was beginning to believe that maybe there was something there between them. More than just the baby. More than just his duty as a father. He liked her. She was sure of it. She could feel it in the look of his eyes. The way he held her hand. The way he stood beside her, almost protectively, as they queued on the stone steps to get inside. His hand in the small of her back. It was just a small touch. Nothing major. But she felt it with everything she had.

As they entered the hall a waitress stood there with flutes of champagne. He walked past her to get to the waitress who held flutes of orange juice, taking two and handing one to Halley.

'You can still drink, you know.'

'I'm driving.'

'You're allowed one, at least.'

'It's fine. I'll have what you can have.'

He was there for her, that much was clear. And every small thing he did? She noticed it. She *noticed*. She couldn't have alcohol, so neither would he. It was a simple thing for someone to do, but it meant something. It meant something coming from him.

Above them, great crystal chandeliers twinkled down upon the assembled guests below, who mingled in their couples and their groups, and then, somewhere off to the left, music started. Someone playing the piano. Halley didn't recognise the music, but knew it was something classical. Something famous. She just didn't know what it was called.

'Want to dance?' he whispered in her ear.

'I do,' she said with a smile.

They put down their drinks on a nearby table and Archer took her hand and led her out onto the dance floor, pulling her close when they reached the middle. He held one hand with his and the other was in the small of her back again and, gently, they began to sway.

Halley glanced at the other couples dancing. She didn't know anyone here and nor did she feel the need to. It was perfectly perfect knowing just Archer. She gazed up into his eyes and smiled at him. 'You're a good dancer.'

'It's just moving from side to side. I think anyone could manage this.'

'And you can't take a compliment.'

He smiled. 'Never had many.'

'Well, then, that's going to change. You are a good dancer and, yes, it may only be swaying from side to side, but you haven't stamped on my toes, so that makes you a good dancer in my eyes.'

'Why, thank you.'

'And…it feels good to be dancing with you.'

Did she feel him stiffen then?

'Thanks.'

'I mean it, Archer. I'm enjoying being here with you tonight.'

'Me, too. But then I'm with the most beautiful woman in the room, so it's not a hardship.'

Her other hand rested on his upper arm. She could feel him tense beneath his suit, felt his chest against hers inhale a large, steadying breath. She wished she could place her spare hand on it, to feel how fast his heart was going. If it was going as fast as hers, that would tell her something.

She looked up to his face, hoping he would meet her gaze, but he was looking at anyone but her. 'Hey. I'm down here.'

He glanced at her then, as if to say, *What? I know. I know you're there.* But then he looked away again.

And she got frightened then, because what if she'd been imagining all of this? All this attraction that she hoped he felt? Maybe he was just the kind of guy that was empathetic? Maybe he was just the kind of guy that was polite? Maybe he was just the kind of guy that knew how to treat a woman right, but was still unable to allow one close?

They'd started this whole relationship off by making it clear to one another, on top of Rookery Point, that they weren't looking for a relationship. That neither of them needed or wanted that.

Ever!

Was she trying to push him in a direction he wasn't ready for? She did this. Rushed into things. Let her emotions run away with her, and could she trust them right now, fuelled as they were with hormones?

'I'm sorry, Archer.'

Now he looked at her, frowning. 'For what?'

'I don't know. I—' She couldn't speak any more. The words got stuck in her throat.

What could she say? *I'm sorry for trying to push this in a direction you're not ready for it to go. I'm sorry for thinking that you might be attracted to me and want more.*

As her throat closed, she felt a panicked feeling and knew that she had to get out. Had to get some air.

'Excuse me.'

She pulled herself free of his embrace and made a dash through a small break in the crowd, leaving him behind. The further she got from him, the more she felt she could breathe, but the more the tears stung the backs of her eyes. She didn't know where to go. Which way was out. So she pushed against the crowd that was still coming in through the front doors and ran down the steps and out towards the gardens, stopping only when she came across a willow tree. She parted the fronds to pass through and hid underneath, leaning against the tree trunk and wiping her eyes.

Had she just made an utter fool of herself?

Archer would be full of questions when he found her. And what would she say? Tell him the truth? That she was having these deep feelings for him and wanted to take their relationship further? But that she was afraid he would say no? But that she was even more afraid he'd say yes? Maybe he'd even go so far as to say it was just her hormones, or something! Caused by the pregnancy and that she'd feel different later.

No. I don't think he would say that. That's me. Worrying that it might be true.

Because for all these years she'd kept herself single. Had dated, yes, but never let it get serious. Had scratched an itch when she'd felt the need. But she'd never felt tempted enough by a man to cast aside all her protective walls and expose her vulnerable heart and soul and be brave enough to take a chance with someone else.

Until Archer.

So maybe the pregnancy, the baby, *was* the defining variable here?

It was the only thing that was different!

Or was it?

When else had she met a man like Archer? He wasn't superficial. He didn't care more about himself than he did anyone else. He was kind, empathetic, a good listener, intelligent, funny. He was a great vet! Unselfish, supportive, steadfast in his beliefs about what would make a good father.

But had he ever expressed how he felt about being a good partner? A good boyfriend or even a good husband?

No. He spoke about the baby and only the baby. He was with her and had her in his life because of that one variable. No other reason.

I need to get a grip here. We had a good scan. The baby is healthy. We heard its heart. I'm feeling better and I'm here at this beautiful place to have a good time! So I need to let myself do that!

Sheepishly, she dabbed at her eyes, sucked in a deep breath and pushed herself away from the tree and headed back towards the house.

It did look beautiful, all lit up at night. She was in a beautiful dress and she felt good in it and they were meant to be celebrating. Halley knew she needed to allow herself to do that. As she climbed the steps, she saw Archer standing at the top.

'There you are! I've been looking all over—are you all right?'

She laughed. Smiled. Nodded. 'I just needed some fresh air all of a sudden, that's all.'

'You're sure?'

'Absolutely.'

As she got closer he touched her arm.

'You're cold!'

'I'm okay! Honestly, let's go inside.'

'Okay. If you're sure you're okay… I think everyone's about to head through to the dining room to eat now.'

'Great! I'm starving.'

He seemed a little perplexed, but she felt that she'd managed to explain herself. Archer would never know the truth of what she'd been feeling and maybe that was a good thing. Maybe she could keep her feelings to herself until *after* the baby was born and re-evaluate then.

'You're sure you're feeling all right? Because if you're not, we can go home. We don't have to stay.'

'Hey! I was promised a night of dining and dancing and I want that. When else will I get the chance again at a place such as this?'

He nodded, but she could see he was holding back some scepticism, so she was determined to prove to him that she was having a good time.

They were sat at a table of eight and spent some time introducing themselves to the other guests. Halley had Archer on her left, but on her right was a young woman who'd recently been voted Veterinary Surgeon of the Year after her recent work with dogs in Romania, performing eye surgeries and campaigning to rescue street dogs. She had some fascinating tales to tell, and Halley allowed herself to give her full attention to everyone else at the table, because it was easier than turning to talk to Archer. Because if she turned to talk to him, she was afraid that something might slip out that she didn't want to slip out. So strangers were easier.

She spoke to one guy called Rupert, who'd spent some time out in Africa tagging rhinos, Wes, who'd been abroad campaigning to stop bear bile farms, and a young veterinary nurse, like herself, who'd been working hard in her own practice to try and bring down incidents of animal diabetes by educating owners on the risks. It was an incredible night, topped by delicious food. A salmon starter. A choice of lamb shank or vegetable chana for main, finishing with a sorbet or lemon meringue pie.

Halley felt pleasantly full as they entered the fundraising part of the evening with a charity auction. Archer bid on a couple of items but didn't win any. But she laughed and had fun, as the auctioneer was quite a funny guy and had lots of jokes. By the time the dancing began again, she'd almost forgotten her upset of earlier and headed onto the dance floor with

Archer and got through three dances before it all became too much and she felt *exhausted*.

'Let's go home,' he whispered in her ear.

She readily agreed, looking forward to the idea of her own bed immensely. As they drove home, they sang along to songs on the radio and Halley realised that all she had to do to be happy was to stop thinking so much. To stop analysing everything between her and Archer. To just *do* and enjoy and be *present*.

When they reached the cottage, she kicked off her heels with a heavenly sigh and headed into the kitchen to get herself a glass of water that she could take up to bed with her.

'It was a good night, wasn't it?' Archer asked.

'It was! A lot of money got raised, so that was great.'

'And you enjoyed yourself?'

'I did. Yes. There were so many fascinating people to talk to and the house itself was beautiful.'

He nodded. 'I thought you looked beautiful, too.'

She blushed slightly and turned to face him. 'That's very nice of you to say so.'

'You look beautiful every day.'

Halley paused, uncertain of what to do or say. She so much wanted to stay and explore this conversation, but it might take them both into waters too deep for either of them to swim in. And they needed to be sensible now. The magical night was over. Reality beckoned. 'Thank you. But I think we ought to say good-night now.'

He nodded and stepped away, so she could pass him.

The tension ratcheted up as she passed him by, falling again as she made her way upstairs away from him. She could breathe again. Freely. Archer saying she looked beautiful every day was just the kind of thing she wanted to hear, but it was dangerous talk. And she didn't want to be in any kind of danger. Not with him. Not whilst it was so good.

She got to her room and closed the door behind her, leaning back against it and sighing heavily before she pushed off it and headed over to her wardrobe to undo her dress and get into her robe. Did she have any energy to read for a little while? She'd been tired before and needed to come home, but Archer's comments had fired her up again and she suddenly felt more alive than she'd felt all evening.

She got into bed and picked up her book. One of the ones that he'd bought for her at that bookstore Many Worlds. She tried her best to concentrate on the words, but she couldn't.

She could hear Archer moving about. Switching off lights downstairs. His footsteps on the stairs as he came up to his own room. His pause outside her bedroom door.

That pause suggested way too much.

That pause suggested that maybe he wanted to say something else. But what? What did he want to say?

She couldn't bear it. It was too much. Halley threw off her covers, went to her bedroom door and opened it, ready to confront him, ready to tell him that he couldn't say nice things like that to her, because it was far too risky! Far too dangerous!

But when she opened her bedroom door and saw his face…she faltered.

He looked to be in some kind of pain. Emotional pain. He looked at her with such longing, with such a need that mirrored her own, she threw all caution to the wind and stepped close to kiss him. Her hands went into his hair as he kissed her back with just as much passion as she was kissing him. She staggered backwards as he pushed her towards the bed and began undoing the buttons of his shirt as he laid her down upon her bed, pushing her book onto the floor with a thump.

'Archer…' There was so much to say. So much she needed to say.

'Do you want me to stop?' he whispered, breathing heavily.

'No.' No, she did not. Maybe later she would regret saying no, but right now? In this moment? All she wanted was him and she felt absolutely sure that he felt the same way.

We can do this. We can find a way to make this work!

He peeled off his shirt and this time, she saw how beautiful he was. The last time it had been dark. Moonlight her only visual aid as they'd made out on Rookery Point. But here? In her bedroom? With the lights on? His musculature was a thing to see. Amazing to touch. She ran her fingertips down his chest, over his sensitive stomach and down. Down towards his belt where she could see and feel that he wanted her. 'Do you want *me* to stop?' she asked, her voice breathy.

He shook his head. 'No.'

She smiled then. Smiled a victory. He was hers and she was his. Exactly how it should be.

Halley made short work of the buckle. His trouser button. His zip. Archer shucked off his trousers, his socks, then he was peeling back her robe to gaze down on her, his lips swiftly following his gaze as he trailed his mouth over her breasts. Her nipples. The underside. Kissing and licking his way over her gently rounded belly and down to the top of her underwear. The last barrier that either of them wore.

He looked up at her as he slid it down her legs. Continued staring at her as he removed his own jersey boxers.

And then he lay on top of her and she could feel every delicious inch of him.

And she was determined she would enjoy it all.

CHAPTER TEN

ARCHER WAS LYING THERE, staring at the ceiling as the morning's early rays began to filter into the room, worrying. Last night had been…amazing. Electrifying! All he'd been dreaming of, thinking of, had happened and he'd thoroughly enjoyed every minute. Halley had too. At least he hoped. But what the hell did it mean? One lapse. Giving in to his physical need for her… Had it ruined everything? Maybe she had just been scratching an itch, too? He'd read somewhere that pregnant women could experience a surge in their sex drives. Was that what last night had been?

He turned to look at her, lying beside him. They'd begun in her room. Had sex, made it to the shower room, soaped each other down in there and then carried on in his bedroom. It was as if they'd been unable to get enough of each other. As if they'd been filling up on how it felt.

Because we both know it can't happen again? Because we both know it shouldn't *happen again?*

His mobile phone at the side of the bed beeped and, groaning, he reached over for it and glanced at the screen. It was the out of hours emergency line. Not wanting to disturb Halley, who looked deeply asleep, he quickly got out of bed and went to stand in the hall, closing the bedroom door behind him.

'Hello?'

It was James. 'Sorry to wake you, Archer, but we've had Sylvie Campbell on the phone. She's got a pygmy goat struggling to give birth and she needs someone to go out to the farm. I'd go, but I need to stay here to monitor our overnight patients. Suzie's oxygen levels keep tanking.'

Suzie was a black lab that had come in with terrible breathing problems yesterday. 'Oh, okay. Call her back and let her know I'll be there in ten minutes.'

'Okay, thanks.'

He ended the call and hurried downstairs, grabbing unpressed clothes from the laundry basket in the utility room. He pulled on boots and grabbed his keys and hurried from the house, glad to be out. Glad to be in the fresh air, away from Halley, where he could think clearly.

What they'd done last night didn't have to change anything. Not really. They could carry on as if it never happened. Sure, the next few days might feel a little odd, but they could do it, right? She'd been tired. They'd had a big night out together, which had been really nice. They'd danced together, which might have created a false belief that something else was happening and maybe Halley just got carried away? She didn't want anything permanent and he knew that for sure, because before they'd gone to bed he'd told her how beautiful she was.

She'd said, 'Thank you. But I think we ought to say goodnight now.'

She didn't want to pursue a relationship with him. Not in that way. Otherwise she would have made it clear! She would have responded. She might have told him that she thought he looked handsome, too, or whatever. But she hadn't. She'd shut him down. Walked away. Created space. He was the one that had pushed. He was the one that had given her a compliment without thinking first. He was the one that had paused outside her bedroom door, in complete agony, because all he'd wanted was to be in her room with her, rather than in his own room, alone.

How many nights had he lain in his bed, knowing she was just in the next room? There was so much he wanted to say, so much that he wanted to change between them, but he didn't think that she wanted him in that way. Sex was fine. Sex was easy. It was a short-term thing. You could even distance yourself from it, if you wanted, but a full-on relationship? Something long term? Something much more committed? That was the big question, and not once had she said she was ready for it, even though he felt that maybe they would have a chance. For some reason, he felt, deep down in his soul, that he and Halley could work.

But she'd given him no sign that that was what she wanted and so he needed to pull himself back again. Put himself back into that box that said he was just the father to her child and her friend and nothing more, because having Halley as a friend was much better than not having Halley at all.

They'd had a minor slip, that was all.

A breach of their control. A lovely breach, but a breach, a mistake, an erroneous event that he didn't think should ruin anything. They were adult enough to move on.

When he arrived at Campbell's farm, Sylvie

was waiting for him in the pygmy goat shed where she bedded them down at night. The goat mother that was struggling was isolated from the others in a small pen, with Sylvie looking on, clutching a mug of steaming tea. 'She's been like this for hours. Keeps trying to push, but nothing's moving. I see hooves, but they keep retracting after each contraction and I'm just worried that it's a really big kid in there.'

'Have you tried to assist?'

'Yes, but since the op, I can't stay kneeling, or bent over long enough to pull so hard.'

'No. We don't need you hurting yourself. Give me a few minutes to get on some gloves and I'll examine her and see what we've got. Hopefully we won't need to do a C-section.'

'You left Halley at home, then?'

'Er, yeah. She was sleeping. I mean, I assume she was sleeping.' He felt heat rise to his cheeks, but Sylvie didn't notice as her phone beeped.

'Oh! Speak of the devil. She's up.' And Sylvie began tapping out a message. 'I'll tell her you're here.'

Archer nodded. Maybe that was a good thing? That way, Halley would know that he hadn't just run out on her. That he was out working. He climbed into the pen, donned his gloves and began to palpate the mother goat. It did feel as if a large kid was coming first and he really didn't want to have to perform a C-section if he could avoid it. He watched her go through a contraction and it was exactly as Sylvie said. The front hooves appeared and disappeared with each contraction. If he could get hold of them and help pull, then maybe they could safely deliver the kid if he could get the head and shoulders out?

Kneeling beside the goat, he waited for the next contraction and tried to hold onto the hooves to help pull the kid out, but there was a lot of fluid, and the hooves were slippery, and he knew he'd need rope. He'd delivered a calf once from a cow the same way, back in his veterinary medicine early days.

'Have you got any rope, Sylvie?'

'Yes, love. Hang on, I'll go get it.'

Archer soothed the goat as she struggled, stroking her fur and whispering gently to her. He knew the second twin was much smaller and that delivery should go smoother. They just needed to get this one out.

When Sylvie arrived with the rope, he tied it around the front hooves and waited for the next contraction and then began to pull. It was a fine line to walk. He didn't want to pull so hard he'd tear the goat internally, but he needed to pull hard enough to have an effect and help those wider shoulders and head pass through the canal. Ensuring a safe delivery would also help prevent future problems as he knew of goats that had suffered with a birthing dystocia before ended up with milk fever, or mastitis, a toxaemia or even a prolapsed uterus. There were many complications and he hoped to avoid them. Helping her now would give her extra energy for the second kid.

The goat kept bleating, calling out in discomfort as he pulled, but he knew he had to do it if both mother and kid were to get through this. The rope was helping and with each contraction he helped the mother with his pulling as she pushed, and there was a moment, an ever so brief moment, when he felt as if this was going to have to be surgical, before he felt the shoulders and head shift past that difficult spot in the mother's hips and the kid slid out in a whoosh of fluid and birthing sac.

'Yes! There we go! Sylvie, can you hand me that towel?' He helped clean some of the fluids off the kid as the mother turned and began washing her baby.

It let out a tiny bleat and shook its head, its two floppy ears wetly flapping around as its mother washed it, seemingly unperturbed by the assisted delivery.

'Oh, thank you, Archer!'

'She did all the work.'

'But you saved her.'

'She just needed a little extra push. Sometimes they're afraid to push past the pain.'

Sylvie nodded. 'We all can be like that. I think you deserve a treat. Want a coffee? I bet you've not had a drink yet this morning.'

He looked at her and nodded. 'Coffee sounds great.'

'I'll make you some breakfast, too. You okay to stay and watch her with the second kid?'

'Knowing breakfast is coming? You bet.'

'Come on in when it's all done. You know the way.'

'Thanks.' He watched Sylvie leave and disappear into the house just as a car pulled up. It looked like a taxi, and he briefly wondered who was visiting the farm that early when Halley stepped out.

Just seeing her made him go all hot and flustered. He'd not expected to see her yet. He'd not thought of what he could say to her.

But he saw her looking around and she must have spotted the lamp on in the shed as she came on over, wrapping her coat around her in the chill morning air.

'You were gone when I woke up.'

'Emergency delivery. I didn't want to wake you.'

No. I wanted to hold you close. Spoon you. Kiss you. But couldn't.

'I thought… I thought you'd panicked.'

He made a short scoffing noise, without looking at her. 'About what?'

'About us. About what we did.'

He looked at her then, saw the fear on her face. Decided to let her off the hook, no matter how hard it was for him to say the words. 'We didn't do anything.'

'We slept together, Archer.'

'But it means nothing! It doesn't mean that anything has to change. I know we promised no flirting, no relationship, but we just scratched an itch, that's all. Nothing more. I'm not going to get worked up about it if you're not.' He hated lying. Hated saying these words. Because he did want to get worked up about it. He wanted to celebrate it. Tell the world that what they had was real!

'But…'

He waited for her to say more, but she didn't. She seemed to be floundering.

'Last night meant nothing to you?'

He thought she was asking because she was clarifying his position. He thought she was confirming how she felt about it too. 'Halley, last night was great, but no, it meant nothing,' he lied.

The goat was beginning to strain again. The second kid was coming. And so he hunkered down to make sure this second delivery would be easier.

'I can't believe you'd say that! Why do I keep doing this to myself?' And she turned and stormed away.

He wanted to go after her, but couldn't. He had a responsibility to this goat and its baby. His own concerns would have to come second.

Archer's mind raced. Halley seemed upset that he'd said last night was nothing! But wasn't that what she'd wanted to hear? How could she want anything else of him? She'd never given any sign. Yes, they got on great and she'd danced close to him last night and the sex was amazing between them, and they could laugh together and gaze at the stars and read the same books and have a child together, but…

Did she want more than that?

He was confused, because she'd always said she didn't!

She is living in my house. Having my child.

Had things changed? Because if he could have a future with Halley, then…

No. It's wrong of me to even hope! It would be amazing, but…what if I lost her? What if I lost them? If it all went wrong and she took my baby with her…

He felt terrified, but he had to concentrate on this birthing goat. This second kid was coming much easier. The front hooves and the head were already out, the goat bleating in between trying to chomp on bits of straw. And then with a big push, the rest of the kid slithered out and suddenly there were twins. The first was already up on its feet, shaky and shivering still, whilst its mum cleaned up the latest one. It was done. It was over. But he needed to stay to make sure both kids latched onto Mum. That she had no post-partum issues.

Maybe he was reading the situation with Halley all wrong, anyway. Maybe she didn't want him to be more than they were, maybe she just wanted to hear that the sex had meant something. That he wouldn't just count it as another notch on his bedpost. Maybe he should go and find her and tell her that of course last night had been amazing and of course she meant something to him. She was the mother of his child! But he would make her see that they were both adults here. Able to separate the physical from the emotional. Even if he was lying to himself.

Is that what my future is going to be? Lies?

Because he shouldn't have to live like that. Hiding away what he felt for her. No, it might not be what she wanted to hear and, yes, she might think that they had made a mistake in moving in together, but he had to be able to tell her his truth.

And what if she did want more from him? What if she'd been lying to herself, too?

Once he was convinced the mother goat and her twins were fine, he packed up his equipment and, with heart pounding madly, returned it to his car, then went looking for Halley. No doubt she'd be in the house with Sylvie. Exasperated? Mad?

But when he went inside, he saw Sylvie drying her hands in the kitchen alone. 'Where's Halley?'

'She went upstairs to her room. I don't know what you said to her, but she's pretty upset.'

'I told her a lie. But I want to tell her the truth. Do you mind if I go up?'

'Truth is always better. Be my guest, love.'

He kicked off his boots in case they were dirty and ran up the stairs, calling Halley's name.

She was sat on her old bed, sniffing and

wiping her eyes with a tissue. It broke his heart to see her so upset.

'I lied to you.'

'Just go away, Archer.'

'No. I need you to hear me. I lied to you just now. When I said that last night didn't mean anything. Because it wasn't true. It meant *everything* to me.'

She frowned, looking confused. 'I don't...' She sniffed, dabbed at her eyes. 'Say more.'

'Being with you...you make me feel whole. You make me feel like anything is possible. You make me think that *we* could be possible.' He paused to take a breath, to gauge how she was reacting to his words.

She didn't seem to be on the verge of telling him to shut up, so he ploughed on.

'Ever since I was a little boy, you brightened my world. I didn't think I was deserving of you back then. I was nothing. A weak kid with nothing to offer you. But when you came back into my life and we made this baby... I told you we could raise it as co-parents without any of the confusing romantic details, because I was afraid of how I might feel if I lost either of you. I kept lying and saying we could be adult about it, but I'm not sure that I can, because every time I look at you I still feel like I'm that weak little kid and that I'm not good enough for you. Not strong enough. Not enough to protect you! That you would leave, that you might walk away, and so, to keep you close, I told you I could deal with it. And I was lying.'

'You're saying that you have feelings for me?'

'No. I'm saying that I love you. I have always loved you and I will always love you. You're my star. You're my reason for getting up every morning. You're my hope. You're my heart and I don't want to be without you. I want us to be together. I want you in my bed every night. I want you to be the first thing I see in the morning and the last thing I see every night. I want to hold you in my arms and keep you safe and I want us to raise our child as a mum and dad who love one another.' He paused. 'But if that is too much for you to accept, then I will step back and I will hold all those feelings inside, as long as you stay and let me see my child.'

'I don't want that,' she whispered.

'Which part?' he asked, confused.

'Living together, but apart.'

Archer shook his head. 'I'm sorry, but I'm going to need you to spell this out for me. What do you want?'

She stood up and gave him a shy smile. 'I

want you, Archer Forde! I want all of what you said and more. Because I've been hiding how I felt, too. I thought it was hormones, I thought it was the baby making me feel this way about you, but it's not! The idea that we could live in the same house for the rest of our lives lying about how we truly felt, because we were both afraid, is terrifying to me! I've always been so afraid of making a mistake in front of the whole village again, I kept hiding my feelings from you without realising I was making the biggest mistake of my life!'

She stepped closer again, until they were mere inches apart. 'I love you with all my heart and I want us to be together. As a couple. I don't think either of us needs to be alone ever again.'

He pulled her towards him then and kissed her. Kissed her with a passion and a need that he no longer had to hold back.

She was his everything and, though once he'd felt he would always be alone, that he *wanted* to be alone, he now knew that he never could and nor did he ever want that.

He had evolved. His happiness had been in front of him his entire life. All he'd needed was a little bravery to reach out and take what was his.

His heart. His love.

Their love. It had called out to him across the many years that they'd been apart, but now, like a star, she had returned to his orbit.

Exactly where she was meant to be.

He pulled back. Smiled. Looked deeply into her eyes. 'Marry me.'

EPILOGUE

IT WAS THE perfect day for a spring wedding. The church looked spectacular as Halley arrived in her bridal car. Grey stone, outlined against the blue sky. The trees were full of cherry blossom and daffodils and narcissus carpeted the grass.

The photographer flitted around her like a hummingbird, taking pictures from this angle, then that, as she alighted from the car in her long white dress, her veil trailing behind her.

She stared at the church. She'd been here before in a white dress. She'd gone into this church full of infatuation and high hopes. In that church, her life had once been cruelly changed.

Archer had suggested that, if it bothered her, they could get married in another church, or in a park, or on the village green if she so wanted, but no. A part of her needed to vanquish the ghost of Piotr. A part of her wanted to be able to stick two fingers up at her past and prove to everyone that she was worthy of a happy ever after. That they didn't have to look down on her with pity as that girl that got jilted. To say, *Look, I got my happy. I found my love.*

Jenny and Hillary were her bridesmaids and they looked stunning in their burgundy dresses, holding miniature versions of her own bouquet.

'Is he here? Is he inside?' she asked Hills.

'He is. And he looks amazing in his suit.'

She smiled. 'He looks amazing in muddy overalls.'

'Well, thankfully, he's not wearing those. Mum would have a fit.'

'Yes, I would.' Her mum got out of the bridal car and stood beside her, holding out the crook of her elbow for Halley to slip her arm through.

She had no dad to walk her down the aisle, and that made her sad. He would have loved this, had he lived. But it felt right that her mum was doing it instead.

'Is Eliana okay?' Halley asked Hills. Their daughter had been born two months ago. Perfectly happy. Perfectly healthy. Doted on by two grateful, overwhelmed parents. Archer would do anything for her and was a great hands-on dad. No doubt, as she grew, Eliana would have her father wrapped easily around her little finger and would become a daddy's girl.

'Stephen has her with the twins.' Stephen was Hillary's husband. 'So she's in experienced hands, don't worry.'

'Okay. Let's do this.' They walked up the pathway to the church, the organ music growing louder with every step. They stopped to fiddle with her veil and dress, making it look perfect for her entrance into the church. They'd invited everyone they knew. Friends. Family. Clients. Regular visitors to the farm. The church was fit to bursting at the seams.

And then 'Wedding March' began and the doors swung open and Halley stepped into the church, with her mother at her side.

All eyes turned upon her and, though that was scary, she knew she could do it. She could get through this because she knew she had a guy standing at the end of the aisle who loved her more than anything in the world. Except maybe for his daughter!

She saw him, dressed in a dark blue suit, and he turned to look at her approach and there were tears in his eyes. He wiped the happy tears away with his finger and tried to steady himself with deep breathing.

He did indeed look amazing! And she couldn't believe she was so lucky!

As she came to stand alongside him, he leaned in and whispered, 'You look beautiful.'

She smiled shyly and passed her bouquet to Jenny as the ceremony started.

'And if there is anyone here present who has reason as to why these two may not be joined in holy matrimony, then speak now, or for ever hold your peace.'

Halley knew there wouldn't be anyone. Not this time. That the church congregation would be silent. And she smiled in triumph.

Her happy ever after was never in doubt. Not with Archer by her side. He was the most honest, the most truthful, the most loyal and loving man she could ever have met.

And he was all hers.

As she slid the ring onto his finger and said her vows, her voice broke. She loved him so much and was so happy to tell the whole village, the whole world, just how much happiness and peace Archer Forde had brought her.

Neither of them needed to be alone ever again.

* * * * *

Sparks Fly With The Single Dad

Kate Hardy

MILLS & BOON

Kate Hardy has always loved books and could read before she went to school. She discovered Harlequin books when she was twelve and decided that this was what she wanted to do. When she isn't writing, Kate enjoys reading, cinema, ballroom dancing and the gym. You can contact her via her website, katehardy.com.

Visit the Author Profile page
at millsandboon.com.au for more titles.

Dear Reader,

When you're in the sandwich generation, sometimes it's a struggle to fit everything in. Your parents need you; your children need you; you have a busy job; and there just isn't time for anything else.

That's the position my hero and heroine are both in—Jenny's a vet who's trying to balance her career in the local veterinary partnership with looking after her frail mother, while James is trying to balance working as a vet and being a single dad to his daughter.

Jenny doesn't want the emotional upheaval of dating again, and James, while knowing that his daughter needs a mother, can't face another relationship after being widowed.

But, now they've both moved back to the village where they grew up in the Yorkshire Dales, they discover that they're a good team at work. Can they be just as good a team outside and make a multigenerational home for all of them?

Read on to find out!

With love,

Kate Hardy

DEDICATION

For Louisa Heaton—it was such fun working with you and planning our duet!

CHAPTER ONE

'SO WHAT DID you want to talk to me about, Jenny?' Archer asked.

Jenny had deliberately waited until the rest of their colleagues had left Burndale Veterinary Surgery after their usual weekly meeting before tackling her business partner. He ought to hear this before anyone else did. 'I'm not sure whether I need to make you a mug of coffee or pour you a large whisky, first.'

'Neither. Just tell me,' Archer said.

'It's Mum,' Jenny said. Jenny had come back to Burndale from Leeds and joined the surgery here so she could keep a closer eye on her mum, knowing that Betty was terrified at the idea of going into a home and wanting to reassure her mum that she'd do her best to keep her in the house she'd lived in for decades. 'Robert came over, this weekend.'

'And?'

She blew out a breath. 'He thinks she's getting a lot worse. She needs more support. And he's got a point. Mum's not really safe to leave alone, any more—not so much the dementia, because that's still more at the forgetful stage than anything else and we can work round that, but she keeps falling, she won't use a walker and I'm worried she's going to end up with a serious fracture. I'm there at weekends and evenings, and I can get friends or our neighbour Sheila to sit with her if I'm called out for work. But I can't get more than three days a week for her in day-care, and I promised her I'd never put her in a nursing home. Which means I need to go part-time for a while.' Until…

No. She couldn't face that.

'I've spent this week exploring every avenue, and I'm coming up blank. Bottom line, it's me or me to pick up the slack.'

'Your brother can't help at all?' Archer asked, his tone deceptively mild.

She knew what he was thinking. Her best friend had said the same thing: Robert had dumped all their mum's care on her. But Jenny knew it wasn't a fight she could win, and she preferred to be practical. The most important thing was keeping her mum safe and as well as possible. 'It's a two-hour drive each way for him. Given the kind of pressure GPs are under, I don't think he'd be able to split the difference with me and do even one day a week.'

'He wouldn't consider doing what you did, and move closer to her?'

'There are the children to think about. It's not a great time for them to move schools.' And it was reasonable to consider the kids' needs before her mum's. After all, Jenny was the childless one. The divorced one. The one who'd have time to spare to look after their mother. She sighed. 'I'm sorry, Arch. I feel really horrible putting pressure on you. Not to mention the fact that it's not really that long since Max retired and I became your partner. But, unless someone invents a way for me to print a working 3-D model of myself, I need to drop down to three days a week at the practice.'

'When?'

She grimaced. 'This is the bad bit. As soon as possible. Within the next month, tops.'

'It's fine. Don't worry,' Archer said, and the lead weight that had been pushing down on Jenny's shoulders ever since her brother's visit finally started to lighten. 'I'll sort it out. We can get a locum in until we can find another vet—someone part-time, or even full-time to give us some extra flexibility.'

'Thanks, Archer. I really appreciate this.' She gave him a bearhug. If anyone had told her twenty years ago that the quiet, gangly lad with his shock of frizzy hair who was two years above her at school would turn out to be one of her closest friends as well as her business partner, she would've been surprised. Jenny had always known that Archer Forde was one of the good guys; but, since she'd come home to Burndale, she'd discovered just how nice he was.

Though they'd never be more than good friends. Yes, Archer was attractive: he'd filled out and got a decent haircut, and nowadays he was very easy on the eye. But there was no chemistry between them. He felt more like a big brother—and, though she felt disloyal thinking it, Jenny knew that her business partner was a lot more supportive than her own big brother was.

'I don't know how to thank you,' she said.

'It's what friends are for,' he said. 'You'd look out for me, if I was in your shoes.'

'Yes,' she agreed. 'Of course I would.'

'Then stop worrying. It's all fixable. Now, go home and make a fuss of your mum.'

'Thanks, Arch.' Jenny wished she could wave a magic wand for him, too. She knew how lonely he was; he'd admitted to her that since he'd lost Amy, his girlfriend, to a brain tumour, he just hadn't wanted to get involved with anyone else.

There were dozens of women who'd jump at the chance to date Burndale's most eligible bachelor, though Jenny wasn't going to insult her friend by trying to fix him up with someone. When he was ready to move on, then maybe she'd give him a nudge or two. But the best thing she could do right now was to have his back, the way he had hers. 'I'll see you tomorrow.'

Maybe now was the right time to move from London, James thought. Before Tilly started school, so she'd have a few months to settle in and make friends at nursery. His family would be thrilled if he went back to Burndale, and Tilly could grow up in the same beautiful countryside that he had. Yes, it would mean a longer trip for Anna's parents whenever they wanted to see their granddaughter, but he'd make sure to find a place big enough for them to stay whenever they wanted to visit.

The idea had been bubbling in the back of his head for a month now, ever since the incident with Sophie, their former nanny. But, before he set things officially in motion, it would be sensible to talk it over with someone else. Someone he'd known for years, and who'd been through the same kind of heartache he had. Someone who avoided relationships for exactly the same reason that he did, because he couldn't face a loss that deep ever again.

'Well, if it isn't Mr Herriot in London,' Archer greeted him when he joined the video-call.

'Indeed, Mr Herriot in Yorkshire,' James teased back. As schoolkids, they'd both fallen in love with the vet's stories, and with them both being science nerds it was obvious that they'd both end up training as veterinary surgeons and following in the footsteps of their hero. 'How's things?'

'Usual. You?'

'Hmm,' James said. 'I've been thinking. Maybe it'd be better for Tilly to grow up outside London.'

'You're moving?' Archer looked surprised.

'I'm seriously thinking about it.'

'What's brought that on?'

James groaned, and told Archer about the incident with the nanny.

Archer winced. 'Ouch.'

'Even if she hadn't walked out on us, the next morning, it was obviously she couldn't stay. Not after that. I've got a temp nanny covering for her, but all this change isn't great for Tilly. She needs stability. And it's made me think. Maybe now's the right time to move.' He took a deep breath. 'This isn't me asking you to give me a job, Arch, because I know you've got Jenny in the partnership and you don't really need a third vet in Burndale. But often people talk about advertising a post before they actually do it, so I wondered if you'd heard of any vet's jobs going within, I dunno, half an hour's drive of Burndale?'

'You're coming back to live in Burndale?' Archer's eyes widened, and then he smiled. 'You know what, James—I think we could do each other a favour.'

'What do you need?' James asked immediately. 'The answer's yes.'

'You're going to get me a visit to the International Space Station for my birthday?' Archer teased.

'If I could, you know it'd be yours,' James said, laughing back.

'Strictly between you and me, because we haven't announced it yet, Jenny's going part time,' Archer said.

'Because of her mum?' James asked, having heard about Jenny's situation from his own mother.

'Yes. I told her I'd get a locum in while I look for someone to fill in the gap permanently. But, if you're serious about coming back to Burndale, you could save me all the recruitment hassle.' Archer looked hopefully at him. 'I can offer you anything between two days a week and a full-time post—we'll work round everyone's needs.'

'That,' James said, 'would be brilliant. Yes. Yes, *please*.'

'That's great. When can you start?' Archer asked.

'I'll talk to the senior partner here tomorrow,' James said. 'They know my situation, so they might agree to use a locum and release me early. I'll call you as soon as I've talked to them. Then we can work out which days you need me and what childcare I need to put in place for Tilly around nursery hours—I don't expect Mum or my sister Vicky to pick up all the slack.'

'Perfect.' Archer smiled. 'It'll be so good to actually work with you, after all these years. Jenny's a sweetheart, so you'll fit in to the practice really well. Plus you'll know nearly all the clients.'

'I'm looking forward to working with you, too. If Anna's job hadn't been in London, I probably would've suggested us going into partnership years ago,' James said.

'I nearly asked you to join us when Max retired,' Archer admitted, 'but I thought you wanted to stay in London.'

Where James could take flowers to Anna every Friday, just as he had when she'd been alive: except nowadays it was to her grave rather than waltzing into the kitchen, handing over the flowers and getting a kiss in return. 'I did,' James said, pushing the sadness down. 'But I have to put Tilly's needs first. And I think it's time for us to come home.'

Archer's smile was slightly tight; James knew his best friend was thinking about the strained relationship he'd had with his own mother, plus his absent father. Archer's mother had never put her kids first, and Archer's brother Axle had really struggled. 'Yes.

You *do* have to put her needs first,' Archer said. 'Call me tomorrow and let me know what your boss says.' His smile broadened. 'And I can't wait to welcome you to Burndale Veterinary Surgery.'

Three weeks later, James dropped Tilly at the nursery in Burndale for her second session.

'Daddy, don't go!' she said, clutching his hand tightly as they stood outside the door. 'I don't want to stay here. I want to go with you.'

He knelt down next to her and wrapped his arms round her. 'Hey, you had a nice time here yesterday. You made new friends and you painted that lovely picture. You'll have a nice time today, too,' he said. 'And Granny will be here to pick you up this afternoon.'

A tear trickled down her cheek. 'But I miss Jas.'

Jasminder was Tilly's best friend at the nursery she'd gone to in London. 'We'll call her tonight, before tea,' he promised. 'She's still your best friend and that's not going to change, just because we moved here. Look at me and Uncle Archer—we've been best friends ever since we were at school together. It didn't make any difference to us being best friends when he came back here while I went to London.'

Another tear trickled down Tilly's cheek, and James's heart squeezed. But he couldn't tear himself in two. Just how did women manage to do this? he wondered. Would Anna have been better at teaching Tilly how to be independent? Was he letting his late wife down as well as his daughter?

'Tilly, I love you very much and of course I want to be with you,' he said gently. 'But I have some poorly animals who are waiting for me to make them better. Can you be brave and let me do that?'

She looked at him with her huge brown eyes under a mop of dark ringlets, so reminiscent of her mother's. 'Yes, Daddy.'

'That's my girl,' he said, and gave her a hug. 'Let's go in.'

Once Tilly was happily sitting at a table, making a dog out of bright pink playdough, James headed for the surgery.

Barb, the receptionist, looked up with a smile as he walked in.

'If it isn't young James Madden. Welcome home, love,' she said.

'Thank you, Barb. It's good to be back,' he said.

Archer appeared from his consulting room. 'Welcome to the practice,' he said. 'You obviously remember Barb, our receptionist. Come and meet the others.'

James followed Archer through to the back rooms.

'James, this is Anu, our vet nurse,' Archer said. 'And you remember Jenny Sutton—Braithwaite, as she was when we were at school.'

'Nice to meet you, Anu,' James said, shaking her hand. 'Jenny. Good to see you again.' He smiled at her and shook her hand; to his surprise, it felt as if an electric shock shimmered across his skin where it touched hers.

What the...?

He'd never had that much to do with Jenny at school. She'd been two years younger than him and in a completely different friendship group; and he'd dated only sporadically in sixth form because he'd been focused on getting the grades to read veterinary medicine at university. Like him, she'd moved away after university. He did remember Jenny, but only vaguely. He certainly hadn't expected to be so aware of the bluest eyes he'd ever seen.

'Nice to see you again, too,' she said politely. 'I'm sorry to hear about what happened to your wife.'

The village grapevine had probably filled her in—or at least given her more than the barest-bones information that Archer might have told her. How Anna had died from an amniotic embolism after the caesarean section when Tilly was born; it was an incredibly rare event, and it had knocked James for six, losing his wife and coping with being a single dad to their new-born daughter all at the same time.

'Thank you,' he said.

'Is your daughter settling in OK?' Jenny asked.

'We had a few tears this morning when I dropped her off at nursery,' he said. 'Tilly misses her friends from ho— from London,' he corrected himself. Burndale was home, now. 'She'll get there.'

'And she starts school in September?' At his nod, Jenny said, 'My best friend, Tamsin, is the deputy head of the infant school. I can have a word with her, if you like, to see if she can give you a heads-up on who's likely to be in her class, so you can sort out some playdates over the summer to help Tilly make friends and settle in.'

'That'd be great. Thank you.' He paused. 'How's your mum doing?'

Jenny gave him a rueful smile. 'Village grapevine filled you in, too?'

'Of course,' he said. Plus, as one of the practice vets, he'd needed to know that she wasn't available on Thursdays and Fridays. Archer had given him the barest bones: enough so that James understood Jenny's situation, but no gossipy details.

'Mum's torn between being relieved that I'm going to be home with her another two days a week, and guilty that she's sabotaging my career. Which she absolutely isn't. It was my choice to go part-time,' Jenny said.

'If it helps, I would've done the same, in your shoes,' he said.

'It's hard to juggle, sometimes,' she said. 'Though I guess it's just as hard juggling things as a single dad.'

'Worrying about whether you're doing the best for them. Tell me about it,' he said with a smile.

'Well, I guess we have patients waiting,' she said. 'Catch you later.'

James's first patient was a springer spaniel with a nicked leg. Mrs Martin, his owner, had fashioned a temporary dressing of lint and micropore tape over the cut. 'I feel terrible,' she said. 'We were giving Alfie a haircut last night—he hates going to the groomers, so we've got our own low-noise clippers and we can keep reassuring him and giving him a break when he needs it. But you know how long hair can get matted—there was a bit on his back leg where we thought we'd better use scissors.' She winced. 'He wriggled, and my husband accidentally nicked him. Alfie didn't make a sound—we didn't even realise what had happened until we saw blood running down his leg.'

'At least his leg wasn't caught on rusty wire, so we don't have to worry so much about infection,' James said. 'When did it happen?'

'Last night. We put a dressing on it, but I wanted to get him checked over properly.'

'That's always a good idea if you're worried—or if the cut's bigger than a couple of centimetres.' James made a fuss of the dog, then removed the dressing and examined the wound. 'It's going to need stitching, I'm afraid,' he said. 'Though it might be a tricky repair. Skin heals best if we stitch it within a couple of hours of the wound happening.'

Mrs Martin looked stricken, and made a fuss of her dog. 'Oh, my poor boy. I wish

I'd called you last night. Is he going to be all right?'

'The cut's in a difficult place,' James said. 'Not so much for me stitching it, but because of the way the muscles move here—it's harder for the stitches to hold the skin in place, plus the flap of skin here is pointing upwards instead of down.' When she bit her lip, he added, 'I can do it—but Alfie will definitely need a collar to stop him licking the stitches and taking them out, because the repair will be quite fragile and we need to give it a chance to heal. When did he last eat?'

'Last night. He had some water about six o'clock this morning—I didn't take him for his usual walk before breakfast,' Mrs Martin said. 'And I held off on breakfast in case he needed stitches.'

'That was the best thing you could've done,' James said, making another fuss of the dog. 'Well, gorgeous boy. We'll be keeping you in, this morning, and I'll sort your leg out at the end of morning surgery. We'll give you a call, Mrs Martin, and let you know when he's round and again when you can collect him.'

A tear leaked down her face. 'He's going to be all right?'

'We'll do our best. But remember you can

always come in and see the vet nurse here if there's a bit of matted hair and we can sort it out for you,' he said, as gently as he could. 'That'll save any future issues like this.'

'My husband's never going to be allowed near a pair of scissors, ever, *ever* again,' she said, and made another fuss of her dog. 'I'll see you soon, Alf. Be a good—' Her voice broke. 'I'm sorry. My daughter left home six weeks ago and I haven't got used to the empty nest, yet. Alfie's kind of taken over as…' She shook her head. 'I know it sounds daft, but he's like my youngest child.'

'That's how a lot of people feel about their pets,' James reassured her. 'We'll take good care of him, Mrs Martin.' James took the dog's lead, but Alfie whimpered and tried to follow his owner out of the room.

'This way, boy,' James said gently but firmly, and led the spaniel into the area at the back where they kennelled animals waiting for an operation.

Jenny grabbed a coffee mid-morning in her break between appointments, adding cold water to it so she could drink it straight down.

She was still shocked by her response that morning to James.

Although they hadn't been in the same friendship group at school, she'd noticed the good-looking teenager back then. She'd really liked his green eyes and his smile, and the way his dark hair flopped over his forehead—just like Orlando Bloom's, her favourite actor at the time—but she'd been way too shy to dare ask him out. He was two years above her. If he'd said no, she would never have lived it down among her own year, and the idea of the relentless teasing had been too daunting. And he'd never seemed to notice her, though maybe it was because he always had his head in his books.

With James being Archer's best friend she'd got to know him by proxy since she'd been working with Archer. Like her, James was single and focused on his family's needs—though in his case it was through being widowed rather than divorced.

And she really couldn't face dating again anyway. The break-up of her seven-year marriage had left her bruised. It had been amicable, to a point—she and Simon hadn't ended up sniping at each other, and they'd been fair in dividing their assets—but, now she looked back, she realised she'd always gone along with what he wanted instead of pushing for more of a middle way.

They'd met as students, but even then Simon had always been much more ambitious than she was, adamant that he didn't want children because he wanted to focus on his career. He'd made consultant at a young age and made a real name for himself in Leeds; Jenny had come to terms with the fact that as they'd got older she'd wanted a family but he hadn't. She had her niece and nephew, even though she didn't see as much of them as she'd like.

The job in London, two years ago, had been the tipping point. He hadn't even told her he'd applied for it—just assumed that she'd go along with him. But, when her mother had been diagnosed with early-stage Alzheimer's, how could Jenny have possibly deserted her?

She didn't regret choosing her family over her marriage, but she sometimes wished that Simon had been prepared to help her find a compromise that worked for all of them. That he'd been there for her to lean on, share her worries and reassure her. But it wasn't who he was, and she knew it was pointless wishing otherwise.

And now she'd met James again. Felt a spark of attraction she hadn't expected to feel again, for someone who had just as many complications in his personal life. Neither of them had time to date someone between work and caring for their closest family member. She'd just have to ignore the attraction and focus on having a good working relationship with him. Keep it professional, she reminded herself. Don't think about how his dark hair flops over his forehead. Or how beautiful his mouth is when he smiles. Or how his eyes are the same green of the moors on a spring day.

All the same, when James caught up with her after morning surgery, awareness of him quivered up her spine.

'I need to repair a tricky cut on a spaniel,' James said. 'Fancy being my anaesthetist?'

Working together would be the best way to help her damp down that attraction and keep it professional, she thought. 'Sure.'

Except she quickly discovered that she'd been very, very wrong.

Seeing the kindness with which James treated the spaniel, his green eyes crinkling at the corners as he made a fuss of the dog before shaving Alfie's paw ready for the anaesthetic injection, made her heart melt.

Seeing the deftness of his hands when the dog was on the operating table and James stitched up the cut—which was indeed in a tricky place—made her wonder how those hands might feel against her skin.

And seeing the smile on his face when she reversed the anaesthesia and the dog woke up made her stomach flutter.

'Good job,' she said, to cover her confusion.

'Good teamwork,' he corrected. 'Though if that had had been any deeper, it would've involved his Achilles' tendon.'

Which, she knew, would've been life-limiting. The spaniel would've been miserable, unable to race around and bounce about as the breed usually did. 'He was lucky,' she said.

'Thanks for your help,' he said, and gently scratched the top of the spaniel's head. 'And I need to phone your mum, Alfie,' he added to the spaniel, 'so she can stop worrying.'

Oh, that smile. It'd charm the hardest heart in the village. And it was definitely doing things to her.

'I'll catch you later,' she said. 'And I'll have a word with Tamsin tonight about school.'

'I appreciate that,' he said. 'Thank you, Jenny.' His eyes crinkled at the corners, again making her feel that weird little fluttering in her stomach. Just like she'd had when she'd known him as a teenager.

She was going to have to be really, really careful not to let herself fall for James.

CHAPTER TWO

'OF COURSE I can suggest people James could get in touch with to sort out a play date,' Tamsin said. 'Give him my number, and I can give him all the info about applying for school places, too.'

'Thanks, Tam.' Jenny smiled.

'How are you getting on with him at the practice?'

'Fine,' Jenny said. 'He's a nice guy.'

Although she'd willed herself not to blush, clearly it hadn't worked because Tamsin gave her an arch look. 'Like that, is it?'

'No. We're colleagues. Friends,' Jenny said. Even though she knew it sounded as if she was protesting a bit too much. 'He's a single dad and doesn't need the hassle of a relationship.'

'Just like you're a carer to your mum and don't need the hassle of a relationship.'

'Exactly,' Jenny said.

Tamsin poured more wine into their glasses. 'You know, it sounds to me as if you both need a bit of fun.'

Not sure where this was going, Jenny didn't answer.

'Jen, it's been two years since you and Simon split up. It's time you made a bit of time for *you* in your life. If he likes you and you like him, why not go out together?'

'Because I don't need the complication of a relationship—I can't leave Mum in the evenings,' she said, knowing it was probably an excuse, but not wanting to admit to how daunting it felt to date again. How did you even meet anyone when you were in your thirties, unless you used a dating app? And anyone she met would have as much emotional baggage as she did. She'd heard so many horror stories. She really couldn't face it. 'Plus he's still grieving for Anna.'

'Or maybe,' Tamsin said, 'it's easier for him to let people think that, and then nobody's going to nag him to get out there and find someone to share his life.'

'Like you nag me,' Jenny grumbled, though she knew her best friend meant well—and probably had a point. 'And he has Tilly to think about.'

'He's just moved back to the village from London—it's common knowledge that he's staying with his parents until his lease starts on the cottage in Richmond Road, and his mum will jump at the chance to spend some time with her granddaughter. And I,' Tamsin said, 'am very happy to come and have a cup of tea and a natter with your mum while you go out for a drink or whatever with James.'

'I…' Jenny knew she should have all kinds of excuses ready to go. But they'd all fallen out of her head.

'You like him,' Tamsin said, 'and he likes you.'

'How could you possibly know that?' Jenny protested. 'Of course he doesn't.'

'Jenny, you're gorgeous. Of course he likes you. Look at you. You're fit from all the physical stuff you do with animals, you're beautiful, there's all that silky blonde hair men would just love to twirl round their fingers, and nobody's going to resist those lovely blue eyes of yours. Don't argue,' Tamsin said firmly. 'Simon needed his head examining, putting his career before you.'

'It wasn't his fault.'

Tamsin scoffed. 'It certainly wasn't yours. He could've had a perfectly good career in Leeds. Commuting between here and Leeds wouldn't have killed him.'

'He would've been crazy to turn down that opportunity in London. It was everything he wanted.'

'He didn't even *try* to compromise, Jenny,' Tamsin said, looking cross. 'He didn't consider there were two of you in that marriage with a good career. Or think that you had opportunities, like the partnership you were offered but turned down because he wanted to live in Leeds. And why didn't he suggest your mum moved in with you in Leeds? He was completely selfish.'

Jenny was uncomfortably aware that it was true. Then again, she hadn't stood up to him, had she? 'It's worked out for the best,' she said. 'I'm a partner in the practice here, and Mum hasn't had to move from the place that's been her home for forty-five years.'

Tamsin sighed. 'OK. I know I'm not going to win *that* battle. But I'm going to win this one, Jenny. All right, I accept you're not in a place right now where you have time for a proper relationship, and neither is James. But some no-strings fun…that'd do you both a lot of good. You've both had a tough time and you deserve a break.'

'I'm fine as I am,' Jenny said.

'No, you're not,' Tamsin said. 'You're doing your best for your mum, you work hard—and you don't have any time left for you.'

'I'm *fine*,' Jenny repeated stubbornly.

And she was. Until the next morning, when James performed the sedation so she could do a diagnostic X-ray on a ginger and white cat.

'What's your thinking?' James asked.

'Sally's—his owner's—mother-in-law came to stay for a couple of days and left her knitting out,' Jenny said.

'Ah. And Pekoe here couldn't resist batting the ball of wool about.'

'Last night,' Jenny confirmed. 'Then, this morning, he wasn't very well. He was vomiting, refusing food and just couldn't seem to get comfortable. Sally's mother-in-law took over Sally's shift in the tea shop so Sally could bring him in for us to have a look at. And when she told me about the playing with wool stuff last night, it made me wonder if we're looking at a linear foreign body.' She blew out a breath. 'I couldn't see any wool caught at the back of his mouth—hence the X-ray, to see what's going on in his stomach.'

The X-ray showed the classic 'string of pearls' sign, indicating that one end of a piece of wool had become trapped in the stomach while the other end had moved through the cat's gastrointestinal tract, and the cat's intestines had bunched up on themselves around the wool, a bit like a concertina.

'Classic presentation of an LFB,' James observed. 'Poor chap. No wonder he wasn't feeling well.'

'Let's just hope the wool hasn't cut through his intestinal wall,' Jenny said. A perforated intestine could be life-threatening. Thankfully Pekoe was only nine years old so he had a better chance than an elderly, less robust cat. Jenny palpated his stomach and intestines. 'I can't feel where the wool's caught.'

'So we're not looking at a simple dislodgement of the wool where we can remove it through Pekoe's mouth,' James said.

'I need to open him up. Ready to go with full anaesthesia?' Jenny asked.

'Yes.' Deftly, he intubated the cat and increased the anaesthesia.

Once the cat was fully anaesthetised, Jenny opened his abdomen at the point where the X-ray suggested it was the most likely place where the wool was stuck.

'Can you see it?' James asked.

'I've found it—and there's no sign of perforation,' Jenny said with relief. She gently dislodged the wool, and managed to remove it. 'And that's good. Just the one cut in his intestines, so he'll heal more quickly,' she said, stitching the cat's intestines with dissolvable stitches before suturing his skin closed. 'Pekoe's definitely used up one of his nine lives this week.'

'Pekoe.' James looked at the cat and smiled. 'Was he named for Orange Pekoe tea, do you think?'

Jenny laughed. 'Given that Sally owns the village tea shop, what do you think?'

James laughed back. 'That's the perfect name for him.'

'We'll keep him in for observations for the next forty-eight hours,' she said, once James had brought the cat round, 'and I'll ring Sally to let her know that he's going to be OK.'

'That'll be the best phone call she has all year,' James said with a smile. 'And that's the lovely bit of our job, telling owners everything's going to be fine.'

'I hate breaking bad news,' Jenny said. 'You can tell what kind of cases I've had in a week, just from my chocolate consumption.'

'I know what you mean,' James said. 'It's so hard for owners saying goodbye—but the good ones remember the love their pet gave them over all the years. They sit with their pet to the end and let them go to sleep in their arms.'

Jenny had to blink away the tears at the thought, and turned away to make a fuss of the still-woozy cat.

'You've got a soft spot for cats, then?' James asked.

'I know you're not supposed to have favourite animals,' Jenny said, 'but I always think of Mum whenever we have cats in. She'd be lost without Sooty.' Or, rather, even more lost than she was gradually becoming, and the knot of worry tightened in her stomach. She shook herself. 'Ignore me.'

As if James could read her thoughts, he said, 'It's tough, seeing your parents become more frail.'

'Especially because Dad died five years ago,' Jenny said. 'It was his heart. Mum started to go downhill about then. My brother Robert and I thought it was grief and a bit of support would help. Except then we realised things were getting more serious.'

'Grief can make you shut everyone and everything out,' James said.

Jenny winced. Of course James was talking from first-hand experience about being widowed. 'Sorry, James. I didn't mean to stamp on a sore spot.'

'You didn't,' he said. 'It's something I've noticed with our older patients—when they're on their own, their pets are that little bit more precious. But, since you raised the topic of grief and loneliness, Anna and I loved each other and we were happy. I'm sad she's gone, and I'm sadder still that Tilly will only get to see and hear her mum in photos and videos. Living in London, we didn't have pets, so I think I would've shut the world out if I hadn't had Tilly depending on me.' He wrinkled his nose. 'What I'm trying to say, in a very clumsy way, is that you have a point about grief making people disconnected from others.'

'It must be hard, coming to terms with what happened to Anna.' It was her turn to wrinkle her nose. 'Sorry. I didn't mean to pry.'

'You're not prying. Most people avoid the subject,' he said. 'What can you say to someone whose partner died in their thirties? And you're right. It's hard to come to terms with it. I'm not a doctor, but I'm a vet and I read every pregnancy book going when Anna was expecting Tilly. Why didn't I notice something sooner?'

'As you said, you're not a doctor,' Jenny said gently. 'It's such a rare complication, half the staff on the ward had maybe seen one case before, if that. You've got nothing to feel guilty about.'

'Mmm,' James said. 'And Tilly has to come first. I'm not going to spend my time wallowing in grief when she needs me. And I'm wallowing now.' He rolled his eyes. 'Tell you what. To make up for my utter rubbishness just now, let me buy you a coffee and a sandwich for lunch, and you can tell Sally the good news in person rather than ringing her.'

'You d—' Jenny began, and stopped herself.

Tamsin had a point.

She worked hard, she looked after her mum, and she needed to make a little bit of time for herself. Becoming friends with James—or maybe even some no-strings dating—would be good for both of them. 'Thank you,' she said. 'That'd be nice. Maybe we can get Archer to join us.'

'Great idea,' James said with another of those stomach-flipping smiles.

Except Archer had been called away to see

a sick cow, so it turned out to be just the two of them for a quick sandwich and coffee in Sally's tea shop.

'Pekoe's really going to be OK?' Sally stifled a sob and hugged Jenny. 'Thank you. Thank you so much. He's nine, and I've had him since he was a kitten. I can't imagine life without him.'

'I'm keeping him in for a couple of days,' Jenny warned. 'He needs pain relief, IV fluids and medications to control nausea and help his intestines get moving again.'

'And then, when he does come home, you need to keep him quiet,' James added. 'It'll take another week and a half for the incisions to heal—and he'll need to come back to have the external stitches out.'

'The internal ones don't need removing,' Jenny said. 'They'll take about four months to dissolve fully, and in the meantime they'll support his intestines.'

'My poor little lad,' Sally said. 'Ian's mum would never have forgiven herself if…' Her voice thickened with tears again.

'He's not the first cat to have swallowed a bit of wool, and he won't be the last,' Jenny said.

'But, yes, you need to keep a close eye

on wool, ribbons, tinsel and the like,' James added. 'They're a magnet for cats—and they can cause a lot of damage.'

'We'll definitely keep a closer eye, in future,' Sally said. She smiled at them. 'You two are obviously close; you virtually finish each other's sentences.'

Jenny could feel heat rising in her face. 'We've both done the job for a long time and we've seen a lot of similar cases,' she said. 'We just think along the same professional lines.'

'Exactly,' James said. 'We're friends. Or becoming that way,' he added. 'We kind of know each other already through Archer.'

'Absolutely,' she agreed firmly.

Once Sally had sorted out their sandwiches and coffee, they found a table in the sunny courtyard.

'Sorry about—well, what Sally said,' Jenny said, embarrassment flooding through her but knowing she needed to make things clear between them to avoid any future awkwardness.

'That's the only thing about living in a small village,' James said. 'They mean well, but everyone sees a single person and they start matchmaking, even though you don't want them to.'

'Tell me about it,' Jenny said feelingly. 'I don't have any designs on you, just as I realise you don't have any designs on me.'

'Exactly,' James said. 'And not making boundaries clear is part of the reason I ended up leaving London.'

It was none of her business, but she said awkwardly, 'Anything you tell me won't go any further.'

'Thank you,' he said, and raked a hand through his hair. 'Actually, it'd be good to get a female point of view, if you don't mind me using you as a sounding board. I couldn't face telling Mum or my sister, because I feel such a fool.'

'I think we've all been there at some point. OK. I'm listening,' she said.

'We had a live-in nanny in London, to cover the gaps between my work hours and Tilly's nursery hours. I was grateful for her help, and I made the mistake of telling her.'

Jenny frowned. 'Why was that a mistake? Everyone likes to be appreciated.'

'Because she took it the wrong way,' James said dryly. 'She thought I meant more than just her job. One evening, I went out for a meal with the others in my practice because Sophie—the nanny—had agreed to babysit for me. But, when I got home, she was waiting for me…in my bed, without a stitch on.'

Jenny winced. 'Awkward.'

'Really, *really* awkward,' James said. 'I didn't know where to look. So I shut my eyes, apologised to her, and explained that I wasn't looking for a relationship—between work and Tilly, I simply don't have space for anything else.'

Exactly as Jenny had told Tamsin: and now she'd had it confirmed. Part of her was relieved, because it would mean he understood her own position; but a little part of her was wistful. How ridiculous had she been, wondering what it would be like to date James, just as she had fantasised about when she'd been a teenager? Better to stick to what he'd said to Sally: they were on their way to becoming friends, and that was it. 'What happened then?' she asked.

'She…um…wasn't very happy about it. I asked her very politely to get dressed and leave my room, and said we'd discuss the way forward in the morning when we'd both had time to think and cool down. And I was sorry if I'd led her to think I regarded her as anything other than as Tilly's nanny.' He winced. 'Obviously I went downstairs and gave her a lot of time to…um…get dressed and out of my bed. The next morning, I found a note from her propped against the kettle with her door key beside it. She said in the circumstances she thought I'd understand that she wanted to leave immediately, and she wasn't prepared to work a notice period.'

'You're kidding. She didn't say goodbye to Tilly before she left?' Jenny asked, shocked that the nanny would abandon her charge like that.

'No.' His mouth tightened. 'Obviously Tilly was upset when I had to tell her that Sophie wasn't going to be around any more. She asked if Sophie had gone to heaven, like Mummy had.' He shook his head. 'God, I know it would've been embarrassing for her, having to face me after she'd made such a blatant move and I'd turned her down. It wouldn't have been great for me, either. But surely Sophie could've put Tilly first and realised how it might affect her?' He blew out a breath. 'Anyway, I told Tilly that Sophie hadn't gone to heaven. It was just that another family needed her to look after them, and she hadn't had time to say goodbye, and we'd find someone else who could look after her when I was at work.'

'It sounds to me as if you handled it the best way possible. Was Tilly OK?' Jenny asked.

'Tearful for a few days, but thankfully she was OK. Luckily my boss was very understanding and told me to take a couple of days off until I could find a temporary nanny, and our admin manager's sister worked at an agency and found a couple of people Tilly liked who could fit us in. But the upheaval made me think about how I'd manage when Tilly started school. The more I thought about it, the more it made me want to come back to Burndale, so I'd got the support of my family as a safety net.'

'When does she start school? September?' Jenny asked.

'January,' he said, 'because she isn't four until the middle of August and she'll be one of the younger ones in the year. I thought about it, and it makes sense to move now and let her get settled in. I rang Archer to see if he knew of any jobs going up this way, and that's when he told me about you needing to go part-time and suggested I join the practice.'

'On a purely selfish note, I'm so glad you did. It made me feel a lot less guilty about letting him down,' Jenny said. 'It's not that long since Max retired, and it wasn't fair of me to ask to go part-time so soon after becoming Archer's partner in the practice. I should've realised how bad the situation with Mum was getting, a lot earlier than I did.'

'When you're with someone every day, you don't notice the small, gradual changes,' James said. 'Don't beat yourself up about it.'

'That's much, much easier said than done,' Jenny said. 'But then I guess you've probably beaten yourself up about your situation with the nanny.'

'I have,' James admitted. 'I've gone over and over how I might have given Sophie the wrong impression, and I just can't see it.'

'What did you say to her, exactly?' Jenny asked.

He looked blank for a moment. 'I can't remember the exact words. I think I said something like I was grateful for her help and glad she was with us.'

'Hmm,' Jenny said. 'I think maybe if you'd said you were glad she got on so well with Tilly because you didn't have to worry about your little girl, it might've made it a bit clearer that you were talking about her in a professional capacity rather than a personal one.'

'There's such a fine line,' he said. 'I was never interested in her in *that* way. And if I had wanted to date her, I would've talked to her about it first and suggested she got another job, so it wasn't like me being a creepy employer expecting the nanny to…well. You know what I mean. Putting someone in an awkward position where they don't feel they can say no in case it affects their job. That's really not OK.' He blew out a breath. 'That's why I'm a bit wary of hiring another permanent nanny, in case I mess it up again—not give her the wrong idea, I mean, but I don't want to go too far the *other* way and make someone feel unwelcome.' He took a sip of coffee. 'I'm hoping that, between me and the nursery, we can cover Tilly's childcare without me needing to rely too much on Mum's help. I know she loves being with Tilly, but I don't want to take advantage of her. It isn't fair.'

'I'm pretty sure your mum understands your situation and she's only too pleased to help,' Jenny said. 'I know my mum would've been, in her shoes.'

'You don't have children?'

'Simon—my ex—didn't want children. He was very focused on his career,' Jenny said.

'And you were OK with that?'

'Yes,' she said, though it wasn't strictly true. 'I went through a broody stage in the first couple of years we were together,' she admitted, 'but he made it clear that he didn't want kids and that wasn't going to change. And I loved him and wanted to be with him, so I made the choice not to have kids.' She shrugged. 'And I love my job. It was fine, until he got the job offer in London. It was a really good opportunity—senior consultant in a London hospital with some teaching that could lead to a possible professorship. Of course he couldn't turn it down. But that's when I discovered my line in the sand: I didn't want to be so far away from Mum. Coming here from Leeds was enough of a trek to see her; coming here from London would've been even further.'

'Couldn't she have gone to London with you?'

If Simon hadn't wanted her mother to live with them in Leeds, he definitely wouldn't have wanted her around in London. 'No,' she said carefully. 'So I told him I was happy for him to go to London, but I couldn't go with him.'

'And he went without you?' James looked surprised.

'Yes.' It had been a shock—she'd hoped that the ultimatum might make him think of a different way forward. But it hadn't; he'd left her behind without a second glance. Though she knew that if he'd stayed, he would've grown to resent her and her mother. The split, painful as it had been, had definitely been the right decision. 'He's found a like-minded high-flyer, now, and they're happy.'

'And are you?'

'I'm fine,' she said, giving him the full-wattage smile she knew everyone expected to see from her but didn't quite feel.

James wasn't entirely convinced that Jenny was telling him the truth. There were shadows in her eyes that told him she shared the same bone-deep loneliness that he felt, the same worry that she was responsible for someone else's health and happiness and was so close to getting it wrong all the time.

And then there was the other thing.

The spark of awareness he felt, every time he saw her.

It was ridiculous. He didn't really know her; yet, at the same time, he'd known her for years. At school, where she'd been one of the girls two years below him; and then, when she'd come back to Burndale, he'd got to know her through what Archer had told him about her. She was a reliable, steady business partner who was easy to work with, good with the patients and their owners, and even charmed their older, more set in their ways clients who didn't think a woman was much use in a calving pen...until she'd proved them wrong by sorting out the difficult delivery they'd asked for help with, and topped it by drinking a mug of strong farmer's tea without wincing.

But it was more than that.

Jenny Sutton was the first woman he'd really noticed since Anna. Which made her dangerous to his peace of mind. Especially as he'd been so clueless about Sophie and the way she'd interpreted his words. What was to say he wouldn't get it wrong here, too?

Jenny had said she didn't have time for a relationship, and it was obvious that, between her job and caring for her mum, she had no time for herself. Just like him. So that made her safe...didn't it?

'It's hard to get the balance right, isn't it?' he asked. 'You put your little one in day-care, and you wonder if you're failing them and you should really be at home with them all the time.'

'It's the same with organising day-care for your parent—you worry you're doing the wrong thing, though you know it's good for them to have the chance to see others their own age, who've got similar life experiences and understand their situation,' she said. 'You feel that they looked after you when you needed them, so now it's your turn to do the same. But that'd mean giving up the career you've worked so hard to achieve, and if you do that you feel you're letting yourself down.'

'Whatever you do, it's wrong. No wonder they call us the sandwich generation,' James said. 'Small children and elderly parents—they have a lot in common.'

She nodded. 'You just do your best to fit in between family and your job. As for all the well-meaning people who suggest you join a dating app and find a partner, too—there just isn't time for it.'

'And then you feel guilty because maybe you're not doing enough. Maybe I should find a mum for Tilly, a partner for me to share my worries and love both of us,' he said.

'A partner who understands I want to look after my mum, share my worries and love both of us,' Jenny echoed.

'I'm assuming your ex…didn't?' He could've kicked himself for saying it, because she'd already pretty much told him that. 'Sorry. My social skills…um…need a bit of work.'

'No need to apologise. You're fine. Simon was a neurosurgeon,' she said. 'The exact man you'd want working on someone you loved, because he was utterly focused and brilliant at his job.'

'But not so brilliant when it came to family matters?' James guessed.

'It feels a bit disloyal to say so, and I don't mean it in a horrible or judgemental way, but Simon just wasn't a family man. When we first met, I was bowled over by his energy, and I didn't even think about anything else. Then, when I hit the broody stage, I discovered he wasn't—I'd thought we could combine a career and a family, but that wasn't what he wanted. And I loved him, so I went along with what he wanted,' Jenny said. 'And I'm guessing nobody can ever replace Anna for you.'

He blew out a breath. 'No. It's been nearly four years, now. Tilly's birthday is always bittersweet for me; I want to celebrate the joy of her arrival in my life.'

'But it's also the day you lost Anna.'

'It felt as if the sun went in and never came out from behind the clouds again,' he said. 'I miss her, even now. And I guess I've kind of used Tilly as a way not to deal with it—if I'm focused on being a dad, I don't have to think about my own loss.'

'You need to make time for you, too,' she said gently. 'And I'm fully aware of how much of a hypocrite I am.'

'Not a hypocrite, at all,' he said. 'Actually, you've made me feel better about it, because you do actually get where I'm coming from. It's the same for you, isn't it?'

'Not quite. It's only two years since we walked away from each other—and Simon's still around,' she corrected.

'And you miss him?'

'I miss the idea of him more than Simon himself. I miss what I wish he'd been for me,' Jenny said. 'Which is very messed up, I know.'

'And you haven't wanted to look at anyone else?'

'I don't want to take any risks. I got it wrong, last time; and I don't want Mum to be collateral damage if I get it wrong again. I'm guessing that's similar for you?'

He nodded. 'I don't want Tilly to be collateral damage. We're pretty much on the same page, I think.'

'You're right,' she said.

'The thing that scares me,' he said, 'is the

day Tilly works it out for herself—that her mum died on the day she was born. I've been practising my speech for that moment for years, to make sure she knows that Anna's death wasn't her fault. I know what I said to you earlier about why didn't I notice, but it really wasn't anyone's fault. Nobody could've predicted an amniotic embolism. And her mum would've loved her just as much as I do.' He swallowed hard. 'Just as much as I loved Anna herself. Even if I do find another partner, in years to come, I'll never stop loving Anna.'

'And anyone who loved you would understand that,' Jenny said. 'Because love doesn't make boundaries, James. It stretches them.'

'That's a good way of looking at it. And I know I need to make the effort to find someone else. Tilly needs someone permanent in her life. Though, after what happened with Sophie, I think I might be as clueless as your ex, when it comes to...' He winced. 'Sorry. That's both feet in mouth, now. I didn't mean to...well...'

Jenny smiled, reached over the table, and squeezed his hand briefly. 'Nicely floundered,' she said. 'Everyone thinks that four years is enough time for you to have grieved for Anna; you're still young and they think you need to move on and start dating, even if you might not be ready.' She paused. 'How long has it been since you dated?'

'Since I first dated Anna. Which is about…' He calculated swiftly in his head. 'Ten years,' he said. 'What about you? I imagine you get the same pressure. "It's time to move on",' he quoted.

'Maybe a couple more years,' she said. 'We met in our last year at uni. So we were together for ten, eleven years—and I haven't dated since him.'

Maybe, just maybe, they could help each other.

James took a deep breath. 'You and I—we sort of know each other, and sort of don't,' he said.

'We know *of* each other,' she agreed.

'Given how we both feel about Archer, I think we'll become friends. Good friends,' he said. 'And we both know there's something missing in our lives—*someone*, really. We need to sort out a relationship, but we haven't got the time or the space to do it. Or, at least, we can't afford to take any risks, because we're not the only ones we have to consider. I have Tilly, and you have your mum.'

'Exactly,' she said.

He pulled a face. 'This is ridiculous. If you were a client worried sick about your pet, I wouldn't be pussyfooting about. I'd know exactly what to say. Whereas what's about to come out of my mouth might be...' He shook his head. 'I'd better shut up.'

'Say it,' she said, 'and I promise not to be offended.' She grinned, and added, deliberately hamming up her accent, 'I'm a down-to-earth Yorkshirewoman. Think of me as Jam*ie* Herriot.'

The warmth of her humour felt as if she'd wrapped her arms round him and given him a hug. 'You, me and Archer—the three James—well, James and Jamie—Herriots,' he said. And the expression in her eyes told him she meant it. She wasn't going to be offended, even if he was horrendously clumsy. It didn't matter that his social skills were so rusty, you could practically hear them screeching when he opened his mouth. 'What I was thinking... We're both out of practice at dating,' he said. 'Maybe we can practise on each other.'

'Fake dating, you mean? So people get off our case about having a life partner?'

'Real dates,' he said, 'but they're also practice dates,' he said.

'How do you mean?'

'We haven't dated anyone for years and we've forgotten how to do it—actually, if anything, things have moved on since we last dated and we're old-fashioned as well as rusty. We can't be let loose on other people, because we'll make a mess of it. But if we practise on each other, we can help each other correct our mistakes until we're ready to go out and find Mr, Ms or Dr Right. We'll be safe dating each other, because we both know we're not in a position for this to go anywhere other than being friends. And whatever happens between us, we'll stay friends.'

'Practice dating,' she said. 'With someone safe.'

A little voice in the back of his head pointed out that Jenny might not actually be as safe as he thought she was, but he silenced it. 'It's not going to affect us working together, because we're not romantically involved and we're both professionals. And we won't take offence when either of us points out what the other's doing wrong.'

Dating—but safe.

And hadn't Tamsin been right about her needing some no-strings fun?

On the one hand, it was the perfect solution.

On the other, there was the fact that James Madden's smile made her stomach flip in a way that hadn't happened to her for years. There was a chance that she could lose her heart to him—whereas he might not lose his heart to her in return. Dating him might be a really bad idea.

'You're asking me to date you,' she said. 'Practice date, but still dating. You've been back in the village a week, James. We hadn't seen each other for years before you walked into the practice yesterday. We sort of know each other, in the way that everyone in a village like ours knows everyone else—but at the same time we don't know each other, really.'

'We went to school together. OK, we were in different years, but we have a connection through Archer,' he said. 'And the bits we don't know about each other will help us, because it means it'll be like dating someone we've never met before and need to get to know.'

'So the idea is to practise dating, and when we think we're ready to let ourselves loose on the world I'll help you find a mum for Tilly, and you'll help me to find someone who'll understand I want to look after Mum,' she said.

'And, best of all, in the meantime it'll stop people nagging us about finding a partner,' he said. 'Plus it'll protect us both from anyone who wants to make a move before we're ready.'

Like his former nanny. 'You're right,' she said. 'What just came out of your mouth was something that would floor a lot of women.'

He winced. 'OK. We've established that not only do I put both feet in my mouth, but they also go in right up to the knee. Maybe I need to pin little bells to my jeans, just above my knee.'

The idea was whimsical enough to make her laugh. 'I'm not quite sure that'd be your best fashion move.'

He looked relieved that she wasn't offended. 'Please just forget I said anything, Jenny. I don't want to wreck our friendship, or our relationship at work.'

'Actually, you made some good points,' she said. 'We could both do with some safe, no-strings dating. Practising on someone who isn't going to get the wrong idea or be offended, because we've been open with each other right from the start. And it'll stop all the well-meaning comments that drive me crackers.'

His eyes widened. 'Are you saying you'll do it, Jenny?'

She smiled. 'Yes.' She held her hand out to him to shake on the deal.

And then she kind of wished she hadn't when he took her hand and every nerve-end in her skin seemed to zing at his touch.

'To honesty,' he said, 'and practising.'

'To honesty and practising,' she echoed. She glanced at her watch. 'We need to get back to the surgery.'

'Of course.' James stacked their plates and mugs. 'I'll just take these back in.'

Jenny liked his thoughtfulness; a lot of people would simply have left the crockery for the staff to collect. 'I'll come with you and say goodbye to Sally.'

And weird how it felt like being on the same team.

CHAPTER THREE

HAD HE DONE the right thing? James wondered. He didn't get a chance to see Jenny between the end of surgery and when he had to leave to pick up Tilly from nursery; then he was distracted by his daughter chattering about her day and the new friend she'd just made. By the time he'd washed up the dinner things, given Tilly her bath and gone through the bedtime story routine, and caught up with his parents, it felt too late even to text Jenny.

But she hadn't texted him, either, so hopefully that meant she wasn't having second thoughts.

She texted him on Thursday morning.

Have a nice day. I'm taking Mum for a look round the market in Burnborough and then lunch out. J.

Burnborough was the next village to Burndale; like most of the other villages in their dale, it had a market square in the centre of the village, flanked on three sides by three-storey honey-coloured stone townhouses with white sash windows and on the fourth side by the parish church. The weekly market supplemented what was usually available from the baker, the butcher, the greengrocer and the general store, and was also a good excuse for the villagers to meet up and catch up in the tea shop or the village pub, depending on whether they wanted cake and coffee or a pie and a pint.

Clearly Jenny was hoping that the outing would give her mum a boost.

He texted back.

You have a nice day, too.

And then, on impulse, he added:

Are you and your mum free on Saturday? Might be nice to go out somewhere with Tilly.

Jenny would want to spend her time off-duty with her mum, the way he'd spend his time off-duty with his daughter.

Are you sure that's a good idea? Tilly's had a lot of upheaval—the temp nannies, and I'm not being judgy or blaming you—plus moving here. Is it fair to let her meet me, knowing we're not really dating each other?

He thought about it. And then he thought again.

We're friends, and that's not going to change after the dating lessons. Why wouldn't my daughter meet my friends—just as your mum meets yours?

It was a while before she replied.

OK, you have a point. In that case, that would be lovely. Where do you want to go?

You know what's around here better than I do. Think of somewhere you'd like to go. Off to surgery now.

Was it really that easy to set up a date?

Then again, this wasn't like trying to think of somewhere that would impress his date. Somewhere with fabulous food, or a show where tickets were hard to come by, or some cultured kind of exhibition. This was an outing that could be anything from a picnic in the Dales to going on a steam train. And they weren't going on their own: they'd have her mum and his daughter with them.

Which meant that this wasn't even the sort of date where they'd be able to hold hands—and he knew deep down that he'd suggested it precisely for that reason, because he wasn't sure if he was ready to hold hands with someone.

But, if he was going to work up to finding a mum for Tilly, he had to start somewhere. This 'date' with Jenny was the first baby step towards it.

On Friday, James was surprised to see Jenny in the waiting room with a cat carrier on her lap. He knew she wasn't on shift, so it had to be something to do with her mum's cat—unless she was helping out a neighbour. Jenny was just the sort to offer help, despite her own life being packed. She had a kind heart. A huge heart. 'What's happened?' he asked.

'Sooty must've got into a fight last night. When I was going to feed him this morning, I could see his ear was torn, and although I cleaned it at home his ear's in a bit of a mess,' she said. 'If you or Archer don't mind doing the anaesthetic, I can stitch him up myself.'

'You're off duty. Archer and I will do it,' he said.

'I'll be on anaesthetic if you do the stitching, James,' Archer said, joining them in the waiting room and overhearing the conversation. 'I assume Sooty's had nothing to eat since last night?'

'Nothing we've fed him, because when I saw the state of his ear I thought I'd better make him skip his breakfast,' Jenny said. 'Though I can't say what he might have scoffed outside the house.'

'We'll sort him out and let you know as soon as he's round from the anaesthetic and ready to be picked up,' James said. 'I'll ring you. Or, actually, I can drop him in on my way home, if you don't mind Tilly being with me—though be warned that she'll want to make a fuss of him and ask a million questions.'

'Thanks—that'd be great. It'll mean I don't have to ask Sheila next door to come and sit with Mum again while I pick him up,' Jenny said, looking grateful. 'By the way, James, you asked me if I had any ideas of something local that Tilly might like to do at the weekend.'

This was obviously her way of suggesting where they could go on their date, but without letting anyone in the waiting room have a clue what was really being said. Clever, James thought. They'd let it leak out…but not quite yet.

'Maybe she'd like to visit Campbell's Children's Farm?'

'That sounds wonderful,' James said.

'Tilly will love cuddling the bunnies,' Archer said. 'And the guinea pigs—Milly, Molly and Moo.'

'How do you know the names of the guinea pigs?' Jenny asked.

Archer's ears went pink at the tips. 'Halley brought them in for their annual check-up, last week. She's…um…looking after her mum and helping with the farm until Sylvie's hip heals.'

Since when did his best friend go all embarrassed and shy? James vaguely remembered Archer having a crush on Halley Campbell at school, but as far as he knew Archer had never actually done anything about it.

Or, if Halley was back in the village, was this maybe Archer's chance to move on from the sadness of losing Amy?

Though he hated people gossiping about him and trying to fix him up with someone who'd heal his own heartache, so he wasn't going to do that to his best friend.

'Guinea pig cuddling it is,' James said. 'I'll give you a ring when Sooty's round, and I'll bring him back to you on my way home.'

'Thank you.' Jenny gave him a rueful smile. 'I feel guilty leaving him. But I feel guilty about leaving Mum, too, and I didn't want to drag her out with me. Her mobility's not great, this morning.'

'Go home,' James said, taking the carrier from her. 'Sooty will be fine with us.'

'She loves that cat as much as her mum does,' Archer said, when Jenny had left.

James nodded. 'And it's hard, caring for someone vulnerable on your own.'

'You'd know all about that,' Archer said.

'I've got it easy, right now, while I'm staying with Mum. It's still a couple of weeks until we can move into the cottage,' James said. 'So Halley's caring for her mum, too?'

'Until Sylvie's properly back on her feet, yes.'

Archer's expression told James he really didn't want to discuss it further, so James decided to give his friend space and shut up. Between them, they worked their way through the morning's waiting room; once everyone had been seen, they turned their attention to the animals who needed surgery.

Sooty's ear was ragged, but Jenny had cleaned it well, and James stitched it up and administered antibiotics before fitting a collar to make sure that Sooty couldn't take the stitches out with a paw. It would mean Jenny would have to feed him by hand, or take the collar off and then make sure she put it back on again straight after he'd eaten, but better that than having to bring him in to be re-stitched.

'Well, little man,' he said, making a fuss of the woozy cat once Archer had reversed anaesthetic. 'You'll be fine. Just try and stay out of fights in future, hmm?'

He called Jenny. 'You can tell your mum that Sooty's round from the anaesthetic and he's fine, if a bit sorry for himself. He's had a drink and a little bit to eat. We've stitched his ear and put on a collar so he can't take the stitches out. But you know the drill.'

'Yes. He might have a cough for the rest of the day because of the intubation, and I need to give him antibiotics and pain relief,' Jenny said. 'Thank you, James. Mum will be so relieved that he's OK.'

'See you later,' James said.

And how weird it was that he found himself looking forward to seeing her again.

This was practice dating, not the real thing, he reminded himself.

When he picked Tilly up from nursery, she was delighted to discover they were on a rescue mission and delivering Sooty back to Jenny and her mum. 'Can I cuddle him?'

'You'll need to ask Jenny,' he said. 'And he might still be feeling poorly after his operation and not want a fuss.'

'Did you make him better, Daddy?'

'I did. His ear was poorly and I had to stitch it.'

'I could help you put a bandage on,' she said. 'Except my scrubs, hat and vet bag are at Granny's.'

James had to suppress a grin. Tilly loved the vet play kit that his mother had bought her—including bright pink scrubs—and regularly bandaged all her soft toys and took their temperatures. When his parents' elderly Labrador, Treacle, had been alive, he'd been patient and not minded her bandaging his paw and his tail, too. 'Maybe another time,' he said.

'And he needs flowers if he's poorly, to help make him better,' Tilly added.

James didn't have the heart to tell her that cats didn't need flowers. And, given that Betty had probably worried about Sooty all day, it might be nice to take flowers to her. He'd find a way to persuade his daughter. 'We'll stop at the greengrocer's and see if they have any flowers,' he said.

They made it into the shop literally a minute before closing time.

'I'd like some flowers, please,' he said.

'Pink ones, please,' Tilly added, 'like those ones.' She pointed to the stocks set in a large bucket of water.

'Are these for your grandma?' Mel, who'd owned the shop from as far back as James could remember, asked Tilly.

'No, they're for Sooty. He's poorly,' Tilly said.

'Jenny's mum's cat. I'm dropping him back to her on the way home,' James explained. 'Tilly, I think maybe Mrs Braithwaite would like these flowers a bit more than Sooty would.'

'Is she poorly, too?' Tilly asked.

Out of the mouths of babes, James thought, exchanging a glance with Mel. 'She's been a bit sad today because Sooty's poorly,' he explained.

'Oh. Then we'll give the flowers to her. And you have to buy some flowers for grandma, too, or it isn't fair,' Tilly said.

'That'll be two bunches of stocks, then,' James said resignedly.

Mel grinned. 'If you want a job selling flowers when you grow up, lass, you come and see me.'

Tilly shook her head. 'I'm going to make poorly animals better when I grow up, like Daddy,' she announced.

She chattered about her day at nursery all the way to Jenny's house, and skipped down the path holding his hand and clutching the flowers for Betty.

'Can I press the doorbell?' she asked.

James smiled, hoisting her up with his free arm while holding Sooty's carrier in his other hand, and she pressed the bell.

Jenny opened the door to find an excited nearly four-year-old bouncing on her doorstep in front of James. 'These are for you, Mrs

Braithwaite, to make you feel happy instead of sad,' she said, thrusting the flowers at Jenny.

'Tilly, this is Jenny, who works with me. Mrs Braithwaite is Jenny's mum,' James said gently.

'Oh.' Tilly's huge brown eyes went wide. 'Um... Sorry. I made a mistake.' She turned to James, looking close to tears. 'But if you give someone a present, Daddy, you can't take it back.'

'You can take this present back,' Jenny said, bending down to Tilly's height. 'It'll be our secret that you gave the flowers to me by mistake. Plus these will make my mum very happy. She'll smile, and that'll be a special present for me.'

'Thank you,' Tilly said, taking the flowers back and looking relieved. 'Daddy says Sooty might feel too poorly to be cuddled, but I could tell him a story to make him feel better. I know one from nursery about mice. And I'll bring my scrubs and my vet bag when we come next time, so I can check his temperature and bandage his ear.'

James had warned her that Tilly could be a chatterbox, but Jenny had half expected the little girl to go shy on her, as it was the first time they'd met. Instead, Tilly was vibrant and sunny—and utterly adorable, with that mop of dark curls. Anna, her mother, must've been stunning, Jenny thought, if Tilly took after her. Though Tilly definitely had James's smile.

'Do you want to be a vet like Daddy, when you grow up?' Jenny asked.

'And make them better when they're poorly, like Daddy made Sooty better,' Tilly said, nodding seriously. 'Daddy's scrubs are green, but I like mine better because they're pink.'

Jenny could imagine the little girl dressed in pink scrubs, carrying a veterinary bag, and the vision was delightful. 'Come in,' she said. 'Then we can let Sooty out of his carrier and you can meet him properly, and my mum.'

'Yay!' Tilly said, and skipped indoors.

Sorry, James mouthed.

'Don't be—she's *lovely*,' Jenny said quietly.

She took the cat carrier from him, and led Tilly into the sitting room. 'Mum, you might remember James Madden from school? He's come to work with Archer and me at Burndale Veterinary Surgery, and he stitched Sooty's ear this morning.'

'I remember young James,' Betty said, even though Jenny suspected maybe she didn't. 'Thank you for helping Sooty, James.'

Jenny braced herself for James looking awkward or with his face full of pity, but instead he smiled, leaned forward and kissed Betty on the cheek. 'Lovely to see you again, Mrs Braithwaite. This is my daughter, Tilly.'

'Hello, Tilly,' Betty said.

'Hello, Mrs Braithwaite. We buyed you some flowers. Daddy said you were sad because Sooty has a poorly ear.' Tilly held the flowers out.

'That's very kind of you, young lady. What a pretty colour.' Betty took the flowers gently from her. 'Thank you very much.'

'Pink's my favourite colour. I choosed them,' Tilly said.

Jenny hid a grin. Given that Tilly was dressed top to toe in pink, including her shoes, it was fairly obvious how much the little girl loved pink.

'I can tell Sooty a story to make him feel better,' Tilly said. 'About dancing mice.'

'I'm sure he'd enjoy that,' Betty said.

So would Jenny. She'd loved reading stories to her niece and nephew, when they were small. She'd forgotten how much fun children could be when they were nearly four. 'I'll put the kettle on—if you have time, James?'

'I'd love a cup of tea, thanks,' James said.

'What about you, Tilly? What would you like to drink?'

'Orange juice, please,' Tilly said.

Jenny angled herself so Tilly couldn't see her face, and mouthed to James, *Can I give her a cookie?*

James nodded, and she smiled back in acknowledgement before heading to the kitchen.

When Jenny came back with a tray of tea and orange juice and a plate of choc-chip cookies, James was sitting on the sofa next to her mother's chair, Tilly was cross-legged on the floor next to Sooty, who was curled up in his basket with the cat carrier next to him, and James and Betty were listening intently as Tilly told the sleeping cat a complicated story about dancing mice.

'The end,' Tilly announced, and James and Betty clapped.

In return, Tilly gave them all a beaming smile.

'Thank you for the drink, Miss Braithwaite,' she said politely when Jenny handed her a beaker of orange juice.

'You're very welcome. And call me Jenny,' Jenny said.

'I'm Betty,' her mother said, not to be outdone.

Tilly entertained them by telling them about

the painting she'd done and the games she'd played at nursery that day, and sang them a song. 'Sooty will like it, because it's all about fishes,' she said.

What Jenny noticed most was how gentle and sweet James was with his daughter—and with her mother, treating her as a normal person rather than a fragile elderly patient with dementia. It was so refreshing, having someone talk to Betty directly, rather than addressing their words awkwardly via Jenny. And she noted, too, that her mother responded to him. It was lovely seeing her mum blossom.

James had a point about them being friends, and staying friends after their dating lessons thing had finished; they'd be able to enrich the lives of her mum and his daughter with that friendship.

And she wasn't going to listen to that tiny voice in the back of her head asking how she'd feel afterwards, if she saw James out on a date with someone else. Because it wasn't relevant. The dating stuff wasn't real.

'We need to go home now, Tilly, because Granny's making tea for us and it's rude to be late,' James said.

Tilly nodded. 'Thank you for having me,'

she said to Jenny. 'And thank you for the juice and cookie.'

'My pleasure, sweetie,' Jenny said, charmed by Tilly's perfect manners.

'Can I come back and tell Sooty another story?' Tilly asked Betty. 'Please,' she added swiftly.

'I'm sure he'd like that. I certainly would,' Betty said.

'Tomorrow?' Tilly asked. 'Daddy doesn't have to work tomorrow and I don't go to nursery on Saturday.'

'I was thinking of taking you out tomorrow,' James said. 'To see some guinea pigs at Campbell's Children's Farm. Maybe Betty and Jenny would like to come with us.'

'And then we can come back here and I can tell Sooty a story?'

James glanced at Jenny, who nodded. 'That's a great idea. He might be feeling a little bit better tomorrow and would listen to you properly.'

'I'd like a kitten,' Tilly said thoughtfully. 'A white one called Twinkle. *And* a puppy called Sir Woofalot.'

Jenny had to suppress a grin at the names.

'We can't have a puppy or a kitten at the moment, darling. Not until we've got our own place and settled in,' James said. 'Now, say goodbye to Betty and Jenny.'

'Bye-bye. See you tomorrow,' Tilly said, blowing them both a kiss and waving madly as James ushered her out of the living room.

Jenny saw them to the front door. 'What time do you need us to be ready, tomorrow?'

'About ten?' James suggested. 'I'll pick you up.'

'Perhaps I'd better pick you up, as Mum's wheelchair fits in my car.'

'It'll fit in mine, too,' James said, 'so I'll collect you both. If you think of anything else I need to know before tomorrow, text me.'

'Thanks for bringing Mum flowers. They really brightened her day—almost as much as Tilly did.'

He looked pleased. 'Good. See you tomorrow.'

For a moment, she thought he might kiss her cheek, and her knees felt as if they'd just turned to jelly.

But instead he smiled and hauled Tilly onto his shoulders, to her delighted giggle, setting her down again by his car so he could strap her into her car seat. They both waved madly to her as they drove off, and Jenny waved back before going back to join her mum.

'It's lovely to have little ones round,' Betty said. 'And she's such a chatterbox. Just like you, at that age.' She smiled. 'And James. He's a nice young man—he's kind, and he makes time for people.'

Jenny knew exactly what her mum wasn't saying. That James was the complete opposite of Simon. A family man.

'Well, we'll be spending tomorrow with them,' she said brightly. 'It'll be nice to have a day out.'

On Saturday morning, James texted Jenny to check that she and Betty were still able to go to the children's farm, then picked them up.

'I wasn't sure if it'd be easier for your mum in the front or the back,' he said, 'but Tilly's in the back, to make the choice easy for her.'

'Front, please,' Jenny said. 'Mum likes to walk a bit, although she can't walk very fast—and it's good for her, giving her confidence that she isn't going to fall. The chair's really just a precaution, for when she gets tired.'

'Got it,' James said.

Betty walked very slowly, and gripped a cane to help her keep her balance; James held the car door for her and helped her into the passenger seat, then put the lightweight wheelchair into the boot of the car.

Jenny climbed into the back with Tilly, who chattered all the way to the farm—and was almost beside herself with glee at the idea of being up close with the animals and being allowed to feed them. Her voice got louder and louder, the nearer they got to the farm.

'Remember, Tilly, you need to use your indoor voice at the farm,' James said as he parked the car.

'So the guinea pigs don't get scared,' she said, nodding solemnly.

'That's right,' he said, smiling. 'Good girl.'

She skipped along beside him happily, and he tried to keep their pace the same as Betty's. After a chat with Halley and Sylvie—and the all-important purchase of a bag of feed—they went to see the animals.

Tilly thoroughly enjoyed cuddling the guinea pigs and was thrilled to be allowed to brush one of the rabbits.

'He's happy,' she said, 'because his nose is all twitchy.'

Jenny caught his eye and grinned. 'You're absolutely right, Tilly. Daddy's obviously been training you so you know if a bunny's nose doesn't twitch, that tells you he might be poorly or not feeling very happy.'

'Happy bunnies hop a lot, too,' Tilly said. 'I'm happy, but you have to be really gentle with bunnies so I'm not going to hop in here, in case I scare them.'

She's adorable, Jenny mouthed at James over the top of Tilly's head.

Yes. She was. And it warmed him all the way through that Jenny could see that, too.

Halfway round the farm, Betty admitted defeat and sank gratefully into the wheelchair. James pushed her chair along the path, while Tilly held Jenny's hand and chattered to her about all the animals they passed.

How Anna would've loved this, James thought, and it put a lump in his throat. How much his wife was missing out on. How much *Tilly* was missing out on.

When they reached the pygmy goats, Tilly asked Betty to help her feed them. James helped Betty out of the chair, and together Betty and Tilly fed the goats, Betty encouraging the little girl to hold her hand flat so the goats could nibble the feed pellets from her hand.

'That's so lovely to see,' Jenny whispered, taking James's hand briefly and squeezing it.

'Mum really feels it that she doesn't see the grandchildren very much—they're heading into their teens so they don't really have the patience to spend time with her, and we're lucky if my brother visits once a month.'

'Yes.'

Obviously Jenny heard the slight wobble in his voice, because she asked quietly, 'Are you OK, James?'

'Yes,' he said. 'And no,' he admitted, a few moments later, knowing it was unfair to push her away when none of this was her fault. They were friends, and she understood his situation a little more than most people because her own was so similar. 'I guess it's all a bit…' He paused, searching for the right word. 'Bittersweet. As you say, it's lovely to see Tilly and your mum making friends with each other and enjoying feeding the goats. But this is the sort of thing I always imagined doing with Anna, when she was pregnant. I thought we'd go to one of these places with our children, watch the joy on their faces when the goats or lambs or whatever ate feed from their hands. And it makes me realise how many things we didn't get the time to share. How much she's missed out on—and Tilly, too.'

'It wasn't your fault that Anna died. You

admitted it yourself. It wasn't anyone's fault. Nobody could be expected to guess that she'd have an amniotic fluid embolism, because it's a really rare complication,' Jenny said softly.

He knew. He'd looked up the stats. Anna had simply been unlucky.

And how hard it was to get past that. To move on.

'Think of it another way. You can still do things with Tilly, and you can talk to her about her mum. You can share things with her. That's important,' she said.

He nodded, unable right then to reply.

'After I split up with Simon—even though it was the right thing for both of us, and there wasn't any real acrimony—I spent a while thinking about all the might-have-beens,' Jenny said. 'All the things we could've done differently. We could've had a family, or persuaded his boss to come to an arrangement with London so he could've worked some of the time in London and some of the time in Leeds. Or we could even have moved to Manchester, with Mum, so we'd be nearer my brother and she could see more of the grandchildren while Simon had the challenge he needed in his job. And it just made me miserable, thinking of all the things we didn't do.'

She took a deep breath. 'It's taken me a while to work it out, but I learned that living in the present and making the most of life made me feel a lot happier.'

James looked at her. Clearly not having children was something she regretted, despite telling him that she'd come to terms with not having a family. And, given the way she'd been with Tilly earlier, James rather thought Jenny would have made a great mum. That part of Jenny's life hadn't worked out the way she might've wanted it to, but she'd done well in her career and she was clearly very close to her mum.

Living in the present. Making the most of life.

That was what he needed to do, now. For his own sake as well as Tilly's.

And move on.

'Thank you,' he said. 'For understanding. And for showing me a different way to look at things.' This time, he was the one to take her hand and squeeze it. 'You're right. It doesn't mean I have to put all my memories of Anna in a box, but I do need to live in the here and now instead of dwelling on the might-have-beens—otherwise, I'll end up realising I've missed things I didn't want to miss.'

'You'll be fine,' she said. 'And so will Tilly.'

Jenny's belief in him was humbling. And he really didn't want to let her hand go. He actually *liked* holding her hand. He liked the warmth of her fingers entwined with his, the silky softness of her skin. After all, this was supposed to be a practice date, of sorts. But he realised he'd gone about it completely the wrong way—or maybe he'd done it so he wouldn't have to make the effort to move on, using Tilly and Betty as an excuse. Right now, he didn't want to have to explain to Tilly why he was holding Jenny's hand, any more than he guessed Jenny wanted to explain it to Betty.

Next time, he'd make the date just for the two of them.

He smiled at her—hoping his expression said more than the words he couldn't quite scramble together—and loosened her hand.

When Tilly had run out of animals to cuddle or feed, James suggested that maybe they could head to the next village for lunch.

'Will they have fish fingers, Daddy?' Tilly asked.

'If they don't,' he promised, 'then I'll make you some tonight.'

He enjoyed driving through the dales, taking a narrow country road with a drystone wall either side that had weathered to a dark grey and was covered in golden moss. There were fields of wheat on either side, interspersed with green pasture where fluffy white sheep with black faces were grazing.

'Look, Jenny! There are lambs!' he heard Tilly squeak from the back.

And then he had to stop as a ewe wandered out into the middle of the road, a lamb trotting along beside her.

'Traffic jam,' he said, and put his hazard lights on so anyone coming behind him would realise that he'd had to stop.

They waited while the ewe walked down the middle of the road, the lamb's tail wagging happily as it walked beside its mum.

'I'm hungry,' Tilly said forlornly.

'I know, sweetheart, but we have to wait for the sheep to move out of the road,' James said. 'We can't rush them. It'll worry them, and that's not kind.'

'Do you know any songs about lambs or sheep, Tilly?' Jenny asked.

It was the perfect distraction, because Tilly loved singing. James was pretty sure he knew exactly what was coming, and just as he'd expected he heard his daughter start singing

'Baa Baa, Black Sheep.' Though, to his surprise, both Jenny and Betty joined in.

'I know another song about sheep,' Betty said. '"Little Bo-Peep".'

'I don't know that one,' Tilly said.

'I'll teach you.' Betty began to sing the nursery song—but then she stalled halfway through. 'Leave them alone, and...'

James could see her shaking her head, out of the corner of his eyes, clearly distressed that the words had slipped away. 'And they'll come home,' he sang, hoping the prompt would help her.

'Wagging their tails behind them,' Betty finished. He gave her a sideways glance and noticed how relieved she looked. He'd just bet Jenny was relieved, too.

'That's a lovely song,' Tilly said.

'And the lamb in front of us is wagging its tail,' James said. 'They're back on the side of the road. Watch its tail as we go past.'

He drove very slowly and carefully past the sheep, then picked up a little more speed when the sheep were safely behind them. Once Tilly got hungry, she started getting grumpy, and he wanted to avoid that.

As if Jenny realised that distraction was still required, she said, 'I know a song about sheep and lots of other animals. Can you guess what it is, Tilly?'

'No,' Tilly said, and there was a touch of plaintiveness in her voice.

'I can,' Betty said, and launched into 'Old MacDonald'.

This time, James found himself joining in with the three of them.

And there was nothing nicer than driving through such beautiful scenery, the verges of the roads frothy with Queen Anne's lace and the odd sprinkle of scarlet poppies and purple meadow cranesbill, while singing nursery songs together.

This felt like being a family. The family he'd envisioned until Anna had been cruelly taken from them.

Except he wasn't going to live in the might-have-beens. He was going to take Jenny's advice and live in the now.

Finally they made it through the winding road to the next village. Like most of the villages in this part of the Dales, the houses were built from honey-coloured stone and slate roofs, with large sash windows; they stood cheek by jowl around the marketplace. James parked, put some money in the honesty box, and they found a table in the café in the square.

To his relief, the waitress was able to sort out some fish fingers and crispy fries with ketchup for Tilly, while he, Jenny and Betty all plumped for a bacon sandwich served with chunky chips and home-made coleslaw.

Tilly ate every scrap, and Jenny gently wiped the tomato ketchup from the little girl's face with a paper napkin.

'That was crump-shuss,' Tilly announced when the waitress came over. 'Thank you!'

'You're welcome, lass,' the waitress said. She smiled at Jenny. 'Your daughter has lovely manners.'

'Jenny's not my mummy,' Tilly said.

James winced inwardly. That kind of flat rejection was one of the reasons he hadn't tried dating yet.

'Jenny's my friend,' Tilly continued. 'She works with my daddy. They make poorly animals better. My mummy's in heaven.'

'Well, I'm sure your mummy's glad you have a nice friend,' the waitress said.

'I agree—and I'm glad, too,' James said. He risked a glance at Jenny, who was smiling.

'Me, three,' Jenny said. 'Mum?'

'Me, four,' Betty said.

Tilly worked it out. 'That's me, five—except I'm not, 'cos I'm nearly four and it's my birthday next month!'

Everyone laughed, and the awkward moment was dispersed, to James's relief.

Tilly dropped off to sleep in the car on the way back to Burndale, and didn't wake when James took Jenny and Betty back to their cottage.

'Thank you for today,' Betty said, kissing his cheek. 'Your little girl is such a sweetheart. And she'll be so disappointed not to have told Sooty a story. Bring her any time.'

'Thank you,' James said with a smile.

A glance over his shoulder reassured him that his daughter was still sound asleep.

'Thank you for coming with us,' he said to Jenny.

She smiled. 'So how would you rate it as a date?'

'Apart from when I went all mopey on you at the farm, and that moment in the café when Tilly said…' He grimaced, not wanting to repeat it and rub it in.

Jenny smiled. 'It's fine. She didn't mean it in a horrible way. And she likes me enough to call me her friend. That's a good thing.' She paused. 'So. Verdict?'

'I enjoyed myself,' James said. 'Actually, it's been the perfect afternoon. I can't remember the last time I relaxed so much—or enjoyed myself so much.' Since Anna's death, though he wasn't going to be tactless enough to say so. And it also made him feel the tiniest bit disloyal towards Anna. 'How about you? Have you had a nice day?'

'I enjoyed myself, too,' she said. 'I think we can say that we both managed a super-safe date-that-isn't-a-date.'

'I would shake on that,' James said, 'but I don't think you're supposed to shake hands with your date. Though I'm out of touch with dating etiquette. Do I ask permission to kiss your cheek?'

'Do you want to kiss my cheek?' she asked.

He held her gaze, enjoying the hint of mischief in those stunning blue eyes. 'What would you do if I said yes?'

The glint in her eyes deepened; she stood on tiptoe, rested her hands on James's shoulders and kissed his cheek. 'That's what I'd do,' she said.

All the nerve-endings in his skin seemed to have come to life in the place where she'd kissed him, and it flummoxed him to the point where he dared not kiss her cheek in case the feel of her skin against his mouth wiped every single word out of his head. 'Well,' he said gruffly. 'That's settled, then.'

'Better get little one home,' she said. 'See you at work on Monday.'

'See you on Monday,' he echoed.

And, even though it had been sunny all day, oddly her smile made him feel as if the sun had just come out again after a long, cold winter.

CHAPTER FOUR

On Sunday morning, James was called out to treat a couple of calves with severe diarrhoea, a condition known as scouring.

The four calves in the isolation pen all had slightly sunken eyes, showing they were de-hydrated.

'Have they been off their feed?' James asked.

'Aye, and the scour's bright yellow,' Reuben Farley, the farmer, confirmed.

'How old are they?' James asked.

Reuben sighed. 'Two weeks. It's just these four affected, right now, but I'm keeping a close eye on the rest. The scouring started yesterday, and they're getting sicker. We vac-cinated the cows before calving, and we made sure the calves had as much colostrum as they could straight after they were born, so they get as much protection as possible against rotavirus, coronavirus and E. coli, and we're very careful with hygiene.'

'Scouring in most calves of this age often has mixed causes, but as you've vaccinated the cows I think it's most likely cryptosporidium,' James said. Cryptosporidium was a protozoal organism, and eggs passed in the faeces of infected animals could survive for months. Because it wasn't a bacteria, antibiotics wouldn't help to treat the infection, and there were no protective antibodies for cryptosporidium in a cow's colostrum. All he could do was give medication if the lab tests showed that the calves were affected. 'I brought some sample pots with me, so we can check the scour samples at the lab to see what's causing the problem. Then I'll be able to sort out the right medication.'

'Right you are,' Reuben said.

'Are they bucket-fed or suckling?' James asked.

'Bucket-fed.'

'OK. The main thing is rehydrating them while we're waiting for the test results. I assume you already have electrolyte solution?'

'Aye, lad.'

'Good. Start the calves on them now, and

I'd advise doing it half an hour before their milk feed.'

'You don't want me to take them off the milk for a day or two, like I usually do?'

James shook his head. 'The milk will help heal their intestines. Don't dilute the milk with the electrolytes, because it'll affect clotting. Obviously you know they need twice as much fluid as usual, to replace what they've lost. I'd suggest frequent small feeds rather than three big ones a day. I'll take the samples straight to the lab, so we should know what's causing the scouring within later this afternoon and I'll bring the medication over.' He gave Reuben a wry smile. Given that he was in his late fifties, Reuben would've seen all this many times before, and he'd know the routine. 'I don't need to tell you how easily the infection can spread.'

'Aye, lad.' Reuben looked grim. 'I know it can pass to humans, so I'll make everyone use gloves and change them between handling the calves, wash their hands thoroughly, change their clothes and disinfect their boots after they've been in this area.'

'Great.' James pulled his rubber boots on and disinfected them before gloving up. 'It's best to get samples fresh from the calves rather than the floor.'

'Shall we split it and do two calves each?' Reuben suggested.

'Two each,' James agreed. Even though he was wearing a boiler suit over his jeans and T-shirt, he'd shower and change his clothes after he'd taken the samples to the lab.

Taking samples of bright yellow liquid faeces from the calves was one of the least glamorous parts of James's job, but it was completely necessary to find out what exactly was causing the scouring so he could recommend the right treatment. He disinfected his boots again once they'd taken the samples and left the pen, and at his car he stripped off the boiler suit and put it in a bag for washing. He accepted Reuben's offer of scrubbing his hands at the farm and a cup of tea, and messaged Archer and Jenny to keep them in the loop. He dropped off the samples to the lab in Richmond, then drove back to Burndale.

The journey was glorious: winding, gentle rolling hills, punctuated with drystone walls and the occasional slate-roofed stone farmhouse. You could see the undulating fields for miles at the top of the dale, bright green pasture with clusters of tress and white dots of grazing sheep across the other side of the valley. At the bottom, a sinuous river carved its way through, looking silver in the sunlight.

It was perfect.

And it was only now that James realised how hard it had been for him to breathe in London. He'd grown used to the city, for Anna's sake, but here in the open countryside was where he realised he really belonged.

Though it wasn't just the beauty of the Yorkshire Dales that drew him.

If he was to be honest with himself, Jenny was a big part of it, too.

But she didn't want a relationship right now; that was the whole reason why she'd agreed to help him to practise dating. It wouldn't go any further between them than friendship, and wouldn't make unfair demands on her time. Much as he liked her—and liked the way she was with his daughter—he needed to respect her situation.

Later that day, the lab texted him with the results, confirming cryptosporidium.

'Mum, would you mind looking after Tilly while I take some medication to one of my farmers?' James asked.

'You're going to a farm?' Tilly's eyes were huge with hope. 'Can I come with you, Daddy?'

James was about to say no: but, then again, she wasn't going to be touching the calves. Plus he liked having his daughter with him. 'As long as you hold my hand all the time we're on the farm,' he said, 'and you mustn't touch the calves or go close, because they're poorly.'

He picked up the medication from the surgery, then drove them out to Reuben's farm and introduced Reuben to Tilly. 'Reuben, this is my assistant—also known as my daughter, Tilly,' he said. 'She wants to be a vet when she grows up. Tilly, this is Mr Farley.'

'Hello,' Tilly said shyly.

'Hello, lass. Always good to follow in your father's footsteps,' Reuben said.

'I promise I won't touch the calves,' Tilly said, 'because they're poorly. And I'm using my indoor voice so I won't scare them.'

'Good lass,' Reuben said approvingly.

Copying James, she disinfected her wellies and followed Reuben to the calves' pen.

'Give this to the calves daily for the next week,' James told Reuben, handing over the medication, 'and it'll stop the cryptosporidium multiplying. Hopefully the calves will all pick up again in a couple of days. They're looking brighter than they were earlier.'

'The rehydration's already helping,' Reuben said. 'I've got another couple of calves I'm isolating in a separate pen, just in case—they're not scouring right now, but their temperatures are up a bit, they're a bit lethargic and lying around, and they're being a bit fussy with their milk.'

'It sounds like you've caught them at the earliest stage, just before they start scouring,' James agreed. 'I'd start the second lot on the cryptosporidium treatment, too, as a preventative.'

'Right you are, lad.'

'Will they get better, Daddy?' Tilly asked.

'They will,' James said.

'Good.' Tilly beamed.

'Come back to the house with us, lass,' Reuben said. 'You can say hello to Mrs Farley. And you can see our Gem's pups, if you like.'

'Puppies?' Tilly's eyes widened. 'Daddy said we can have a puppy when we move into our new house.'

'Oh, aye?' Reuben smiled. 'Well, most of these ones have new homes lined up already, I'm afraid. And they need to stay with their mum for another month or so.'

James could almost see the wheels turning in his daughter's head, and knew exactly what was coming next. 'Will we have our new house by then, Daddy? Can we have one of Mr Farley's pups?'

'Maybe,' he said.

'It's my birthday next month,' she reminded him.

Yes, and she'd made it very clear what she wanted.

'When I get a puppy, I'm going to call him Sir Woofalot,' she told Reuben.

The farmer grinned. 'Well, now. That's quite a name for a dog.'

'And we're going to have a kitten called Twinkle,' Tilly added.

Reuben's grin broadened as he looked at James. 'Sounds as if you're going to have your hands full.'

As James could've predicted, Tilly fell in love with the litter of springer spaniel puppies, and thoroughly enjoyed sitting on the floor with them while they clambered over her. Though James couldn't resist giving a couple of the pups a cuddle, too.

'She's a bonny lass, your girl,' Susan, Reuben's wife, said. 'Good with animals. Knows how to give them space.'

'Going to be a vet, just like her dad, she says,' Reuben told her. 'After a pup, she is.'

He tipped his head towards the puppies and tapped his nose. 'And it's her birthday next month.'

James groaned. 'When we've moved into the cottage we're renting and settled in, provided the landlord doesn't mind us having pets, maybe we'll look for a pup.'

'You're renting a place from Ben Williams, aren't you? He loves dogs,' Reuben said. 'Can't see it being a problem.'

'The runt of the litter's made himself quite at home on her,' Susan remarked. 'And nobody's booked him, yet.'

'He'd be much happier as a pet than as a working dog,' Reuben said. 'And your lass'd learn a lot from having a pup and training him how to be a good boy. You have a think about it, James. That little one's yours, if you want him. And he can stay with us a bit longer, if you haven't moved by the time the pups are ready to leave their mum.'

'It wouldn't be fair to leave a pup at home on his own all day,' James said, as a last-ditch attempt.

'I'm sure your mum and dad would help you out. I know they miss their Treacle,' Susan said.

That was the thing about living in a village.

Everyone knew everyone—and they knew all the details of everyone else's lives, too.

'Maybe,' James hedged. But he had a feeling that the liver and white springer pup currently asleep on Tilly's lap would end up going home with them in a few weeks. 'Tilly, we need to go home now, love,' he said.

Susan scooped the sleeping pup off Tilly's lap and, reluctantly, Tilly said goodbye to the rest of the puppies and got to her feet. 'Thank you for letting me see the puppies, Mr and Mrs Farley,' she said politely.

'You're very welcome, lass,' Susan said. 'You can come and see them any time your dad's free.'

Tilly beamed. 'Thank you!'

Later that evening, James sent Jenny a text, telling her the sorry tale of how he was close to being talked into letting Tilly have one of the Farleys' pups.

She called him. 'How can you possibly resist a pup?' she asked. 'Those warm, fat little tummies, that lovely popcorn smell when you nuzzle them, those lovely big eyes…'

'Not to mention the puppy breath,' he countered. 'Tiny teeth that feel like needles every time they shred your skin. The joy of getting up in the night and accidentally standing in a puddle of puppy pee.'

She laughed. 'Oh, you *fraud*. I bet you had a cuddle with the pups as well.'

'Yes, I did,' James admitted. 'It's one of the privileges of being a vet. You can cuddle as many puppies and kittens as you like, but you can also give them back.'

The grin was obvious in her voice when she said, 'I have a feeling Sir Woofalot might be coming home with you.'

'Even if I've moved into the cottage by the time the pups are ready to come home, the landlord might not want me to have a pet,' he protested.

'James, anyone who rents a cottage in the Dales to a vet *knows* there will be animals in the house. Besides, Ben Williams loves dogs. I don't think he's going to have a problem if you want a pet.'

He really didn't have a choice with this, did he? 'Tilly wants a kitten called Twinkle and a puppy called Sir Woofalot.' He groaned. 'But I can't leave a pup at home all day.'

'You won't have to,' Jenny said confidently.

'I can't take him to work, either.'

'I know, but your mum bumped into Mum and me in the baker's the other week and she told us how much she misses taking Treacle for walks.' Jenny paused. 'Ask her what she thinks about the pup. I bet she offers to help you out while the pup's still tiny.'

Exactly what Reuben and Susan had said. Was the whole village ganging up on him? 'Maybe,' James said. Wanting to head her off, he changed the subject. 'I was going to ask you: could we have another practice date this week? I thought maybe we could go for a drink one evening. Just you and me.'

'When were you thinking?'

'Mum has her dance fitness class on Tuesday and her book group's on Wednesday,' James said. 'Any other evening, she'll be happy to look after Tilly.'

'How about Thursday?' Jenny suggested. 'Maybe seven, so we can be out for a couple of hours. I'll see if Tamsin can sit with Mum. If she can't, then maybe Friday?'

'That'd be great. Thanks. I'll see you tomorrow at work,' he said.

It turned out that Tamsin was free on Thursday, and James picked Jenny up, as arranged.

They drove to a village that sprawled along the stream at the bottom of the dale. The local pub was ancient, with a stone floor and a huge fireplace, and it had a pretty garden shaded by apple trees. James bought their drinks, and they found a quiet table in the garden, sitting next to each other rather than opposite and watching the bees hum lazily over the lavender flowers in the border.

Now it was just the two of them, James felt weirdly shy.

'What's wrong?' Jenny asked, clearly picking up on his discomfiture.

'It's been so long since I was at the early stages of dating someone, I don't even know how I'm supposed to act,' he said. 'Do I hold your hand? Put my arm round you?'

'That's why we're doing the practising, isn't it?' Jenny asked. 'What do you want to do?'

Kiss her.

Though this was Jenny. His *friend.* He wasn't supposed to be thinking about her like that. 'What do you want me to do?' he countered.

She laughed. 'You can hold my hand, if you like. But mainly talk to me, so I can get to know you.'

'You already know me. You work with me,' he pointed out.

She coughed. 'Practice dating means practising what you'd do on a date. Tell me about your social life—what you enjoy doing.'

Feeling slightly awkward, he laced his fingers through hers. 'Is that OK?'

'It's fine,' she reassured him. 'Relax, James.'

But holding her hand made him feel all flustered and he didn't have a clue what to say next.

'Your social life?' she reminded him gently.

'Right now,' James said ruefully, 'it consists mainly of visits to the playground and the park, learning to do really good different voices when I'm reading bedtime stories, and visits to zoos and sea life centres.'

She grinned. 'Actually, that sounds like fun. I'm rather fond of jellyfish, myself. They're fascinating creatures. It's a few years since I took my niece and nephew to a sea life place, but I remember they had these huge tanks for the jellyfish, under a purple light. I could've watched them for hours.'

'Tilly's favourites are the sharks,' he said. 'The bigger, the better. And the giant rays.'

Jenny shivered. 'Sharks are magnificent to watch, yes; but the rays always scare me. I think it's their mouths. I'm glad we don't have any sea-life centres as clients. The idea of having to treat one, with those huge teeth…'

'They have suction plates, not teeth,' he said. 'So they're not going to hurt you or bite you when you feed them. If anything, their jaws make them more like a cow chewing the cud.'

'Except they're chewing anchovies and shellfish,' Jenny said. 'Which is *not* like chewing grass.'

'Fair point.' He smiled. 'Tilly's fascinated by them. You can guess what I'm planning for her eighth birthday, the first time she'll be old enough to feed them.'

'A VIP ray-feeding trip? She'll love that,' Jenny said. 'But rather her than me!'

'What about you?' he asked. 'What do you do in your social life?'

'Visit gardens,' she said. 'I take Mum to a stately home most weekends, especially the kind of places that have all-terrain paths for wheelchairs in the grounds. And then,' she added with a grin, 'hard though it is, we force ourselves to head for the tea shop and have a pot of tea with scones, jam and cream.'

'What a tough life,' James said, mirroring her light tone. 'Actually, I'm a bit envious. Tilly's not a fan of scones. When we eat out, she wants fish fingers or sausages and *lots* of ketchup.'

'Fish finger sandwiches,' she said, 'are a thing of joy.'

Clearly he didn't look convinced, because she smiled. 'You might like the foodie version. Sourdough bread, with little gem lettuce and sliced plum tomatoes. Mayo on the bread next to the lettuce, tartare sauce on the fish finger side, all served with some crispy sweet potato fries.'

'Actually, that does sound nice,' he said.

'Let's make it a lunch date,' she said. 'Mum likes fish finger sandwiches, too. Tilly can help me put the sandwiches together, and we'll do a mixture of sweet potato and skinny fries so she can try them both.'

'That'd be lovely, but won't that be a lot of work for you?' he asked, mindful that her free time was limited.

'Not with an air fryer,' she said with a wink. 'It's the best labour-saving device ever. Especially on days when I'm working and pick Mum up from the day-care centre on the way home—that and the slow-cooker mean I don't have to spend huge amounts of time in the kitchen sorting out dinner instead of spending time with Mum.' She gave him a rueful smile. 'And if it's a day when Mum's struggling with cutlery, I can do finger foods so she keeps her independence.'

'Sounds as if you're a brilliant organiser,' he said. 'I had to learn the hard way how to organise a home and cook for a child. Anna and I tended to eat out or get takeaways, and if we had friends round for dinner she'd do the cooking and I'd do all the clearing up.'

'At least you shared the work,' she said.

He raised an eyebrow. 'Your ex expected you to do everything?' OK, so she'd said he was a neurosurgeon; but Jenny's job was demanding, too.

'Looking back, I probably should've been a bit less accommodating,' she said. 'But you can't change the past, so it's a bit pointless dwelling on it.'

'True.' He paused. 'So, apart from visiting gardens, what do you like doing?'

'I used to like walking in the Dales, when Dad was alive,' she said. 'But Mum can't manage uneven ground or steep slopes. It's fine. Like I said, we find places with good accessibility. Places where we can potter around without worrying.' She smiled. 'What about you?'

'Live music, theatre, the cinema,' he said.

'Anna and I made a list of all the hidden corners of London and worked our way through it—everything from a candlelight concert in one of the churches through going on a tour of the bits of the Tube that aren't usually open to the public. And we both loved street food.'

'That sounds good,' she said. 'I used to like the cinema, too. There was a fabulous cinema with comfy sofas in Leeds city centre, and a pop-up cinema during the summer in the grounds of Kirkstall Abbey ruins.'

'Maybe we can go to the cinema, some time,' he said. Maybe holding her hand in the dark would be a little bit less unsettling than holding her hand in the daylight.

'Maybe,' she said. 'And it's always lovely walking by the canal or a river. If I'd lived in London, I would definitely have done the Thames Path.'

'Maybe we can do some walks by the canals locally,' he said. 'Hebden Bridge, or Skipton—if it's dry, your mum's wheelchair would cope just fine with the towpath. And if we see narrowboats going through the locks, it'll be interesting for her and for Tilly.'

Jenny nodded. 'That's a nice idea, as long

as you don't mind us taking up time on your weekend.'

'Of course I don't. Tilly likes you,' he said. 'Plus there will be shops selling ice-cream, which just about beats fish fingers for her.'

She laughed, and he noticed how pretty she was when she laughed, with those stunning blue eyes crinkling at the corners.

'Do you miss London?' she asked.

'I've only been back in Burndale for a couple of weeks, so it's probably not quite long enough for me to miss it,' he said. 'Though I admit I miss how everything was on my doorstep—we lived in Hackney, so we were only half an hour away from the centre of the city. Then again, much as I like Hackney Marshes, nothing quite compares to the Yorkshire Dales.'

'It was a bit of a shock to the system when I first came back to Burndale,' she said. 'Going from small animal work to treating farm animals—it felt like being a rookie again.'

'I'm lucky,' he said, 'because I got to do farm animals in London.'

'How?' she asked.

'One of our clients was a children's farm,' he said. 'A bit bigger than Campbell's Children's Farm—there were sheep and pigs, and a couple of cows. Though I admit it's nice coming back and seeing proper herds in the fields again. I missed that.'

'Talking of herds, is there any news on Reuben Farley's calves?'

'They're doing well. The second lot went down with scour the next day, as he suspected, but because we caught them at an earlier stage they haven't been as sick,' James said.

'And Sir Woofalot?' she asked.

'I talked it over with Mum,' he said. 'She's all for it. She thinks it'll be a good way of teaching Tilly responsibility—making sure the pup has plenty of water, proper feeding times and exercise, as well as grooming and teaching some basic obedience.' He wrinkled his nose. 'Actually, she gave Reuben a ring and went over to see the pups while Tilly was at nursery on Monday. It seems there was another pup left in the litter apart from Sir Woofalot. A black and white one.'

'Which is now your mum's?' Jenny asked.

He nodded ruefully. 'I wish I'd realised how much she missed Treacle. I would've suggested her getting another dog sooner.' He glanced at his watch. 'And I guess we need to make a move. We said we'd only be a couple of hours, and we're a good twenty minutes away from Burndale.'

'I've enjoyed this,' Jenny said.

'Me, too,' James said.

In the car, he turned to her. 'If I kiss you goodnight at your place, it's going to fuel rumours, and I'm not quite sure I'm ready for that just yet. So may I kiss you now?'

She smiled, and stroked his cheek. 'Yes.'

He pressed a kiss into her palm, then drew her hand down and leaned over to kiss her. Just lightly, his lips brushing against hers, a whisper of a kiss.

When she slid her other hand round the back of his neck and kissed him back, it felt as if a slow fuse had lit and heat started shimmering through him. For a moment, he was dizzy. He'd forgotten how it felt to kiss someone, the teasing friction that made you want to get closer and closer.

When he finally broke the kiss, he was shaking. Somehow he had to bring back some lightness, so Jenny didn't realise just how much that kiss had affected him. 'Not bad for a practice kiss,' he said.

'Eight out of ten,' she said.

He nearly suggested a second kiss, to see if he could improve his score, but held himself back. This was Jenny. His colleague. His friend. She was supposed to be *safe*, not putting him into a spin.

'Uh-huh,' he said, and drove them back to Burndale.

'Do you want to come in, just to say hello to Mum?' she asked when they arrived at the cottage.

It would be horribly rude not to, James thought. And Jenny had probably told Tamsin the truth about their 'date'; the deputy headteacher wouldn't gossip, in any case. 'Sure,' he said, following her into the cottage.

Betty was sitting in her chair in the living room, and made to get up.

'You don't need to get up for me, Betty,' he said, going over to her and kissing her on the cheek. 'I need to get back to Tilly, but I just wanted to pop in and say hello to you before I go.'

'It's lovely to see you.' Betty smiled at him. 'Did you both have a nice time?'

'Very nice, thank you,' he said. 'We found a lovely pub near the river, with a garden full of apple trees and lavender.' He smiled at Tamsin. ‘Hi, Tamsin. Nice to see you. Thanks for that list you gave me—it’s very helpful and I’ve got a couple of playdates arranged for Tilly.’

‘Good.’ Tamsin gave him an assessing glance.

Remembering that she was Jenny’s best friend, he decided to drop her a text to reassure her that he and Jenny were friends, and he’d never do anything to hurt her.

‘Would you like to come for lunch on Sunday, James?’ Betty asked. ‘Tilly can read Sooty a story, and I’ll make my apple pie.’

‘That’d be lovely. Thank you, I’d like that,’ James said. ‘Jenny was trying to convince me how nice fish finger sandwiches are.’

‘They’re lovely, the way my Jenny makes them,’ Betty said.

‘It’s a date. Fish finger sandwiches and apple pie,’ James said, and kissed her cheek again. ‘I’ll sort out the time with Jenny. Bye, Tamsin.’

‘I’ll see you out,’ Jenny said. ‘I think you might’ve made Mum’s day,’ she said when they were at the front door.

‘I like your mum, very much,’ James said. ‘She was the secretary at school, wasn’t she? I remember her being very kind to me in Year Seven when someone tackled me a bit too hard on the sports field and I thought I'd broken my wrist.' He rolled his eyes. 'Luckily it was just a bad sprain, but I appreciated her looking after me while I was waiting for Mum to come and pick me up.'

'You'll have to tell her about that,' Jenny said. Her smile held a tinge of sadness. 'It's far back enough for her to still have a clear memory of it.'

'Hey. You're doing a brilliant job, looking after her. She's safe and she's happy.' On impulse, he leaned forward and kissed the tip of her nose. 'And *you* are amazing. I'll see you Sunday. Text me later to tell me what time to be here.'

Jenny watched him drive away.

Holding hands with James on a practice date was one thing. Kissing him in the car had been quite another; it had thrown her that she'd wanted to respond to him so much. Her cheeky marks-out-of-ten comment had been designed for self-preservation, and thankfully he hadn't noticed that he'd put her in such a spin.

And now this completely unexpected, very sweet demonstration of affection had made her gulp. Hard.

She was really going to have to keep a grip on her emotions. It would be very easy to let herself fall for James Madden—and that would make life way too complicated. For both of them.

CHAPTER FIVE

On Sunday, James and Tilly arrived for lunch.

Tilly handed a painting to Jenny with a huge smile. 'It's Sooty. I made it for you.'

'It's gorgeous,' Jenny said. 'I'll put it on my fridge.'

'I was going to bring wine,' James said, 'but I wasn't sure if your mum likes wine, so I brought these.'

He'd bought locally made cordials from the farm shop just outside Burndale: elderflower, and a deep ruby-coloured raspberry and lemon, along with a bottle of sparkling water.

'Thank you, James. That's really thoughtful.' She reached up to kiss his cheek, and there was a hint of a smoulder in his green eyes that sent an answering smoulder through her blood. 'Come in. I'll sort out drinks, and then get the fish fingers going. Tilly, would you like to help me?'

'Yes, please! And I brought my favourite book.'

It was about a black cat rather than a white one, and Jenny smiled. 'We can read it to Sooty together after lunch, if you like.'

She'd already set the table in the dining room; James went to chat with Betty while Jenny tucked a clean tea-towel around Tilly to protect her clothes. Between them, they seasoned the fries with smoked paprika—probably a little more than Jenny would normally have used—and put them in the drawer of the air fryer.

'How high can you count, Tilly?' Jenny asked.

'A hundred,' Tilly said proudly.

It was a while since Jenny had counted with a small child, but she was pretty sure that her brother's children had struggled with the teens at that age, and they'd been bright. 'That many? Wow!'

'Daddy taught me,' Tilly said. 'One, two, skip a few, ninety-nine, one hundred!'

Jenny laughed. 'That's clever! How high do you count at nursery?'

'Twelve. I get a bit muddled after that,' the little girl confessed.

'OK. We need twelve pieces of lettuce, and eight tomatoes,' Jenny said. 'Can you count them out for me?'

Once Tilly had done that and Jenny had washed the vegetables and sliced the tomatoes, they cut the sandwiches together and added the sauces—tomato, of course, for Tilly. When the air fryer beeped, Jenny sent Tilly to call Betty and James to the table.

'I helped,' Tilly said proudly. 'And I counted to a whole hundred.'

Jenny caught James's eye. *Skip a few*, she mouthed, and he grinned back, sharing the joke and enjoying it.

Right then, he looked relaxed and happy, and that grin took her breath away.

Weird how the house felt like a family home again, Jenny thought. Tilly chattering was like the way she and her brother had talked at the dinner table, eager to share what they'd done at school. And Betty was as attentive to Tilly as Jenny's own grandparents had been to her.

Although Betty had burned the apple pie, Jenny tried to avoid serving the worst bits of the crust and covered it with custard. Both James and Tilly declared the pudding delicious; the sheer joy on Betty's face put a lump in Jenny's throat. It was good to see her mother relaxing and unwinding, too. James even got Betty singing snatches of Abba songs and telling stories of the day she'd seen them play in Manchester—something she hadn't talked about in years.

James insisted on doing the washing up, and then Tilly entertained them after lunch, reading her book to Sooty. 'It's all about a greedy cat,' she told Sooty. 'He's a black cat, like you. And, look, that word says "cat",' she said, picking out the word. 'C-a-t,' she spelled, clearly proud that she could read some words.

Although the full text was obviously beyond Tilly's reading ability, she told the story to Sooty with the help of the pictures.

'I've read it to her so often, she knows it almost by heart,' James said very quietly.

And, from the way Tilly was pointing out details in the pictures to Sooty, clearly James had spent time with her rather than rushing it or seeing reading to her as a chore.

Jenny could see from her mother's expression that the little girl had charmed her hugely, too.

Was this what it would've been like, had she had a child with Simon?

Though somehow she couldn't imagine Simon having the same kind of patience with a pre-schooler than James had. He wouldn't have had the same gentleness in his tone when he corrected her on a word.

'Thank you for having me,' Tilly said at the end of the afternoon. 'I've had a lovely time, and so has Daddy.'

And so have we, Jenny thought. James and his daughter had brought a real brightness with them.

'Come and see us any time,' Betty said. 'And I'll dig out my old records, James.'

She'd got rid of the vinyl and the record player years ago, Jenny remembered with a pang. But she'd look on her streaming app and make a special playlist, instead, filling it with the songs her mum could remember.

'I'd like that,' he said with a grin. 'Tell you what, Betty, I think we'd be a good team on a pub music quiz.'

'Let's do it,' Betty said.

'I'll find out when the next one is locally,' James promised.

Jenny saw him to the front door. 'Thank you. Mum's had a lovely afternoon.'

'So have we—haven't we, shrimp?' James asked, sweeping Tilly's mop of curls out of her eyes.

'I'm not a shrimp, I'm a girl.'

'You're a shrimp, and I'm a shark who's going to chase you across the swimming pool this evening,' James teased, and Tilly shrieked with laughter.

'Thank you, Jenny.' He took her hand and squeezed it. 'I enjoyed spending time with you. Maybe we can have dinner sometime this week. Go into Ripon, maybe. Somewhere dressy.'

'Provided you let me pay,' she said.

'We'll argue that later.' He leaned forward and brushed his mouth against hers. 'See you tomorrow,' he said, his voice husky and full of promise.

Jenny stood waving as she watched them go, but mainly because she didn't trust her knees to hold her up after that sweet stolen kiss.

When she went back into the living room, Betty said, 'You've chosen a good one, this time.'

'James is my friend, Mum. My colleague,' Jenny protested.

'He doesn't look at you like a friend,' Betty said. 'I like him. A lot. He's a man with a heart.'

And that was what Jenny was afraid of. Because it would be oh, so easy to let herself fall in love with James Madden and his little girl.

On Monday, James was doing the annual vaccination and health check for a ten-year-old pug called Percy. He noticed that the dog had developed a bit of a pot belly, and his coat was thinning on his flanks.

'Tell me a bit more about Percy, Mr Reynolds,' he said to the owner. 'How's he been, the last six months?'

'I know he's getting a bit fat and his hair's thinning a bit and fading in colours,' Mr Reynolds said, 'but they do say pets look like their owners.' He laughed, patting his own pot belly. 'Seriously, though, he's doing OK. He's maybe eating a bit more than usual, but he's enjoying his walks and he hasn't seemed unwell.'

'Has he been drinking more?'

'And panting a bit, but it's July. Even in England, it can get a bit hot,' Mr Reynolds said.

Which sounded to James as if Mr Reynolds was trying very hard not to notice any changes, worrying that it might be something serious and not being able to face it. 'Have you noticed anything different in the way he's behaved?'

Mr Reynolds thought for a moment. 'I guess he's started wanting to go out for a wee in the middle of the night—but he's ten. Isn't that normal?'

'Not really,' James said.

Mr Reynolds looked anxious. 'Is there something wrong with him, do you think?'

'I think he might have developed a medical condition,' James said, 'but, if it's what I think it is, it's something we can give him medication for and he'll do just fine.'

'Me and Percy, we've been together ten years. He saw me through when I lost my wife,' Mr Reynolds said. 'Without him…' He swallowed hard. 'What's wrong with him?'

'I'd like to do a blood test to check, but I think he might have a bit of a problem with his hormones.'

'He's not going to die?'

James knew he had to phrase this carefully. 'Most dogs with this condition are absolutely fine with medication,' he said. 'May I do a blood test?'

Mr Reynolds' eyes widened as he took in

the possible severity, and he rubbed the top of the pug's head. 'Yes, of course. Whatever you need. And I'll do whatever it takes to make him well. I know I let him have too many treats, and if it's my fault that he's fat…'

'No, it's not your fault,' James said, seeing the anxiety in Mr Reynolds' expression. 'But I agree, it's a good idea to scale the treats back a little bit. Dogs are like humans; as they get older, they don't need quite so many calories.'

He deftly took a blood sample, and then made a fuss of the dog. 'I might need to do a second test, depending on the results of this one. Would you be able to sit in the waiting room for a while, Mr Reynolds, or would you rather come back tomorrow?'

'I'll wait,' Mr Reynolds said. 'I want my boy made better.'

'Thank you,' James said.

He ushered Mr Reynolds and Percy out of the consulting room, then went into the back room where Anu, their veterinary nurse, was assessing the animals who'd come in for a procedure.

'Are you rushed off your feet, Anu, or can you run a couple of blood tests for me, please?' he asked.

'I can run the tests. What do you need?'

'Baseline,' he said, 'and I want to take a close look at liver enzymes, thyroid and cortisol levels.'

'Hormone tests?' Jenny asked, coming into the room and clearly overhearing the last bit.

'I suspect we have a dog with Cushing's,' James said. 'Depending on what the blood results are, I'm planning to do a low-dose dexamethasone suppression test.'

'Which dog?' Jenny asked.

'Percy.'

'Mr Reynolds' pug,' she said. 'I noticed at Percy's last check-up that he'd put on some weight. I was thinking possible thyroid, given Percy's hair was thinning and losing colour, but Cushing's makes sense. Let me know how he gets on. Mr Reynolds lives on the same road as Mum and me, and I see him pass our house every morning on his walk. He always waves to Mum, or stops and has a chat if she's out in the garden. If I can do anything to support him, I will.'

'Will do,' James said.

His next patient was a kitten in for vaccinations and microchipping; by the time they'd finished discussing worming and neutering, the blood tests were done.

'High liver enzymes, low thyroid, and too much cortisol,' James said.

'You're right. That definitely sounds like hyperadrenocorticism,' Jenny said.

He nodded. 'I'm planning a low-dose dexamethasone suppression test.' It meant giving the pug an injection of steroid and taking blood samples over the next eight hours to measure Percy's cortisol levels; dogs with Cushing's found it harder to lower their cortisol levels after an injection.

'If there's a tumour…just to warn you… Mr Reynolds lost his wife to cancer five years ago,' Jenny told him quietly.

'He did say he'd lost his wife, but it felt rude to ask how. Thank you—I'll make sure I'm careful how I phrase it,' James said.

She patted his arm. 'I know you'll be careful. I just thought you could do with a heads-up, in the circumstances.'

James called Mr Reynolds and Percy back into the consulting room, and made a fuss of Percy. 'He's a lovely little fellow.'

'My best boy. Mary and I couldn't have children,' Mr Reynolds said. 'What did the blood test say? Is he going to be all right?'

Remembering what Jenny had told him, James faced Mr Reynolds and smiled in reassurance. 'I think he has a condition called Cushing's disease—it's where the body produces too much cortisol. The good news is that we can give him medication to control the symptoms, so you should find his fur's in better condition, he doesn't drink so much or need to go out in the middle of the night, and he'll lose that little pot belly.'

Mr Reynolds' shoulders sagged. 'Thank God. I thought you were going to tell me…' His voice broke.

'He should be with you for a few years yet,' James reassured him. He drew a quick sketch. 'Now, I've checked Percy's records, so I know he hasn't suffered any allergies or an immune disorder that needed to be treated with steroids, which is a possible cause of Cushing's.'

'So what's causing it?' Mr Reynolds asked.

'It's a hormone imbalance. The pituitary gland is here, at the base of the brain—' James marked it on his sketch '—and it sends a message to the adrenal gland to produce cortisol.' He marked the adrenal gland next to the kidney, and chose his next words very carefully. 'Sometimes there's a benign growth on the adrenal gland or on the pituitary gland, which affects the way the hormones are produced and causes the kind of symptoms Percy's been getting.'

Mr Reynolds paled. 'Percy's got cancer?'

'No,' James said. 'It's usually a benign growth.' And he really, really hoped that this wasn't one of the rare malignant cases.

'Will he need an operation? I mean, he's not a young dog, any more. If he…' Mr Reynolds dragged in a breath. 'I'm sorry I'm making such a fuss.'

'Don't be. You and Percy are family, and it's always a shock to hear when our dogs aren't well,' James reassured him. 'In most cases, there's a growth—and again, I'd like to emphasise they tend to be benign—on the pituitary gland, but sometimes it's on the adrenal gland. I need to see which gland is affected, so I can give Percy the right treatment. The good news is that the treatment's a capsule, and you can disguise it in a treat.'

'Don't you need to send him for a scan?'

James shook his head. 'I could, but apart from the fact scans are expensive it also means he'll need to be sedated to keep him still while he's being scanned. As you said, he's not a young dog, so I'd rather not put him through that if we don't have to. I can find out what I need to know by giving Percy an injection of steroids, then doing a couple more blood tests over the rest of the day. It'll be a lot easier on his system.'

'All right,' Mr Reynolds said. 'Can I wait with him?'

'I know it's hard,' James said gently, 'but it'll be easier if you go home, Mr Reynolds. Percy can settle here and rest without worrying about you. And I promise I'll call you the minute I've got the results, and then he can come home.'

Mr Reynolds bit his lip, then made a last fuss of Percy. 'Be a good boy for Dr Madden, here.'

'He'll be fine,' James said. 'And he'll get to have a fuss made of him by every single person in the practice. We all love dogs and we all want to see Percy his usual well and happy self.'

Mr Reynolds nodded, took a deep breath—clearly he was close to tears—and handed Percy's lead to James. 'I trust you with my boy.'

'We'll take good care of him,' James said.

Once Mr Reynolds had gone, James gave Percy an injection of steroids and found him a comfortable spot in the kennels area. He did the first blood sample an hour later, between seeing patients in morning surgery, then caught up with paperwork over a sandwich at his desk before beginning the afternoon surgery.

With it being summer, it was prime tick season; he had a couple of dogs in with swollen armpits, and taught the owners how to spot ticks and remove them safely with a tick-twisting tool before advising them to add tick and flea treatment to their worming routine. 'It doesn't stop the ticks biting, but if they're infected it kills them before they can spread Lyme disease,' he explained.

One of the dogs had reacted particularly badly to the tick bite, so he prescribed antibiotics. 'Keep an eye on him. If he's still off his food in a week, or if you notice any sign of swollen joints, lethargy or a fever, bring him straight back,' he said. 'I'll have a note on his file, so even if we're busy we'll make sure we see him.'

Jenny was checking a cat who'd needed some teeth out in the back room when James checked his last sample.

'Is that Percy's blood test?' she asked.

'Yes. It's definitely Cushing's, and it's the pituitary involved,' James said.

'So you can treat him with daily capsules

rather than putting him through surgery. Good,' she said. 'I meant to ask—is there any news on your house, yet?'

'Moving day's confirmed for a week on Saturday,' he said. 'Which gives me another two weeks to get the house sorted out ready for Tilly's birthday party. Sophie organised the pre-schooler party for me last year, and I'm ashamed to say I haven't a clue where to start. I've spent the last three nights looking things up on the internet.' He wrinkled his nose. 'So far, I've got a list of party games, and I know I need to make sure that everyone wins a prize or a sticker in every single game, with a slightly bigger prize for the winner. And that needs to be a different person each game, too.'

'That sounds pretty good to me,' she said. 'What are you doing for a birthday cake?'

'Cake-making isn't in my skill set. Luckily, Mum's coming to the rescue. She's borrowing a cake tin in the shape of a number four.'

'Good idea,' she said. 'What's the theme?'

'Theme?' He looked blankly at her. 'Is "pink" a theme?'

'I guess,' she said. 'Or fairies, or unicorns.'

'I did think puppies,' he said. 'But Sir Woofalot isn't coming home until after her party. I thought ten excited four-year-olds might be a bit too much for a pup.'

'Definitely,' she agreed. 'You're having Reuben's pup, then?'

'I asked Ben if he'd mind us having a pup, and he said it was fine. So, yes,' he said. 'Reuben's happy—oh, and his calves are all doing well. The first lot will be out of quarantine in a day or two, and the second lot had a much easier time of it because we caught them early.'

'That's good. It sounds as if everything's coming together for you. That's lovely.'

'Thanks.' And everything in his new life was going to plan. A job he loved with colleagues he really liked, his daughter had settled at nursery and made friends that would help her settle in to school, and they were about to move into their own place and get a pup.

The only thing missing was someone to share it with.

Though Jenny was helping him with that, overcoming his rusty social skills.

'Is Tamsin able to sit with your mum on Thursday night?' he asked.

She nodded. 'Did you want to run birthday stuff past me over dinner?'

'I was thinking more the other project,' he said.

Just for a second, she looked flustered. And then she smiled. 'Sure.' She glanced at her watch. 'You'd better call Mr Reynolds.'

'And Percy will be thrilled to see him,' James agreed. He called Mr Reynolds to tell him Percy was ready to be picked up. When Mr Reynolds came in, his eyes were rimmed with red, as if he'd been crying with relief.

'The good news is, we can treat Percy with a capsule once a day to reduce the production of cortisol, and it will help his symptoms,' James said. 'You need to give him the capsule whole, with a meal, so I'd suggest disguising it in a treat before you give him his dinner.'

'I will,' Mr Reynolds said.

'You might find the hair loss gets a little bit worse before it improves,' James warned, 'but you should start to see a difference in a couple of weeks. I've printed off a leaflet for you that explains everything, but ring me if you're the slightest bit worried.'

'What if I forget to give him a dose?' Mr Reynolds asked.

'Then you just wait to give him his normal

dose, the next day—don't give him double,' James said. 'Most dogs tolerate the treatment just fine, but if Percy's sick or has diarrhoea, bring him straight back to us. I'd like to see him once a week for the next three weeks, to see how he gets on, and then we can go a bit longer in between visits. But I promise we'll keep a good eye on him, Mr Reynolds.'

'Thank you,' Mr Reynolds said, shaking his hand.

It was good to be able to help with someone's worries and bring a bit of sunshine into their life, James thought. Which was what Jenny was doing for him. And maybe he could find a way to do that for her, too.

CHAPTER SIX

DINNER.

This wasn't just a meal with a friend, where it didn't matter what she wore. It was a practice date. One that made Jenny realise just how rusty she was when it came to dating. Thankfully her favourite little black dress still fitted, and it was a classic style that wouldn't look dated. She made an effort to style her hair into soft waves, instead of pulling it back into a scrunchie, the way she normally wore it, and dredged out a pair of high heels. A touch of lipstick and mascara, and she was ready.

'You look lovely,' Betty said. 'Are you going out with James?'

'We're just friends, Mum,' Jenny said. Explaining the situation would be too complicated, and her mum would worry. 'We're simply having a nice time together, as colleagues, relaxing after work.'

'Hmm. Is Archer going as well?' Betty said.

'He can't make it tonight,' Jenny fibbed, feeling guilty that they hadn't asked Archer.

'Well, I like James.'

'So do I. As a *friend*,' Jenny emphasised. Secretly, she was beginning to suspect that she liked him as a little bit more than a friend, but she didn't have the headspace to work it out.

Tamsin came over with a playlist on her phone, some home-made cheese shortbread and a bottle of a non-alcoholic cocktail to share with Betty; then, at precisely seven, the doorbell rang.

James was wearing a dark blue suit with a white shirt and copper-coloured tie, and he didn't look like the slightly scruffy but professional colleague she was used to.

'You look lovely,' he said.

'Thank you—so do you,' she said, feeling oddly shy.

After he'd exchanged a few words with Betty and Tamsin, James drove Jenny to the foodie pub, two villages away, where he'd booked a table.

'I can't remember the last time I went out to dinner like this,' he said. 'I'm more used to places that do the kind of food Tilly likes.'

And Jenny wasn't used to going out to dinner at all, any more. She glanced down the menu and chuckled. 'You can bring her here, you know—they offer cod goujons.'

'Ah, but they're *posh* fish fingers,' he said, laughing back.

'The menu's fabulous. It's really hard to choose,' she said. In the end, she chose salmon served with Tenderstem broccoli, asparagus, courgettes and new potatoes, while James plumped for pie and mash with greens.

'That's so blokey,' she said with a grin.

'It's a treat,' he corrected. 'Because I'd never cook pie and mash for myself.'

'I was under the impression,' she said, 'that you cooked.'

'I can shove something on a tray in the oven and forget about it for thirty minutes,' he said, 'and I think anyone can manage vegetables with an electric steamer. But that doesn't really count as cooking, does it?'

'Not really,' she agreed.

'Mum taught me a few basics before I went to university,' he said, 'but I was never really interested in cooking. Some of my friends could woo their girlfriends with home-made lasagne, but mine would get cheese on toast if they were lucky. Or pasta mixed with pesto.'

'Maybe we should put the practice dating on hold and do some cookery lessons instead, once you've moved into the cottage,' she said. 'Tilly can join in.'

'A small child and a sharp knife?' He looked horrified.

'A small child, a wooden spoon and a mixing bowl,' she corrected.

'If you're really offering, then, yes, please,' he said. 'Just don't let on to my mum quite how hopeless I am.'

'It'll be our secret. And Tilly's and Mum's,' she added.

'What you were saying about putting the practice dating on hold.' James looked at her. 'You're struggling as hard as I am with this situation, aren't you?'

'It's just…odd,' she admitted. 'At work, you and I talk about our patients. In Burndale, we have Tilly and my mum with us. But here…' It *felt* like a real date, despite their protests that it wasn't. And that made her insides feel as if they'd done an anatomically impossible backflip.

'If it makes you feel better,' James said, 'I'm relieved that you're finding it difficult. That means I'm not alone.'

Which meant that she wasn't alone, either.

But the conversation stalled again, and they just looked at each other.

In the end, James laughed. 'You know what?' He picked up his phone. 'I know it's rude to check my phone when we're out, but we're both very obviously stuck on this. Let's ask the internet what you do on a first date.'

They'd agreed on the way to the pub to keep their phones on the table, face down, in case of emergencies—even though they knew Tilly would be perfectly fine with James's mum and her own mother would be fine with Tamsin, they both wanted the comfort of knowing that they were only a phone call away if there was a problem.

'Questions to ask your first date. Are you an early bird or a night owl?' James read. 'Oh, wait—this is a good one. Are you a cat person or a dog person?'

Jenny laughed. 'As vets, we're both—and both.'

'Hobbies—right, we both have time for them. Not.' He rolled his eyes.

'Actually, that's a good one. Archer makes time for his sky-watching. What would you do, if you had the time?' she asked.

'Visit every single castle in Yorkshire, and

make sure I get the best view from the highest point,' he said. 'You?'

'Actually, that's not so far off what I do at weekends,' she said. 'Mum and I tend to visit the gardens rather than the stately homes or ruined castles—unless they've got good accessibility.'

'And ruins, by definition, don't,' he said. 'But we could make it work. Take it in turns to explore the inaccessible bits while the other one eats ice cream in the tea shop with Tilly and your mum.'

'Let's add that to our list,' she said. 'What else?'

'To add to our list?' he asked.

She shook her head. 'We're not discussing the safe stuff. What else would you do, if you had the time?'

'Travel,' he said. 'Anna and I used to love city breaks. We'd do maybe one or two of the top ten tourist attractions in the city, but then we'd wander off in the back streets and see what we could find.'

'Living in the city, Simon and I always headed for the countryside rather than the city,' Jenny said. 'I think my favourite break was in Iceland. We got to see a geyser, loads of waterfalls—that was fabulous, because there were rainbows everywhere, and the best one we actually got to stand behind the waterfall and look out. And there's this amazing beach that had hexagonal columns of basalt. I loved that—the contrast between the turquoise sea and the black sandy beach.'

'It sounds great,' he said. 'I've always wanted to do the coast-to-coast walk from Whitehaven to Whitby. But I couldn't possibly expect Tilly's little legs to keep up on something like that.'

'We could do bits of the walk, in the Dales,' she said.

He smiled. 'We could—but if we start planning things like that, making a list of the parts that'd be accessible for your mum and Tilly, it takes us out of dating territory.' He glanced at his phone. 'Back to the list of questions. Is Iceland your favourite travel memory?'

'Yes, because the landscape's so different,' she said. 'I loved the waterfalls, and then the little hot pot spa pools—there seemed to be one in every town.'

'Did you see the Northern Lights?' he asked.

'We went in summer, so we saw the midnight sun instead,' she said. 'It was a real experience, walking by the harbour in Reykjavik at midnight and watching the sun just about setting over the sea.'

'I'd like to see that, one day,' he said. 'And the Northern Lights. If we could all have time off together, I'm pretty sure Archer would be up for a Burnham Veterinary Surgery bonding trip to see the Northern Lights.'

'He would,' Jenny agreed. 'They're on my bucket list, too. But they've been seen in Yorkshire. I'm pretty sure Archer gets text alerts or something about potential aurora nights.'

'Maybe we can have a team Northern Lights-spotting outing, with him in charge, next time he gets an alert,' James said with a smile.

'What's your favourite travel memory?' Jenny asked.

'Venice,' he said immediately. 'Dancing in St Mark's Square on a late spring evening when hardly anyone was about. We put one earphone in each and played something soppy on my phone.'

'Simon wasn't really one for dancing,' Jenny said, feeling a twinge of envy.

The relationship she'd had with Simon sounded like a shadow of what James and Anna had had. And she could really see James's problem. He clearly loved Anna so deeply that, despite him saying he wanted and needed to move on, she wasn't sure he'd be able to. How would any woman be able to measure up to memories like those?

'If you like dancing,' he said, 'we can find somewhere to dance.'

The idea of having a slow dance with James, under the lights of the stars and the moon, made a shiver of anticipation run down her spine. What would it feel like to be in his arms? Cradled close, swaying together to a slow beat…

But it wasn't going to happen, and she couldn't afford to let herself dream about it. 'I'm not really one for clubbing. What's the next question on your list?' she asked.

'What matters to you?' he asked. 'But I know that. Your mum and your job. Just as you know my answer.'

'Tilly and your job,' she said. 'Next?'

He scanned the list. 'An awful lot of them are things we already know about each other. This isn't helping.' He flicked to another page. 'Oh, and here are topics not to talk about. Wait for it: family, parents and exes.' He groaned. 'Oh, dear.'

She laughed. 'We've done just about all of those.'

'According to this, we should keep conversation light and unpressured. Casual chit-chat.'

'Which would bore you silly,' Jenny said.

'And you,' James said.

'What's your idea of the perfect romantic day?' she asked after their food had arrived.

'It'd be spring,' he said. 'Breakfast on the coast, somewhere we can see the sunrise—preferably with a bacon sandwich, and a mug of tea you can stand your spoon up in. Then a walk on the beach, to see if we can find fossils. Heading out through the Dales, along one of the back roads where you see lambs skipping about in the fields and new calves all wobbly on their legs. Lunch in a little old pub somewhere—and, because we'd be walking it off, that'd involve Yorkshire pudding, locally produced sausages and cauliflower cheese. A walk round a ruined castle, watching the sun set somewhere, and then dinner somewhere like this followed by dancing under the stars.'

It sounded like her idea of the perfect romantic day, too. Which was really unsettling, because now she could imagine sharing something like that with James, and it made butterflies rampage in her tummy.

'You?' he asked.

She thought about making up something exotic, but he already knew her so well that he'd spot at once that it was a fib. 'That'd work for me, too,' she said. 'Though I'll switch that tea for good coffee, and there had better be scones with cream and jam in the afternoon. Actually, I think I'd start in the Dales, going via a waterfall or two, and head towards the coast. Then the dancing after dinner could be barefoot on the beach, seeing the moon make a path on the sea.'

'That,' he said, 'sounds even better than my version.'

The possibility hung in the air between them.

A romantic day. Just the two of them. Nothing to worry about other than holding hands, having fun, dancing under the stars and kissing in the moonlight.

Jenny was shocked to realise that she was actually leaning slightly towards him, as if they were already together on that date. Which was crazy, because no way did either of their lives have room for a day like that. 'It's fun to dream,' she said instead, trying to get the lightness back between them instead of the sudden tension. 'And now you've got your benchmark for your dates. On the first day, you ask her about her idea of a perfect romantic date. If it doesn't match yours, then maybe you're not suited.'

Though she didn't dare meet his eyes, in case he could see what she had a nasty feeling might be written in hers.

The following weekend, James spent Saturday moving into the cottage. He'd put most of his personal things plus his furniture into storage; he'd hired a removals company to bring it to the cottage, and Archer, his parents and his sister were helping him to move and unpack.

Jenny had suggested that Tilly could spend moving day with her and Betty, so James wouldn't have to worry about his daughter while he was getting the house straight.

'I can't ask you to do that. That's above and beyond friendship,' he said.

'It's what friends do for each other,' she contradicted. 'Anyway, you're not asking me. I'm offering. And I'd really like you to say yes, because Mum's looking forward to fish fingers for lunch, and doing a bit of singing with Tilly and playing games with her.'

He gave in gratefully. 'Thank you,' he said. 'It's really appreciated.'

The cottage was typical for the area: stone, with a slate roof and a front garden bursting with old-fashioned cottage garden flowers that scented the air. There were three good-sized bedrooms: one for himself, one for Tilly and one for guests. He took Tilly to the house first, to show her where they were going to live, and let her choose which bedroom she wanted before dropping her off at Jenny's. Predictably, she chose the one with pink curtains that overlooked the garden and was next to his.

His parents, his sister and Archer arrived and helped him move all the furniture and boxes, as well as putting Tilly's new princess bed together with its filmy pale pink drapes.

'She'll be thrilled to bits when she sees that,' his mum said with a smile.

James had bought a new bed for himself, too, wanting a new start. He'd given the bed he'd shared with Anna to a women's refuge, knowing his wife would've approved thoroughly of his decision.

They worked solidly throughout the day, only stopping briefly for the bacon rolls and Yorkshire parkin James had ordered from

Sally at the café—and which Sally had insisted on delivering herself.

'You OK?' James's mum asked.

He nodded. 'It's just a bit…strange. It's home, but not home at the same time.'

She gave him a hug. 'I know you loved Anna, but she'd be the first person to tell you to move on. And Jenny's lovely. She was so kind to me when we had to say goodbye to Treacle. She gave me all the time I needed to be with him on that last morning, let me weep all over her and even made me a cup of tea.' She paused. 'Anna would've liked her very much.'

There was a lump in his throat. James agreed. Anna would've liked Jenny.

But.

'Jenny's my friend.'

'I know, love, but all I want is for you to be happy. I'm just trying to say, I can't see any barriers to making your friendship something more.' She hugged him again. 'Our Tilly's taken a real shine to her.'

Which was a relief, but he knew it wasn't a given that Jenny would want to make a family with them. 'We're friends,' James insisted.

But when he'd gone out to dinner with Jenny and talked about their perfect romantic day, they'd been really in tune. They'd wanted the same things. She'd even told him to use it as a benchmark when he started dating. Did that mean she'd use their shared idea of a perfect romantic day as a benchmark, too? Would she consider dating him for real, despite the fact that he came as a package?

Though Jenny had her own complications to deal with. James wasn't entirely sure whether she was still quietly in love with her ex and using her mum's illness as an excuse not to date anyone. The last thing he wanted was to scare her off.

'Speaking of Jenny, she's had Tilly all day. I'd better call her and let her know I can pick Tilly up,' he said, and took his phone out of his pocket.

Jenny answered quickly. 'Hi, James. How's the moving?'

'All done,' he said. 'I can come and collect Tilly now.'

'I have a better idea,' she said. 'Why don't I bring Tilly and Mum, and stop at the fish and chip shop on the way? I can pick up an order for everyone,' she said, 'and we can celebrate your new house. And we can eat from the wrappers, so you're not left with a pile of washing up.'

She really did think of everything. 'That would be wonderful,' James said. 'Thank you. But only on condition that you tell me how much it is, so I can transfer the money to you. I really think I should be the one treating everyone.'

'We'll sort it out later,' Jenny said. 'Go and ask everyone what they want, and text me the order. See you in a bit.'

James checked with his family and Archer, and texted the order to Jenny.

A few minutes later, Jenny arrived with her mum, Tilly and the food.

'I had a really nice day, Daddy,' Tilly said. 'I drawed you a picture of Sooty, and me and Betty read to Sooty, and we did singing, and we made fairy cakes with sprinkles.'

'Otherwise known as pudding—we brought them over,' Jenny said with a smile, and handed him a carrier bag containing two bottles of Prosecco and two bottles of sparkling elderflower cordial. 'Plus some bubbles to celebrate your new house, including the non-alcoholic version.'

'You,' James said, meaning it, 'are a marvel.'

She shrugged it off, but he could see the sparkle in her eyes and the heightened colour in her cheeks.

'I stirred everything,' Tilly said when everyone had finished their fish and chips and Jenny had brought out the tin of cakes, 'and I put it in the cake cases, and Jenny put it in the oven. And then I stirred the icing and put it on top with the sprinkles. Lots and lots and lots of sprinkles.'

'They're perfect,' James's mother said, giving her a kiss.

'Do you want to come and see your room, Tilly?' James asked.

Tilly nodded with excitement and clutched Jenny's hand. 'Jenny, will you come and see my room, too?'

Jenny was touched that the little girl wanted her to see the room; but, at the same time, maybe this particular moment should be for just James. She glanced at him for guidance, and he smiled at her. 'Come and have a look round,' he said.

'You've all done wonders. I was expecting to see lots of boxes, still,' she said.

He laughed. 'I've barely touched my books, but Tilly's room is done.'

'Daddy! You made me a real princess bed! A pink one!' Tilly squealed in delight as she opened the door. 'I love it!'

There were fairy lights twirling round the columns at the corners of the bed, too, and round the fireplace.

'And you put Mummy's picture up,' she said, looking happy.

Of course Jenny couldn't resist glancing at the framed photograph on the mantelpiece over the fireplace.

Anna was stunningly beautiful, with the same long dark curls and huge brown eyes as Tilly, and it looked as if Tilly had inherited her mother's bone structure, too. But it wasn't just that Anna was beautiful on the outside: her personality shone through the photograph, the kind of smile that told you she was the sort who loved life and made everyone else's life just that bit brighter for being in it.

How much both James and Tilly had lost.

Jenny's heart ached for them. 'Your mummy looks lovely,' she said. 'She's got a beautiful smile. And she's so like you.'

Tilly looked pleased. 'My other nanna says I'm her spitting image. And my nanna here says I'm as sweet as my mummy was.' She smiled. 'You're lovely, too, Jenny. You're all smiley and nice.'

'Thank you, sweetheart.' Jenny didn't dare look at James. It would be just too awkward. She wasn't in competition with Anna and she didn't want him to feel that she was trying to take Anna's place. 'You have a pretty view over the garden.'

The little girl nodded. 'That's where Sir Woofalot and me are going to play, when I get my puppy. One day,' she added wistfully.

This time, Jenny did look at James; behind Tilly's back, he winked at her and put his finger to his lips in a 'shh' signal. Clearly the puppy was going to stay a secret for now—as was her grandmother's new pup.

'We'd better go down and join the others,' Jenny said. 'Your room's lovely, Tilly.'

When they went back downstairs, Jenny could see that her mum was getting tired. 'We need to get back,' she said with a smile. 'Catch you on Monday at work, James. Bye, Tilly!' She took her leave of the rest of James's family and Archer, and drove Betty home.

She still wasn't sure if James was really ready to move on.

And, if he was—would it be with her? Or would he be better off with someone who had fewer complications?

CHAPTER SEVEN

PERCY THE PUG came in for a check-up, the following week. 'He's doing really well,' James reassured Mr Reynolds, his owner. 'He'll be on the daily treatment for the rest of his life, and we'll do regular checks and blood tests to keep an eye on him.'

'He's definitely more his old self—not panting so much, and not hungry all the time. That little pot belly's starting to go,' Mr Reynolds said.

'I'm really glad,' James said.

He caught up with Jenny at lunchtime. 'Good news—Percy the pug came in for a check-up and he's responding to his meds. I'm happy with the blood test I did today.'

'Oh, that's fabulous,' Jenny said. 'I bet Mr Reynolds is relieved.'

'I'm glad I've caught you both,' Archer said, walking into the staff room. 'Just letting you know that we have a vacancy for a part-time vet nurse—Anu handed her notice in yesterday morning. She wants to move to Hull with her boyfriend.'

'I had a feeling that might be on the cards,' Jenny said. 'We'll miss her—she's so good with the owners as well as their pets.'

'She wants to go earlier rather than stay to work out her notice,' Archer said.

'Can you get hold of a locum so she can go?' James asked.

'Better than that,' Archer said. 'I've got someone locally who's happy to step in for a little while.' His ears went very pink again. 'Halley. She…um…it'll be just for a few months.'

'And will she stay on when her maternity leave ends?' Jenny asked very gently.

He sighed. 'The whole village is talking about it, aren't they?'

'About the fact that she's pregnant and you're moving in together?' James asked. 'I've heard a mention or two. But it's not gossip, Arch. Everyone's really thrilled for you both.' He clapped a hand on Archer's shoulder. 'I remember you liked her years ago, when we were at school. I couldn't be happier for you.' He left it unspoken, but was pretty sure that his best friend would be able to read it in his eyes: after all the sadness he'd been through with Amy, Archer deserved a break.

Archer looked at them. 'As we've brought up village gossip, I'm not the only one they're talking about. Is there anything you want to tell me?'

'I need a mum for Tilly. I haven't dated for ten years—so I need a female friend to bring me up to speed on the dating front, which is where Jenny comes in,' James said, not looking at Jenny.

'And, with Mum to look after, I just don't have the headspace for a proper relationship right now,' Jenny said. 'So being James's dating coach works for me. It means I get to have some fun without the pressure, and Mum stops worrying that she's wrecked my social life—which of course she hasn't, but she's worried anyway.'

This time, James did look at Jenny, and was relieved to see her smiling. 'Though it's a shame we're being talked about. I thought we'd managed to avoid people seeing us together.'

'By going for a drink in a pub that's only a couple of villages away? I think you'd have to go to the other side of the North York Moors before you'd be off the Burndale gossip radar,' Archer said ruefully.

'Jenny and I are just good friends—and colleagues,' James said.

'Absolutely,' Jenny agreed.

'Hmm.' Archer didn't look entirely convinced. 'Well, anyway, I just wanted to let you know about Halley joining us.'

'Was he trying to deflect what's going on between him and Halley, or are people *really* talking about us?' James asked when Archer had left.

'They're probably gossiping,' Jenny said. 'But you know what it's like in a small village. Blink and they'll be talking about something else. How are the plans coming on for Tilly's birthday?'

'We've invited all the girls she's friends with at nursery, so if they all come there will be about ten of them, including Tilly,' he said. 'I've come up with a menu Mum agrees with—cream cheese sandwiches cut into stars, cocktail sausages, cherry tomatoes, carrot sticks, pitta chips and hummus, and then we're doing a "build your own sundae" with ice cream, strawberry slices, squirty cream in a can, sprinkles and a chocolate flake.'

'That sounds messy, but fun,' she said. 'What about a birthday cake?'

'Mum's making the cake for me and icing it.' He grinned. 'Guess what colour it's going to be?'

'Let me think—oh—could it possibly be a shade of flamingo, cerise or carnation?' she asked, laughing back.

'Certainly is,' he said. 'I need to put together some goodie bags. Going by what Tilly likes, I was thinking bubbles, coloured pencils and a colouring book, some playdough and a cutter, and maybe a pack of flower seeds. And I can pack them in pink paper carrier bags.'

'Sounds good,' she said. 'You've really got this sorted.'

'Once I stopped panicking and made a few lists, it got a bit easier,' he admitted.

'Good.' She smiled at him.

'Are you busy Thursday evening?' he asked. 'For…um…project planning? I thought we could go to Aysgarth and have a walk, then a picnic by the falls.'

'That'd be lovely,' she agreed.

Thursday evening was perfect weather for a walk, warm enough not to need a jacket but not humid. James's mum was babysitting

Tilly and Jenny's neighbour Sheila was keeping Betty company. Jenny had put together a picnic, and he drove them out to Aysgarth.

The falls were a popular tourist spot, but it tended to be busier in the daytime and quieter in the evening, so they had no trouble parking. James thoroughly enjoyed wandering along the bank of the River Ure with Jenny until they reached the broad limestone steps of the waterfall.

Although he hadn't intended to hold her hand, his fingers brushed against hers several times and it felt natural to link his fingers through hers. She didn't pull away, and James told himself that this was just how it would be on a date with a stranger…except somehow he rather doubted it, because he couldn't imagine holding hands with anyone else. It was *Jenny's* hand he wanted to hold.

But he also didn't want to scare her away, so he didn't draw attention to the fact that they were holding hands.

They kept the conversation light, and he took several photographs of the two of them with the waterfalls in the background, as well as some of the round holes in the rock made by spinning water over the years, and a video of the water gushing over the limestone.

'Tilly would love this. We need to do this again in the spring,' Jenny said. 'Even better if we do it a day or so after there's been a lot of rain, so we get to see the waterfalls in full spate. And spring means the primroses and bluebells will be out.'

If she wanted to make plans for months in the future, that was fine by him. 'Great idea,' he said.

He enjoyed the picnic, too, once he'd helped Jenny spread the picnic rug on the ground and unpack the basket. She'd packed fresh bread, a large chunk of crumbly Wensleydale, sweet plum tomatoes and home-made sausage rolls spiced with chili jam, followed by raspberries and Greek yogurt and some sticky Yorkshire parkin he guessed she'd made herself.

'This was perfect,' he said, when she'd packed everything away in the picnic basket.

'Thank you.' She smiled at him.

He took a risk. 'Or almost perfect. There's one more thing that would make this perfect.'

Her blue eyes went wide. 'What?'

'Dance with me? I'm a bit out of practice, but I'll try not to bruise your toes.' He stood up and held his hand out to her. When she took his hand, he drew her to her feet, then took a wireless earbud from his pocket and handed it to her. Once she'd put it into her ear and he'd switched on his own earbud, he started playing the music he'd prepared earlier in the week.

'Just so you know,' he said quietly, 'this isn't what I danced to in Venice with Anna. This one's a song that makes me think of you.'

As soon as Jenny heard the opening notes, she recognised One Direction's 'What Makes You Beautiful'.

This song made him think of her? A song about someone who didn't know how beautiful she was?

The idea made her catch her breath. He'd just strayed well over the lines of 'practice date' territory. She ought to take a step backwards, make some kind of excuse and not dance with him.

But, for the life of her, she couldn't resist the temptation to be in his arms.

She moved closer, resting her head on his shoulder and swaying with him to the beat of the music. It was just the two of them, dancing on the grass by the river, with the rush of the river acting as a backbeat for the music playing in one ear.

He followed up the song with a ballad from

Take That, Eva Cassidy's version of 'Fields of Gold', and Norah Jones—the sweetest, most romantic music she knew. He'd really put some thought and effort into this, and she appreciated it.

When he shifted slightly so his cheek was next to hers, how could she resist kissing the corner of his mouth? And, when he moved a little closer and kissed the corner of her mouth, how could she not respond and move a little closer, until they were really kissing?

The way he kissed her drove every coherent thought out of her head. With her eyes closed, all she was aware of was the warmth of his arms around her, the way his heart thudded against her and the sweetness of his mouth moving against hers.

When James finally broke the kiss, there was a huge slash of colour across his cheeks, and his pupils were so huge that his green eyes looked almost black.

'Sorry,' he said. 'I know I've crossed a line.'

'You have. But I was with you all the way,' she admitted.

'So what do we do now?' he asked.

'I don't know.' She dragged in a breath. 'With Mum's health, I just don't have the space in my life for anything more than friendship.'

'I understand.' He stroked her cheek. 'If I'm completely honest, I don't really have space in my life, either. Not with Tilly. But, if I did, I'd want to share that space with you.'

'Same for me,' she admitted. 'I know you're looking for a mum for Tilly, and I don't want to get in the way.'

'Maybe,' he said, 'we can just avoid making a decision for now.'

'Leaving us both in limbo?' That would be the worst of all worlds, not knowing where they stood or what either of them wanted.

'No. I mean giving us both space to decide what we want,' he said. 'I know I said I want a mum for Tilly, but I don't have to rush into finding a partner. Neither do you.'

'So, what? We stick to being just good friends?'

'Or maybe,' he said, 'we just take the pressure off and see what happens. See where this thing between us goes. I like you, Jenny, and I think you like me.'

She did.

Very much.

But, if it went wrong, the way she'd got it wrong before with Simon, this time there would be collateral damage, and that wasn't fair. Tilly and Betty didn't deserve to be hurt. 'We can't be selfish about this.'

'I know. But let's not overthink things. Maybe there's a way to get what's best for all of us. I know you're a planner, but we don't need to work it out right this very second.' He leaned forward and kissed the tip of her nose, and the cherishing gesture nearly undid her.

'Right now, we both need to be getting back,' he said. 'Even though I'd like to dance with you properly in the moonlight.'

'Next to a waterfall's probably not the best place to do that,' she said, her voice slightly shaky. 'If we trip over a root or an awkward bit of stone…'

'We'll end up falling in. You're right,' he said. 'We need a flat, sandy beach or a lawn.'

She could imagine dancing with him under the light of the moon, to the sound of the waves swooshing onto the shore or the sweet harmony of a nightingale or a robin singing in the garden, and it made her weak at the knees.

He folded the rug, tucked it into the top of the picnic basket, and carried it in one hand while he slid his other arm round Jenny's waist.

'James,' she asked, 'is this a good idea?'

'Yes,' he said. 'I've just kissed you until my common sense went over the edge with the waterfall. *And*,' he added, 'you kissed me back. So I reckon holding each other close is a good idea.'

It was also a dangerous one. But she couldn't for the life of her think of a reasonable argument. Probably, she admitted silently, because she liked having his arm round her.

Back at the car, he put the basket and picnic blanket into the back of his car and she gave him back his earbud.

'How long did it take you to make that playlist?' she asked.

'Quite a while,' he said. 'I tried to find some really recent stuff, so it wouldn't make you think of Simon or me think of Anna—but I think I must be officially heading for middle age, because none of the chart stuff worked for me.'

She grinned. 'You're thirty-seven and I'm two years younger. We don't *quite* count as middle-aged.'

'Yeah, well. I played it safe and went for the stuff that was around when we were students,' he said.

'I liked it,' she said. 'Dancing to slow songs

from the kind of artists I'd sing to in the car when I'm out on the way to a client.'

'And it's a little more fun than singing "Old MacDonald Had a Farm" for the gazillionth time,' he said.

'E-I-E-I-O,' she retorted, and he laughed.

And that made things easy between them again, breaking the tension. It stopped Jenny wondering what would happen if she slid her arms round his neck and kissed him again—because right now they couldn't take this anywhere and they'd simply have to stop. It made James safe again, which she was pretty sure was a good thing.

As usual, when he dropped Jenny home, James went indoors with her to say hello to her mum and their neighbour Sheila. He showed them the video he'd taken of the waterfall.

'I'd love to see the falls again,' Betty said wistfully. 'But I don't think I'd manage to walk there now.'

'I'll find a wheelchair-accessible waterfall in the Dales and take you,' he promised, and Jenny knew he'd keep that promise. Because James Madden *cared.*

She didn't see him over the weekend, though she knew he'd be up to his eyes organising Tilly's birthday for the following weekend. But it warmed her that he made the time to text her with a link to the official web page for Cotter Falls.

There's a path for pushchairs and wheelchairs. Maybe we can all go there for a walk, the weekend after Tilly's birthday?

That would be lovely, she replied.

And you and Betty are very welcome to come to Tilly's birthday party next Saturday, if you're not busy and don't mind ten lively pre-schoolers running round. My parents and my sister will be here, too. Starts at three, but come at twelve and have lunch with us.

Jenny was pretty sure he was inviting her as his friend and colleague. And that meant she could accept the invitation, with pleasure.

On Tuesday morning, James was called out to see three orphaned lambs.

'I'm glad you're here while the kids are out,' Joanne Foster said. 'If I'm right, this is going to break their hearts.'

The Fosters had been farming longer than

James had been a vet, so he was pretty sure Joanne's assessment of her lambs was right. 'Talk me through it,' James said.

'We had three orphans, this year—one of them, the mum rejected her; another of the ewes just didn't have enough milk for her lamb; and we lost the mum of the third one and I couldn't get any of the other ewes to take the lamb on,' Joanne explained. 'We've been bottle-feeding the three of them on formula. The kids have been doing feeds before school, after school and just before bed, I've done the midday feeds, and the lambs were doing well. We had a pen in the barn for them with nice fresh bedding and a heater, and they've had plenty of cuddles and socialisation because the kids' friends have all wanted to come and spend time here.'

'Did any of the lambs get colostrum?' James asked. This was the fluid that the ewes produced just before their milk came in, and was full of important antibodies and minerals.

She nodded. 'The biggest one did—the one whose mum didn't have enough milk.'

'It might be worth taking a tiny bit of colostrum from each ewe and freezing it in an ice cube tray, in future,' James said, 'in case you need it later in the lambing season.'

'I wish we'd done that this year,' Joanne said. 'Because I think our little orphans have got coccidiosis.'

Coccidia was a single-celled parasite that infected nearly all lambs and peaked when they started to eat grass at the age of five to six weeks. Only two of the eleven different types of coccidia were a problem, and they tended to affect lambs with lowered immunity—often bottle-fed lambs who hadn't had the antibodies in their mother's milk to protect them. The parasites damaged the lining of the lamb's gut so the lambs didn't get enough nutrition from their milk.

'You've noticed weight loss and scouring?' James asked.

Joanne nodded. 'And, if you pop your finger in their mouth, they're cold.'

James knew the old shepherd's trick; with young lambs, if the mouth was warm they were OK, but if it was cold they needed more calories.

'How are the rest of your lambs doing?' he asked.

'Fine,' she said. 'We make sure the creep feeders are moved every day to prevent the build-up of infection.' Creep feeders were feeders that the lambs could access easily but the grown sheep couldn't. 'We've grazed the late lambs on different pasture to the early lambs, and there's a low density of lambs.'

'Sounds like perfect hygiene to me,' James said, 'though I think it'll be a good idea to give all the lambs oral drench to combat the infection.'

'You're right,' she said. 'I'll get some in.'

When James saw the orphan lambs in their pen in the barn, it was clear that one of them was really poorly; she was bleeding slightly from the mouth.

'Jo, I'm sorry. I could treat her, but I'm pretty sure this little one's not going to make it and we need to do the kind thing,' he said.

She blinked away tears. 'Sorry. I've been around sheep all my life. I should be used to this.'

James gave her a hug. 'Nobody ever gets used to this. It's the bit of my job I really hate. I can give the other two antibiotics, and they should pull through. But this little one's too poorly.'

'She wasn't bleeding when I called you,' Joanne said. 'I'd never let any of my sheep suffer.'

'I know you wouldn't.'

'James—I can't bear the usual way of euthanising lambs. Not for my little orphan girl,' she said quietly.

He nodded. 'I'll use an injection so she just goes to sleep. Can you weigh her for me so I can get the right dose?'

'Yes,' she said, her voice breaking.

He sorted out the antibiotics for the two bigger lambs; Joanne weighed the littlest one, then sat on the straw with the lamb on her lap.

'She's six kilos,' she said.

'All right.' James prepared the injection and euthanised the lamb while Jo held her close.

'My poor little Buffy,' Joanne said, stroking the lamb while tears slid down her cheeks. 'Dreadful names the kids gave them. Fluffy, Buffy and Puffy.' She stroked the lamb. 'They've been doing video diaries about them at school. They'll be in bits when I break the news to them.'

Just like Joanne herself was in bits, now. Whoever said that farmers were hard-hearted, James thought, didn't have a clue. Even though death was part of every flock cycle, every death was felt—and orphan lambs were always mourned hardest.

His mood was still sombre by the time he got back to the practice.

'Are you OK, James?' Halley asked when he walked into the staff kitchen.

'No. Jo Foster's orphaned lambs have coccidiosis and the littlest one didn't make it,' he said. 'She's really upset, and her kids will be devastated when they get home and learn what's happened.'

Jenny, overhearing the last bit, came over and gave him a brief hug. 'Sounds like a rough morning. I'll stick the kettle on.'

'Mum was going to have one of the lambs at the Children's Farm,' Halley said. 'I'll let her know what's happened. She'll give Jo a ring.'

'I think she needs a listening ear, right now.' James headed for the cookie tin. 'And I need comfort food. I hate this bit of our job.'

'We all do. But think of it another way,' Jenny said. 'That little lamb was poorly and in pain. You saved her from any more suffering.'

'That still doesn't help,' James said. 'I might have to go to the Farleys on the way home and have a cuddle with Sir Woofalot and Cookie, before I pick Tilly up from Mum's.'

'Good idea,' Jenny said. 'Your mum's calling her pup Cookie, then?'

He nodded. 'Their official names are Farley Swale and Farley Ribble—the whole litter's named after rivers. But Cookie's a sensible name—short, and something you wouldn't mind calling across the park.'

'Indeed.' Jenny's mouth twitched. 'Maybe you can talk Tilly into thinking of something a little simpler to call her pup.'

'My daughter is the princess of stubbornness, once her mind's made up about something,' James said with a sigh. 'He'll probably end up answering to Woofy, and over time we can maybe change that to Woody. I can't imagine her calling him Sir Woofalot when she's a grumpy teen.'

'No.' Jenny laughed. 'But the main thing is, he'll always be loved.'

'Like those little orphaned lambs.' He blew out a breath. 'Sorry. I'm not being professional.'

'You're human, James,' Jenny said. 'I'd be the same, in your shoes.'

'And me,' Halley agreed.

It took three biscuits, two cups of tea and a pile of paperwork to settle James before afternoon surgery, and the Farleys were sympathetic when he phoned to ask if he could pop in to see the pups on his way home.

'Saying goodbye to a stock animal is almost as hard as saying goodbye to a pet,' Susan Farley said, handing him a mug of tea, when he told her about how much his morning had upset him. 'And it's worse when it's a baby you've been hand-rearing. I know how I'd feel if we lost one of our calves. Poor Jo must be in bits. And the kids.'

James nodded. 'As a vet, I'm supposed to be detached. But some cases really…' He had to swallow hard to dislodge the lump in his throat. 'I kind of needed a litter of puppies romping over me to cheer me up before I pick Tilly up. I don't want her realising I'm upset and I definitely don't want to explain why.'

'That's what makes you a good vet. You *care*.' Susan patted his arm. 'You're welcome here any time. And I bet your lass will be thrilled to bits when her pup comes home. Does she know her gran's having one of the pups?'

'That's a secret, too, right now,' James said. 'Mum's going to look after Sir Woof-alot while I'm at work and Tilly's at school. Two springer pups.' He groaned. 'It's going to be utter chaos.'

'That's the best kind of chaos in the world,' Susan said with a grin.

The following weekend was Tilly's birthday. She was up early on the Saturday morning, too excited about her party to sleep. And she was thrilled to bits with the pink bicycle James had bought for her and hidden in the garage, wrapped in brown paper and tied up with a bright pink ribbon. His parents had bought her a pink cycling helmet, knee and elbow pads to go with it, as well as training wheels and every pink cycle accessory that a four-year-old could possibly dream of, and she thoroughly enjoyed pedalling her new bicycle up and down the pavement with James at her side.

Jenny and Betty arrived in time for lunch, with special birthday cupcakes iced in pink and with candles to blow out. 'I know your gran has made you a proper cake for your party, but I thought you might like these with your lunch—because you can never have too many candles on your birthday,' Jenny said with a smile.

Tilly was thrilled to bits with the parcel Jenny gave her, wrapped in iridescent pink paper and tied with a white chiffon ribbon. 'Daddy! Look, fairy wings!' she said in delight as she opened the parcel. 'And a fairy crown. And…' Her eyes widened as she saw the magic wand.

'Let me switch that on for you,' Jenny said. 'Now wave it and see what happens.'

The star at the end of the wand lit up, and there was a magic 'twinkling' sound that made Tilly beam her head off and do a magic spell for everyone.

Jenny really paid attention to detail, James thought. She'd chosen exactly the kind of wrapping that Tilly loved, the perfect present…and she'd even hand-drawn the birthday card, a picture of Sir Woofalot that he recognised from a phone snap he'd sent to his mum and she'd clearly shared it with Jenny.

'Daddy, look at my card! It's just like the puppy I want!' Tilly hugged Jenny. 'Thank you! I love it. I love you, too.'

James stilled, panic flaring through him. Would that declaration make Jenny back away?

But Jenny simply hugged the little girl back. 'I love you, too, Tilly. It's always good to tell your friends you love them.'

He thought that message was probably for him rather than for Tilly, a suspicion that was confirmed when she met his gaze and smiled.

Of course she wasn't going to back away from the little girl, even if this thing between them didn't develop the way he'd like it to. She'd said from the start that they'd be friends, and she wouldn't let his daughter or her mother be collateral damage.

'You doing OK?' she asked gently.

There was a lump in his throat. She'd remembered how this day would be bittersweet for him. All he could do was nod.

'OK. But if it gets tough and you need a break at any point, give me the nod and I'll get the girls singing or playing,' she said.

'Thank you,' he said, meaning it from the bottom of his heart. It felt so good to have someone so in tune with his feelings. Jenny Sutton was incredibly special, he thought.

They settled Betty in a comfortable chair in the garden. After lunch, Jenny helped him make the sandwiches with a heart-shaped cutter, and they set up everything in the fridge so all they'd have to do when it was time for the party tea was take everything to the table in the garden. The party bags were all ready on the kitchen dresser, along with a 'Pass the Parcel', stickers, and larger prizes for the main winner of each game.

The weather was perfect, sunny but not too hot, and the garden soon filled with a dozen pre-schoolers and their mums.

Tilly gratefully accepted the presents that her friends had brought to the party.

'She's going to open them after the party,' James explained, 'so she'll have time to enjoy them properly—I know she can't wait to play party games with you all.'

He started off with songs, with a little help from Jenny and his sister Vicky. The girls were all excited and threw themselves in to doing the actions for 'The Wheels on the Bus', 'Heads, Shoulders, Knees and Toes' and 'If You're Happy and You Know It'.

He put Betty and his mother in charge of the music for musical statues. 'Everyone needs to dance,' he said, 'and when the music stops you need to strike a pose.' He demonstrated a silly, gangling pose, and all the little girls laughed. 'Nobody's out,' he said. 'Betty and Christine will choose the person with the best pose in each round, and that person will get a sticker.'

'Yay!' the little girls yelled.

Once everyone had won a sticker and the overall winner had won a sparkly hairband, James put on a green bucket hat that had been customised with a woolly sheep glued onto it, and explained the rules of Simon the Sheep Says. 'So if I say "Simon the Sheep Says", you do what I say,' he said. 'And if I don't say "Simon the Sheep Says," then you stand still. And if you get it wrong, you'll get a sticker. The last person to get a sticker wins.'

Jenny was a great help, whispering ideas to him, and the little girls were soon quacking like a duck, hopping like a bunny, waving their right hands or walking like an elephant. The prize for the winner of this game was a rainbow bangle, and the girls were clearly having a wonderful time.

After some more dancing, they played a few rounds of 'Duck, Duck, Goose'; and then it was time for the birthday tea.

'I think I've got them all a bit too excited,' James said. 'They're never going to sit down for tea and birthday cake.'

'Leave this to me,' Jenny said with a smile. 'Everyone, we're going to play "Sleeping Lions". Do you know how to play it?'

'No,' the girls chorused.

James had never heard of it, either.

'Everyone has to lie down,' Jenny said. 'I'm going to walk round, and anyone who wriggles or giggles is out—you'll get a sticker, if you're out, and you have to help me wake the lions by telling a joke. And the winner is the one who can stay still the longest without wriggling or giggling. Who's going to be my most sleepy lion?'

'Me!' the little girls yelled. 'Me! Me!'

But then Jenny put her finger to her lips. 'Shh! The lions are sleepy,' she said in a loud whisper, and they all lay down and were all still. There were wriggles and giggles, and lots of shushing, but eventually everyone had a sticker and the chance to tell a joke, and the winner ended up being presented with a pink hair scrunchie.

This was just the sort of thing that Anna would've done, James thought—knowing how to calm little girls down and get them ready for the birthday tea party.

Meanwhile Vicky and Christine had quietly ferried out the plates of sandwiches, mini sausage rolls, cherry tomatoes, carrot sticks and crisps from the kitchen to the low tables James had set out.

It had been a long time since Jenny had been to a child's birthday party. She could see that Tilly was having a wonderful time with her friends; the little girl's face was bright pink and full of smiles.

Once the girls were all seated, Jenny went round with a jug of juice, filling everyone's cup. The mums helped, too, passing plates of food and making sure that everyone had something to eat. Jenny was pleased that they chatted to her as if she was one of them, even though she didn't have a child at the party; she knew them all either from their own school-days or as a client at the practice.

If things had been different, she and Simon could've hosted birthday parties like these… Except she knew Simon would've hated every minute of it, whereas James had seemed to be enjoying himself as much as the children were.

When the girls had finished the savouries, Jenny helped Christine bring out the dishes, ice cream and bowls of toppings, and the mums helped the girls make their own ice-cream sundae with sprinkles, strawberries, raspberries and a chocolate flake.

Finally, they cleared the table. Jenny took her phone from her pocket and filmed James lighting the candles on the bright pink birthday cake, and then everyone singing 'Happy Birthday to You'.

'Take a deep breath, and make a wish inside your head when you blow out the candles,' James told Tilly.

She did so and blew out all the candles, while her friends clapped and cheered.

Christine took the cake back to the kitchen, ready to be sliced, wrapped and slipped into the party bags, while Jenny and Vicky got the girls playing pass the parcel and then another game of 'Musical Statues', where this time the girls had to do an animal pose when the music stopped.

Finally, the party was over. James helped Tilly to give out the party bags as her friends went home, then finally flopped into a garden chair.

'That,' he said, 'was exhausting.'

'But huge fun,' Vicky said. 'It feels like for ever since mine were that small. You forget what they're like at that age. So sweet and full of fun. When they get to ten, the boys only want to play football or video games.'

The next day, James and Tilly popped round to Jenny's with a huge bouquet of flowers. 'We just wanted to say thank you for everything you did yesterday,' he said.

'No problem. That's what friends do,' she said.

The problem was, she was starting to think that she wanted more than friendship from him. But how could she offer him anything when she knew her mother would need more of her time and attention as the months went on?

CHAPTER EIGHT

ON SUNDAY, James dropped Tilly over to his mother's so he could check that he had all the bits of puppy paraphernalia he needed for their spaniel and make sure that the house and garden were puppy proof without Tilly asking questions. He secured wire netting to the wrought-iron garden gate so the pup wouldn't be able to squeeze through or under it, and planned distractions so she wouldn't notice. On Monday, after work, he drove his parents and Tilly to pick up Farley Ribble and Farley Swale—better known as Sir Woofalot and Cookie—from the farm and took them all back to his parents' house.

Tilly was beside herself with joy, having two puppies to play with, and he noticed that his mum was smiling. Clearly having pattering paws and waggy tails in the house again was helping to stop her missing Treacle so much.

Both Tilly and Sir Woofalot fell asleep in the car on the way back to the cottage. James woke them both so Sir Woofalot could go out into the garden to start his bedtime routine of having a wee, and Tilly could clean her teeth, then tucked his daughter up in bed with the pup cuddled up next to her. He read them stories until Tilly fell asleep with the pup in her arms. He couldn't resist taking a picture of them together and using it as his phone's lock screen. Cuteness personified, he thought.

But they'd agreed that the pup would sleep in the kitchen, so he gently disentangled the pup and took him downstairs, before sending photos to his sister and to Jenny.

Vicky texted back.

Mum looks so happy. We should've talked her into this before. Have a good first night with Sir Woofalot—hope he doesn't live up to his name! xx

James took a selfie of the pup asleep on his lap and sent it back to both her and to Jenny.

Sir Sleepalot, I hope. x

Jenny texted back.

Gorgeous! Have a good first night x

He suppressed the wish that she was here to share it with him. That wasn't their deal. He suppressed the sudden wave of loneliness, too. He couldn't possibly be lonely, not with his daughter and a tiny puppy to fill his time. And yet he was. He and Jenny had agreed to be friends, but dancing with her by the waterfalls and kissing her had thrown him for a loop and made him realise just how much he missed sharing his life with another adult.

How was he going to persuade her that this thing between them could work—that they could have time for each other as well as looking after Tilly and her mum?

'You're the walking epitome of the owner of a new puppy,' Archer said when James walked into the practice on Tuesday morning.

Jenny had to agree. There were dark shadows under his eyes, and she had to resist the urge to smooth his hair and stroke his cheek. 'How much sleep did you get?' she asked.

'Not very much,' James admitted. 'I bought one of those special teddies for him with a heated pad and a ticking sound to remind him of his mum's heartbeat—but it didn't seem to work. He woke five times last night and cried.'

'And you went down to him each time, so he's learned that howling gets him attention,' Archer said, tutting. 'Bet he ends up sleeping on your bed.'

'No, he won't, and I've told Tilly he can't sleep on her bed, either.' James yawned. 'I need coffee.'

'Try putting the radio on, tonight,' Jenny said. 'So you get the white noise between the stations. That might help him settle.'

'You,' James said, 'live with a cat. I'm not taking puppy advice from *you*.'

Halley came in to hear the last bit, and laughed. 'Oh, dear. New pup-owner all grumpy from lack of sleep, are we?'

'Just you wait. Babies are worse than puppies,' he grumbled.

'Your Tilly's an angel, and you know it,' Halley teased.

'Huh,' James said, and made everyone a hot drink. Jenny noticed that he put twice as much coffee as normal in his own mug and added enough cold water that he could drink it straight down. 'I have patients waiting,' he said.

Jenny couldn't help it. She gave a soft puppy

howl, and he groaned, leaving the staff kitchen to gales of laughter from his colleagues.

At lunchtime, James still had shadows under his eyes.

'Here.' She made him a mug of coffee.

'Thanks.' He took it gratefully. 'Would you like to bring your mum over to meet the puppies on Thursday evening? At my mum's place—stay for dinner.'

She raised an eyebrow at him. 'It's a bit rude to invite myself over with no notice—and to invite myself for dinner.'

'It was Mum's suggestion,' he said. 'She told me you were lovely with her when she had to say goodbye to Treacle.'

'It's the hardest bit of being a pet owner. Of course I'd be kind,' Jenny said.

But on Thursday evening she duly took her mum over to Christine's house, along with a bottle of wine and a bunch of flowers.

'Oh, they're wonderful,' Betty said, making a fuss of the puppies.

Tilly was beyond excited, and was carefully teaching the pups to sit. 'This is puppy nursery school, like my school,' she told them, offering them a tiny slice of cocktail sausage when they sat nicely. 'You'll go to big puppy school next.'

Village hall, James mouthed to Jenny, and she knew exactly who was running the puppy training classes.

It was incredibly charming, watching Tilly with the pups; she was gentle and sweet, and so like her father that it made Jenny's heart squeeze.

Particularly when she realised that, actually, she *did* want a child.

A child like Tilly.

She wanted Tilly—*and* Tilly's dad.

Not that she was going to pressure James by telling him how she felt. They'd agreed that they'd just see how things went. No risks, no worries.

On Sunday afternoon, James picked Jenny and Betty up and drove them out to Cotter Falls. He ended up pushing Betty's wheelchair while Tilly skipped along, holding Jenny's hand and chattering to her about the waterfall.

Betty was really grateful. 'I can't remember the last time I came here. I miss—' She shook her head as the word escaped her, but James knew what she meant. She missed having freedom to go wherever she wanted instead of having to rely on a chair when she got tired. 'You're so thoughtful, James.'

'I always keep my promises,' he said. 'I would never make a promise that I have no intention of keeping.'

She nodded. 'You're a good man.'

It was good to know that she approved of him. But her daughter was the one he needed to persuade to give him a chance.

On the way back, they stopped at James' parents' house so Tilly could show off the new tricks Sir Woofalot had learned, offering his paw for a treat and sitting nicely when she asked.

'Shall we take him out for a walk, Tilly?' he asked.

Jenny felt her eyes widening. As a vet, of course he'd know that puppies were vulnerable to infections until a couple of weeks after the second lot of vaccinations, so they weren't advised to go out for walks until then.

As if he'd guessed her thoughts, James said, 'Socialising is good for him, and his feet won't be touching the ground.' He picked up a baby sling he'd customised for the pup, settling the spaniel into the sling so he was safely cuddled against James's chest.

They looked unbelievably cute together, and Jenny's heart felt as if it had done a somersault. 'Let me take a picture of this for your mum and your sister,' she said.

And the fact it would be on her phone so she'd be able to keep it had nothing to do with anything, she told herself.

'I'll stay here while you youngsters go out,' Betty said, 'if you don't mind, Christine.'

'I'm glad you're staying with us,' James's mum said, 'because I'd like to ask your opinion about a new cake recipe I tried today—I can't work out what's missing. Let's have a cup of tea and you can try the cake and tell me what you think.'

Jenny loved the fact that James's family were so inclusive, making her mum feel part of them. Christine was a few years younger than Betty and much more mobile, but she treated Betty as a valued equal rather than as an object of pity, and Jenny appreciated that.

They walked into the village, with Tilly holding Jenny's hand. Various people were sitting at tables outside the pub and Sally's café, and waved at James and Jenny in acknowledgement. James let Tilly introduce the pup to everyone he knew, and Sir Woofalot thoroughly enjoyed having a fuss made of him.

'Are you and James…?' Sally asked, outside the café.

Jenny smiled, hoping that she could stop this particular bit of village gossip before it spooked James. 'We're friends and colleagues. Tilly's a sweetheart. And who can resist taking a new puppy out for a bit of socialisation?'

'Not me,' Sally agreed, and went to make a fuss of the spaniel.

On Monday morning, Cally Bywater brought her fourteen-year-old cat in to the surgery.

'He's not eaten for the last twenty-four hours, so I know he's not right, and this morning he was sick,' she told James. 'I don't like the way he's miaowing. I think he's in pain.'

James had seen from the file that Boots had a history of pancreatitis but managed well with dietary management. It was possible that this was a flare-up, but it might be something else.

'Let me examine him,' he said.

The cat was salivating much more than usual. James checked his temperature, which was on the low side, and when he examined Boots the cat clearly had a tender abdomen.

'I'd like to admit him for some investigations, to see if it's his pancreatitis flaring up or if there's a new problem,' James said. 'I'll check his bloods and give him some pain relief and fluids, and then tomorrow if he's well enough we'll sedate him and give him an X-ray to see what's going on.'

'I know he's getting on a bit,' Cally said, 'but he's been well up until this week.' Her voice wobbled. 'I'm not ready to say goodbye yet.'

'Hopefully it won't come to that,' James reassured her. 'And in the meantime we'll keep him comfortable.'

'Thank you.'

She was clearly close to tears, and he patted her arm. 'Try not to worry. I know that's an easy thing to say, because he's been part of your life for years.'

'He was a rescue kitten,' she said, 'my twenty-first present from my mum—and Mum's not with us any more. I can't lose him yet.' She blinked back the tears. 'I just want him well and happy and back with my family.'

'I'll do what I can,' James promised.

When she left, James took a blood sample from Boots. 'Let's get you comfortable, boy,' he said, and gave the cat some pain relief along with anti-sickness medication. He took the cat to the kennel area in the back, making a fuss of him.

'Is that Cally Bywater's Boots?' Jenny asked, coming in.

'Yes. Actually, I could do with your help,' James said. 'Have you got ten minutes?'

'I can make the time,' Jenny said.

'Thanks. He's been sick and he's not eating, plus he's hyper-salivating. I've just given him some pain relief and anti-emetics, but I need to get some fluids into him. Tomorrow, if he's perked up, we'll sedate him and do an X-ray to see if it's his pancreatitis or something else.'

'What do his bloods say?' Jenny asked.

'I've just given them to Halley,' he said. 'I'll tell you in a few minutes when she's run them through.'

Jenny sat on a chair, and cuddled the cat. 'I assume we're giving him subcutaneous fluids?' she asked.

James nodded. They both knew that putting some fluids underneath a cat's skin, where it could be gradually absorbed into the body, was a good way of getting fluids into a dehydrated cat; and most cats tolerated it really well.

He set up the hanger for the drip, put the bag of electrolyte solution on the hanger, then swiftly got the fluid set in place, checking the tubing to make sure there were no blockage or leaks.

'Are you sitting comfortably?' he asked, knowing it would take ten minutes or so for the fluids to be administered.

'Ready,' she said, stroking the top of Boots's head. 'We're doing all right, aren't we, Boots?'

Gently, James picked up a loose roll of skin above the cat's right shoulder blade and inserted the needle into the tented space between the skin folds, all the while talking to the cat while Jenny soothed him, then adjusted the lock on the fluid set so the electrolyte solution gradually came through.

Once it was done, he removed the needle and discarded it safely in the sharps bin.

'Well done, little man,' James said. 'Let's get you comfortable, and hopefully you'll feel a bit better by this afternoon.'

When the cat was settled, he checked the blood results. 'ALT's high and potassium's low,' he said to Jenny.

'So at this stage it could be pancreatitis or possibly an infection,' Jenny said. 'You said he'd been vomiting and not eating, so that's probably why his potassium's low.'

'We'll give him some potassium in with the

next lot of fluids,' James said. 'That'll help with the hypersalivation, too.'

The next day, Boots seemed a lot brighter; he was better hydrated and hadn't vomited again.

Jenny did the sedation while James did the X-ray.

'It looks like severe pancreatitis to me,' he said. 'But Boots also has gallstones, and they're partly blocking his bile ducts. No wonder he's been in pain, poor boy.' He grimaced. 'He's fourteen and he's had a good life. I know Cally's not ready to say goodbye, but I'm not sure I'd want to put him through surgery. Maybe the kindest thing would be to let him not wake up.'

'But he's been well until recently, and he's stable,' Jenny argued. 'You could remove his gall bladder, and feed him by tube for a few days until he's able to eat properly again. He'll pull through.'

'Maybe,' James said. 'I'll have a word with Cally and see what she wants us to do.'

He came back from the phone call. 'She's asked us to do the surgery,' he said. 'I've told her I'll need to remove his gall bladder, and he'll be here for a few days so we can feed him by tube to make sure he gets the right nutrients while he's recovering from his operation. We can give him his meds that way, too; it'll be less stressful for him.'

Jenny deepened the sedation to full anaesthesia and James worked swiftly, taking out the gall bladder and the stones obstructing the bile tract. Once he'd sewed up, he fitted a nasogastric feeding tube through Boots's nose, and protected it with a dressing.

Jenny brought the cat round and gave him a cuddle, while James called Cally to let her know that Boots was round from the anaesthetic and doing OK, and he'd call her tomorrow after morning surgery with an update.

On Wednesday, Boots was definitely starting to perk up and ate a little bit of fish on his own. He was still being fed mainly by tube, but he was clearly more comfortable.

'Can you text with me an update, tomorrow?' Jenny asked. 'I know we're not supposed to have favourites, but…'

'Of course I will,' James said.

But on Thursday evening, just before James put Tilly to bed, he was called out to the Davidsons' farm; they had a cow in stage two of labour, but she wasn't progressing.

James called his mum to let her know the

situation. 'I don't know how long it'll take,' he said.

'Bring Tilly and Sir Woofalot here,' Christine said. 'They can have a sleepover.'

'Thanks, Mum.' Though he had a feeling that he'd need a hand with this particular case. On the way to the farm from his parents', he tried to get hold of Archer but the senior partner wasn't around. Feeling guilty, he called Jenny. 'Sorry, I know this isn't fair because you don't work on Thursdays, but I can't get hold of Archer and I have a funny feeling about this. Lee Davidson knows what he's doing, so if he's called me for help there's a chance it's really serious. I might need to do a section. Could you help?'

'I'll get Sheila next door to sit with Mum, if need be,' Jenny said. 'Call me when you get to the farm and you've had time to assess the cow.'

'It's her third calf, and she hasn't had a problem in previous calvings,' Lee, the farmer, told James. 'I think this calf is a big one.'

James checked; the calf was big and the cow's cervix was tight. The calf was viable, but she definitely needed help.

'How long has she been in labour?' he asked.

'Early hours of this morning,' Lee said.

'I could give her an epidural and we can try traction again, or we can do a section,' James said.

'I'm not taking any risks with my Heather,' Lee said scratching the cow's poll. 'Let's get the calf out of the side.'

'I'm calling Jenny in to give me a hand,' James said, and did so. Then he gowned up, gave the cow a local anaesthetic to keep her comfortable and then slid the big needle in for the vertebral spinal block. He gave the cow an anti-inflammatory as well.

Heather mooed. She was clearly still having contractions, but the calf wasn't moving.

By the time James had prepared the surgical field, shaving the cow's hair away from her skin, Jenny was there, scrubbed up and gloved.

'We're going in on the left flank,' James said. The cow was haltered to a ring in the wall, and her tail was tied loosely to a rear leg to keep it out of the way of surgery.

James checked that the anaesthetic had reached an adequate level and scratched her poll. 'You're a good girl, Heather. We're going to help you with your baby,' he said. He looked at Lee Davidson. 'She's more relaxed now. We can make a start.'

He used scrub and surgical spirit on the surgical area, then made the vertical skin incision before cutting through the muscle layers, careful not to damage the rumen.

'I've got a calf leg,' he said as he explored Heather's abdomen. 'Ready to do the uterine incision. Can you two pull the calf out for me?'

He made sure the incision was big enough so the calf could be extracted safely, and got two of the calf's legs out. 'I need one of you on legs and one supporting the calf as it comes out,' he said.

'I'll do the support—you do the legs, Lee,' Jenny said.

Under James's direction, Lee pulled the calf out and Jenny supported the calf so there wasn't any strain on the incision, and then Jenny attended to the calf.

'It's a girl,' she said. She cleaned the membranes off the calf's face so she could breathe, then put her elbows underneath her, sitting her like a frog so her pelvis was square. 'This puts a bit less pressure on the lungs,' she told Lee. 'The calf's doing well, James.'

James closed the uterus with Jenny's help, washed out the incision with saline solution and sewed up the muscle layers and skin, then finally gave the cow some antibiotics and sprayed the incision with silver spray to minimise the risk of infection.

Lee stripped some colostrum from the dam and tube-fed the calf, then gave Heather a good drink.

When he placed the calf with her mum for bonding, the calf tried to stand, wobbled a bit and fell back into the soft straw.

Heather mooed and went over to her, sniffed her, licked her, and the calf stood.

'That's brilliant,' James said. 'I love this moment.'

'Me, too,' Jenny said, hugging him.

He enjoyed her warmth and closeness, the moment of joy when a new life had just begun. And, when she pulled back, he missed that closeness.

They said goodbye to Lee, leaving him to check on the cow and the calf, and headed for their cars.

'I need to decompress,' James said. 'Come back to my place for a cup of tea? Tilly and the pup are at Mum's tonight, because I wasn't sure how long I'd be and I didn't want to keep Mum out half the night.'

Back to his place.

Where they'd be alone.

This might not be a good idea. They were both emotional, and probably shouldn't be on their own together—especially after that kiss by the waterfall.

But, at the same time, he had a point; she needed to decompress before she went home. They didn't do that many caesarean sections on cows, and there was always the worry with a complicated delivery that a calf might not make it.

'All right,' she said.

She followed him home and parked in the street outside his cottage; he waited for her by the front door.

'There's a clean towel in the downstairs cloakroom if you want to wash your hands and arms,' he said.

She smiled, knowing that despite changing out of her scrubs she still smelled of cow. 'Thank you.'

When she came out, he'd clearly washed his own hands and arms at the kitchen sink because he was putting a hand towel into the washing machine.

'That's better,' he said. 'Thanks for coming out and helping, tonight.'

'I wouldn't have missed it for the world,' she said. 'It's so special, seeing new-born calves wobbling over to their mums.'

'Isn't it just?' He switched on the kettle and threw a couple of teabags into two mugs.

'Tsk. My mother would tell you to warm the teapot and do it properly,' she said, teasing him.

'Properly, hmm?'

Then she realised he was looking at her mouth, and all of a sudden her stomach swooped. She found herself looking at his mouth, too. Remembering what it had felt like, against hers…

She wasn't sure which of them moved first, but then she was in his arms, the kettle and the tea forgotten. He nibbled her lower lip, and she opened her mouth to let him deepen the kiss. Eyes closed, all she was aware of was the warmth of his lips against hers, the steady thump of his heartbeat, his clean male scent. And it just wasn't enough. She wanted more.

He broke the kiss and drew a trail of kisses down the side of her neck, making her shiver and tip her head back.

'Jenny,' he whispered against her collarbone. 'We shouldn't be doing this.'

She knew. But, for the life of her, she couldn't marshal her common sense and tell him to stop. The words that came out of her mouth came from a deeper place. 'I don't care.'

'Jenny.' Her name sounded hoarse, as if it had been ripped from him. 'Tell me to stop.'

'I don't want you to stop,' she said.

He pulled back and looked her straight in the eye. 'You sure about that?'

No. It was utterly insane. 'Yes.'

He drew her back into his arms, kissed her, then scooped her up and carried her up the stairs.

Even Simon hadn't swept her off her feet like this, and it made her feel all fluttery.

He set her back on her feet outside the door she knew led to his bedroom.

'Just so you know,' he said quietly, 'I've never shared this bed with anyone.'

He was telling her that there were no memories of Anna. That he knew exactly who was going to be in his bed, and he wasn't pretending she was someone else.

'Thank you,' she said. 'That's…' She swallowed the lump in her throat.

'It's been a while for me,' he said. 'Just as I'm guessing it's been a while for you.'

She nodded.

'No expectations. No pressure. But right now I want you so badly, I can hardly see straight.'

'That makes two of us,' she said, and stepped back into his arms.

He kissed her; then he opened the door and led her inside.

'I'm at the back of the house,' he said, 'and nobody can see in. But if you want me to shut the curtains…'

She shook her head. The soft, gentle light filtering into the room was perfect.

'Kiss me, Jenny,' he said.

She reached up, slid her hands round the back of his neck and drew his head down to hers. He was trembling, she noticed, guessed he felt as nervous and excited and mixed-up about this as she did.

When she broke the kiss, she stroked his face. 'Sure about this?'

'No. Yes.' He gave her a wry smile. 'I don't want to think with my head, right now.'

'Me neither,' she said.

'Then let's not think. Not talk. Just…'

In answer, she slid her fingers under the hem of her T-shirt and drew it over her head before dropping it on the floor.

He gave a sharp intake of breath. 'You're beautiful.'

She put her finger to his lips. 'You're the one who said no talking.'

He raised his eyebrows at her, sucked the tip of her finger into his mouth, and all the words in her head vanished.

He traced the edge of her bra with the tip of his finger, making her breathing quicken, and then stroked his way up her spine and unhooked her bra. With shaking hands, she grasped the hem of his T-shirt and pulled it upwards. His shoulders were broad and his chest was muscular—from his work rather than from the gym—and there was a light sprinkling of dark hair across his chest. His abdomen was flat, and she couldn't resist tracing one finger down the arrowing of hair.

My turn, he mouthed, and cupped her breasts, rubbing the pads of his thumbs across her hardening nipples.

But touching wasn't enough.

Even though she didn't say it, maybe it showed on her face, because he dipped his head and took one nipple into his mouth. She gasped and slid her hands into his hair, drawing him closer as he teased her with his lips and his tongue.

He undid the button of her jeans, and then the zip, before sliding the soft denim over her hips.

She shimmied, but they stuck at her knees. Stretch denim might be great for work, when you had to bend and stretch while you dealt with animals, but they were the worst clothing in the world when you wanted to remove them quickly.

'Let me give you a hand,' he said, and dropped to his knees in front of her. He nuzzled her abdomen, sending sparks of desire through her, and gently tugged the denim down. She stood on one leg, letting him pull the material over one ankle, then the other.

He pressed a kiss to her inner thigh, then rose to his feet. 'I'm in your hands,' he said.

Her fingers were trembling as she undid the button and zip of his jeans and drew them downwards. His erection was obvious through the soft jersey of his underpants.

This was crazy.

They weren't even dating properly.

But, for the life of her, she couldn't stop. She needed him. Wanted him as much as he wanted her. Seeing the evidence of his arousal made her feel like a goddess, strong and gorgeous.

'Jenny.'

He kissed her again, and time stopped. She had no idea which of them took off which bits of clothing, but the next thing she knew they were in his bed, she was straddling him, and he was looking at her as if she was the most gorgeous woman in the world.

'I have just about enough sense left,' he said, 'to ask you to open the drawer in front of you.'

She felt the colour flood into her face. She hadn't even thought about a condom.

'And it's not because I made assumptions,' he said. 'I knew I was going to look for a partner. It made sense to be—well, sensible about it. Make provisions.' He looked at her. 'If you've changed your mind, all you have to do is say so. I'd never push you into anything.'

She shook her head. 'I just feel stupid that I hadn't thought of it.'

He sat up, and kissed the tip of her nose. 'You've very far from being stupid. We got carried away. Which was entirely my fault.'

'I was with you all the way,' she said, and wriggled slightly against him. 'I don't care if it isn't sensible. If we stop now, I'm going to spontaneously combust.'

'Me, too,' he said, and kissed her again.

She reached over to his drawer for the condom. Helped him slide it on, unsure whose hands were shaking more, his or hers. And then she lowered herself onto him.

Afterwards, they showered together and made love again.

And then they got dressed and he led her downstairs. 'Let me make you that tea.'

'I ought to get back,' she said. 'Sheila's sitting with Mum, and it's not fair to stay out.'

'I know,' he said, 'but stay long enough to have a mug of tea. Just a few minutes. Because I'd really like to sit in the garden with you in my lap and watch the stars come out.'

How could she resist?

They didn't talk about what had just happened between them, just sat at the table on the patio with the mugs of tea in front of them, with her on his lap and his arms wrapped round her, her head resting on his shoulders.

Right at that moment she felt perfectly content—knew this was a moment out of time, that she needed to savour it, but would've been happy for this one moment to last and last and last.

In the distance, they heard the hoot of an owl, and then an answering hoot.

'Oh, that's lovely,' she said. 'It sounds like barn owls. I love it when you see one flying across the fields.'

'Me, too.' He stroked her hair.

The tea sat on the table, untouched, neither of them willing to move away from each other for long enough to pick up a mug.

They heard the owl again and she knew she couldn't stay any longer, much as she wanted to. She kissed him lightly. 'I need to go, James.'

'I wish you didn't, but I'm not going to be unfair.' Reluctantly, he let her slide off his lap; then he walked her to the car and kissed her goodnight. 'Sweet dreams. I'll call you tomorrow.'

James lay in bed, the curtains still open, thinking. He could still smell Jenny's floral scent on his sheets and he wished she was still there beside him, maybe asleep in his arms.

Tonight had changed everything.

But where did they go from here?

Both he and Jenny were wary of things going wrong because of the potential collateral damage to Tilly and Betty. But, the more he thought about it, the more it was obvious that their fears were unfounded. Both Jenny and Betty had taken to Tilly; and his daughter had taken to them, too. He was pretty sure that Betty and Tilly would both be happy for him and Jenny to be more than just friends.

Though the next step would be actually merging their lives…and that would be huge.

And a little voice in his head reminded him that he'd never expected to lose Anna. Could the shockingly unexpected repeat itself? This time, Tilly would be old enough to be hurt…

He shook himself. What had happened to Anna was tragic and incredibly rare. Besides, his relationship with Jenny was still in the early stages. He should be enjoying it instead of worrying and overthinking things.

Once Jenny had thanked Sheila for helping her mum to bed, told her about the new calf arriving safely and said goodnight, she checked on Betty, who was sound asleep, and headed for bed.

Though sleep evaded her.

What had just happened between her and James had been bubbling underneath their friendship for weeks. Their shared kisses, dancing together by the waterfall—it had all led up to that moment, heated up by the urgency of that difficult calving. They'd celebrated the wonder of a new life.

But had they just made a huge mistake?

They couldn't simply please themselves. They had Tilly and Betty to think of. And, although Jenny was pretty sure that Tilly liked both herself and Betty, and she knew that Betty doted on Tilly, merging her life with James's would be an enormous step. Betty's health would continue to decline, and Tilly's needs would change as she grew older. It would be a big ask, for all of them. There would need to be compromises—some of them difficult.

James wasn't like Simon. As her mother had pointed out, he was a family man. He was reliable as a colleague and as a friend. He'd proved himself to be a generous lover, too, wanting to cuddle her afterwards.

If she could make this work with anyone, it would be James.

But.

What if it went wrong? They worked together, too. Everything would come crashing down round her ears.

And, no matter how she tried to shake it, the fear wouldn't go away.

CHAPTER NINE

JAMES AND JENNY spent the next couple of weeks circling round the issue. James was busy with Tilly and Sir Woofalot, and Jenny was busy with Betty. The way the caseloads panned out, James was out on farm visits when Jenny was seeing patients in Burndale Veterinary Surgery, so they barely passed each other at work.

They both knew they were avoiding each other and making excuses not to see each other outside work; and the longer the time went on, the more awkward it felt.

On the Wednesday, they were both in together and had to work together to treat a spaniel who had a grass seed stuck in her ear. The dog had been scratching vigorously and shaking her head, and when Jenny looked in her ear the signs of inflammation were obvious. She could see the grass seed but it was very deep in the spaniel's ear and would be painful to remove. The only solution was sedation.

She needed James to do the anaesthetic while she used an endoscope and tiny tweezers to take out the grass seed, then gave the dog antibiotics and pain relief.

'Thanks for your help,' she said to James.

'Pleasure. It's a good reminder for me to make sure I check Sir Woofalot's ears and paws after every walk.'

She nodded in acknowledgement.

'Are you and Betty busy on Sunday?' he asked.

She paused a fraction too long. Now if she said they were busy he'd know it was a deliberate brush-off, and that wasn't fair. 'I'm not sure,' she said carefully.

'Tilly and I are taking the pup for his first visit to the sea,' he said. 'The plan is to go to Filey, paddle in the sea, make a sandcastle, have fish and chips, and then Woofy and Tilly can both have a nap in the car on the way home.'

It had been a long while since she'd been to the sea. Even longer for her mum, she'd bet.

She blew out a breath. 'James. After…' She

could feel the colour shooting into her face and she couldn't bring herself to say the words *after we made love.* 'It's difficult.'

'It's simple,' he corrected. 'The seaside, a puppy and chips. I'm asking you as Tilly's friend.'

'That's emotional blackmail.'

'It's not meant to be,' he said. 'It's meant to be taking the emotion out of it. An afternoon out, and it'll be fun for all of us, whether it's sunny or it's raining.'

Could it really be that simple?

'Have a think about it,' he said. 'Text me and let me know.'

He'd really messed things up between them, James thought. He'd taken it too far, too fast. He should've stuck to offering Jenny a cup of tea after the calf was born, and nothing more than a cup of tea. Better still, he should've let her go straight home from the Davidsons' farm.

Unlike his own marriage, Jenny's hadn't been entirely happy. She'd been the one to make all the compromises, and Simon had pushed her to her limit. James knew he needed to be fair, now, and back off until she was ready.

Though he didn't want to lose her friendship. He needed to find a way of making that clear to her.

Waiting was torture, but finally on Friday morning she texted him.

Mum and I are delighted to accept your and Tilly's invitation to Sir Woofalot's first trip to the seaside. Let me know what time.

He hadn't realised just how tense he'd got until it felt as if his shoulders had just shed a huge weight.

He replied.

Tilly will be delighted to see Betty. And I'm glad I haven't quite ruined our friendship. Pick you up at half-past nine.

So was he saying that now they were just good friends, and nothing more than that? Jenny wondered. Well, it was what she'd wanted. Safe. So she shouldn't feel disappointed that he was doing what she'd asked.

She typed back.

We'll be ready.

On Sunday, she felt oddly shy with him. He helped her mum into the back seat; Tilly was in the back in her booster seat, and Sir Woofalot had a harness attachment that clipped to the seatbelt and kept him safely on his blanket, settled between Tilly and Betty.

Jenny's hand accidentally brushed James's as they both put their seatbelts on, and the glance he sent her was loaded with meaning. But they couldn't talk about the situation here, in front of Tilly and Betty. It would have to wait, and she'd have to play this as if she and James were no more than friends.

Despite the worries churning in her head, Jenny enjoyed the drive to the east coast.

'Filey's quite dog-friendly. There's a bit where dogs are forbidden, but a lot where they can go,' he said, 'plus it's good for wheelchairs.'

He parked the car and got Betty's chair out; while she helped Betty into the chair, James got Tilly and the puppy out of the car.

He was strict with Tilly when it came to suncream and hat-wearing, and also gently applied suncream to Betty's face and arms.

'Can I put suncream on your shoulders?' he asked Jenny. 'I don't want you to burn.' Then he added in a lower voice, so only she could hear, 'I'm asking you as your friend.'

Her friend, not her lover. Well, that worked for her. 'Thank you,' she said.

Her mum actually had a paddle in the sea and really enjoyed it, and they all loved watching Sir Woofalot's reaction to the sea. At first, the spaniel backed away, unsure of the swishing movement of the incoming tide; but then Tilly walked into the sea until her ankles were covered in water, and the pup grew braver, trotting by her side with James holding a long lead.

Five minutes later, Sir Woofalot was happily splashing in the shallows with Tilly, under the supervision of James.

Sir Woofalot had a nap on Betty's lap while James, Tilly and Jenny built a sandcastle together, including seaweed that Tilly had collected to decorate the castle and shells to serve as windows. James dug a moat round it, and Jenny helped Tilly to collect buckets of water to put into the moat.

She took a selfie of all of them next to the castle, and then headed back to the promenade with Tilly to get fish and chips while James sat with Betty and Sir Woofalot. The pup sat very nicely and lifted a paw to ask for a flake of fish, which he happily licked from James's hands.

It really was the perfect family day out, Jenny thought.

At the end of the day, the pup was tired, so James put him in the baby sling. 'Oof, pup, your weight must've doubled since last week!' he grumbled, though he was smiling.

'I'm tired, too, Daddy,' Tilly said.

'All right, honey. It's been a busy day. Do you want me to give you a piggyback?' James asked.

'You can sit on my lap if you want, Tilly,' Betty said. 'And then maybe your dad can push both of us.'

James glanced at Jenny, who nodded.

'That's kind, Betty,' James said. 'Thank you.'

'Thank you, Betty,' Tilly said, and climbed onto her lap.

'You can give me a hand pushing, if you like,' he said to Jenny.

She took one of the handles while he took the other, and they pushed the chair back up the ramp to the promenade.

She wasn't quite sure how it happened, but his hand was curled round one of hers on the handle, and it made her heart skip a beat. This felt like being a proper family. Could she—dared she—try to make a family with James and Tilly?

James's fingers were laced through Jenny's. And today had felt like a real family day out. As if they belonged together.

Could he and Jenny make a multi-generational blended family?

He'd always love Anna, but now he was ready to risk his heart again with Jenny. He already knew that Tilly adored Jenny and Betty, and it was mutual; he liked Betty very much; and he was pretty sure that Betty liked him, too.

But how did Jenny feel about him?

He liked her. More than liked her. If he was honest with himself, he'd fallen in love with her common sense, her ready smile, her warmth.

They were friends. They'd been compatible as lovers, too; there was no reason why they couldn't make this work.

Admittedly, life would become more complicated as Betty's health declined and her needs changed, but he was prepared for that. He wanted to support Jenny.

But, given how she'd been let down before,

would Jenny trust him to do that? And how could he make her see that she could trust him?

The following day, James had an invitation to a former colleague from London's fortieth birthday party in York, in a fortnight's time. He persuaded Jenny to go with him as his plus one; Tamsin agreed to keep Betty company, and Tilly was thrilled that she and Sir Woofalot got to have a sleepover with Cookie at her grandmother's.

'You look lovely,' James said when he collected Jenny.

'Thank you. You don't scrub up so badly yourself, Dr Madden,' she said with a smile.

He smiled back in acknowledgement, hoping that tonight he'd get the chance to be close to her and tell her how he really felt about her.

As he expected, she got on well with his old colleague and his family, and Tom took him to one side when Jenny went to the ladies'.

'I'm so glad you came tonight, James. And I like your Jenny.'

She wasn't really his Jenny—not yet, anyway.

But Tom didn't give him the chance to protest. 'She's lovely. She's perfect for you—and Anna would've liked her very much.'

'Yeah.' He had a lump in his throat. 'It's still early days.'

'The way you look at each other,' Tom said, 'it's obvious where this is going. And I'm really pleased for you. You deserve a bit of happiness.'

'Thanks,' James said, clapping him on the back. And he needed the subject changed before Jenny came back; he didn't want to risk her being spooked by the conversation. 'Now, I need to buy the ancient birthday boy a drink.'

Tom laughed, as James had hoped, and let himself be taken to the bar.

When Jenny came back, they spent the rest of the evening dancing to the kind of music that had always filled the floor in their student days. And then, at last, the DJ slowed everything down. Finally, Jenny was in his arms, just the way James had been aching for her to be all evening. He held her close, swaying with her to the music.

Was she, too, remembering the evening they'd danced by the waterfall?

Was she, too, remembering the night they'd

made love and then sat in the garden, watching the stars come out?

It was a risk—but he had nothing left to lose. If she said no, he'd still be in the friend zone, where he was languishing right now. If she said yes…

His heart rate sped up. Please let her say yes.

'It's a bit stuffy in here,' he said when the tempo of the music went up again. 'Want to come and get some fresh air?'

She nodded, and he led her out of the crowded hall. Thankfully there was a quiet garden, and he was able to find them a more private space.

'Jenny.' He took her hand and lifted it to his mouth, pressing a kiss into the palm and folding his fingers over it. 'I wanted to tell you, I…' He chickened out of using the word he wanted to use. 'I like you.'

Her eyes were huge in the moonlight. 'I like you, too,' she said.

It encouraged him enough to tell her the truth. 'But it's more than that,' he said. 'This brushing up of my dating skills—it turns out there's only one person I want to date. And not just date, either.' He took a deep breath.

'I love you, Jenny. I want to make a family with you.'

'James.' Her voice was husky. 'I… We haven't really known each other that long.'

Technically, they'd known each other for decades. But he knew what she meant. 'It's long enough for me to be sure,' he said.

'I…' She blew out a breath. 'James, this whole thing scares me.'

'I know,' he said. 'All I need to know is how you feel. The complications don't matter, because if we work together we can find a way round them.'

Could it really be that easy?

Four little words. That was all she had to say.

Someone opened the door to the pub's function room, and the chorus of 'Three Little Birds' blared out.

It was almost like a sign, telling her to stop worrying. Of course everything would be all right. James had a point: they'd work together and find a way round all the tricky stuff.

'I love you, too,' she admitted. 'I'm scared, but I love you.'

He wrapped his arms round her. 'No need to be scared. I'm here. I'm not going away.'

He kissed her lightly. 'I never thought I'd be happy again, after I lost Anna. But then I came back to Burndale, and I met you, and the world was suddenly full of sunshine again. I told myself that you were my friend—but you're so much more than that.'

'James.' Her heart was too full for words. Instead, she kissed him.

When he finally broke the kiss, he stroked her face. 'I need to get you home, Cinderella—and, much as I'd like to take you back to my house and have you all to myself for a while, I know Tamsin's waiting for us. We'll find time for us, later.'

He understood. He *really* understood. And she loved him even more for it.

When he dropped Jenny off in Burndale, Tamsin gave her a hug. 'You look happy,' she said.

Jenny nodded. 'James and I… I think it's going to work out.'

'Good.' Tamsin gave her another hug. 'For what it's worth, I think you're really well suited.'

'Me, too,' Jenny said. 'We're not going to rush things. But right now I feel happier than I have in years.'

The floating feeling was still there the next morning. Especially when James texted her.

Good morning. I love you.

She replied.

Good morning. I love you, too.

Happiness got her through the chores and even the bit of weeding she'd been avoiding in the back garden. She was smiling to herself, remembering the way James had kissed her, when she heard a yell.

The sound galvanised her into action; pulling off the gardening gloves as she went, she ran into the house.

Betty was on the floor in the kitchen.

'I tripped,' she said. 'I was making tea, and I tripped.'

'It's an accident. Nobody's fault,' Jenny reassured her. Though she knew it was her fault. She'd been mooning about over James instead of paying attention to her mum.

'I wanted to surprise you with a cup of tea.'

'That's lovely of you, Mum. Does anything hurt? Your arm? Your leg?' Jenny checked.

Reassured that there wasn't an obvious

fracture, she helped Betty to her feet and then to a chair.

'I'll make us that cup of tea, Mum,' she said.

Her mum was fine, apart from having a bit of a shock at the fall. But it could've been so much worse. Betty could've fallen and pulled the boiling kettle down and scalded herself. She could've hit her head on the corner of the table and given herself a subarachnoid haemorrhage. She could've ended up in hospital and then a nursing home, because she wasn't safe enough with Jenny.

And all because Jenny hadn't been paying proper attention.

Later that evening, when her mum was in bed, she video called James to tell him about Betty's fall. 'Thankfully, she's all right—but it's what *could* have happened that worries me.' She took a deep breath. 'James. I'm sorry. I can't offer you anything other than friendship.'

He frowned. 'Last night, you said you loved me.'

'I do,' she said. 'But Mum needs me more. I don't have room in my life for anything else. We can't see each other, any more.'

His face tightened. 'I think you're using your mother as an excuse.'

She glared at him. 'That's not fair.'

'I think, deep down, you're scared of having another relationship in case you make a mistake and you end up being hurt, the way Simon hurt you,' he said. 'And instead of seeing this as an accident that could've happened at any time, you're seizing on it as a reason to avoid seeing me.'

His words stung, and she lashed out. 'Says the man who hasn't tried to have a real relationship, since his wife died.'

'That,' he said, 'isn't quite true. I recognised I needed someone in my life and I wasn't in the right place to offer anyone a relationship. I asked you to help me work on my dating skills.'

'I'm glad you're admitting that nothing between us was real,' she said tightly.

'Oh, but it was,' he said. 'It started out as friendship and it quickly became something more. I fell in love with you, Jenny, and you admitted that you feel the same way about me.'

'Mum has to come first,' she repeated stubbornly.

'I'm not saying she doesn't,' he said, raking

his hand through his hair. 'In any true partnership, there's give and take. There's compromise. Sometimes you have to put someone else's needs first for a while. There will be times when we need to put your mum first, and times when we need to put Tilly first. And there will be times when we put *us* first,' he said.

She shook her head. 'I don't have the headspace for this. I can't be with you any more.'

'You're being a coward,' James said.

'That's unfair.'

'Is it? I think you're scared because deep down you believe I'll let you down, the way Simon did. But you're not giving me the chance to show you that I'm not like Simon.'

'And I'm not Anna,' she said, nettled.

'I don't expect you to be like Anna. You're *you*. And I've learned to face my fear of losing someone again—it probably won't be to an amniotic embolism, but it could be to a road accident, a virus, or something completely out of the blue. I've come to realise that if I try to avoid the risk of losing someone by keeping myself locked away, I'm actually losing far more. Anna would've quoted the Tennyson thing about it being better to have loved and lost than never to have loved at all. And it's true. It hurts when you lose someone,' he said, 'but it hurts you a lot more if you lock yourself away and don't give yourself the chance to open your life up to love.'

She knew he had a point, but she couldn't get past her worries. 'I can't do this, James.'

He sighed. 'All right. Talk to me again when you're ready to face your fears,' he said.

But she couldn't, she thought as she ended the call.

She was stuck.

CHAPTER TEN

'ARE WE SEEING Jenny and Betty, tonight, Daddy?' Tilly asked, several days later.

'No.'

'Why not?'

'They're busy, sweetheart,' James said.

'What about tomorrow?'

He shook his head, hating the way the light dimmed in his daughter's face as it sank in that they wouldn't be seeing Jenny any time soon.

'But I taught Woofy to sit and stay,' she said, sounding devastated. 'I want to show them how clever he is.'

'I know, darling,' James said.

He needed to fix things between himself and Jenny so they could at least go back to some kind of friendship.

But she was barely talking to him, except at work. And even then, it was only when they were both working on a patient. Like the dog they'd worked on this morning, who'd eaten a knuckle bone at the weekend and then started vomiting, and the worried owners had found bone shards in the dog's vomit and diarrhoea.

Jenny had felt a firm mass in the dog's intestines, and thought maybe some of the knuckle bone had become lodged in the dog's bowels. She'd asked James to handle the sedation for an X-ray, which revealed a blockage in the dog's intestines; he'd deepened the sedation to full anaesthesia so Jenny could remove the blockage before it ruptured the dog's bowel. Given a few days, the dog would make a full recovery.

His relationship with Jenny had a far less certain prognosis.

Jenny took a second reading with the no-contact forehead thermometer. Despite Jenny getting her mum to take sips of water, sponging her face and arms with tepid water to cool her skin down and patting it dry, and giving her mum paracetamol, Betty's temperature was still climbing. It was above thirty-eight degrees centigrade now, so it definitely counted as fever.

And Betty was getting agitated, mumbling to herself.

The GP's surgery and the local pharmacy were both closed, so Jenny couldn't ring them for advice. The chances were, this was another urinary tract infection—Betty had had them before. Jenny knew they were more common among elderly women, because their urine flow was weaker and the bladder didn't empty completely, which could lead to a build-up of bacteria. A UTI could cause confusion—and infections could also speed up the progress of dementia. Betty had bounced back from the last one, but she hadn't been as agitated.

Her brother was two hours away, but he would at least listen and give her some professional advice, enough to stop her panicking.

'Rob? I think Mum might have a UTI. She's got a temperature, and she's a bit agitated and confused,' she said.

'When did you last give her paracetamol?'

'Two hours ago, and her temperature's still climbing. I'm getting her to take sips of water, but I've got a bad feeling about this.'

'I think you're right and it's probably a UTI,' Robert said. 'I'd try and get a urine sample, if you can, then get her to the emergency department. If it's a UTI, they'll give her antibiotics. Don't wait until your GP's surgery opens tomorrow.'

'OK,' she said.

'Do you want me to come over?'

'It's fine,' she said. 'I know you're busy.'

'Keep me posted,' he said, 'and if you need me to talk to anyone, call me. I'll make sure my phone's free.'

'Thanks, Rob.'

She called an ambulance, only to be told that there would be a three-hour wait.

The quicker she could get her mum diagnosed, and treated with antibiotics if her suspicion that it was a UTI was correct, the better.

'Come on, Mum. I'm going to take you to see a doctor to make you feel better.'

'We can't go until the coalman's been paid,' Betty said, twisting her hands together.

Coal? It must be several decades since her mother had lived in a house heated by coal. Clearly she was stuck in the past, not knowing where she was now.

'It's all right. I'll pay the bill over the phone,' Jenny said, wanting to reassure her mum.

She put Betty's shoes on, texted their neighbour Sheila to say that she was taking Betty to hospital and would keep her posted, texted Robert to say she was taking their mum to hospital, and drove to the hospital in Harrogate.

The staff at the emergency department triaged Betty, took the urine sample and tested it, and admitted her to a ward for treatment with antibiotics and a drip to get fluids into her. Jenny stepped outside for long enough to call Rob and Sheila with an update, and to let Archer know she wouldn't be in for her usual Wednesday morning session, then went back to her mother's side.

'Go home and get some rest, love,' the senior sister advised.

Jenny shook her head. 'Mum's confused, and I don't want to add to the worry. At least if she sees me, she'll know she's here for a reason.' She gave the nurse a wry smile. 'And if I go home I'll drive myself crackers, worrying about her. I'd rather be here.'

On Wednesday, James came in to Burndale Veterinary Surgery, prepared for another difficult day working with Jenny, only to discover that she was at her mum's bedside in hospital.

'Do you know how Betty is?' he asked Archer.

'They're struggling to get her temperature down, Jenny said this morning,' Archer said.

'She must be worried sick.' And, being Jenny, she'd be dealing with it on her own.

He quickly texted her.

Archer told me about Betty being in hospital. Give her our love. Anything I can do to help, let me know. Will pick up messages after surgery. J x

Her reply was polite.

Thank you.

It told him nothing.

But there was one person who might know more. He rang Sheila, who told him Jenny was staying at the hospital until Betty improved. 'If you talk to her, tell her I'm feeding Sooty for them and keeping an eye on the house.'

'I will,' he promised, and called his mum.

'Of course you need to go and see them,' Christine said. 'I'll collect Tilly from nursery.'

'Thanks, Mum. I owe you,' James said.

After he'd seen his last patient and sorted out the paperwork, he headed for the supermarket to pick up some grapes and some lemon barley water for Betty—most hospitals had a policy of not allowing flowers—and a card, then drove to Harrogate.

He called in to the geriatric ward and checked with the nurse on Reception, who directed him to Betty's ward.

Jenny was sitting by her mother's bed, holding Betty's hand; there were deep shadows beneath her eyes. She clearly hadn't slept, the previous night.

'Hey,' he said. 'I know sometimes when you're not well, it tempts you to drink if there's something flavouring the water, so I bought Betty some lemon barley and some grapes.'

'Thank you.' She bit her lip. 'I didn't expect to see you.'

'And you didn't ask me to come. I know. But I thought you could do with a bit of support. Which is exactly what you'd do for me, if I was in your shoes,' he said, before she could start arguing. 'When did you last eat?'

She shook her head. 'I'm not hungry.'

'So not since yesterday. OK. See you in a bit.'

He headed for the cafeteria and bought her a cup of strong tea, a chicken salad sandwich and a banana. He added a chocolate brownie, and went back to the ward.

Her eyes widened as she saw him. He smiled, put the food on Betty's bedside cabinet, then fetched another chair. 'Move,' he said. 'I'll hold Betty's hand while you eat that sandwich and drink your tea.'

'But—'

'Not buts,' he said firmly. 'You need to

look after yourself as well, Jenny. If you're not well, how are you going to be able to look after your mum properly?'

She clearly couldn't argue with his logic, so she gave in, muttering her thanks.

James chatted to Betty, telling her all about Sir Woofalot and how Tilly was doing at nursery, until Jenny had finished her sandwich and the tea.

To his relief, the colour in her face was slightly better.

'Now, your mum needs to rest,' he said, 'and she's not going to be able to do that if she's worrying about you. So this is the deal, Jenny. I'm driving you back to Burndale now, and I'll drive you back here in the morning before I go to work. It's up to you whether you want to go back to your own house, stay at mine, or stay at my mum's, but you are most definitely going to sleep in a bed tonight instead of half dozing on an uncomfortable chair for the second night in a row.'

'But Mum—'

'Is in the best hands,' he said firmly.

'What about Tilly?'

'It's fine. Mum or Vicky will drop her at nursery tomorrow. That's what families do, pitch in and help when it's needed,' he added softly. ‘You need to get some rest. Otherwise you’re going to be too exhausted to sit with your mum tomorrow. You need a shower and a comfortable bed.’

Colour slashed across her cheeks, and he realised how she might have taken his words.

‘That’s not me trying to get you to sleep with me,’ he said swiftly. ‘I mean you need to rest. Your mum’s asleep now, and there’s nothing you can do apart from wait for the antibiotics to kick in. Say goodnight to her, and I’m driving you back to Burndale.’

Clearly wanting to stay, but also knowing that he had a point, Jenny kissed her mum’s forehead. ‘Night, Mum. I’ll be back in the morning.’

‘And I’ll keep an eye on your girl, Betty,’ James added.

‘My car’s still here. I’ll drive myself,’ Jenny said.

‘You’re shattered. Don’t drive tonight,’ he said. ‘I’ll take you wherever you want to go, and I’ll pick you up tomorrow and bring you back here.’

He was as good as his word, taking Jenny back to her own house, then feeding Sooty and making her a mug of hot chocolate with hot milk while she had a shower, changed into her pyjamas and wrapped herself in a fluffy towelling dressing gown.

'Lock up behind me, drink the chocolate and go to bed,' he said firmly.

'What if the hospital calls and says Mum's worse?' Without her car, she'd have to rely on a taxi, and she didn't want to waste time that her mum might not have.

'Then you ring me, and I'll drive you in,' he said, cutting through the jumble of fears in her head. 'Goodnight, Jenny.'

And then, the bit that made her tears spill over after he'd left, he gave her a hug and kissed the top of her head. 'Betty's in the right place. I bet in the morning you'll see a difference in her. Get some rest, and things will look better tomorrow.'

Jenny thought she'd never be able to sleep, for worrying about her mum; but she made herself close her eyes and, perhaps worn out from her vigil by Betty's bedside, she fell asleep almost instantly.

The next morning, she was up and ready before James arrived, called the hospital to see how her mum was doing, and had just boiled the kettle when James rapped on the kitchen door and walked in.

'Breakfast,' he said, handing her a bacon roll. 'Because I'm guessing you haven't eaten anything this morning.'

'Not yet,' she admitted.

'How's your mum doing?'

'She had a good night, but her temperature's still up and she's still not making sense.'

'You and I both know that's a common side-effect of a UTI and it can take time for antibiotics to kick in,' he said. 'It doesn't mean her dementia's suddenly taken a dive.'

But it was still a possibility, one she dreaded. When that day came, she'd need to give up her job completely for a while. Instead, she said, 'The kettle's boiled. Can I make you a mug of coffee?'

'If you've got a travel mug, that would be lovely,' he said. 'Thank you.'

He came up to the ward with her to see Betty, then kissed her mother on the cheek and told Jenny he'd be back after work.

'You really don't have to come,' she said. 'I had a good night's sleep. I'm safe to drive myself home.'

'OK,' he said. 'Provided you promise you'll call me if you need anything.'

'I will. And thank you for everything you've done.'

Her brother Robert arrived at lunchtime. 'I got a locum for this afternoon,' he said.

She bit back the comment that it was about time he'd made the effort. 'I'll give you some time alone with Mum,' she said, and headed for the cafeteria.

He came to find her, an hour later. 'Mum's asleep—before you ask, that's the only reason I left. And I don't want to have this conversation with you in the ward, in case she wakes up and overhears.'

'What conversation?' she asked, her stomach dipping.

'Jen, when she's recovered from this, I think she's going to need more help than you can give her.'

Jenny shook her head. 'She'll be fine when she's over the infection and comes home.'

'Jen, you need to face this. She has dementia, and she's not going to get better,' he said. 'Every day, we're going to lose a bit more of her. Some days she'll be on an even keel, and other days she'll dip down further.'

'I know.' Did he think she was stupid? As soon as their mum had been diagnosed, she'd read up on the condition.

'She needs nursing care.'

'Where she'll be stuck in a chair in front of

a television, in a room that's way too hot so it keeps her quiet? No.'

He sighed. 'Not all nursing homes are like that.'

'They don't want to be like that, I know—but they have to manage with not enough staff. I promised Mum I'd never put her in a nursing home,' Jenny said. 'I intend to keep that promise, Rob. Even if she gets to the stage where she doesn't know where she is, *I'll* know—and that's what counts. I can look after Mum myself. She's at day-care three days a week, while I'm at work, and the rest of the time I can look after her. It's fine.'

'It's not fine,' Robert said. 'It's a really heavy burden, being a full-time carer and working. You've got yourself to think of, too.'

She noticed that he didn't offer to share the care. Then again, he lived two hours away and had teenage children to think of.

'I'm fine as I am,' she said. 'If you've come here to have a fight, I'm not interested. I think you should go home, now.'

'Jen—' he protested.

'No, really. Just go home, Rob.' She stood up, put her hands on her hips and glared at him. 'I'm the one who's been looking after Mum for the last couple of years. You ring her once a week, visit once a month if she's lucky—so, no, you don't get to swan in and tell me what to do. Go home.'

He glared back at her, then muttered something rude and stomped out of the café.

And Jenny was so fed up with being bossed about that when James texted her to ask if there was anything she needed, she snapped back her reply.

Nothing, thank you. I appreciate your kindness earlier but we don't need any help.

Something had clearly upset Jenny, James thought, looking at the text—hopefully nothing he'd done or said. But when she pushed him away for the third day in a row, he was at a loss what to do.

'It's impossible. She's putting a brick wall round herself,' he said to Archer, handing his friend a mug of tea after surgery had finished.

'She's worried about her mum,' Archer said. 'Give her time.'

'Time to make that brick wall even higher, and maybe add climb proof paint and a bit of barbed wire?' James asked.

'There is that,' Archer said. 'What's actually going on with you and Jenny?'

'We have…feelings for each other,' James said. 'More than friendship.'

Archer grinned. 'Yeah. I know that one.'

'You and Halley.' James smiled ruefully. 'I envy you.'

'She taught me I need to reach for the dream,' Archer said. 'Maybe you can learn from me. If Jenny's your dream, then what are the obstacles?'

'I think the real obstacle's Jenny herself,' James said. 'She seems to have this idea that she has to do everything herself, on her own—whereas in a proper relationship you support each other.'

'You know the situation with her ex,' Archer said. 'He left her to do everything—and he wanted her to move to London with him when he knew she was worried about her mum.'

James frowned. 'But I'm not her ex. She knows that.'

'Talk to her,' Archer advised. 'Be honest. It's all you can do.'

The hospital really wasn't the right place to have a conversation with her but, short of stalking her house, how would he know when she was actually home?

Maybe it was time to enlist some help.

He asked his sister to pick up Tilly, bought some flowers, and went to see Jenny's neighbour.

Later that evening, Sheila rang him. 'She's just got home from the hospital, love. See if you can talk some sense into her,' she said.

'Thank you. I'll try,' James said.

He drove over and knocked on Jenny's kitchen door.

She looked bone-deep tired and miserable when she answered.

'Not now,' she said.

'Jenny, have you eaten today?' he asked.

She sighed. 'Don't nag, James. I'm not in the mood to cook.'

He lifted up the tote bag he'd brought with him. 'I guessed as much. Which is why I brought you a tub of home-made pasta with pesto, chicken and grilled peppers,' he said. 'Works hot or cold. Let me in, and I'll stick it in a bowl for you and get you a drink.'

'You're not going to take no for an answer, are you?' she asked wryly.

'Absolutely not,' he said. 'No more talking

until you've eaten. Do you want the pasta hot or cold?'

She closed her eyes momentarily, as if she was giving in. 'Cold, please.'

He scooped the salad into a bowl, fished cutlery out of the drawer and made her sit at the kitchen table. Jenny took a couple of mouthfuls, clearly intending to be polite, but then polished off the lot.

'Thank you. That was really...' A tear leaked down her face, and she scrubbed it away crossly. 'Ignore that. I'm fine.'

'Jenny, you've had days of worry about your mum. Nobody would be fine, in your shoes. And you don't have to be fine. I'm here.'

'You don't have time. You're a single dad.'

'With a supportive family who lives nearby.' Exactly what she didn't have.

A muscle worked in her jaw. 'Rob thinks I should put Mum in a home. He says I can't look after her on my own.'

'He has a point,' James said.

Her eyes sparked in outrage. 'I think you'd better leave. Now.'

'Hear me out,' he said. 'You're running yourself ragged right now, working and looking after your mum. I know you love her, and

I know you want the best for her. But what happens to your mum if you get the flu, say?'

'I'll sort something out.' She folded her arms and glared at him.

'I'm not saying you should put Betty in full-time care. What I'm saying is that you can't do it all on your own. You need support. I learned something, the other day.'

She frowned. 'Where are you going with this?'

James reminded himself that this wasn't the real Jenny. Right now she was tired, worried sick and over-burdened, and that was why she was snapping at him. 'I finally got round to finishing the unpacking, the other day. When I was putting the books on the shelves, a post-card Anna had been using as a bookmark fell out. It had a quote from John Donne—her favourite poet—on it. "No man is an island." I think you're trying to be an island, Jenny, doing everything yourself.'

She rolled her eyes. 'That's how it is.'

'But it doesn't have to be.' He sighed. 'I'm making a mess of this. What I'm trying to say—without putting any extra pressure on you—is that I want to be a family with you. Being apart from you, these last few days, has really brought it home to me how important you are to me. I've missed you—at work, and outside.'

Her eyes filled with tears. 'I've missed you, too.'

'Then stop pushing me away. I love you, and you've admitted you love me. Let's make a life together.'

'It's too complicated,' she said quietly.

'Is it? Because I think we could make this work. You, me, Betty and Tilly. We'll support each other. Tilly gets a mum who can do all the girly stuff with her that I can't. Betty gets a son-in-law who'll spend time with her and can lift her when she needs it. And you and I—we get each other,' he said with a smile. 'We get to fall asleep in each other's arms, and wake up in each other's arms. We get our private moments. We might need to sneak them in, sometimes, but that's all part of being a family.'

She looked at him as if she couldn't quite believe it was possible.

'You and I, we're not islands,' he said. 'We both come as a package. And, yes, we'll need to move—but to a place that has a ground-floor bedroom and a wet room for Betty, and where she'll be part of a bigger family. Where we all contribute. And where we're together because we love each other.'

She swallowed hard. 'You'd do that for me?'

'*We'd* do this for *us*. All of us,' he corrected. 'As for Sooty and Sir Woofalot—they might be a bit wary of each other at first, but they'll learn to rub along. Just like we will. It's what being a family means.' He smiled. 'We can have it all, Jenny. All I need from you is one little word. I love you. Will you marry me?'

He meant it.

And, as she stared at him, the penny finally dropped. He wasn't like Simon. He meant it about being there for her. About being a partnership. A team. A family.

And that knowledge was enough to dissolve her fears.

'I love you, James,' she said. 'Yes.'

'About time, too,' he said, and kissed her.

EPILOGUE

One year later

'NANA BETTY! I made a picture of you and me and Sooty and Woofy,' Tilly said, scampering into the open-plan kitchen/living room in front of her father and handing a picture to Betty, who was sitting in a chair by the French windows overlooking the garden. She'd labelled the figures painstakingly in wobbly handwriting.

'That's lovely, Jenny,' Betty said.

'I'm Tilly,' Tilly corrected with a smile. 'Jenny's my mum.'

'Certainly am, lambkin,' Jenny said, bending down to give the little girl a hug and a kiss hello.

Tilly had asked her if she could call her 'Mum' the day that she and James had told the little girl that they wanted to get married and make a family together, and over the last year Jenny had discovered how much joy a little girl could bring into her life—and her mother's. 'That's a beautiful picture. Where do you want to put it?'

'Nana Betty's room?' Tilly said.

'No. Keep it here,' Betty said. 'Where everyone can see it. Put it on the…thingy.' She waved a hand towards the kitchen area, to indicate she couldn't quite remember the word.

'Fridge,' James supplied, kissing her cheek. 'Good idea, Betty. Go and see where we've got a space, Tilly, and I'll lift you up so you can stick your drawing to the fridge with a magnet.' He turned to his wife to kiss her. 'Good day?' he asked quietly.

'More than good,' she said, her voice equally quiet. 'I have news for you.'

'What kind of news?'

'Complicated,' she said. 'Or it will be, in about seven months.'

James's eyes widened as he worked out what she meant. 'That's the best kind of news,' he said. 'I know Tilly still wants a white kitten called Twinkle, but I think she'll settle for having a little brother or sister. Betty will love having a baby around.' He kissed her. 'And I didn't think you could possibly make me any happier, but you have. I'm the luckiest man in the world.'

'We're the luckiest family in the world,' she corrected. 'Because we have each other.'

'We have each other,' he agreed.

* * * * *

Keep reading for an excerpt of a new title
from the Western Romance series,
SWEET-TALKIN' MAVERICK by Christy Jeffries

PROLOGUE

NEARLY EVERYONE IN our small Montana town had attended some sort of event in the newly renovated Bronco Convention Center. But only one other couple had thrown an actual party inside of it. Of course, the last weekend in January wasn't exactly the time of year for a large outdoor gathering, and the crowd tonight was definitely a large one.

Everyone knows that when the beloved mayor invites the whole town to celebrate his thirtieth wedding anniversary, it's not a question of *if* you'll go. It's a question of what you should wear and who else is going to be sitting at your table. Sure, you could miss the annual Christmas tree lighting or a rodeo on occasion. Those types of events brought in enough tourists that your absence might go unnoticed. However, tonight's party celebrating Rafferty and Penny Smith was strictly for the locals. And anyone who was anyone in Bronco, Montana, had RSVP'd yes before the invitations were even printed.

"Thank you all for coming out to join me and Penny on this momentous occasion," Mayor Rafferty Smith began his speech welcoming everyone. The man was a great speaker and an even better storyteller. It was no wonder he kept getting reelected. "You know, when I first asked Penny to marry me, I wasn't sure she'd say yes. In fact, I don't think *she* even knew she was going to say yes. But we were just a couple of young kids in love back then, flying by the seats of our pants. We had no big plans other than making it through each day and having as much fun as we could. Nobody tells you how much work a marriage takes… I mean, nobody except all the boring adults who know better than you. But you ignore them because you've got too many stars in your eyes. Then, as time goes by and you begin to look back on all the ups and downs, all the good times and the bad, you begin to realize what you've actually accomplished. Personally, my biggest achievement is sharing the past thirty years with the woman I love."

Everyone oohed and aww'd as the mayor pulled his wife onto the stage beside him. "Penny, you've stuck by my side all this time and there is nothing I could give you that would even come close to everything you've given me these past years. But I couldn't show up here completely empty-handed." The crowd chuckled politely, then applauded as Rafferty presented his wife with a black velvet jewelry case. "They say pearls are traditional for the thirtieth anniversary, but if you ask me, there is nothing traditional about you, Penny Smith. Like this necklace, you are one of a kind and I can't wait to see what the next thirty years have in store for us."

Rafferty made a big show of fastening the stunning heirloom pearl necklace around Penny's neck, causing the guests to cheer uproariously when he hauled his wife into his arms for an over-the-top kiss.

Everyone in the crowd agreed—the party was already off to a fabulous start.

CHAPTER ONE

DYLAN SANCHEZ FORCED himself to come tonight because he didn't want to be the only business owner in Bronco who refused the mayor's invitation. Oh, and because his parents and siblings would've never let him hear the end of it if he'd skipped.

At the rate the Sanchez family was growing, though, it wasn't just the opinions of Dylan's two brothers and two sisters he had to contend with, either. He'd assumed that when his sisters got married and his brothers got engaged, they would find better things to do with their time than remind him that he was now the odd man out.

Clearly, he'd been wrong about that.

Not that Dylan wasn't proud to be the last Sanchez standing. Growing up in a competitive family, if he wasn't going to be the first one to do something, then he sure as hell was going to outlast everyone else. It was just that being surrounded by so many happy couples, talking about anniversaries and upcoming weddings, could start to wear on a happily single guy.

Plus, he hated crowded events.

"Aren't these tables only supposed to seat ten people?" Dylan muttered to his father. "How did we manage to get thirteen chairs crammed around one tiny space?"

"Thirteen chairs *and* a stroller," his brother Dante said as he rocked his and his fiancée Eloise's daughter back to sleep in her little buggy. Merry, Dylan's eight-week-old niece, was officially his favorite family member, and not just because she kept her opinions to herself.

A few minutes later, when Dylan mentioned the lack of elbow room, his sister Sofia replied, "Boone and I are going to sit with the rest of the Daltons once they pass out the cake. You can put up with being squished for that long, Dylan."

"Yeah, but I don't know how long I can put up with Felix stealing my beer." Dylan snatched the pint glass from his older brother's hand. "The bar's right over there if you want to go get your own."

Felix had the nerve to smile unapologetically. "Shari and I are going to head that way for another round as soon as she and Mom get done talking about bridal shower themes. In the meantime, you can share."

Uncle Stanley returned from the buffet line with two full plates and his fiancée, Winona Cobbs. As the older couple took their seats, there was even less space to move.

Dylan turned toward his sister Camilla. "I think your in-laws are looking for you."

"No they're not," Jordan Taylor, Camilla's husband, replied. "My dad and uncles are busy holding court with the mayor."

"If you need to get away from us, Dylan," Camilla said as she nodded discreetly at a table with several young women, "there's room over there."

"Stop trying to set me up. Between the car dealership and the new ranch, I don't have time for a girlfriend right now."

"When have you ever had time, Dyl?" Sofia asked. "Aren't you getting tired of the dating scene? You're not getting any younger."

"Uncle Stanley is eighty-seven and *he* just got engaged. So there's not exactly an age limit for someone getting married. In fact, I don't have to get married at all." Dylan knew he sounded defiant, possibly even stubborn. But the more his family talked about weddings, the more determined he became to stay single.

"Don't forget, kiddo, that I was already married once and there's nothing better than sharing your life with someone." Uncle Stanley, who'd been a widower for some time, turned to Winona. "Speaking of which, we should probably be setting our own wedding date soon."

Winona, a ninetysomething-year-old psychic who was prone to mystical statements, shrugged noncommittally. "We will when the time is right."

"You're not having second thoughts, are you?" Uncle Stanley asked, concern causing the wrinkles around his eyes to deepen.

Winona shook her head, her messy white bun tipping to one side. "Of course not. But love cannot be rushed. It *will* not be rushed." Then she pointed an age-spotted hand covered with several rings at Dylan. "But it cannot be avoided, either. Love always finds a way."

Dylan opened and closed his mouth several times, unsure of how to respond. Or if he should. He reclaimed his beer once again from his brother and drained the glass before changing the subject.

"Anyway, the ranch has me so busy lately, I hired two new salespeople for the dealership to cover for me. But January is normally a slow month for car sales. I need to think of something to get business moving again."

"You could try not spending so much time at Broken Down Ranch," one of his sisters suggested.

"It's called Broken *Road* Ranch," he corrected. His family had always been supportive of his dream to own land, but several of them had recently questioned his decision to own *this* particular property. The place was a bit of a fixer-upper and most of the buildings had seen better days. But it sat in one of the best spots in the valley and, hopefully, the grass would return this spring and make it look not so...well...run-down.

"What about a car wash?" Dante, the elementary school teacher, suggested. "My school did one before summer break last year and made a decent amount."

Dylan frowned. "I don't need a onetime fundraiser. I need to get more people on my lot. But without being one of those cheesy salespeople who resort to gimmicks or corny commercials just to make a buck. You know how I hate public speaking."

"What about a game of hoops?" Their father had raised his children with a passion for sports. "We could do a tournament, like we do with the rec league. I'll be the referee."

Several people at their table groaned, including Dylan's mom, who had attended more than her share of basketball tournaments over the years.

"That would take an awful lot of time for people to form teams and have practices," their mom said. "You need to put something together sooner and you need a theme."

"Valentine's Day is coming up," Sofia said a bit too casually and all the women were very quick to agree. Suspicion caused the back of Dylan's neck to tingle.

"You guys want me to do something on a commercialized holiday created for the sole purpose of selling romance to people? What am I going to do? Have a Valentine's dance?" Dylan snorted at the absurdity. "No wait, maybe I should send everyone who wants to test-drive a car on a ride through a tunnel of love."

Uncle Stanley raised his hand. "I vote for the tunnel of love idea."

Dylan needed another drink. "Buying a vehicle is a big decision, you guys. When someone comes to my dealership, it's to make a practical purchase. They're not there for all that mushy stuff."

And neither was Dylan. He didn't do mushy. He certainly didn't do grand gestures like Mayor Smith had done up on the stage a few minutes ago when he'd given his wife that necklace in front of the whole town.

"Valentine's Day is one of the biggest nights of the year in the service industry," Camilla, who owned her own restaurant, pointed out. "Trust me, when it comes to gifts, some people want more than flowers and chocolates."

Dylan grimaced. "So I just get some big red bows and hoist up a new banner? Maybe dress up as Cupid and shoot arrows at the potential customers?"

Winona lifted her wineglass. "Lots of gals in this town wouldn't mind seeing the Sanchez brothers dressed up like Cupid and wearing nothing but a tiny white toga."

Thankfully, that suggestion got a resounding set of *noes* from Felix and Dante. Several more ideas were offered and rejected before Dylan excused himself to go to the bar while his family wore themselves out discussing the most absurd concepts that would never come to fruition. He told himself that he'd grab another beer, maybe a plate of food, and by the time he got back to the table, his family would have moved on to another subject.

However, Dylan got sidetracked talking with a few buddies about the upcoming baseball season, speaking to one of the city council members about a permit application for some electric vehicle charging stations and checking the score on the college basketball game. When he returned to the party, he ran into Mrs. Coss, the older lady who owned the antiques mall next door to his dealership.

"I think it's a great idea, Dylan. I'll even be willing to lend you a few pieces from my 1920s rolling pin collection as long as they're just used for display purposes."

He smiled politely despite his confusion. "What's a great idea, Mrs. Coss?"

"The bake-off. Maybe I'll put out a shelf of my older cookbooks and a rack of mid-century aprons to do a little sidewalk sale." The band began playing their rendition of the "Cha Cha Slide," and before Dylan could ask her what she meant, Mrs. Coss said, "This is my song. We'll talk more about cross-promotion tomorrow." She patted him on the arm and dashed onto the dance floor before he could say another word.

Dylan heard the word *bake-off* several more times on his way back to the table. By the time he arrived at his seat, most of his siblings and his mom were already gone, blending into the crowd. His dad was still there, though, holding baby Merry and serenading her with the off-key lyrics of the line dancing song.

"Where'd everyone go?" Dylan asked his dad.

"They're spreading the word about the bake-off."

Dylan's temples began pounding. "Please tell me that this doesn't have anything to do with my dealership."

"Hey, Dylan," LuLu, the owner of his favorite BBQ joint, called out from two tables over. "What's the prize for the bake-off?"

His dad responded before Dylan could. "A year's worth of free mechanical service. Oil changes, new brakes, tire rotations, that sort of thing."

All the color drained from Dylan's face as he stared at his dad in shock. "I was gone for thirty minutes."

Apparently, thirty minutes was all it had taken for Dylan's entire family to come up with a harebrained idea to hold a Valentine's Day–themed bake-off at his place of business. Oh, *and* promise the winner a prize valued at potentially thousands of dollars. But it was too late to call the thing off. Gossip spread like wildfire in Bronco and Dylan was officially on the hook for a contest he hadn't authorized.

"Nobody even asked my permission," he told Dante, the first sibling who returned to the table.

"Have you met Mom and our sisters? You walked away midconversation. That's practically giving them your blessing to proceed however they see fit."

Dylan rolled his eyes. "It's a car dealership, not the set of some cooking show. You've seen my break room. I have an old microwave and a toaster that sets off the smoke alarm anytime I want a bagel. How do they think they're going to hold a bake-off there?"

"I don't know. Something about a giant party tent and one of Camilla's suppliers who rents out restaurant-grade ovens." Dante took his baby from their dad. "I wasn't really paying attention, man."

Could this evening get any worse? The pounding at Dylan's temples revved into a full headache and he was about to call it a night. But if he left the party now, what other crazy schemes would his family come up with in his absence? Needing to ward off the gossip and do damage control, he rose from the table.

Unfortunately, he didn't get more than two feet when the mayor thwarted his plans.

"Dylan!" Rafferty Smith reached out to enthusiastically shake Dylan's hand. "I hear we're holding an exciting town event at the dealership next month. Penny loves that British baking show, by the way. Obviously, I'd be honored to help judge the contest. I'll tell my assistant to clear my schedule for that day."

Okay, so having the mayor make an appearance at his dealership could actually be good for business. Plus, Dylan was in the middle of working on a bid proposal to supply the city officials with a fleet of vehicles. Since he didn't want to risk losing that contract, he had no choice but to clench his jaw, smile and act as though this ridiculous bake-off plan could actually work. That it wouldn't be nearly as embarrassing as him running around dressed like Cupid. "Great. It should be a lot of fun. I look forward to having you join us."

Mayor Smith then took a step closer and lowered his voice. "Just between us, any chance you happened to see a pearl necklace around here?"

"You mean like the one you gave your wife less than an hour ago?"

"Shh. Keep your voice down. Penny had it on when we were on the dance floor, but it must've fallen off somewhere. I'm trying to ask around discreetly because I don't want to cause a—"

"Attention, ladies and gentlemen," the lead singer of the band interrupted as he spoke into the microphone. "We have an announcement to make. If anyone finds a pearl necklace, please bring it up to the stage so we can reunite it with its owner."

The crowd's hushed murmurs quickly grew louder as everyone realized whose necklace had gone missing. Rafferty Smith muttered, "So much for doing anything discreetly in this town," before striding away.

Dylan couldn't agree more.

Surely someone would find Penny's necklace soon. Dylan doubted his own reputation as a serious businessman would be recovered as easily.

ROBIN ABERNATHY WAS better on the back of a horse than she was in front of an oven. But she'd been known to have a few tricks up her sleeve when it came to the kitchen. Or at least a few recipes.

Okay. Two recipes. One of which, fortunately, was a

batch of cookies. Besides, she didn't want to actually win the Valentine's Day bake-off. She just wanted to get one of the judges to notice her.

She parked one of the ranch trucks at the curb in front of Bronco Motors, then stared at her reflection in the rear-view mirror. Her summer tan had long faded, and her complexion could benefit from a swipe of blusher. Too bad she didn't own any makeup. She dug around in her purse and came up with a tube of colorless lip balm. Oh well. She yanked the elastic band out of her hair, ditching her usual ponytail. Maybe she'd look more feminine with her hair down.

For the first time in thirty-one years, Robin asked herself why she couldn't be better at the whole flirtation thing. Probably because she spent too much time with her brothers and the other cowboys out on her family's ranch. If she couldn't find the time to go out on many dates, then she certainly didn't have the time to put much effort into her appearance. If a guy didn't appreciate her for being herself, what was the point in bothering with a second date?

But that was before Dylan Sanchez had smiled at her during Bronco's annual Christmas tree lighting event. She hadn't been able to stop thinking of the man since then.

She'd planned to casually run into him at the Smiths' anniversary party, but a last-minute emergency with one of her client's horses had kept her away. Maybe it was better this way since his recently announced bake-off might prove to be a better opportunity to talk to the man without such a huge crush of people around.

As if on cue, she saw him striding across the dealership lot and heading into the office. Robin wasn't used to the feeling of butterflies in her stomach because it was rare that her nerves got the best of her. Before she could overthink what she was about to do, she exited the truck and slammed the driver's door, closing off any doubt and leaving it behind her.

You can do this. Gripping the printed flyer tighter in her fist, she entered the building that served as a couple of offices and a showroom for a brand-new 4x4 truck. She'd purposely picked a time when she thought the dealership wouldn't be busy and, from what she could see, it appeared she'd planned well. Nobody else was around.

Dylan's voice made its way through an open door and then a second voice responded from what sounded like a speakerphone. Not wanting to interrupt his call, she casually walked around the vehicle on display, reading the information on the back window sticker.

It wasn't that she was trying to eavesdrop, but it was hard not to hear him in his office ten feet away. It only took her a few moments to figure out the extent of the conversation. His small herd had been overgrazing in the same spot for years and he couldn't move them until he had time to repair some fences. The other voice clearly belonged to a fertilizer salesman trying to convince Dylan to invest in an untested anti-erosion soil product. The last phrase sent a warning bell to Robin's brain and she found herself inching closer to the office.

Dylan was pacing back and forth in the small space, the lines on his forehead deeply grooved. When he caught sight of her, she immediately took a step back, but not before she saw his face transform from concern to a veneer of charm and grace.

"Let me call you back, Tony," he said as Robin pretended to be absorbed in reading about all the off-road features listed on the truck's sticker price.

"Welcome to Bronco Motors," Dylan told her with that same smile and those same cheek dimples that she'd been seeing in her dreams the past several weeks. "Are you interested in trying this out?"

She almost said yes, then realized he was talking about the car between them. "Oh, um, not today. I came to sign up for the bake-off."

She held up the flyer, as if to prove that was her sole intention in coming here.

If Dylan was disappointed that she wasn't there to buy a car, he covered it well. "Right. So full disclosure, my mom and sisters did the flyers this past week and posted them all over social media before I even got a chance to create any sort of official sign-up or even come up with contest rules. I wasn't really prepared for the amount of interest I've already gotten." He walked over to an empty reception desk and retrieved a clipboard. "So I've just been having people put their contact information on this sheet. We'll reach out when we have all the details finalized."

Whoa. Up close, the man smelled even better than he looked. Trying not to let the scent of his cologne go to her head, Robin took the clipboard from him and it only took a quick glimpse at the other names on the list to see that it was all women. Apparently, she wasn't the only one in town who wanted an excuse to get up close and personal with the last single Sanchez brother.

She paused with the pen in her hand. This was so foolish. What was she even doing here? Someone like her wouldn't have a chance of winning a baking contest or attracting a guy like Dylan. But as he stood there watching, another thought occurred to her. He'd just asked her if she wanted to go for a test-drive. Her parents bought all their ranch vehicles from this dealership, including several of this exact same model. If Dylan knew who she was, then he would know that Robin wouldn't need to test-drive a car she often used at work.

Which meant he had no idea who she was.

Robin wasn't sure if she should be relieved or offended. Until he added, "I should probably warn you that the bake-off is on Valentine's Day. In case you're already busy that day. Or, you know, have plans."

She looked up quickly and was rewarded with the sexiest smile and the most smoldering pair of brown eyes she'd ever seen. At least this close. Was he suggesting that she might have some sort of date for the most romantic day of the year? Her sister, Stacy, teased her about being oblivious to men flirting with her. Was this one of those times?

Since Robin couldn't just stand there staring at him in confusion, she mumbled what she hoped sounded like, "No, I'm available." Or at least it would've sounded like that if her tongue wasn't all tied up in knots.

She scribbled her name on the list, along with her cell number and email address. Her face was flushed with heat by the time she returned the clipboard to him, but he didn't give it so much as a glance before tucking it under his arm.

His phone rang from his pocket and he pulled it out long enough to glance at the screen and then silence it.

"I should probably let you get back to work," she said, jumping on the excuse to get away before she did or said something else that made her seem like a lovesick fool.

"Only if you're sure I can't interest you in a test-drive."

No, Robin wasn't sure at all. But her whole goal in coming here today was to meet the man in person and see if this crush she'd developed on him from afar was just as foolhardy as she'd been telling herself. And the answer was yes.

"Nope, I'm all set," she said, pivoting to leave. Before she executed a full turn, though, she stopped in her tracks. "Actually. I know this is none of my business, but someone needs to stop you from making a huge mistake."